The Blue Coat Saga

BELLEAMIAUTHOR.COM

FROM THE BESTSELLING AUTHOR OF
The Girl Who Knew Da Vinci
& The Last Daughter

BELLE AMI

Published Internationally by
Tema N. Merback
Thousand Oaks, CA, USA
Copyright © 2020 Tema N. Merback
All rights reserved.

The Blue Coat Saga
Cover Design, Interior Book Design
and Formatting: Joanna D'Angelo
Editor: Joanna D'Angelo

Ebook ISBN: 978-1-7359423-6-0
Print ISBN: 978-1-7359423-3-9

For permissions or inquiries, contact:
Belle Ami belle@belleamiauthor.com
www.belleamiauthor.com

AUTHOR'S NOTE AND ACKNOWLEDGMENTS

Six million. A number almost too big to fathom. How do you comprehend a number like that? You can't. Because it's not just a number. The true meaning of six million is lost to us forever. Six million Jewish men, women, and children who lived, loved, and laughed. Six million individuals who might have gone on to paint great works of art, or write beautiful novels, or just live out their lives in peace. Six million human beings. We can never forget them.

Fifty-thousand. In ten years it is estimated there will be less than fifty-thousand survivors left. Elderly, with fading memories, and frail health. These are the Survivors of the Holocaust. A living memory to a past where evil almost ruled the world. Thousands of memories passed onto children, grandchildren, and great-grand-children. We must keep their memories alive.

One. Dina Frydman Balbien. My mother. A Holocaust survivor. She has inspired every aspect of my life. From a young age I realized my mother was different. Sometimes her tears would gush down her cheeks as though for no reason—no reason my child's mind could understand. My mother's nightmares would make my legs tremble with fear in my bed. Not for me, but for her. What were these horrors that haunted her, even in sleep?

When I was nine years old, I learned the truth. I found out why my mother was different from the mothers of my friends. I was an inquisitive child and I began to ask questions. I begged her to share her stories and she did. That process of telling me her terrifying experiences of World War II allowed her to heal.

I have never forgotten.

Eighty-one years have passed since Hitler invaded Poland and the Nazi scourge spread across Europe. I am often reminded that what happened during those darkest of times will never be forgotten. Many museums have been built and dedicated to the remembrance of the Holocaust. Countless films have been made, and thousands of books have been written about every aspect of the Holocaust. I suspect thousands more will be conceived and written in years to come. It would seem we couldn't possibly forget, and yet...

Anti-Semitism and Holocaust denial are on the rise. Acts of violence perpetrated against Jews occur daily throughout the world and even here in the United States. According to the Anti-Defamation League (ADL), there have been 2,100 acts of anti-semitism in the US, so far this year. The highest since the ADL began tracking in 1979.

As a writer, I have a voice. I can put words to paper and tell stories. Stories inspired by my mother and countless other survivors. Stories inspired by those who did not survive. Stories inspired by those who fought against evil.

As a daughter of a Holocaust survivor, I have tried to impart a truth about the evil that still exists, and that must be stopped by shining a beacon of truth in as many dark corners as our light can reach.

The Blue Coat Saga is both a time-travel journey into the past and a mystery/thriller woven through the darkness. It is historical fiction that takes place in two eras and in two lifetimes. It is also a love story—or rather two love stories, both poignant and soul-stirring. And finally, it is a metaphoric guide—that shows us the empowering strength that can pass down from generation to generation—as long as we keep telling our stories.

I hope you enjoy *The Blue Coat Saga*. And I hope it will inspire you to share your own stories and your history with present and future generations.

I thank and acknowledge every survivor who has shared their story whether in a book, a documentary, or speaking at schools or other public forums. You have honored yourselves and you have honored your mothers, your fathers, your siblings, and the six million beacons of light whose light shines on in your truth.

This is for you, Mommy

God made man because He loves stories.
— *Elie Wiesel*

PROLOGUE

December 12, 1972
Rapperswil, Switzerland
Privatklinik für Psychiatrisches Wohlbefinden

"I found her."

"Found who? What are you talking about, *sohn*?"

Heinrich Brandt shoved a stack of photographs at his father, Horst. "The woman — Nadia Sauvage."

All color drained from his father's face. He stared at the photos as if mesmerized. "You found Nadia." He whispered her name as if he were whispering the name of a saint. His gaze fixed on the photos, devouring every inch of the images. Finally, he lifted his eyes to Heinrich's. "*Mein Gott,* where is she? You must tell me."

The joy that filled his father's face should have warned Heinrich but he was so filled with bitterness, he failed to see the minefield ahead.

"She lives in New York."

"New York." His father's voice trailed off as if suddenly aware of his audience. He cleared his throat. "You will give me her address, Heinrich," he commanded.

Bile rose in Heinrich's throat as he thought about *her.* The woman who'd reduced his father to a love-struck fool. The red diary Heinrich had found when he was seventeen years old had loomed large for ten years. Now at the age of twenty-seven, he was ready to destroy it — the diary, and everything it represented.

In a ritual he'd performed since the day he'd discovered the journal, he removed the worn leather book from his desk and opened it, his gaze riveted to the slanting curves of his father's handwriting. He meant to destroy it, this nauseating testament to his father's weakness. Just as he intended to extinguish his father's love for Nadia. After today neither would exist.

Horst had fallen in love with a woman — a prisoner in Auschwitz — and he'd never found his way free from that passion. Page after page of impassioned poetry and sonnets all in praise of this Mata Hari who'd seduced his father — cringe-worthy, to say the least.

After the war, Horst built a successful *klinik,* and when it grew into a smoothly running operation with a well-trained staff, he would go off on his mysterious trips. Researching and building contacts, he'd claimed, were the reason for his disappearances. But eventually, Heinrich learned the truth.

Every month Horst would abandon Heinrich and his mother to make his pilgrimage to Paris. There he sat in cafes and restaurants searching the faces of strangers for the one woman who obsessed him. Nadia.

As far as Heinrich knew, his father never found her. Over the years, Heinrich watched his mother wither away — a slow death her reward for her sacrifice. Her passing was just another day in his father's life, hardly worth a tear. Heinrich was devastated when his mother died. Even though her husband had failed her, she'd never failed her son. As a boy, he would sit in her lap for hours while she cuddled him, her tears wetting the top of his head. As he grew older, she would retire to her rooms and sleep the weeks away until her husband returned. Then she would light up once more and greet her husband with a joyful cry.

Heinrich was nearly as bad as his mother. Torn in two each time his father left, he would watch his mother withdraw from the world, not knowing how to coax her out of her gloom. Then upon his father's return, he would sit beside his papa, across from his mother. Together, they listened to every word, every story Horst shared about his travels — laugh at all the funny parts and nod at all the fascinating observations his brilliant father made.

He had no idea that everything Horst told them was a lie.

Heinrich followed in his father's footsteps and became a psychiatrist, guaranteeing succession in the *klinik*. But beneath the façade of dutiful son grew a hatred and a desire to get even. To get even with that woman — Nadia. And to right the wrongs of history.

That day had finally arrived.

His mother was dead and could no longer be touched by his father's betrayal. Determined to find the mysterious French woman, Heinrich had hired a team of private investigators, and they had succeeded where his father had failed.

"I must contact her," Horst said again, this time with his voice raised in anger.

"I don't think so, Papa," Heinrich replied smoothly. "You wouldn't want to risk our lives for her, would you?"

"What are you talking about?"

"All of these years, you've deluded yourself, obsessing about *her*. As if you and she could have ever had a life together. You destroyed Mama because of her and made my life a misery. What for Papa? I'll tell you what for —a Jew. Your precious Nadia is a

Jew, a dirty Jew who should have perished in the gas chambers of Auschwitz."

The light of joy in his father's eyes dimmed. "You fool," his father whispered. "You don't know anything. You are still a stupid little boy. And you will always be so."

"I am not the fool, dear Father," Heinrich spat. "You are the fool. You allowed your unnatural attraction to that Jewess to destroy Mama's life and mine. Oh, yes, all of your love letters to her in your pitiful diary. I read everything. EVERYTHING!"

The slap echoed in the stillness. Heinrich stood frozen as Horst pulled back his hand.

He stared into his father's eyes and saw anger, bitterness, hatred, love — or perhaps he saw his own feelings.

"Congratulations, *mein sohn*. If you think I didn't know she was a Jew, you are wrong. I knew."

Horst turned and walked out of the room.

That was the last time Heinrich saw his father alive. He stood in the wake of his father's leaving, his anger simmering, boiling, incinerating his ability to think.

He pictured his father calmly packing his bags, making arrangements for a flight to New York. To find *her*. His Jewess.

Heinrich ran up the stairs, wanting to stop his father, stop this madness, make him see reason.

Shouting his father's name, he threw open his father's office door — the crack of gunfire assaulted him. "No!" he screamed.

The scene froze inside his brain for all eternity.

The German Luger inside his father's mouth, then brains, bone, and blood splashing against the wall.

CHAPTER 1

January 10, Present day
Lower East Side, New York
Mount Sinai Beth Israel Hospital

L *ive, Bubbie. Please don't die. I'm not ready for that. I don't think
   I'll ever be.*

Rose Levi was weary. She'd been at the hospital for almost two
days straight since her grandmother Leah was admitted. Leah had
fought battles her entire life. She'd fought uterine cancer five
years ago and won. The cancer was back. Metastasized in her
bladder. There would be no more chemo. It was too much for
Leah's frail body. And now pneumonia had set in and Leah lay in a
coma, hovering between life and death.

In the past two days, a steady stream of friends and relatives
had said farewell to a woman they both adored and admired. Now
it was time for Rose and her immediate family to gather around
their beloved matriarch and wait.

The gathered Manheims and Levis had left a few minutes before to replenish their dwindling coffee cups or grab a bite of food, leaving Rose, who refused to leave Leah's side. The only sounds were the beep of the heart monitor and the respirator pump clicking up and down with its constant hiss of oxygen into the mask, supplementing Leah's final breaths. Rose held Leah's hand gently in hers, the paper-thin skin soft as the downy feathers of a bird.

Rose found comfort in talking to her grandmother, even if the old woman couldn't answer. "Bubbie, you've always been here for me, much more than a grandmother. You're my best friend and confidant. The person I've always turned to for advice." Rose wiped away a tear that rolled down her cheek. "I can't imagine life without you. I know you wanted to see me married, and I'm sorry I let you down. You always told me not to settle for anything less than true love. I never found it, and I don't think I ever will."

The door opened with a swoosh, and Kelly, the nurse, came in to check on Leah. She lay a gentle hand on Rose's shoulder. "How's she doing, honey?"

"The same." Rose patted Kelly's hand. "Kelly, do you think she can hear me when I talk to her? Sometimes I feel her hand squeeze mine a little when I speak. Like she wants me to keep talking."

While she answered, Kelly checked the monitors and the chart, and changed out the fluid bags attached to the IV. "Honey, I don't want to get your hopes up too much. Patients in this twilight state show physical signs, sometimes. Mostly they're tremors and whatnot. But in Leah's case, who knows? Your grandmother is a feisty one, that's for sure. She had those doctors jumping through hoops with her constant questions. Your granny wouldn't listen to any medical babble, she wanted everything laid out plain and simple. No sugar-coating of the truth for her. She's a brave one."

Rose smiled through her tears. "She can be pretty bossy some-times. I think that's why my mother ended up a psychotherapist. Grandmother and Mom were always a bit at odds." She caressed her grandmother's cheek. "It's just that I never got to say goodbye, and it's killing me. One minute she was here, and the next minute she disappeared into the coma."

For a moment, Kelly studied Leah's face. "She looks peaceful now, doesn't she? No more pain. I saw that tattoo on her arm. She's known her share." Kelly shook her head, her eyes dimmed with compassion. "I've seen a lot of Holocaust survivors die in this hospital. Soon there won't be any left. Who will carry the torch when they're gone?"

"Their children and grandchildren. It's all been recorded and documented with irrefutable evidence. The history will live on."

"History can be manipulated — altered — forgotten. My little brother's a reporter at the *Times*. The stuff he tells me would curl your toes. Evil people twisting the truth whatever way suits them."

Kelly turned to go. "Don't be so hard on yourself. You loved her when she was alive, and you're loving her now as she makes her final journey. That's what really matters. I'll be back to check on her in an hour."

Kelly's words echoed in Rose's mind long after she'd left. Rose pressed her cheek against Leah's hand, marveling at the life her grandmother had led. Leah had spent decades after Auschwitz preserving the memory of the Holocaust. She'd served in various organizations and sat on dozens of charitable boards. Proudly she'd served on President Clinton's Advisory Commission on the Holocaust with Elie Wiesel and served on the board of the Holo-caust Museum in Washington. Leah had personally underwritten a "Meals on Wheels" program to deliver hot meals to needy Holo-caust survivors. An outspoken and articulate voice, she'd fought tirelessly for the survivors and the preservation of the truth. "Never again" was their mantra.

Rose, in her own small way, had followed in her grandmother's footsteps. She'd become a librarian and worked at the David Berg Rare Book Room at the Center for Jewish History. Rose tended to the precious manuscripts and books where over seven hundred years of Jewish history was preserved. She shook her head. *It's ridiculous. There's no way the Holocaust could be forgotten or denied.* Closing her eyes, she rested her cheek against Leah's hand. The sterile hospital room with its peculiar sounds and stringent scents slowly receded into the background.

"Open your eyes, Rose. You must promise me something."

"What?" she murmured, half asleep.

"I need you to look at me, darling."

"Bubbie?" Rose raised her head. Stunned and speechless, she gazed into the bright green eyes of her grandmother. Leah was sitting up, the oxygen mask off, her cheeks rosy pink with life. Her "don't mess with me" smile a reminder to any who dared challenge her. "Bubbie, you're awake. You've come back to us. My prayers have been answered."

Her grandmother's French accent, melodic and mesmerizing, as sweet a sound as Rose had ever heard. "I will never leave you, *mon tendre*. But, right now, I need something from you."

"What? Anything. I'm so happy to see you feeling better. I can't wait for Mom and everyone else to get back. We'll celebrate this miracle."

"Yes, my love. But I need you to do something for me. Promise me you will take my place. I've felt it since you were a child, and now I'm sure. *You* are the chosen one."

"Take your place? Chosen for what? I don't understand."

"Chosen to carry on my work. In life, we are given choices, sometimes dangerous choices. During the war, I was forced to make choices I couldn't have fathomed. So much was at stake. But now, humanity is facing another terrible danger. Promise me. Promise me you will do this."

Leah's gaze was so intense, so focused, that Rose had a hard time taking it all in. Leah cupped Rose's cheek and smiled. "My darling girl, I promise you that great things will happen if you take that leap of faith. You have more courage than you know. And that courage will guide you in life and love. I promise you. You will find him. He is out there."

Rose covered her grandmother's hand with her own. "Bubbie, I don't understand any of this, but if I can be half as courageous in my life as you've been in yours, then I'll be happy with that and know that I achieved something."

A light illuminated Leah's face. The lines around her eyes faded away. "You will understand, *chérie*. One day soon, you will understand everything. Your destiny. I'm counting on you, *ma chère grand-fille*. Your journey is just beginning. We'll see each other again, I promise. Close your eyes and I will tell you a story just like I did when you were a little girl."

Rose's eyes grew heavy, and the soothing voice of her grandmother filled her with warmth and love. She rested her cheek once more against Leah's hand. "I'm so happy you're back, Bubbie...so happy..." Her words drifted away as sleep overcame her. The last thing she remembered was the press of her grandmother's kiss on her head.

"*Adieu, chéri*, until we meet again."

Rose's eyes flew open, and she jerked her head up. She looked at Leah's hand, still in hers. She studied the pale face of her grandmother. Leah's eyes remained closed; the oxygen mask was still in place.

Was it a dream?

She tugged on Leah's hand, hoping for a response. "Talk to me some more, Bubbie," she pleaded. "Tell me what you want me to do."

Silence except for the sound of the oxygen machine and the beeping of the monitors.

Rose pressed her cheek to Leah's hand and gave herself over to the flow of tears.

CHAPTER 2

December 10, 1942
Paris, France
11th Arrondissement

Merde. The Englishman was late.

Leah Manheim shivered and pulled up the collar of her blue coat. An icy wind sliced through the streets of Paris, bringing with it more snow. Looking up at the stone-gray sky, frosty snowflakes drifted down, dampening her face. In the fading light, the church of Saint-Ambroise loomed behind her, its edifice a gray ghost misted in dark clouds.

I can't feel my toes. Stamping her feet, Leah began to pace. "*J'attendrai...*" she sang in a feathery voice. The Rina Ketty song, *I Will Wait*, never failed to lift her spirits.

"*J'attendrai*
Le jour et la nuit, j'attendrai toujours
Ton retour
J'attendrai."

The pacing and singing kept her blood flowing and calmed her frazzled nerves. She'd heard it was the coldest winter on record. Just the other night, the temperature had dropped to minus twenty, and the river Seine had frozen over. It was as if Mother Nature had taken it upon herself to punish Parisians for allowing the Nazi vermin to invade France and steal her riches.

Where is he? Every minute was torture. Their rendezvous was set for 5:00 p.m. Already, the light was gone. *Cher Dieu, something must be wrong. I hope he wasn't apprehended. I'll give him two more minutes and not a minute longer.*

She decided to venture up the icy steps of the church and stand under the awning, away from the sharp wind that cut through the empty street. On the top step, it happened. Her feet shot out from under her, and she went down with a tumble on her tailbone. Her cry of *"Mon Dieu!"* pierced the silence.

A nun exiting the church ran to her. She carried a heavy walking stick with a silver metal knob at the end. "Mademoiselle, are you all right?"

"Oui, oui."

The nun grabbed an elbow, and leaning on the stick, helped her up. Leah rubbed her back, wincing. *"Merci, Soeur."*

"Ce n'est pas sûr, ma fille," the nun whispered in Leah's ear. The old woman's sharp gaze swept the street. "They are always watching."

The good nun was right. It was dangerous to loiter and could draw unwanted attention. The Carlingue had eyes everywhere. The French police were often more brutal than the occupying Germans and had rightly earned their moniker "French Gestapo." It was madness to be out on the streets with no real purpose so close to curfew.

Ah, but I do have a purpose. A crucial one. Where is he? "Thank you, Sister. I'm supposed to meet my fiancé — we live in such worrisome times — I always fret when he's even a minute late."

"I hope he comes soon." The nun glanced at the sky. "You don't want to be out on the streets tonight. May God bless you and keep you safe." The nun hurried down the steps, thumping her cane as she disappeared along the Boulevard Voltaire.

The nun's warning reminded Leah of her last conversation with her parents. She'd been sneaking out for weeks, hoping her late-night excursions did not cause them undue worry.

One night her father confronted her. "Where are you going?" he asked. "Curfew is soon, Leah, and the streets are not safe."

She assured him she would be fine. She was going to a friend's apartment to meet a few of her girlfriends. "Don't worry, Papa, if it gets too late, I'll stay the night."

There were things she wanted to keep secret from her mother and father, but she should have known better. Her astute parents figured it out a few days later.

Leah had begun training with *La Résistance*, France's underground rebellion against the German occupiers.

"*Ma fille chérie*," her mother, Estelle, cried. "Please don't put yourself in danger."

"I will not stand by and let others dictate our fate, *Maman*."

"But what can you do?" her father, Adam, asked. "You're only a child, eighteen years old. You can't fight off these Germans."

"I'm not going into battle if that's what you mean, Papa, but there are things I can do to help — to resist."

Her mother's tears and pleas had kept her home that night. She'd explained everything to them. Most of all, she wanted to reassure them. The truth was, she no longer felt like a child. There was too much darkness in the world, too much hate. The war had forced her to cast aside any whimsical ties to her girlhood.

That night seemed such a long time ago, yet it was only a year since Leah's parents left Paris — she'd gotten them out — and she'd acquired a new identity. Leah Manheim had disappeared, and Nadia Sauvage from Bayonne was born. She rubbed away the tears that bloomed. She didn't know when or if she'd see her parents again.

"Two more minutes," she muttered. Her heart pounded in her chest as she fingered the half of a theatre ticket in her pocket. With her other hand, she brushed the gathering snowflakes out of her hair, wishing she'd worn a hat or at least a scarf.

Leah, what are you doing? She castigated herself. *What if you accidentally damaged the ticket?* She withdrew her hand from her pocket and blew on her gloved fingers, trying to relieve the numbness caused by the frigid temperature. *Oh, what I wouldn't give for a hot bath and a café au lait. Dear God, where is he?*

"There you are *mon amour*. Sorry, I'm late." A tall, lean man ran up the steps. He smiled, but beneath his hat brim, his sky-blue eyes narrowed as he stealthily glanced across the street. "You're being watched," he whispered. "Kiss me."

CHAPTER 3

January 12, Present day
Brooklyn, New York

Rose answered the door as another group of mourners arrived for the shiva. She recalled the first time she attended a shiva with her grandmother. "In Judaism, 'sitting shiva' for seven days following the funeral is very important," Leah had told her when Rose was ten years old. An elderly friend of the family had passed away, and Leah had taken Rose's hand and said it was time for her to learn a lesson about life.

"But this is so sad," Rose whispered to her grandmother as they walked into the house full of mourners.

"When we lose a loved one, it is very sad. We cannot hide from that fact," Leah whispered back, squeezing Rose's hand. "But it helps ease the grief when family and friends sit shiva because we are celebrating the life of the person we love."

Rose had looked up at her grandmother and saw the tears in

her eyes. It was the first time she'd seen Leah cry. "Oh, Bubbie, you're crying. Now I'm going to cry too."

"Sweet Rose, tears are nothing to be ashamed of — nothing to run away from."

Now here she was answering the door for a shiva for her grandmother. A shiva that she would give anything not to attend. Rose welcomed the newcomers and ushered them into the house, thanking them for their offered condolences. She glanced outside and shivered. Dreary and cold, the day perfectly reflected the sadness surrounding her heart. She sighed, shutting the door. The shiva was supposed to bring comfort, but Rose felt none. She was still reeling from the reading of Leah's will and its ramifications.

Taking in the room with its classic Biedermeier furniture, she still couldn't grasp that her grandmother had left everything to her. The house, the bank accounts, the stocks, the books, and the jewelry. All of it. Not that it amounted to a fortune, but she'd bypassed her own daughter. Of course, Leah knew that her mother Edith needed nothing, as she was a successful psychotherapist, and Rose's father was an esteemed heart surgeon. Both were successful beyond measure. But still, Leah's will flew in the face of tradition. Her mother professed happiness for her, but Rose wondered if deep down, this rejection cut like a knife.

She returned to the living room and found a chair in the corner. Word of Leah's death must have spread like wildfire because the nineteenth-century brownstone was packed with people. Leah had been a force of nature and a colorful figure, but Rose was still taken aback by the mourners filling every inch of the spacious old brownstone. Fortunately, Edith had ordered enough food for an army. Rose imagined her mother's order had covered a week's overhead for Jack and Lloyd's Kosher Deli. Rose made a mental note to take the leftovers to the Mainchance homeless shelter tomorrow. Besides, the following six nights of shiva would be held at her parents' Upper Eastside apartment with different catering every night.

Being French, her grandmother had never taken a shine to delicatessen food, and neither had Rose. Leah's idea of comfort food was French onion soup, seafood bouillabaisse, or steak frites. Rose would never forget weekly Sunday nights at Boucherie with Leah. The first Sunday of every month, they would get all dressed up and enjoy a leisurely dinner at the fine French restaurant. It had begun when Rose was but a child. French children are made to sit through laborious meals at a very young age, but Rose had loved every minute of her grandmother's recitations about food, wine pairings, and the art and joy of cooking. Rose wiped away the tear that slid down her nose. There would be no more of those beloved Sunday outings.

Turning her attention to the colorful assortment of visitors took her mind off her sadness, her grandmother's will, and the perplexing dream she'd had just before Leah's passing. The dream was something she hadn't come to terms with, and she'd buried it in the back of her mind. Something about being chosen for some secret mission, an inherited pursuit that Rose was meant to continue. She'd chalked it up to exhaustion, grief, and her grandmother's stories about the war. Without her *grand-mère,* her world would never be the same, and the dream had been a manifestation of her fear.

The outpouring of love for Leah filled every room. It was an elderly crowd, most born of the same pre-World War II generation as Leah. Many were Holocaust survivors. They whispered sotto voce in small groups, their eyes studying each new arrival. Always suspicious and on alert, their eyes darted around the living room.

Being a Holocaust survivor's granddaughter, she'd met many survivors over the years. And, of course, her librarian status at the Center for Jewish History meant she was exposed to nearly every book written on the subject. But, hearing a survivor recount aloud what happened to them during the war in the ghettos, work camps, and concentration camps brought to life what happened — made it vivid — made it undeniable. Soon those precious voices would be silenced by the passage of time. Like her grandmother, the survivors would pass on, and the living witnesses would fade into the pages of history.

Perhaps that was why she couldn't get Kelly's words at the hospital out of her mind. "History can be manipulated — altered — forgotten. We see it every day. The media, educators, they spin the truth whatever way suits them." Rose was sure her grandmother would have concurred with the nurse's analysis, and it distressed her.

Rose was deep in thought as two elderly women approached, pushing a third old woman in a wheelchair who peered at Rose through milky blue eyes, her bristly white brows raised in question. Her gnarled fingers clutched something in her lap.

"Is this the *eyniklekh*?" The tiny woman resembled a bird in form and in her chirpy high-pitched voice.

"Yes, I'm Leah's granddaughter." Rose smiled at the three women.

"She doesn't look so special." The bird-like woman frowned, glancing up at the friends hovering behind her.

"Esther, she *is* the one, the chosen," the shorter of the duo chimed in.

"Remember what Leah told us," the taller one said.

The woman in the wheelchair leaned forward to scrutinize Rose more closely. Rose held onto her smile, reminding herself these elders were Leah's long-time friends.

"*Oy, Gott in Himmel!*" The woman's wail made Rose jump. "What will become of everything we've worked for? How can this child stop the evil that is beginning again?" Something about the way the old woman bemoaned to God reminded Rose of the last words of the wicked witch in the *Wizard of Oz*, "You cursed brat, look what you've done! *I'm melting*! Ohhhhh, what a world, what a world!" Rose was glad the old bird couldn't read her thoughts, or she probably would have melted.

"I'm sorry, but I don't understand." Rose looked at each of the old women, hoping one of them would explain. The chair-bound babushka continued to moan in Yiddish, her muttered words indecipherable to Rose.

"We apologize for the confusion," the taller of the duo said. "My name is Frida Goldsmith. We met when you were a child, and these are Leah's friends, Sonia Leon and Esther Finklestein."

"I'm happy to meet my grandmother's dear friends," Rose said. Frida, elegantly attired, reminded her of Leah with her beautifully coiffured snow-white hair pinned in a bun. Chubby and smiling, Sonia nodded. Rose pictured her with an apron around her waist baking cookies, her kitchen smelling sugary and sweet.

"Esther, it must be passed to her." Frida's face conveyed worry as if her conviction wasn't absolute. "Forgive her, Rose, Esther is distraught and means you no ill. We've all worked tirelessly to keep the flame alive, Leah, most of all. Your grandmother chose you, and that's good enough for me. We entrust the sacred brooch to you." Prying the pouch from Esther's fingers, she handed a black velvet bag with gold corded ties to Rose. "We meet once a month in Esther's apartment and would love you to join us once you finish sitting shiva."

"I-I...of course, I'd be delighted. I'm sure Bubbie would want me to." She stuffed the pouch in her pocket. It couldn't hurt to pay these ladies a visit. They were her grandmother's friends, after all. The doorbell rang, and her gaze darted to her mother sitting on the couch. She wept, dabbing her eyes with her father's handkerchief, while her father held her hand, whispering soothing words.

The bell chimed again, and she jumped up. "Excuse me, but I'd better get the door." Like synchronized swimmers, the old women nodded as one. Rose wouldn't have been surprised to see them pirouette in a circle, their arms raised above their heads in perfect harmony. She held back a chuckle, not wanting to offend them.

Rose opened the door expecting more gray-haired mourners. Instead, she found herself face to face with a young man. His steel-gray eyes sized her up from head to toe. *How rude.* Had she forgotten to button her blouse? His scrutiny made her feel naked. Her hand lifted to her chest. Perhaps it was the shock of his disheveled chestnut hair powdered with snow. But the way he stared at her was so disconcerting that it was a good thing his lips crinkled into a smile, or she might have slammed the door in his face.

"I'm here to see Leah Manheim." He stuck out his hand. "Ethan Blackwood, and you are?"

Rose realized she'd been standing there mute. "Rose Levi," she shook his hand. "Leah, you're looking for Leah?"

He stared at her as if she might be mentally challenged. "That's what I said." He stepped back, looking at the address number on the house. "This is Leah Manheim's house, isn't it?"

"It is...I mean, it was. My grandmother passed away three days ago."

"Oh my God, I'm so sorry. Please forgive me." He looked around as if confused as to what to do. "I'm sorry I bothered you." He hunched his shoulders and stuffed his hands into the pockets of his leather jacket, turning to leave.

"You knew my grandmother?"

"Yes, we emailed often. We had an appointment...but that doesn't matter anymore."

Rose was confused, but more than anything, she was curious. "Why don't you come in, Ethan? Maybe you can tell me a little about your relationship with my grandmother. I'd love to hear what you talked about."

He glanced around as if mulling the question. When at last, he returned his gaze to Rose, she was sure he had x-ray vision and could see through her. "I wouldn't want to impose on you or your family."

"It's no imposition. We're sitting shiva, and the house is filled with people, most of whom I don't know. There's a lot of food and," she glanced past him, noticing the snow had begun to come down heavier. "You might as well get out of the cold for a bit." Rose's curiosity was piqued, she couldn't imagine what her grandmother and Ethan Blackwood emailed about. There it was again, that penetrating stare of his. She wasn't sure whether she shivered from the intensity of his gaze or the cold. "Please, hurry and make up your mind," she added. "It's freezing, and there are a lot of elderly people inside who won't be thrilled when an Arctic wind blows through the house."

The dark storm brewing in his eyes transformed with his smile. "Of course, how selfish of me." He walked into the house, and she closed the door behind him. He turned, taking in the clerestory entrance until his eyes alit upon the stained-glass window above the door, and he drew in his breath. Rose followed his gaze to a heavenly view of the ancient City of David. Jerusalem, surrounded by the hills of Judea, glimmered beneath a glowing star of David. The *Magen* David depicted as a metaphorical sun, its rays illuminating downward, turning the ancient walls surrounding Jerusalem to gold. "The shield of David," he whispered.

"I beg your pardon?"

"In Hebrew *Magen* David means the shield of David." He looked at her quizzically, and she felt foolish.

Probably because she'd seen the jeweled window all her life,

21

Rose had never really looked at it closely. But now it was as if she was seeing it for the first time. Rose noticed that below, the majestic city of Jerusalem was an inverted view of the gates of Auschwitz. *How could I have missed that?* Upside down, were the words "Albeit Macht Frei" "Work Makes You Free." The symbolism was clear — the juxtaposition of the paradise of The Holy City and the Hell of the concentration camps. *Heaven and Hell.* "How odd, I've looked at that window a thousand times and never really saw it."

He nodded. "Not surprising. It's human nature to turn a blind eye to things that are part of our everyday world. Things we take for granted become invisible. But I can assure you your grandmother commissioned that stained glass for a reason. She made a point of explaining to me the true symbolism of the Star of David. She said the six points of the star encompass the direction of God's rule." His fingers traced the direction of each point. "The points represent the Lord's dominion over the North, South, East, and West. In other words, the whole universe. She also said it symbolizes the clash between good versus evil and the physical world versus the spiritual world. She was quite adamant that the greatest battle was yet to come."

"My grandmother said that to you? It seems so unlike her. I mean, she was an activist when it came to the Holocaust, but the notion of a battle being fought on some higher plane between good versus evil sounds — spiritual and out of character." Rose was having difficulty wrapping her head around her bubbie being involved in such mystical undertakings. Leah, if anything, was such a pragmatist that Rose often wondered if the horrors of war had destroyed her belief in God. For Leah to embrace the metaphysical didn't seem possible.

"You would know better, of course," he replied. "I'm probably putting too much emphasis on an old woman's imaginings."

Reluctantly she drew her gaze from the window. She sensed a smugness in Ethan's reply. As if he questioned whether she knew her grandmother as well as he did. *Better to ignore it. What difference does it make anyway? He's only here to pay his respects, and then he'll be gone.*

As they entered the living room, Rose caught the questioning look on her parents' faces. She suppressed an eye roll, knowing what they must be thinking: *Who is the tall, good-looking goy, and what is he doing here?*

It was annoying how traditional her parents were. They had never dreamed of marrying outside of the Jewish faith, and their expectations were the same for her. Her grandmother had been a bird of an entirely different color. She'd married an American GI she'd met in Paris after the war. That they were both Jewish was a coincidence and not of importance to either one of them.

Leah had told Rose of their meeting so many times, Rose had it memorized. They met at a little café in Paris. Leah had been immersed in a book, sipping *café au chocolat*. It was a particularly poignant moment in the book, and Leah had sniffled, dabbing the tears from her eyes with her napkin. A man's voice interrupted, "Excuse me, but are you okay? Are you crying over a book?"

She'd looked up, embarrassed. "It's a sad passage from *Tess of the d'Urbervilles*. It's the moment when her husband realizes he doesn't love her. She's crying, and her tears do not move him."

"Well, I sure as hell am moved by your tears. Life is cruel enough without having to read books about it. After what I've seen from war, I want to find happiness, and seeing you cry saddens me."

It had struck Leah in that instant that this man wasn't about to dwell in tragedy — he was going to build a life that mattered. It appealed to her. It was time to move on and leave the past behind.

Their conversation continued, and they met several times for lunch over the next few weeks, building a friendship.

Bernard had remained in Paris after the war to set up connections for the import-export business he would establish. He'd rightly determined that European goods would be highly sought in the States after the war. When Bernard concluded his business and returned stateside, he and Leah stayed in touch. When she moved to New York, they resumed their courtship, and they eventually married. Sadly, Bernard passed away when Rose was only two years old. He'd left her grandmother financially independent, and Leah had never remarried.

The magnificent reddish-brown mahogany table in the dining room was covered with a white Alençon lace tablecloth. Arrayed on the table were numerous crystal bowls and silver platters piled high with delicatessen and salads.

"I hope you like Jewish deli. Even with the large crowd that showed up, I think we might have gone a little overboard. If you want, I can wrap some food up for you to take back to your place. We're never going to eat all of this."

"Thanks, but I'm staying at a hotel. I'm only in town for a few days. My flight was delayed because of this abominable snowstorm. To be honest, I'm really not a deli kind of guy," he quipped. "Never developed a taste for it, except for bagels, I do like bagels." He eyed piled platters and bowls. "Right now, though, I'm so hungry I could probably eat the proverbial horse."

"Deli's not my thing either, but it is a traditional food for New York Jews." For some reason, she felt a twinge of disappointment that Ethan didn't live in New York. Rose watched him take a Limoges plate from the stack. Methodically, he began to build a sandwich upon two pieces of Russian rye bread. He heaped on mustard, pastrami, cheese, coleslaw, and Russian dressing. *You might not be Jewish, Ethan Blackwood, but your deli sandwich skills beg to differ.*

"Where do you live?" She hoped she didn't come off as nosy.

"D.C. I live in Georgetown. Truth is, I came here mostly to meet with your grandmother. We were planning on working on a project together." The sandwich had risen to a towering height. She held back her laughter when he garnished the plate with a surrounding wall of dill pickles. Unknowingly he'd built a daunting, edible castle and fortress. She was looking forward to watching him eat his creation. She placed a wager with herself on whether he could open his mouth wide enough to even take a bite.

"I hope you're not going to make me eat alone." He handed her a plate and waited, his expression one of infinite patience.

"My apologies." Her lips tilted up in a smile as she scooped up a spoonful of egg salad, tuna salad, and her own humble pile of pickles. "I'm curious what project you and Bubbie were working on."

"I was hoping you'd ask." He nodded. "Is there a quiet place where we can eat and talk?"

CHAPTER 4

December 10, 1942
Paris, France
11th Arrondissement

A chill that wasn't from the cold crept up Leah's spine. As a rule, the Germans were less suspicious of women. But Leah was under no illusions — if discovered, she would be arrested and taken to La Santé Prison, and torture would be her reward.

When the man grabbed her, pulled her against him and kissed her passionately, her knees went weak. When he broke the kiss, overcome with surprise, she leaned limply against him. What little breath she had, stolen from her.

He whispered, "My identity is Lucien Bruguès, and you are?"

Still dizzy from the kiss, she nearly forgot. "Le — I mean, Nadia...Nadia Sauvage." Regaining her composure, with trembling fingers, she brushed aside a thick, dark, forelock that had fallen across his brow. She whispered, "You know I can't trust you until you prove who you are."

He grinned, running his hands up and down her arms. "I've missed you, *ma chérie*. You are such a coquette." He whispered through his teeth. "If I show it to you now, we'll probably both be arrested. Why don't we get out of this blasted cold? I need coffee."

She didn't dare look around and draw attention from whoever was watching them. She hadn't noticed anyone on the street, but it didn't mean they weren't there. Instead, she took Lucien's arm, leaned her head on his shoulder, and gazed up at him with total adoration. "*Oui, mon chou chou*. My body is so numb from the cold that even your delightful kiss failed to ignite it."

His laughter rang in the silence. "I think it best we remedy that, Mademoiselle Sauvage."

They walked two blocks to a small café and sat at a booth in the back with a clear view of the cobblestoned street that had begun to disappear beneath a blanket of snow. A bartender stood behind the small bar wiping the counter, and one other customer sat on a stool, nursing a glass of amber liquid.

After seating Nadia, Lucien went to the bar and ordered. He returned and slipped into the booth beside her. He draped his arm around her shoulder and pulled her close against him.

"Is this necessary?" she whispered.

"It most definitely is. Besides, I don't know about you, but I could use a bit of warming up."

"Do you think we were followed?" She peered out the window but couldn't see a thing with the thickening snowfall.

"I can't tell until we're on the move. When we leave, we'll take a couple of false turns and make sure we're not being followed before going to your flat. It seems unlikely someone would wait outside freezing their arses off in such abominable weather."

Carrying a tray, the bartender set down two steaming cups of ersatz coffee and two snifters of amber liquid.

"Oh, I can't possibly drink alcohol," she protested.

"You most certainly can. It will warm you up and relax you. What I need is a convincing performance from you for safety's sake. If we're not affectionate, our story won't hold up. Let's face it, only a couple of madly in love fools would be out in bloody weather like this anyway."

Under the table, Leah felt his hand on her leg, and she stiffened.

He breathed in her ear. "See what I mean? Relax, I'm trying to pass you the other half of the ticket, and you're acting as if I'm trying to seduce you." His lips brushed her ear, causing goose-bumps to rise. "Which I'm not."

"I'm sorry." Reaching her hand under the table, she took the other half of the theatre ticket. Pulling her half from her pocket, she put them together. A perfect match. It wasn't a trap. She crumpled the halves up and tossed them into the ashtray. Lucien lit a cigarette and placed the lit match on top of the ticket, and it burned into ash.

"Okay, now that we can trust each other, I need some questions answered, Nadia Sauvage."

"*Bien sûr*, ask."

"I don't want to insult you, but you seem to be a novice at this. Have you helped any other soldiers out of France before?"

"I-I..." She straightened her shoulders and lifted her chin. "To be honest, none. You are my first assignment, but I promise I won't fail you."

"Great." He sipped his coffee and gagged. "*Merde*, this coffee tastes like mud." Lifting the snifter, he downed the brandy. "Ahh... much better." Waving at the bartender, he called, "*Un autre, s'il vous plaît.*" The bartender delivered another snifter and returned to the bar. Lucien swirled the amber liquid in the glass and met her gaze. "I'm sure your intentions are good, but let's be honest, your track record is nonexistent, which isn't very reassuring." He chuckled, shaking his head and downed the second snifter. He flicked his fingers again, and the bartender immediately came and refilled his glass.

It was true, this was her first mission for the French armed resistance, but she had been trained well. The resistance sent her to a secret camp in the Haute-Savoie, where she learned the use of firearms and coded communication. She would sacrifice her life to see Lucien safely out of France. She was terrified to die, but there was no other choice, was there? Either way, the Nazis would come for her.

Swallowing her fear, she'd volunteered to become a *passeur,* a people smuggler. It was one of the most dangerous missions for a female fighter to undertake. If captured, it would land her in La Santé Prison. Known as the *château de la mort lente*, the castle of slow death was infamous for torture. She'd heard the frightening tales survivors told — little food, no heating, stone walls that dripped a putrid substance, and infestations of fleas and lice. But the most terrifying stories were of the beatings with batons, lashings with leather whips, burnings with blowtorches, and victims being near drowned in freezing tubs of water for hours.

Since the summer, hundreds of executions were carried out. It was only a matter of time before women in the resistance would join their male compatriots in transports to the Eastern internment camps, and God knew what. As terrible as this would be for her if caught, for Lucien, it would most likely mean death. Failure was an unacceptable option.

She placed her hand on his cheek. "I'm trying to gain your confidence, but you've already written me off as an amateur."

"Perhaps, Mademoiselle, I have, but you need to understand how I came to place my life in your hands."

"Please tell me, Lucien."

He swirled the liquid in his glass. "I am a Royal marine

commando. A week ago, a British submarine delivered my mates and me off the coast of France. In five canoes, we paddled sixty miles inland up the Gironde estuary to the Garonne River. We paddled at night and hid during the day. The water was freezing and rough, and two of the canoes capsized..."

"What happened to the men in the canoes?"

He took another sip of brandy. "We all knew the risks. We had to leave them."

She laid her hand on her chest. *Mon Dieu, would that I could be so strong.* "I pray they made their way to safety."

Lucien nodded. "We traveled separately, each canoe leaving at different times. A third canoe never reached our destination. We have no idea what happened. Only mine and one other made it to the port of Bordeaux. Three days on that bloody river in freezing temperatures to reach our targets. We found six ships in the port, fully loaded and ready to supply Germany with plunder from France. In the stealth of night, we attached explosives and blew up all six. A bloody marvelous sight, I must say, a firework display not soon forgotten." He clinked his glass to hers.

She took a tentative sip, squinting as the fiery liquid burned its way down her throat.

"Mission accomplished." He touched his glass to hers again. "To us!"

Is he toasting the destroyed ships or the fact that I took a sip of his poison? She took another sip and gagged, her body shaking in a coughing spasm.

Lucien patted her on the back. "Breathe," he chuckled. "As you might imagine, the Germans are none too happy with our success. The bastards would love nothing better than to catch and execute us as a warning, but I have no intention of dying here. So, made-moiselle, your plan better be good."

His blue eyes were intense. Leah admired his bravery and

bravado. "It is a good plan. You're my new husband, and we're going to meet my parents for the first time. First, we'll travel to Bordeaux and then to Bayonne. From there, you'll be taken to a safe house in St. Jean de Luz and guided over the Pyrenees to San Sebastian in Spain, then Gibraltar, and home to England. The resistance has smuggled many pilots out this way. Our chances are very good that you'll make it home."

He grinned. "I like that, especially the husband part." He winked.

"You're rather cheeky considering the danger we'll both be in." She was reluctant to admit it, but she liked him, this English commando with the sky-blue eyes. If she were to be honest, she was in awe. He was a hero, risking his life to save humanity from the German brutes. Leah lived in a constant state of fear, but his devil-may-care sense of humor made her feel stronger — braver. Life was so uncertain, his flirting almost made her forget the danger.

"I apologize if I've offended you. I place my life in your hands." He took her hand and kissed her knuckles as if she were a queen, and she trembled. His eyes met hers with a mischievous twinkle. "But I think we need some practice."

"What do you mean?"

"Well, when a newly married man and woman are together, they have an easy banter. They touch, caress, kiss. They flirt. We need to be as familiar with each other as possible, or we're not going to fool anyone that we're enjoying connubial bliss. If we get into a spot of trouble, we'll have to be very convincing."

A young woman approached the table and set a plate down in front of each of them. "What's this?" Nadia asked.

He nodded to the girl. "*Merci beaucoup, mademoiselle.*" The pretty girl nodded and returned to the kitchen. "I took the liberty, *ma chérie,* of ordering us a croque-Monsieur. I hope you don't mind because I'm starving, and you look as if you could use a good meal."

"How can you tell? It's so cold I haven't taken off my coat."

"Ah, and a lovely coat it is. A gorgeous shade of blue that enhances your natural beauty." He picked up the hot ham and grilled cheese sandwich and bit in. "Bloody damn delicious," he moaned and pointed at her with his sandwich. "Your cheekbones are sharp, and your cheeks are hollow," he chewed, "good bone structure, but too thin. Come on, *mon amour*, eat up."

Leah's blush rose from the tips of her toes to her ears. She didn't know how to answer his outrageous comment, so instead, she picked up her sandwich and took a small bite. The cheese melted in her mouth and tasted like heaven. Leah hadn't realized how hungry she was. She chewed, slowly savoring each bite. Sitting in a café with a man and sharing a meal felt like... it felt normal. It was such a treat she wanted to relish it for as long as possible.

It only lasted a moment before her thoughts returned to the present. It was essential to her that Lucien understand what life under German occupation was really like. She placed her sandwich on her plate. "I'm thin because we're all suffering from forced rationing, especially the children, who are bone thin. The Germans are bleeding us dry. The monsters have given us the immense pleasure of paying for their three-hundred-thousand occupying soldiers as if we invited them here. They've requisitioned eighty percent of all food production. The farmers don't have enough grain to feed their livestock. I'm praying the resistance gets me a ration card for you, or it's going to be difficult. Our allotments are barely above the starvation level."

"Don't worry, Nadia, I have cash. There is a black market, I presume?"

"Yes, the black market thrives. The thieves are gouging the

people with exorbitant prices. If you have money, it's easier to survive. But it's not just food that is scarce. Fuel for vehicles and heating is nearly non-existent. We're not only starving, Lucien, but we're freezing through the coldest winter ever to hit the continent."

Lucien turned his glass in his hands. "Hitler is slowly strangling France, yet the French as a whole seem content to make do and not fight."

She sighed, sensing the underlying bitterness in his comment. "Yes, it is shameful how so many have acquiesced to the Nazi occupation. I don't know how they can stand by and do nothing. It truly angers me beyond reason. Paris reminds me of Miss Havisham in *Great Expectations*. Arrayed in a white wedding gown and suffering from delusions. Most Parisians exist on the fantasy that if they ignore the truth, the reality of occupation will go away. I'm quite sure, if they could, they'd stop the clocks or turn them back. I, and many like me, have made up our minds that it is better to die for liberty than to barely exist under servile domination. We'll fight to the bitter end."

They sat quietly within their own thoughts until Lucien broke the silence.

"Pip and Estella, such a tragic love story. You're a reader, I see."

"Yes, I've always loved literature. Books are my secret escape from this war." The warmth of the brandy had lightened her head and loosened her tongue. "Lucien," she rested her chin on her hand and stared into his eyes, "thank you for risking everything to defeat the Nazi scourge."

"I can't see a future for any of us unless we do."

She nodded and took another bite of her sandwich. They ate in silence for a few moments. Leah delicately patted her lips with her white linen napkin. "Lucien, you have no reason to believe in me, but I'll do whatever it takes to see you to freedom." She hiccupped, covering her mouth, embarrassed.

"I'll drink to that." He winked and clinked his glass to hers. "You know, *ma petite amie*, I am beginning to believe in you."

She smiled and sipped the brandy, enjoying the warmth that traveled through her body. Since the war had begun, she felt as if she hadn't taken a breath. With Lucien, she suddenly felt she could breathe. She felt alive again.

CHAPTER 5

January 12, Present day
Rapperswil, Switzerland
Privatklinik Wohlbefinden für Psychiatrisches

"She's dead."

Heinrich Brandt filled his lungs as if he'd just run a marathon. As if he'd just crossed the finish line. He trembled from head to toe, fighting to stop the dizziness that threatened to topple him.

He'd waited for this day. Wished for it. And now it was here. "How long?"

"She died two days ago."

The woman who'd destroyed his family was dead, and the danger she harbored over his life and organization buried with her. He croaked past the knot in his throat, "I don't think her daughter poses a problem, do you? What do we know about the granddaughter?" His gaze wandered to the windows and the snowy landscape beyond.

"The daughter certainly not. As for the granddaughter, she's a librarian. What kind of danger or power could she possibly wield?" Ernst chuckled. "No, I don't expect any danger coming out of that little mouse."

"I'm sure you're right, but I think it's a good idea to keep an eye on her. At least for a time until we know for certain she's innocuous. Find out everything you can about her. The next few weeks will be telling. I expect a detailed report."

"I'll see to it, Heinrich. But I'm certain there is no threat coming from this timid girl."

Heinrich's brain started to function again. Adrenaline surged through his veins with the realization that his enemy was no more. The one person who threatened his plans was kaput.

"They're Jews, so they'll be sitting shiva for a week. I need you to go to Washington first and meet with our people in Congress. Calm their nerves before Brussels. I'll send you an encrypted document to share with them. I'll concoct some proof that the old girl took her secrets with her to the grave. My reassurance should be enough. Besides, we have no reason to believe our identities have been compromised, or that there is any credible threat to the organization." He was back in control. A feeling of power spread through his limbs. Heinrich leaned back in his chair, his arms behind his head, his chest expanding with a calming breath. "You need to impress on them that they need to act now. The time is right to drive a wedge between Israeli-U.S. relations. The prime minister of Israel is weakened and might not be able to form a government. I think the old adage of 'kick them when they're down' should direct our actions. War will soon ignite again in the Middle East. The time is ripe to inflict significant damage to the Israelis."

"I'll leave tomorrow for D.C. and be back in New York in a few days. Plenty of time for me to gather intel on the granddaughter. In the meantime, I can send you photos of the girl."

"Yes, I'd like to see what she looks like." He gazed out the window where snow had begun to fall. "I'm going to put my agent at Credit Suisse Bank on notice. He will alert us if there's any activity on the account. It can't hurt to have our people ready for action."

"I should say not, especially if the evidence is in that vault. We must do whatever it takes to make sure the list never sees the light of day."

"We are in agreement. Anyone who tries to access the account must be dealt with," said Heinrich.

"Anyone who tries to access it will not be seen again."

CHAPTER 6

December 10, 1942
Paris, France
11th Arrondissement

From the corner of his eye, Aidan McQueen saw the waitress whisper in the ear of the bartender. Should he be concerned? He was always on alert, but he was exhausted. He'd made his way from Bordeaux to Paris as Lucien Bruguès. And now, dumb luck had plunked him into the arms of Nadia Sauvage. Sitting in a café with a lovely woman whose attention was entirely on him was heady, to say the least. Or was it the four snifters of brandy he'd had? Damn, he was tired. He was looking forward to sleeping in a warm bed.

It barely registered in his mind when the bartender and the one other customer, a skinny, tall man, walked to the front door. The chime tinkled when the door opened and again when the door closed on the customer. The bartender locked the door and strode back to the bar.

He was about to ask the bartender why he'd locked the door, but Nadia interrupted his thoughts. "We should be leaving. We need to be off the streets before curfew at nine o'clock."

"We'll go now. Let me pay the check." Aidan went to the bar and settled the bill. "Monsieur, I see that you locked the front door. My *fiancée* and I are ready to leave."

"*Oui, oui, Monsieur,* I hope you don't mind leaving through the back entrance. We're closing, and my daughter and I are in a hurry to get home. I'd rather not be bothered with any last-minute customers."

"No, that will be fine. It will actually cut some time off our journey home." He couldn't have planned it better. If they were being watched, their tails wouldn't have a clue that they'd left from the rear entrance.

Aidan followed Nadia through the kitchen to the back of the café. The daughter of the bartender bid them goodnight and locked the door behind them when they exited.

The snow was coming down in a blanket of white, and Aidan pulled his collar up. "I hope your apartment is not too far from here."

"Not far," she answered.

Out of the shadows, three men appeared suddenly and surrounded them. Aidan sobered immediately and pulled Nadia behind him, slowly turning and shielding her from the threatening trio.

He cursed, forgetting to speak French. "Bloody ass, what the hell do you buggers want?"

"*Alors, mes amis,* what do you think the going rate is for British spies?" The tall, gangly man of the group sneered. Aidan cursed under his breath, recognizing the same man who'd sat at the bar. They'd been set up.

His companion, a man with a drooping jowl and a flattened

nose that had seen its share of fists moved in closer. He was thick and muscularly built like a bouncer. Aidan quickly assessed him and decided the bouncer posed the most significant threat.

"I say we turn them into the Carlingue. The Brit will probably fetch a tidy reward," said the bulldog-faced man, "but not before we enjoy a taste of the *jolie caille.*"

"How dare you? Is there no decency in you?" Nadia hissed.

The third man wore a black beret that slouched down over his forehead to his thick black brows. There was a prettiness to his face that belied the hungry gleam in his gaze as it roved over Nadia as if she were a meal waiting to be devoured. "Such a morsel. I can't wait to sample her wares."

"If you think I'd let you lay your filthy hands on her, you are mistaken." Aidan knew these crude individuals were not the authorities. He was sure they were thieves. He also knew his only chance was to go on the offense. He swung hard and fast and made contact with the ugly brute's bulldog-like nose. Blood spurted, and Bulldog fell backward in the snow gurgling curses. The other two men pounced on Aidan, beating him with their fists. Pretty-boy grabbed Aidan's arms, restricting his movement, but he kicked forward and landed a boot on Skinny's groin.

Skinny's hands flew to his privates. "*Sacrebleu!*" His response fell on deaf ears as Nadia grabbed his hair and yanked his head back. Fearlessly she tore at his greasy locks, digging her nails into his scalp and clawing his face.

He snarled, "Get this bitch off my back." He shoved her hard enough that she lost her balance, sprawling backward.

Aidan flushed with rage. He swung hard at Pretty-boy, hoping to take him out of the fight and landed a fist in his solar plexus. The thug crumpled forward, spewing vomit. He rolled back and forth in the snow clutching his stomach.

Aidan focused his attention on the bastard who dared lay a

hand on Nadia. Roaring like a warrior of old, Aidan dove for the thug's knees, and the two men rolled in the snow. Bulldog growled as he lumbered to his feet, one hand holding his nose to staunch the flow of blood. Distracted, Aidan failed to block Skinny's punch to his temple. He stumbled, shaking his head, trying to regain his balance.

Bulldog pulled Nadia up, and before she could resist, bent her arm behind her back. She cried out, and he wrenched her arm harder.

"You finish the English bastard," he spat. "I'm going to enjoy the *tarte sucrée.*" He pulled a gun from his pocket and pressed the muzzle into Leah's back. She kicked and screamed, despite the danger.

Still dizzy, Aidan glanced over his shoulder as Bulldog dragged Nadia down some steps into a darkened doorway.

"I think it's time to find out what lies beneath your skirt, *petite fleur,*" the brute said.

Bloody hell. I'm going to kill him. A raging fire of anger blasted through Aidan. He needed to get to Nadia, but he had to kill this bastard first. Skinny got his second wind and came toward Aidan again. He pulled a knife, and Aidan focused on the gleaming blade.

The two men circled each other, breathing heavily like bulls in a corrida. Aidan was trained in hand-to-hand combat, whereas he assessed his opponent had most likely learned his skills in the streets. Skinny began slashing the air, but quick and agile, Aidan danced away.

"I'm going to cut you into little pieces," Skinny raged. He shifted the knife back and forth between his hands, then leaped forward. The blade sliced through Aidan's coat sleeve, tearing into his shoulder and down his arm. Aidan gasped and stumbled backward, clutching his arm.

A black shrouded figure swooped into the alley. Far more worried about this new intruder, Aidan forgot about his wound. If this was another accomplice, their odds had just worsened.

Nadia's scream drew the black figure down the steps.

Desperate to get to Nadia, Aidan kicked out, catching Skinny off guard, and the knife flew out of his hand. The two men froze, their gazes fixed on the glinting blade, watching as it turned end-over-end in a slow arc above their heads. Aidan sprang into action first and caught the knife, plunging it into Skinny's neck. Howling like a stuck pig, the dead man crumpled, and Aidan turned toward the darkness.

LEAH KICKED AND SCRATCHED AT THE UGLY, POCK-MARKED FACE OF her attacker. The squat brute rammed her against the brick wall. Dazed, her breath wheezed out of her, and she went limp. Bulldog pocketed the gun, yanked open her coat, and began to paw at her breasts. His rancid breath coated her face, and she begged him to stop.

She squeezed her eyes shut, held her breath, and prepared for the worst. At the sound of a hefty whack and the cracking of breaking bones, her eyes popped open. Bulldog, without so much as a moan, collapsed on top of Leah. She screamed and managed to shove his slumped body off her. *"Mon Dieu!"*

The nun from Saint-Ambroise stood a few feet away from Leah, her hand still brandishing her cane as a weapon. The nun smiled benignly at her. "Mademoiselle, are you all right?" Her savior in a habit lowered her deadly walking stick and wrapped her arms around Leah, hugging her.

"I'm fine, but how is this possible? What are you doing here?"

Leah looked down at her attacker. He lay unconscious with blood seeping from a wound on his head. The nun had cracked it open like an egg with the yolk spilling out.

The sister raised Leah's chin, drawing her eyes away from the bloody mess at their feet. "I had a sneaking suspicion when we met at the church. God put the notion in my mind that you were in danger."

"Thank you, *bonne sœur*."

"I help the resistance any way I can." The nun bent and searched the man on the ground. Finding his gun, she slipped it into her pocket. "To protect the church," she whispered with a wink and a genuflect.

Leah grinned through her tears and hugged the nun.

Lucien came running and stopped dead in his tracks. "*Dieu merci, tu es en sécurité, mon amour.*"

"Yes, I'm safe, the good sister arrived in time."

"I don't understand."

The nun interrupted, taking charge. "Explain it to your young man later. Right now, we must all get away from here. Evil lurks everywhere these days. Please, let us be gone."

Leah took Lucien's hand, and he winced. "You're bleeding."

"It's nothing, I'll be fine. The good nun is right, we need to get out of here."

Leah was worried about Lucien, but she knew every minute they remained in the alley increased the danger tenfold. "I'll tend to your wound when we're safe in my apartment." The three hurried away, leaving their assailants to their fate, and at the end of the alley, the nun and Leah embraced.

"Go with God, *ma fille*. And you too, monsieur." The nun brushed her hand over Leah's cheek and turned on her heel, walking briskly away thorugh the swirling falling snow.

Au revoir, dear sister. May God protect us all.

CHAPTER 7

January 12, Present day
Brooklyn, New York

E than did his best not to gape.

While Rose placed a tablecloth on the antique chess table, he held their plates and gazed around the library. Ethan took a few steps toward the books. He was a bibliophile and the collection of books drew him like a bee to honey. The bookshelves lining the walls rose to a towering ceiling anchored in the center by a chandelier of sparkling cut crystal drops that cast colored prisms of light over the leather-bound volumes. A red Persian rug covered most of the parquet wood floor, and the only interruption in the seemingly endless rows of books was a fireplace against one wall and a gold-leafed mirror tarnished with age that hung above it.

He was seized with curiosity. All he wanted to do was run his fingers along the spines of the treasure trove of volumes. "No need for you ever to go to the library. It would take a lifetime to read what's here."

She laughed and joined him. "Actually, I am a librarian. I work at the David Berg Rare Book Room at the Center for Jewish History."

"Really?" For some reason, he hadn't pictured her as a librarian. But that explained the tightly wound bun and the horn-rimmed glasses. "I've never been there. Do I need an appointment?" He couldn't resist an opportunity to tease, especially now that he knew she had to be a bookworm.

But Rose took the bait and responded in kind. She placed a finger in the dimple in her left cheek, her eyes lifting to the ceiling in a classic pose of contemplation. "Not if you have friends in high places."

"I don't suppose knowing a librarian who works there counts, does it?" He was enjoying this repartee with Rose. Maybe a little levity would lift her spirits, given the circumstances.

"I'll give you my card before you leave. I work Sunday through Thursday. Why don't you stop by and find out?"

"I might take you up on that. It's always nice to meet a fellow book lover."

"My grandmother instilled in me a love of books." She winked and leaned in with a conspiratorial whisper. "Books never betray or judge you."

She was charming to be sure, but naïve as well. "I'm not sure I agree with that," Ethan said in a blunt tone. "Books can also be filled with untruths and propaganda. They can promote destructive ideas and hate. Case in point, Hitler's *Mein Kampf*."

"*My Struggle*," she repeated the translation aloud. "I'm familiar with the tome. A fitting title for a madman's book."

"A madman who nearly succeeded in taking over the world and destroying an entire race of people."

"Those days are over."

"Are you sure about that?"

Her eyes narrowed. "Of course, they're over. I've read many books about the Holocaust. They're an important reminder of what happened. Fortunately, Hitler was defeated, and hopefully, we've learned our lessons."

"I repeat, are you sure about that?"

She shrugged off his question and looked at the wall of books. Tears welled in her eyes. "They're all mine now."

"The books?"

She wiped at her tears. "Yes. She left them all to me."

His voice gentled. "It's a wonderful gift. Leah must have loved you very much."

"She did love me very much, and the books are an incredible gift. But the cost — losing her — is too much of a price to pay. I don't know if I can bear it."

He understood the pain of loss. Anguish comes in many forms and in different doses. Every person handles sorrow differently. It's not a contest of who hurts more, it's the damage that comes from a broken heart.

Ethan had been happily engaged to Christie, a freelance journalist he'd met while based in London. A whirlwind romance had them "shacking up" in a cozy flat in Kensal Rise in North London and planning their future. Six months later, after one too many late nights working on her deadline and crashing at a friend's place, Ethan's phone buzzed. It was a brief text from Christie: *Sorry love, I just can't do this right now*. She hadn't even had the decency to face him, or at the very least, talk to him on the phone. Dumped by a text. A few days later, she collected her things while he was at work. The anger faded to pain and frustration, and finally, that faded away too. Trouble was, she was fiancée number three. Third time's the charm. Or, in his case, the straw that broke the camel's back.

Ethan had steered clear of long-term relationships after that. And marriage? No way. A year later, he began his new assignment in D.C. and had locked up his heart for good. Besides, his career didn't mesh well with a relationship. At least that's what he kept telling himself.

"It takes time to heal. Remember the good times and the love," he advised. "That's what carries us through."

Her scrutiny made him uncomfortable. "Sorry, maybe I've said too much." He focused his attention back on the books, and a title came into focus. *The Abandonment of the Jews,* David S. Wyman's book that documented and condemned the United States and its allied partners during World War II for their lack of effort to save the Jews of Europe. When he'd read the book in college, it had changed Ethan's life forever. He'd asked himself the question a thousand times. If nothing else, why hadn't the allies bombed and destroyed the train tracks that led to Auschwitz or any of the other death camps? It was true they couldn't have stopped the genocide of the Jews already there, but they might have saved thousands or even hundreds of thousands of lives by stopping the transports.

His own theory was that anti-Semitism lay at the root. Throughout history, the song and dance had never changed. The Jewish people, since time immemorial, had always been the scape-goat for the ills of society. Israel was the latest trope. The old dog of anti-Semitism had grown another tail.

"It sounds as if you're saying this not only for my benefit but for yours."

It took him a moment before he realized Rose was speaking to him. "I'm sorry, what did you say?"

"I said it sounds as if you're saying this not only to me but yourself."

Perceptive. "You're probably right. Anyway..." The impressive library of books again drew his gaze. "I envy you the hours you'll spend in this room."

"If you ask my mother, she'll tell you my grandmother did me no favors. She thinks I hide behind books."

"How so?"

"I guess she thinks I should read less and go out more — that I prefer books over people." A red glow painted her cheeks. "Sorry for the over-share."

"Not at all." Not wanting to embarrass her further after her confession, he stared at his plate with yearning.

"I'm sorry for keeping us standing here. Shall we eat?" She invited him to sit, and he placed the plates on the table and sat down across from her.

"Bon Appétit." He took a bite and couldn't suppress a moan of appreciation. "I may have to change my opinion about deli-catessen. This is really good."

"Jack and Lloyd's Deli will be thrilled they have your approval," Rose said with a straight face.

Methinks she has a sense of humor. Ethan bit into a pickle, pleased it was crunchy and not one of those limp atrocities.

After a few minutes of chewing in silence, Rose wiped her lips and asked. "I'm dying of curiosity. How did you come to know my grandmother, and what's this project you mentioned?"

He swallowed and took a sip of cream soda. "Leah contacted me. I work for an organization whose mission is to combat anti-Semitism."

"That makes sense. Bubbie dedicated her life to fighting anti-Semitism. But what exactly did she contact you about?"

"She told me she had crucial information about a worldwide network bent on distorting and denying the Holocaust."

Rose's brows lifted. "How is that possible? How could my

grandmother have possibly come across such insidious information? We're talking about an elderly woman living in Brooklyn." Her brows furrowed. "It's true that Leah was involved in community work over the years, especially when it came to recording and videoing for posterity the lives of Holocaust survivors. But where would she stumble across something like that?"

"I don't know, but she did, and she was alarmed by it. The fact is, we've seen a dramatic rise in anti-Semitism over the last few years around the world. Did she share any of this with you?"

Rose stared at her plate. "No, no, she didn't. I wish I could help you, but I can't." The young woman seemed caught off guard by this revelation about her grandmother. Had he imagined it? Or was she hiding something.

"Rose?" A voice echoed in the hallway. The door opened, and a blonde, middle-aged woman entered. Her bluntly cut chin-length hair and bangs gave her an air of scholarliness. "Rose, what are you doing?" Her face and words reflected her displeasure as she stared first at him and then at her daughter.

"Mother, I'd like you to meet Ethan Blackwood, he... he was a friend of Bubbie's."

"Pleased to meet you, Mrs..." Standing, Ethan stretched out his hand towards Rose's mother.

"Levi, Edith Levi." She weakly shook his hand. "That's odd, I don't recall my mother ever mentioning you, Ethan." He sensed her distrust and was amused by it. *Maybe she thinks I'm going to make off with the sterling silver.*

"Leah and I never actually met in person. We corresponded by email."

"I see." She turned to her daughter. "Rose, I don't think it's appropriate for you to disappear like this. We have guests."

"I'm sorry, Mother. I'll be right in."

Edith Levi turned her attention back to him. "Thank you for stopping by, Mr. Blackwood."

"I'm very sorry for your loss. Through our correspondence, I grew very fond of your mother."

"Yes, thank you. My mother touched so many lives." She turned to leave. "Rose, dear, don't be too long."

Edith left, leaving the door open. Rose stood and gathered up their plates.

Ethan followed her down the hallway to the kitchen. Edith Levi had been less than welcoming. In fact, he found himself amused by her cold reception. What did she think? He suspected it wasn't just the sterling silver she was worried about; it was seeing him alone with her daughter. But what difference did it make? The whole exercise of coming to New York had been a total failure. He'd come away with nothing. Leah had died with her knowledge, and now he was no closer to identifying the mystery man and his organization than he'd been before. Rose apparently didn't know a thing and her mother, well she was nothing like Leah, or Rose, for that matter. Families were like that. His own relationship with his father and mother was strained, to put it mildly. Not that he cared or dwelled on things in the past. He didn't. It was time to call a cab and be on his way.

"Thank you, Rose, for the sandwich and taking time away from your guests. I should get going," he said.

Her green eyes held his gaze. *She's quite pretty*, he thought, *and there's something enigmatic about her she's not even aware of*. He'd never been attracted to redheads, but there was always room for an exception. *I wonder what she looks like with her hair pulled out of that old-lady bun? Too bad we live in different cities. I'd have asked her to meet me for coffee sometime.*

"Wait just a second." She opened a drawer and pulled out a purse. "I want to give you my card in case you'd like to see the library. It would be my pleasure to give you a personal tour. Next time you're in town, perhaps."

Beneath that shy, librarian persona, this woman goes after what she wants. He was impressed.

Rose continued. "It's really an extraordinary experience, especially for a book lover."

It seemed he wasn't the only one who was experiencing an *I'd like to see you again* moment.

Rose couldn't hide her blush or her intent.

"I'll take you up on that sometime." He took the card and offered his hand. She placed her hand in his.

"Ethan, if I learn anything about what my grandmother had in mind when she contacted you, I'll get in touch."

"Thanks, I'd appreciate that. Here," Ethan reached in his pocket and drew out his wallet. "Here's my business card just in case you learn anything."

She stuck it in her purse. Ethan felt her eyes on him as he left.

CHAPTER 8

December 10, 1942
Paris, France
11th Arrondissement

They arrived at the entrance to a six-floor walk-up. Despite the darkness, Aidan could tell the building was old and run down. He clutched his wounded left arm, cursing under his breath as he stumbled on the stairs. He'd been wounded worse before and under far rougher conditions, but he cursed because what happened was his own bloody fault. Seeing Nadia in danger and desperate to get to her before that brute raped her had nearly cost Aidan his own life. *I need to keep my wits about me, especially around this slip of a girl.* Next time they couldn't expect divine intervention.

"I probably should have warned you about the number of steps," Nadia whispered, gripping his good arm. "Take heart, we're almost there."

"No wonder you're so thin," Aidan muttered. "How many times a day do you walk these bloody stairs?"

"I try to plan my day well ahead."

"Good thinking, but I wish you'd planned our night as well," he said, trying for humor, but it came out as a grunt. They reached the top floor, and Aidan, huffing and puffing, followed Nadia down a dingy hallway. She opened the door, exclaiming, "*Voila!*"

Aidan tumbled down on the only comfortable place to sit — the bed.

"I guess I don't have to invite you to make yourself at home." Nadia giggled.

He caught his breath and looked around. Through the window, the silhouette of the Eiffel Tower rose in the distance. When Paris used to be known as "*La Ville Lumière*," the view was something to behold. The lights from the tower had illuminated everything surrounding its glow, including the Dôme des Invalides on the Avenue de Tourville and the Rodin Museum. But with the descent of the Nazi darkness came the forced blackouts — the "city of lights" was snuffed out. The French Republic's motto of *Liberté, Equalité, Fraternité*, were now hollow of meaning. "How long have you lived here?"

"A month — the longest I've stayed in one place for some time."

"Where are you from?"

"Paris. We lived on the left bank. My father was a professor of economics at the Sorbonne, but soon after the occupation, he was fired." She rushed from the room and returned a moment later with a bowl of water, cloths, bandages, and a bottle of a red tincture that he felt sure would sting like hell.

Aidan shrugged off his coat, and Nadia helped him remove his shirt. "Bloody hell." He gritted his teeth as she inspected the wound. "Why was he fired, Nadia?"

She paused as if considering her answer while unscrewing the cap from the bottle. Dampening the cloth with soap and water,

Nadia cleaned the cut. Quick and efficient, she soaked the rag with the red liquid and began dabbing at the wound. "I know we have to get comfortable with our fake identities as soon as possible, but I want you to know who I really am. My real name is Leah Manheim. My father is Jewish, my mother is a Rabbi's daughter from Alsace."

He couldn't stop his sudden intake breath from the searing iodine. "Go on."

"The cut is not too deep. It should heal without leaving much of a scar."

"I'll live. Go on."

"One of the first things the Germans did when they took Paris was to begin severing the Jews from society. All the Jewish professors at the universities were fired. Our home and everything else was confiscated. The underground helped me get my parents out of Paris. They're living in Le Chambon-sur-Lignon, a tiny Huguenot village in the Haute Loire region. I pray they'll be safe in the mountains."

"And you didn't go with them?"

She wrapped the bandage around his arm and secured it with a safety pin. "I — I couldn't live with myself if I didn't stay and do something." She swallowed and turned away from him, packing the medical supplies away. "I'm not brave like you. I'm no warrior. I know that some women fight like men, close to the front lines —
"

Aidan lay a gentle hand on her delicate shoulder. "Leah," he whispered. "You are indeed a brave woman."

She glanced at him and nodded, her lips trembling. "Thank you, Lucien."

"Aidan." He smiled. "My real name is Aidan McQueen."

She nodded again. "Aidan McQueen," she said in her accented English. It sounded like a sweet melody.

He cleared his throat and glanced around the tiny room, observing the lace curtains on the window, the café table with its checkered tablecloth and bistro chairs, and a single touch of luxury to cheer the spirit — a spray of violets tucked into a glass preserves jar. Leah helped him put his shirt back on.

Aidan's gaze returned to her face. A gentle girl forced by circumstances to be tough and live rough when she should be making dinner for an adoring young husband and hoping for a sweet babe to cuddle. *She's Jewish. That makes her all the more vulnerable.* He'd heard enough stories to turn his stomach. Horrifying tales seeping out of eastern Europe about the Jews who fell into Nazi clutches as the blitzkrieg devoured the land. Stories of Jews herded onto trains for resettlement and then never heard from again. It was beyond reason to imagine what was happening to the women, children, the old, and the infirm. Of what use would they be to the Nazis? And if they were of no use, what would happen to them? He watched Leah as she walked down the little hallway returning the medical box to its rightful place. What had happened to the soul of humanity? Didn't the Jews have their rightful place as well? Leah was right about needing to do something to stop the Nazis. What choice did she have? What choice did any of them have? "I've heard dreadful rumors about what's happening to the Jews," he said when Leah returned.

"It's beyond reason," she whispered. "In July, more than eight-thousand Jews — half of them children — were rounded up and held at the bicycle *Vélodrome d'Hiver* before being deported to internment camps, purportedly for resettlement. The truth is we don't know what's become of them." The sorrow in her eyes made his heart ache.

"Does it frighten you?"

"Yes." Her lips trembled. "But if I dwell on my fears, I will go mad."

Aidan wanted to reach out to her, to pull her into his arms, but she'd turned away to fuss and tidy the room. He understood all too well that kind of madness. Madness born of terror. He'd witnessed too many soldiers, most of them boys barely out of the school-room, overwhelmed by it. He gazed out the window to the silhou-ette of the Eiffel Tower, his thoughts in turmoil.

"You must be exhausted." Leah's voice snapped his attention back to her. "The bathroom is over there," she pointed to the little hallway. "I don't mind waiting for you if you'd like to get ready for bed first. You're probably going to want to sleep in your clothes because, as you can feel, there's no heat. I told you about the shortages."

He looked around, realizing there was only one narrow bed to sleep on. "We can sleep in the bed together. I trust you." He winked.

She blushed, her hands fiddling with a lock of red hair.

"Look, I can sleep on the floor. I don't want you to be uncom-fortable in your own flat."

"It's all right. We're both adults. As you said, we need to behave like a married couple. I mean, the more convincing we are, the better, *oui*?" She gave a little shrug, but her cheeks were still pink. "I left a razor, shaving soap, and toothbrush in the bathroom for you." She hesitated. "Oh, and don't worry if I'm not here when you wake up in the morning. I get up early, but I'll be back with break-fast and some clothes for you. I'll pick up some more bandages. We'll need to keep the wound clean and change the bandages regularly."

He stood. "Righto, then, Florence Nightingale. Have they told you how long before we leave?"

"I think it may take several weeks. You and I need to get our stories straight, and your documents need to be prepared. I'm afraid you're stuck with me for a time. I'm sorry, but you won't be able to leave the flat. It's safer."

"That's fine. I've seen worse." He turned, walking toward the bathroom. "If you can manage it sometime in the future while you're out and about, I wouldn't mind some books to read."

"I'm sure I can manage that. Anything you prefer?"

"French literature. I might as well bone up. Thank you, Leah, for your help. I won't be too long."

Aidan stared at the ceiling, the woolen blanket pulled up to his neck. The sounds of Leah preparing for bed reached his ears.

Damn! I'm only human, and she's bloody beautiful. It's been months since I've touched a woman.

And then he heard something that melted his heart. Leah's voice rang clear and pure through the walls of the tiny apartment like a bell chiming. He was spellbound, and tears filled his eyes. She sang, "I'll Be Seeing You." It wasn't so much the song, although that one was a tearjerker. Leah had the voice of an angel. The sad love song was one of the most popular on the radio, reflective of every fighting man and woman's dearest wish. The prayer to go home to loved ones. The prayer this war would someday end.

If he wasn't smitten before, he was now. That they were ships passing in the night did not escape him. A month from now, he'd be back in England waiting for his next assignment, and Leah? Where would she be? Facing unspeakable dangers, he was sure. He tried not to let his protective nature wreak havoc with his reason. His first impulse was to keep her safe. But the truth was, she was self-sufficient, and her fate was not in his hands. The most important thing to do was to stop the Nazis from destroying the world, and then every man, woman, and child would have a better future. His task had been carved out for him. He owed his allegiance to God, country, and family.

The door to the bathroom opened, and Leah returned. She froze as her gaze landed on him. For all of Leah's bravado about their being adults, he was sure she had to be at a loss of how best to sleep in the same bed with a man she barely knew. He doubted she'd ever been intimate with a man at all. Her response when he'd kissed her on the steps of the church spoke volumes. *Pure as the driven snow.*

He tried not to stare but couldn't pull his gaze away from the lovely young woman. She was dressed demurely in a flannel nightgown that reminded him of the one his childhood nanny had worn. Her wet, thick auburn hair was braided and hung over her shoulder, the end of the braid grazing her breast. He sucked in his breath. He could barely make out the outline of her full bosom, and yet he couldn't suppress the charge of desire that flowed through his body.

Damn! Too bad she doesn't look like Nanny — I wouldn't be in such a bloody quandary.

"I won't bite," he offered, trying to break the tension.

"It's not your fault. It's me. I've never slept with a man before." Even in the half-light, he could see the flush in her cheeks against her milky white skin.

Exactly, what I thought. This is going to be tougher than blowing up the damn ships.

"I can assure you, I'm a gentleman and you will wake up in the morning exactly as you are now." Although he doubted he'd get much rest and predicted a restless night. He patted the mattress. "Come on now, no need to worry."

She sat, lifted the blanket, and shifted onto the bed. Aidan moved to the edge of the mattress, and somehow, they managed a few inches between them. She smelled as sweet and clean as a morning after a rainfall.

The no-go-zone was the few inches between them. Aidan chuckled at the ludicrousness of the situation. It would have made a stellar scene in a Noël Coward play.

"Are you laughing at me?" The huffiness of her tone, he was sure, a cover for her embarrassment.

"No, love. It's just that the situation warrants a bit of humor, don't you think?" He rolled over to face her, making sure not to intrude on her space. He'd much rather rest his eyes on her flawless skin and the pale sprinkling of freckles across her nose.

Charming.

She turned and faced him. "I suppose you're right. I'm sure it will get better, and after a few days, it won't be a factor. That's how life is. You get used to things."

"Some things, yes, but I'll never get used to the bloody Boche trying to take over the world." What he didn't say was that he was pretty sure he'd be happy to stare at her face forever.

"No, never that." She smiled.

He loved the way her green eyes tilted up. *Dear Lord, she is lovely.*

"Maybe I'd feel more comfortable if you told me a little about yourself."

A perfect segue to keep my head on straight. "Born and raised in *Cair Grauth,* Grantchester, a hop and a skip away from Cambridge University on the River Cam. Prettiest place you'd ever want to see. I'm a proud Cantabrigian,"

"A Cantabrigian?" She carefully sounded out the word.

Delightful accent. "A name for students at Cambridge. When this bloody war ends, I plan on returning to Cambridge to finish my doctorate. My father is a Protestant minister, old-fashioned as the day is long, the second son of a proud old Scotch family. I have two brothers and two sisters, who are all involved in the war effort. The McQueen progeny are a feisty bunch, always brawling among ourselves to the great dissatisfaction of our poor mother, an angel if ever there be one. And lucky for our devilish souls, it is that she was placed on Earth. These Germans are going to have their hands full when they meet the McQueen clan."

"Your family sounds so lively. I'm an only child, and I always longed for brothers and sisters." She leaned her chin on her fist. "Tell me more. What is your course of study, and what do you plan to do with your life?"

"Mathematics at Trinity College. I suppose I'll teach or perhaps research. We'll see where the road leads." He usually didn't like talking about himself, but it was quite dazzling the way Leah's green eyes glowed with excitement and the intensity of her focus as she listened. "How about you? You're the professor's daughter, so how do you see your future?"

Her brows knit in contemplation. "I don't really know. I hope I'll be able to go back to school, but that may not be a possibility. My parents will need me." When she averted her eyes, he knew she was hiding something. The realization felt like a punch to his gut. *She doesn't believe she'll survive the war.* He wanted to lift her chin and tell her everything would turn out well, but he had no right to build her hopes up or his own, for that matter.

"Don't you want to get married and have children someday?"

Her face lit like a Christmas tree. "Yes, I do. I want lots of rowdy children, just like you and your siblings. With that much noise and commotion, I might even be able to forget this war."

"Here, here!"

The way her eyes sparkled when he talked about his home made him want to tell her everything about his life and family. She was so different from any woman he'd ever known. So self-contained and so honest. So sincere in her interest in who he was. Her smiles and laughter were like rare gems, but once he caught a glimpse of one, all he wanted was to experience another.

"Thank you for sharing a little about yourself with me, Aidan. It makes me believe there's hope for tomorrow."

"Are you daft, woman? Of course, there is."

"Sometimes the losses get to me. I forget that anything worth having is worth fighting for, and in the end, evil will not win."

"They will not win. They can't. You and I, and millions more like us, will not let that happen."

She placed her hand on his cheek. "There's not a negative bone in your body is there Aidan?"

"Can't see the point of it. We need to win this war so we can get back to doing what God intended us to do. I, for one, have dreams to accomplish."

"And you will, Aidan. I feel it."

He was so focused on the warmth of her hand on him, he didn't answer. When her hand slipped away, all he wanted was to feel it again.

"It's getting late. I suppose we should say goodnight." She started to turn over.

He was disappointed she'd cut their conversation short. "Leah?"

"Yes?" She looked over her shoulder and met his gaze.

"For what it's worth, I think you're swell."

"*Merci beaucoup*, Monsieur McQueen. Now that we know a little about who we really are, I think we will do well as Madame and Monsieur Lucien Vernier." She pulled the blanket up to her chin. "I think you're swell too," she said softly. "*Bonne nuit*, Lucien."

"*Bonne nuit*, Nadia."

CHAPTER 9

January 13, Present day
Brooklyn, New York

She was running through a snowy landscape. Her breath came in short sharp gasps. Dogs barked, and angry shouts grew louder. They were coming. And then she heard it, the gunshot, deafening as it echoed in the forest. She turned, expecting to feel the bullet, her pounding heart extinguishing her ability to think.

Rose woke with a gasp. The dream was so real that the barking still rang in her ears. She shook her head, trying to rid herself of the nightmarish sound. Suddenly, she realized that the barking was coming from a dog somewhere in the neighborhood. She let out a sigh of relief. *You're not going crazy.*

She'd spent so many happy sleepovers in this house, playing chess and drinking hot chocolate. Now that the house was hers, she'd be damned if she'd be haunted by anything except happy memories. Ethan's words returned to her. "It takes time to heal.

Remember the good times and the love you shared. That's what carries us through." She wondered if she'd ever see Ethan again. She wondered why she wanted to.

Driving those intense gray eyes and his face from her thoughts, she got up and tucked her feet into her slippers and grabbed her robe. Coffee, she needed coffee, and then she'd begin the task she'd set for herself. Today she'd go through Leah's closet and box up her clothes. She braced herself for the tears and the memories that would flow. Later she'd deliver the clothes and the leftover deli to the Mainchance Homeless Center. At least Leah's beautiful clothes would live on and help a less fortunate woman.

Hours later, the scent of Chanel No. 5 lingered in the air. Her grandmother's favorite perfume. Fighting back tears, Rose blew out a deep breath. Packing up Leah's clothes had provided some closure. She was about to close the closet door. A shadow on the back wall caught her eye. Rose stepped into the walk-in. *How did I miss this?* She lifted the hanger and brought it out into the light. It was a blue wool coat, faded, moth-eaten, and worn. *I don't remember ever seeing this coat before. Never. Why would she keep this?*

Everything her grandmother owned was in perfect condition. Even a tiny snag in a sweater was enough for Leah to give a garment away. Leah couldn't bear to wear worn clothing. They were a reminder of the war years and all the deprivations she'd suffered. This coat wasn't fit for anyone, it was a rag. Rose shook her head, perplexed. In less than twenty-four hours, she'd discovered things about her grandmother that didn't compute. It was unsettling and confusing. How many more things about Leah were going to be revealed to her? She rolled the coat up, determined to be rid of it. She placed it in the trash bag on the floor and pulled the ties tight, knotting them securely. When she left for the homeless center, she'd take the bag out to the trash can.

THE SUN HAD MELTED MUCH OF THE SNOW FROM YESTERDAY'S storm. Rose took the Brooklyn Bridge over to the F.D.R. Drive toward 34th Street and Midtown, to the Mainchance Homeless Center. The streets were bumper to bumper, usual for Manhattan, and the sidewalks were crowded with an endless throng of people busily pursuing the daily drill of living. New York. No other city equaled its constant rhythms. Bustling, grinding, bursting with energy, New York moved forward into the future. A future without Leah.

Rose blinked back tears and swallowed the perpetual lump in her throat. Loved ones die, but life propels the living forward.

Leah told her that even in the camps amidst the dying and the dead, everyone fought for one more minute, one more breath of life. The struggle to live was all-encompassing, and each person was acutely aware, even amidst the hopelessness, how precious life was. Rose recalled a story she'd read about the Theresienstadt ghetto in Czechoslovakia, where 88,000 Jews were interned. One in four died of starvation and disease. Many of those who managed to survive later met their deaths at Auschwitz and other concentration camps.

One man's rebellion against the hopelessness of the camps was to carve a Chanukiah, a Chanukah menorah out of wood for the lighting of the holiday candles. Whether it was the Jews trying to survive the Greek and Syrian conquerors or the Jews trying to survive the Nazis, it was life they thirsted for. Hope, kept barely alive and clung to, still lived among the doomed and dying. For the prisoners, the phrase "life is for the living" was not lost on them. They fought to live even though they believed they would be forgotten after they stepped into the gas chambers. Erased. Who would remember them or mourn their deaths when everyone they'd ever loved was also dead?

I remember. We all do. The survivors. Never forget!

Leah's words echoed in Rose's ear.

What were you trying to tell me at the hospital, Bubbie?

Rose had never experienced any form of psychic sight, nor did she believe in it. But the dream, coupled with the stained-glass window that referenced some ongoing battle between Heaven and Hell, continued to haunt her. Mysticism made her uncomfortable, and she considered it pure fantasy. Stopping some shadow world conspiracy designed to change the historical record was crazy, especially for her practical grandmother, let alone a sensible young man like Ethan. Rose wanted to forget the whole thing, but it gnawed at her, refusing to be forgotten.

After she dropped off the last of her grandmother's things at the homeless center, Rose drove to her apartment in Chelsea. It had taken less than a day to rent her furnished flat. A definite bargain, she probably could have held out for a more substantial monthly sum, but she was pleased to find a trustworthy tenant. Her parents had bought her the unit when she'd begun to work for the Center for Jewish History. Now that gift would offset the increased maintenance and care that her grandmother's old brownstone would require. Leah had left her very comfortably off, but that money was to secure her future. She was determined to keep it invested and not touch the principal. In honor of her grandmother, Rose was eager to use a portion of profits toward various Jewish charities. Particularly for the elderly survivors who struggled on little.

Bubbie, I want to make you proud.

She packed up the rest of her personal belongings and clothes and set the bags by the door. Sipping one last cup of coffee, Rose gazed out the living room window of her Chelsea flat. The sturdy London plane trees that grew so well in the urban landscape were in winter slumber. Without their leaves, their branches appeared to be living sculptures, their twisted limbs reaching to the sky. Whether Rose liked it or not, her life was changing, and this move to a new home represented the end of one chapter and the beginning of another. Her residence was changing, but what about her life? Would her life change, would she? Her life had become so predictable, she couldn't imagine what could possibly change the endless cycle of her routine. She sighed, reminding herself she was lucky.

By the time she got back to the brownstone, the light had begun to fade from the sky. Rose had opted out of tonight's shiva, telling her parents she needed the time to re-orient herself in Leah's home. But it wasn't anymore Leah's — it was hers. Rose sighed as she carried the boxes up the steps of the stately house and then up the stairs to the second floor.

Bubbie, I may live here now, but this will always be your home.

Rose opened the doors to the walk-in closet in the bedroom, her arms laden with Ann Taylor skirts and jackets, and stopped in her tracks.

"Impossible!"

The blue coat that she'd bagged and thrown away was hanging in the same place at the back of the closet. *Did I imagine throwing it out?* The hairs on her arms stood on end.

She yanked the coat off the bar and carried it out, her heart pounding in her chest. This time she'd make sure the pesky garment met its proper end. She grabbed a plastic garbage bag and stuffed the annoying rag into it. "Ouch!" She dropped the bag and stuck her finger in her mouth, tasting blood. Something had pierced her skin.

With shaky fingers, she pulled the coat from the bag and carefully searched the pockets. She gingerly removed the velvet pouch she'd been given by her grandmother's gray-haired sisterhood. She must have inadvertently stuffed it in the blue coat's pocket. *I have to be more mindful.* She shook her head at her own carelessness.

She set the velvet pouch on the bedside end table and stuffed the coat back in the bag. She scampered down the stairs and out the front door to the trashcan on the street. Opening the lid, she dropped the bag inside, banged the top down on it, and exclaimed with satisfaction, "There!" She was fully aware she'd just thrown out the musty old coat. Giving her hands a swipe for good measure, she marched back up the stairs and went inside, locking the door behind her.

Rose went to bed early that night, her nerve endings still vibrating. She was positive that her misplacement of the coat and the velvet pouch were because of her grief. *Time will heal.* She repeated the mantra over and over until she finally fell asleep.

The next morning, she woke with a start with little or no recollection of her dreams. No running through forests, no shouting from pursuers, no barking dogs. A flash of lightning filled the room with pellucid light. The flash was followed by a crash of thunder. The rain hit in a deluge pounding upon the eaves and roof. The house creaked as wood and stone moaned from the onslaught. Had she not grown up in the old brownstone and loved it as much as she did, she might have been frightened by the looming shadows, clanging sounds, and ghostly moans common in old houses.

Rose stretched, yawning, mulling her options. She considered huddling down under the covers and going back to sleep. She had a full day ahead of her before she returned to work tomorrow. But being lazy wasn't part of her DNA.

Rose padded downstairs to the kitchen and made a cup of

coffee. She turned on the TV and was greeted by a panel discussing a recent poll about the rise of anti-Semitism paralleling the exact moment in time that the memories of the Holocaust among Europeans were fading. "I find it incomprehensible that one-third of the Europeans in this poll say they know little or nothing at all about the Holocaust," one of the analysts said. Rose's stomach churned at the statistic. Surrounded by books and manuscripts every day at the library, Rose wouldn't have thought the words "never again" could fade away into the ether. Had she been living in a bubble?

George Santayana, the philosopher, had warned, "Those who cannot remember the past are condemned to repeat it." Rose had no idea how to stop the merry-go-round, or how to draw attention to the problem.

Promise me you will take my place.

A cold swirl of air tickled the back of Rose's neck. "What do you want me to do, Bubbie?" she whispered.

The brooch!

CHAPTER 10

December 11, 1942
Paris, France
11th Arrondissement

Leah rechecked her handbag for the fifth time. All French citizenry were required to carry a variety of documents. And even though hers were expert forgeries, it still made her nervous every time she went out. She sighed. Everything was in order, her ID card, a ration card, a tobacco voucher, travel permits, and work permits were all in an envelope. Soon Lucien, too, would have his own new set of forged papers.

Leah took the Paris Métro from the Saint-Ambroise station to Châtelet Metro station. Emerging from the Métro, she pulled her wool scarf up around her chin. It was freezing, but a pale-yellow sun was struggling to burn through the gauze of clouds in the morning sky. She walked the banks of the Seine with her memories.

When she reached the green stall of her favorite *bouquiniste,*

Leah combed through a selection of French literary novels. Paris's renowned booksellers of antique and used books had plied their trade on the banks of the Seine for hundreds of years. Every Sunday, she and her father perused the shelves in search of the one book that would ignite their imaginations. It was a game they played to see who would discover a gem to discuss over the dinner table. She shook her head, pushing away those thoughts of family and life before the war. It was better not to dwell on what had been, better to focus on what was now. Walking around crying would only bring curious stares. Stares that could lead to unwanted attention.

She'd left Aidan sleeping in the flat. She imagined that after everything he'd been through, he could probably sleep for days. Especially after their encounter in the alley. *Thank heaven his wound is superficial.*

Last night she'd been so nervous lying beside Aidan in that small bed that she'd spent most of the night awake listening to his gentle snores. Even in the cold, her cheeks flushed with heat remembering. When she woke in the morning, she was surprised to find herself snuggled into Aidan's back. Of course, it made sense that in her sleep, she'd sought the warmth of his body. She hoped and prayed he hadn't noticed or would not think less of her if he had. At first, she'd been flabbergasted at herself, but it had felt so right, so *naturel,* that she just laid there, her body pressed against him, not wanting to pull away. It was beyond her experience, the scent of a man, and the power that emanated from him. A brazier couldn't have warmed her more. It took all her better sense to extract herself from the bed in the morning.

Her fingers lightly brushed the leather spines sitting on the shelf, coming to rest on Alexandre Dumas's *The Three Musketeers.*

Perfect. Leah added the book to her growing pile, which included Gustave Flaubert's *Madame Bovary,* and Victor Hugo's *Les*

Misérables, her favorite book of all time. At the last minute, she added Hugo's *The Hunchback of Notre-Dame,* which she couldn't resist. *I'm certain Aidan will enjoy it.* Excitement bubbled up inside her. She hoped he would like all of her selections, and they could discuss the books just as she and her father had.

An hour later, she let herself into the flat, surprised to find Aidan seated at the small table smoking a cigarette. He jumped up when he saw her, relieving her of the cloth sacks she'd toted up the stairs.

"Good Lord, Leah, how the hell did you manage all of this up those bloody stairs?"

"I'm used to it." She emptied the bags he'd set on the counter and then handed him the stack of books. "For you."

His eyes widened. "Smashing! I didn't expect you to bring them so soon." He brushed his fingers over one of the embossed titles. "I read *Les Misérables* years ago, but I could do with another go. I've always found the clarity Hugo delineates between good and evil revealing. Just like this war and our fight to defeat the Nazis. Good versus evil is not up for question." He met her gaze and reached for her hand. She didn't pull away. "This is jolly good of you. I do appreciate it."

"*Pas du tout.*"

"It may be nothing to you, but to me, your thoughtfulness means everything."

THE DAYS FLEW BY, WITH THE WEATHER ONLY GROWING COLDER. BUT inside the flat on the *rue Alexandre Dumas,* Leah kept warm in Aidan's company. They took turns reading to each other, filling their evenings with Guy de Maupassant's *Bel Ami,* Andre Breton's

Nadja, and George Sand's, *Indiana.* They read, argued, and discussed the books long into the night. And for a time, Leah forgot the darkness that loomed down the road.

It was nearly Christmas when the day came — the day Leah dreaded. She returned to the flat from her rendezvous that morning to find Aidan on the bed reading. It had become a dear and familiar sight, a warm memory she would tuck away in her heart during the cold nights ahead.

Leah shut the door and stood, trying to memorize every detail of Aidan's dear face. His eyes met hers, and as hard as she tried, she couldn't hide it. Didn't even bother wiping her eyes. She'd been crying all the way up the stairs.

He rose, and they both stared at one another for what seemed like an eternity.

"What is it?"

"Our *laissez passe* documents have come through," she whispered. "We leave tomorrow."

He closed the distance between them. Leah fell into his arms, sobbing.

"Shh, sweetheart, why the tears?"

Her face was wet when she gazed up at him. "I'm happy for you, really, I am. It's just that..."

His gaze made her breathless. Those sky-blue eyes filled her vision and made her yearn for something she could never have. And then he claimed her lips, and the world spun around her. She kissed him back with such heated fervor she had to drop her coat to the floor to cool down. They both drew ragged breaths. She could not, would not, drag her gaze away from his.

Without thinking — thinking was impossible — thinking might have called for reconsideration — she didn't want to think. All she wanted was to feel. She loved him. Truly. Completely. Hopelessly. Their lips and tongues met again in a symphony of passion. Aidan swept her up in his arms and carried her to the bed. The bed that had seemed so small was now perfect.

They made love for hours until exhaustion claimed them. They slept naked in each other's arms, and when they woke, it was dark, and they made love again.

It was joyous. Unquenchable. Everything Leah had imagined. Her mind sang, her body sang, and unable to restrain herself, she hummed, "You'll Never Know." Her head rested on his shoulder, her fingers gently playing with the hair on his chest. She kissed his neck, unable to get enough of him.

He smoked a cigarette. "I love that song, Leah, and I love it when you sing. I don't think I'll ever forget the first time I heard you in the bathtub, singing, "I'll Be Seeing You." I bloody cried my eyes out."

She watched the rings of smoke rise in the darkness, still marveling at the perfection of what they'd shared. "I'm glad you like my singing. At one time, I dreamed of being a professional singer."

"Don't stop dreaming, darling. When the war is over..."

"Yes. When the war is over." She looked away, wiping her eyes.

"Why are you crying, love? You're not sorry, are you? About us?"

"Sorry? Oh, God, no." She lay her hand on his cheek. "This. Us. It's the most beautiful thing that's ever happened to me."

"I'm not sorry, either. I'm torn. Angry at the unfairness of it all."

"What do you mean?"

He kissed the top of her head. "I can't bear the thought of leaving you, Leah."

She rose to her elbow and searched his face. "I can't either, but we both know it has to be."

He gazed at her, and she saw the love in his eyes.

"I love you, Aidan. I never expected to feel like this. I know what we've shared is only *une brève affaire,* but I wouldn't change it for the world. I feel as if I've lived a lifetime in these past few weeks. I will treasure this time we've shared forever."

"Oh, Leah, my love." He kissed her sweetly, endearingly, as if to imprint himself with her lips. "When this bloody war — "

She placed her fingers on his mouth, silencing him. "Let's not make promises we might not be able to keep."

"But — "

"No, buts."

He extinguished the cigarette in the ashtray and gathered her up in his arms. "Why don't we get married for real? Right now."

"And then what?"

"Then, we'll share a commitment to finding each other when it's over."

"It's too late, *mon amour.* We don't have time to get a marriage certificate or find someone to do the honors." Her fingers combed through his dark waves. "But, thank you for asking me. If it's worth anything to you, know that I'd marry you in a heartbeat."

"No matter what you say, Leah, when this nightmare is over, I'm going to find you and hold you to that."

"Just make love to me again, *mon coeur.*"

CHAPTER 11

January 14, Present day
Brooklyn, New York

The black velvet bag was on the nightstand just where she'd left it. Opening the pouch, she dumped the contents on the coverlet. It was a golden pin, a brooch about the size of her palm. Another lightning strike lit the room, and Rose gasped. The pin seemed to glow, radiating its own light.

Her pulse thrummed in her ears as she tentatively picked it up to examine more closely. Turning it in her hand, the heat from the talisman reverberated through her body. It had the weight of solid gold and was a perfect duplicate of the Ark of the Covenant. But how had it come to be and what did it mean to those three old women and her grandmother?

Snapping a picture of it with her phone, she began a search on Google and then stopped herself. Changing course, she logged onto the secure server housing the archives where she worked.

The brooch was a perfect duplicate of the biblical Ark of the Covenant. The *kapporet,* or cover, of the tiny gold amulet held two cherubs, angels who served God. They knelt in supplication with the tips of their wings touching. Where their wings touched, they formed what has been described as the Mercy Seat, purportedly where God listened once a year on Yom Kippur to the High Priest's plea for forgiveness and for the Lord's atonement to his people.

The Ark was said to contain the two stone tablets of the Ten Commandments, one broken and one intact. The first had been hurled and broken by Moses when he found the tribes worshipping the golden calf, and the other was God's gift of forgiveness, a duplicate given to Moses when he returned to Mount Sinai. Also carried within the sacred sarcophagus was the staff of Aaron, which had performed the miracles that freed the Jews and gained them exodus from Egypt. Most notably, Aaron's staff had magically become a fearsome snake that had proven the power of the Lord when it devoured the snakes conjured by Pharaoh's magicians. And finally, the Ark was also said to hold a golden bowl containing manna. During their forty-year trek through the desert, the Jews survived on manna that rained down from Heaven.

In a description from the book of Shemot (Exodus) chapter 25 Rose read that the Ark of the Covenant carried the essence of God, and as such, it represented God's covenant with the Jewish people.

The brooch entrusted to Rose was an exact replica. She was mystified by its glow and the heat it emitted. But what was she to do with it?

Goosebumps rose on her arms when she heard a creak coming from the closet.

Carefully, Rose set the brooch down on the coverlet, then stood and inched her way to the closet. Opening the door, she flicked on the light, and her knees buckled at the sight. There at the back of Leah's closet hung the blue coat. Dazed, she tried to come up with some reasonable explanation for it. But nothing could explain this.

Trembling, she lifted the worn garment off the hanger. She carried it from the closet, and feeling compelled, she gently laid it on the bed. She didn't understand how the old coat kept reappearing, but she had to accept that the strange heirloom was here to stay.

You are the chosen one, Rose.

No amount of rationalization or explanation could alter what was undeniable — this tattered old blue coat and the Ark of the Covenant brooch had been bequeathed to her by her grandmother and were hers to protect.

Rose's hands shook as she pinned the brooch to the lapel of the coat. At first, the changes were nearly indiscernible. But with every second, the royal blue color of the coat grew richer, deeper, brighter. The loose threads of the garment bonded together, sealing holes and snags. A few moments later, Rose stared in awe at a coat as new as the day it was first made.

The coat was beautiful. Lifting it from the bed, Rose examined it more closely. The wool was soft and pliable. A freshly stitched satin label on the inside of the lapel read *Au Bon Marche, PARIS.* The coat must have come from the venerable old department store.

Tears sprang to Rose's eyes. It had to be Leah's.

"Why, Bubbie? Why did you never show me or tell me anything while you were alive?"

Questions tumbled in her mind. How had it survived the war? How had Leah managed to hold onto it in Auschwitz? Most of all, why didn't her practical, talented grandmother tell her that magic was real? She sure hoped it was magic and that she wasn't developing schizophrenia.

The sounds from the storm faded away, and a warm glow

surrounded Rose, like a hug from her grandmother. "Try it on, *ma belle fille*," a whisper cajoled in her ear. Like fingers strumming the strings of a harp, she was being played, and the music was other-worldly.

Standing before her grandmother's antique gold full-length mirror, Rose slipped first one arm and then the other into the sleeves. She ran her hands down the front of the soft material and turned in front of the mirror. The coat fit as if it had been made for her. The Ark of the Covenant brooch emitted a dazzling light that seemed to grow stronger as she gazed at herself in the mirror.

Rose's body tingled, and her skin shone with a pearlescent glow, but then her image in the mirror began to fade.

What's happening?

She looked down at her hands, and they seemed unchanged. But when she lifted her eyes to look in the mirror, her image had grown transparent, and before she could remove the coat, the image faded into nothing. No reflection. She'd disappeared.

The room began to spin around her, and her knees buckled. Golden threads of light wrapped around her body and pulled her through the mirror. This was no gentle tug. Rose twisted and turned, her body hurtling through a tunnel of light. She was so dizzy it was all she could do not to throw up. She had no idea where she was headed, so she closed her eyes tight, wrapped her arms around her body, and prayed she would make it through alive.

Rose flew for what seemed like an eternity but couldn't have been more than a few moments. She screamed in panic until a soothing voice reached her ears, "*Calme-toi, ma chérie*, you will get there soon enough."

Rose grunted as she tumbled onto a hard surface. A crash resounded behind her, and she opened her eyes and saw her grandmother's antique gold mirror crack and splinter. Rose screamed again and covered her head as shards of glass flew out in every direction. And then it stopped. Silence. Blessed quiet. Slowly, Rose lifted her head and opened her eyes.

CHAPTER 12

December 26, 1942
Bordeaux, France

The countryside flew past the window in a blur of white as the train sped toward Bordeaux. Leah twisted the gold band around her wedding finger, her body jostling against Aidan's while he slept. They'd boarded the train in the thirteenth arrondissement at the Gare d'Austerlitz station without incident, their identification papers holding up to scrutiny. Leah was used to rubbing shoulders with the Germans daily, it was *un fait de la vie,* a distressing fact of life, but she was certain Aidan wanted to kill each of them with his bare hands. He'd been cooped up in the apartment and hadn't really witnessed what the German occupation was like.

And now everything had changed. There was only a scant chance they would find each other, yet it was all she could think about. A tiny flame of hope kindled in her heart. She looked down at the ring on her finger. It was a fake in every sense of the word, but for her, it symbolized her dearest wish.

The train ground to a halt, wheels screeching, and Leah peered out the window, realizing they'd arrived at the Gare de Bordeaux-Saint-Jean. She smiled and turned to Aidan, who hadn't moved. He had an uncanny ability to grab his sleep when needed. How he filtered out the noise of the train was beyond her. She was wide awake, her senses on high alert. She had to assume his military training had taught him to sleep anywhere, anytime, and under any conditions. Bringing her lips to his ear, she whispered, "*Réveille-toi, chérie*, we're here."

Aidan's eyes blinked open, and he smiled. "I look forward to someday waking every day to your voice in my ear." He kissed her and then stood, grabbing their bags from the mesh storage net above their heads. She suppressed a giggle, recalling that first night when he scolded her on the importance of being a convincing couple. *I'd say we're more than convincing now.*

They followed the queue of passengers out to the platform where billowing clouds of white steam condensed in the air. Without dawdling, they left the station and walked across the street to the Café Rouge where they were to be met by the first of their contacts from the *Réseau Comète*.

The café was empty. *Where is he?*

Leah tried to control the butterflies in her stomach. Her nerves raw, she could barely swallow. Loitering could spell disaster, especially when moments later, two German officers entered the café. Upon seeing them, Aidan nodded to a table in the far corner near the window, as far from the Germans as he could muster.

How does he do it, she wondered. *How does he remain so calm?*

Aidan lightly drummed his fingers on the table, waiting for the waiter, who took the German officers' orders first. The waiter, no fool, understood where his priorities lay. Leah noticed the double lightning bolts on the officers' collars and shrank back in her chair.

When the waiter finally came to their table, Aidan maintained his composure and ordered for both of them. Several times the Germans glanced at them, their appraising eyes drifting approvingly over Leah. Their guttural German tones made Leah's skin crawl, and their glances made it hard for her to breathe. But Aidan, sensing her discomfort, came to her rescue. He leaned in to steal a kiss and said just loud enough for the Germans to hear. "And what would my pretty wife like?"

"*Café au chocolat, s'il-vous plait.*" She regained her composure, ignoring the Germans and focused her attention on the man who meant everything to her. She caressed his face; she didn't have to act.

The Germans' got the picture and turned away, resuming their conversation.

Leah had been instructed to wear a flower in her hatband so their contact would easily recognize her, but with two Germans in the café, it was unlikely the man would ever approach.

Their coffees arrived, and after he took a sip, Aidan's smile told her the black liquid wasn't the tasteless fake brew available in Paris. At least his hand didn't shake when he lifted the cup to his lips, which was more than she could say about hers. She tried not to spill coffee all over the table and herself. When they finished, Aidan stood and grabbed their carry-ons. Remaining in the café with the Germans was impossible.

"*Allons-nous, ma chérie.*" Without making eye contact with the Germans, they left the café. Their proximity to the train station meant there were plenty of people milling about. Leah marveled at the sight. Regardless of the war and German occupation, life went on — the French clung to their routines as if determined to prove everything was normal.

"What are we going to do?" asked Leah.

"We can't stand here, that's for sure. Come on." They walked, falling into step behind a woman who seemed to know where she was going. They crossed several streets, distancing themselves from the Germans and the café. Aidan surreptitiously glanced back several times. "I think we're being followed. Don't look."

Her heart thundered in her chest. Could it be one of the Germans from the café? "What should we do?" she whispered.

The woman they'd been following crossed a street ahead of them. "We'll turn right at the next block and see if he turns and follows us."

Fear altered Leah's perception. Every footstep behind them was a Nazi closing in, every tree hid a collaborator ready to pounce, every glance from a passerby was suspicious. It was all Leah could do not to break into a run. When the tap on her shoulder came, she nearly fainted dead.

"Madame and Monsieur Vernier, follow me."

"But why?" she begged. "We've done nothing."

"Shhh, relax, do as he says," Aidan said.

Startled, she turned to Aidan.

"It's okay. He's one of us."

"How do you know?"

The man raised his gray fedora in greeting, the toothy smile on his face reassuring.

The hat! Of course. She sighed with relief. In her panic, she'd forgotten, and then, of course, how would he have known their names. *I'm such a fool.*

"You can call me Henri Dupris. I've been following you since you arrived. I was supposed to meet you in the café, but the Germans — " He shook his head. "You understand, it was better

I didn't make myself known to you. I'm taking you to a safe house only a few blocks from here where you'll stay the night," he whispered. He linked his arm through Leah's, and in a louder, jovial voice he said, "It's wonderful to see you, dear sister," as he guided her down the street with Aidan following close behind.

The apartment was on a narrow, cobblestoned street, the houses butting up against each other. Henri inserted a key in the door of an old brick walk-up with red painted shutters. "Up the stairs, *s'il-vous plait*." Henri locked the door behind Aidan and followed them up a rickety set of wooden stairs to the third floor. Their steps creaked, echoing in the dimly lit stairwell. Leah stood back as Henri unlocked the door with its yellowing, chipped paint. The flat was small and dingy with an unmade bed in the corner. The sheet and blanket were thrown aside as if whoever had slept in it had just jumped up and fled.

"Sorry, my wife wasn't feeling well today and couldn't come to tidy up and change the sheets. A pilot slept here last night, and this morning he left early for Bayonne."

"I hope your wife feels better soon," Leah offered.

"The freezing temperatures and lack of coal have taken a toll on everyone, I'm afraid. We've been trading off colds all winter." He sighed. "I can't stay long." From the inside pocket of his coat, he removed two train tickets and handed them to Aidan. "Your departure is at nine a.m., get there early and find seats in the front. It looks less suspicious. Tomorrow is Sunday, so most of the Germans will be hungover and hopefully won't be traveling on the early train. Just remember, if you're questioned, your parents live on the rue d'Espagne — Paulette, and Michele Sauvage. They have a small antique shop near the Cathédrale de Sainte-Marie in the old city on the left bank of the Nive River. You and Lucien married a month ago, and you're here, Nadia, to introduce your new *mari* to your family. I'm sure you have your stories down pat by now."

"What happens when we get to Bayonne?" Aidan asked.

"You'll be met by a woman who will billet you for the night in another safe house. She will be wearing a yellow rose pinned to her dress. In the morning, you'll be given bikes, and you'll ride to Saint Jean de Luz. One more night at an isolated farmhouse, and you will be handed over to the *mugalari,* the local Basque smugglers. They will guide you over the mountains out of France and into Spain. *Voilà,* you'll be on your way home." He buttoned up his coat. "Good luck, *monsieur.*" He turned to Leah, *"Mademoiselle,* safe journey back to Paris." Henri stepped to the door and stopped. "Oh, I nearly forgot. There's some food for you in the icebox. *Au revoir et bonne chance."*

AIDAN LAY AWAKE, HIS GAZE FIXED ON LEAH AS SHE SLEPT. WITHOUT a camera to preserve his memory, he studied her face, imprinting her beloved features in his mind. It wouldn't be possible to forget what she looked like, would it? But he knew time could be cruel, and even the most profound memories of loved ones were apt to fade like photographs with the passage of years. There was no way of knowing how long the war would last or when he would find her again.

He was painfully aware of the hours and minutes counting down their time together. Two more nights was all they had. Perhaps it was this pending loss that fueled his passion. But every time he made love to her, the fire grew stronger, and his desire to remain with her tortured his soul. He wanted to capture her kisses in a glass and slowly sip them for the rest of his life. He wanted to stay awake all night, drinking in her beauty, illuminated by moonlight filtering in through the small curtained window. There would be plenty of time to sleep after.

In the morning, they walked in silence through the streets back to the Gare de Bordeaux-Saint-Jean. The closer they got to pending separation, the more words became superfluous. After all, what could be said that hadn't already been said? They boarded the train and sat in the front just as Henri had instructed. Aidan leaned his head back against the seat and closed his eyes. It was approximately two hours to Bayonne, and he finally allowed sleep to claim him.

He had no idea how long he'd dozed off, but suddenly his eyes flew open. A woman's cry followed by guttural shouts of men and the vicious barking of dogs pierced his sleepy consciousness. Leah gripped his hand. Her face was bone-white, her eyes stark.

"Run to the back, Aidan! Get off the train!"

He peered out the window and cursed under his breath. The police and their dogs were everywhere. It was impossible to know what had happened. Had they been denounced? Was this routine? "I can't leave you."

"Don't worry about me. I'll be fine. You must escape. Please, I beg of you, go!"

He stood, grabbed his bag, and turned to her. "I'll find you. I swear, I'll find you."

Tears stained her face. "Live my darling. Live for both of us."

LEAH TOUCHED HER LIPS, STILL WARM FROM AIDAN'S BURNING KISS. Their final kiss? It had happened so fast there'd been no time to think. She stared out the window, hoping to catch a glimpse of him, but she saw only German uniforms. She prayed. She prayed for Aidan's safety. She prayed they would find each other again. She prayed for the end of this brutal war.

The shouts from the Gestapo as they searched each compartment stormed around her. Leah leaned back against the seat and closed her eyes.

Live, my darling.

CHAPTER 13

January 14, 1943
Limousin, France

A frigid wind blew through her hair, and icy drops of moisture landed on her face. Carefully, she stood on wobbly legs. She looked down and noticed she was wearing a pair of antique leather boots she'd never seen before. Only they weren't antique, they were brand new. But they looked like shoes her grandmother would have worn as a young woman. Rose took a few tentative steps and managed to keep her balance. The ground beneath her feet was frozen. She squinted into the darkness of night, trying to see through the snowflakes that clung to her lashes and drifted silently down around her.

Out of nowhere came the distant echo of laughter. She turned — ahead was a tall stand of trees — a forest. She narrowed her eyes, searching the black void that surrounded her, then spied a flicker of light. From a distance, she again heard muted laughter.

Trudging forward through drifts of snow toward the voices and the beckoning warmth, she swallowed her fears — her instinct told her this was where she was supposed to go.

The snow crunched beneath her feet. Surprisingly, the blue coat kept her warm, except for her hands, which had become numb from the cold. She stuck them in her pockets and was surprised to find a pair of gloves. Gloves that hadn't been there before. She slipped them on and held up her hands in the darkness, realizing they were the same blue as the coat. She blew out a deep breath and trudged onward toward the flickering light in the distance.

The light was coming from a campfire. Rose's heart palpitated in her chest as she stepped over fallen logs and trudged through deep banks of snow. Having reached the clearing, she moved slowly, fearful of what she might find.

Around the campfire, a dozen men huddled together, passing a silver flask among them. When she stepped on a twig, they all jumped up, pointing guns and rifles at her. She raised her hands, indicating she wasn't a threat.

"*S'il vous plaît, ne tirez pas,*" she said in French. "Please, don't shoot," she repeated in English.

A rough voice asked in French. "What are you doing here in the middle of the forest? How the hell did you get here?"

Another man barked, "Don't trust her. She's probably a spy working for the *krauts*. Shoot her!"

Bile burned her throat. "I'm not a spy. I-I'm lost."

"Poor little Bo-Peep has lost her sheep," yelled another man. "The little sparrow has probably led the Germans right to our door. I say we kill her."

"*Non,* I'm alone," she called back. "Help me, please, I don't know where I am."

Cynical laughter reached her ears. "Poor little damsel in

distress. Why don't we take turns with her? It seems like years since I've lain with a woman. A redhead no less, and pretty."

From somewhere behind the threatening group, a man pushed forward. "Shut-up, you animals, can't you see she's harmless? Think of your mothers, your sisters. Besides, I know this woman."

"You're just trying to keep her for yourself," another man growled.

The man with the British accent pulled his gun and pointed it around the circle, aiming with deadly intent at each of them. "Any of you want to die tonight, just touch a hair on her head. She's a *passeur* with *La Résistance*."

Rose held her breath. She had no idea who the man was, but she sensed she could trust him. It was better to deal with one man than a dozen. But how could he possibly know her?

The man must have held sway because the rest of the men backed down. They holstered their weapons and resumed their places around the fire, whispering among themselves.

The Brit walked toward her. He was tall and lean, but with the fire behind him, she couldn't make out his features. When he reached her, he studied her face. Hoarse, his words were thick with emotion. "Dear God, Leah, I thought you were dead."

Rose stared at him with wide eyes, unable to speak. *He thinks I'm my grandmother! Dear God, how did this happen?* She swallowed hard. From the men's clothing and their mention of the resistance, Rose assumed she'd been hurtled back to France during World War Two, but beyond that, she knew nothing.

"Never mind, you can tell me everything later," he whispered. "This is a rowdy bunch of *maquis* fighters. I don't trust them as far as I can throw them. Don't say anything until I tell you it's safe. Voices travel easily at night. I need to get you out of here." He took her arm and led her past the resistance fighters, his hand still holding the pistol.

They walked deeper into the forest. From the corner of her eye, she glimpsed sky-blue eyes and dark wavy hair. He had a scraggly beard and mustache, no doubt from the rough conditions living in the wilderness. But who was he, and how did he know her grandmother? Leah had always said Rose looked like her as a young woman, even though there were no photos of Leah before she immigrated to America. But for this man to mistake her for Leah seemed impossible. But then, she reminded herself, nothing about what had happened since she put on the blue coat made any sense.

They reached a small encampment with a makeshift tent. A large breed of mastiff standing just outside the tent let out a low growl.

"It's okay, Winston," her rescuer said.

The dog suddenly transformed into a gigantic puppy and loped up to them, his tail wagging. He sniffed Rose's coat and deciding she was acceptable, turned to greet his owner, licking his hand and making those delightful universal dog grunts of happiness.

"You have a dog?"

"I rescued him from a stream shortly after I got here. He'd escaped from somewhere, and the rope around his neck had gotten caught between two rocks. We've been together ever since. Since then, he's saved my life a time or two." The man smiled, and his gaunt face transformed with his mirth. He was very handsome. "Are you cold?" he asked.

"No, I'm fine, just scared."

Before she could protest, he pulled her into his arms and pressed a kiss to her lips. "Darling, I prayed, but I never dreamed I'd find you again. When we parted, I thought my life had lost all meaning. Nothing has changed about the way I feel about you." His kiss was so tender, tears sprang to her eyes.

A few moments later, he pulled back and cupped her cheeks with his hands. "I can't believe fate has brought you back to me. You must tell me how you got here. Dash it! You're the most beautiful thing I've ever seen." His blue eyes glowed with tenderness.

How could she tell him the truth? Surely, he'd think her mad. Rose didn't know what to do or say, so she decided to pretend to be Leah for a while until she could figure out how best to manage the situation. Whoever this man was, he clearly had deep feelings for her grandmother. She swallowed hard. "*Mon amour*, I've dreamt of this moment. Tell me everything about what happened since we parted." She covered his hands with hers.

He chuckled. "This will take some time. Come," he nodded to the tent. "Welcome to my humble abode." He took her hand and led her to the entrance. He patted the dog on his head. "*Garde, Winston,*" he commanded in French. The dog sat at attention, his gaze fixed on the landscape. "*Bon chien.*"

He opened the flap. "*Après vous.*" She knelt and crawled in. The space was tiny, scarcely large enough for one person, let alone two. A bedroll took up most of the space. A backpack sat in the corner. A rifle rested against the side of the tent. He followed her gaze as she inspected the small space. "It's not much, darling, but you're safe. No one will bother us with Winston keeping guard."

She nodded and sat with her legs tucked beneath her. The Englishman lay next to her, resting his head on his hands and staring up as if gazing at a star-filled sky. "I guess I should start when I ran from the train in Bordeaux. Leaving you tore me in two. But I knew you were right, I had to flee. Had they caught us together, they would have arrested us both, and I could not have protected you. Without me there, no one would question a girl going to visit her parents."

He grabbed his backpack and pulled out a leather case with cigarettes. He lit one, pausing to take a drag and exhaling.

Rose wasn't used to being in such close quarters with a smoker. She'd never smoked a day in her life, and none of her friends were smokers, either. A friend had set her up on a blind date once with a guy who vaped, and that was a definite deal-breaker for Rose. That, and he turned out to be a jerk. This man seemed the opposite, despite his bad habit. The word *hero* sprang to mind. The only explanation was Leah had fallen in love with an English soldier fighting with the resistance. Whatever had happened, they'd become separated and lost track of each other.

"After I escaped," he continued, "I did my best to blend into the crowd. I had nowhere to turn, so I headed back to the flat where we spent our last night together." He released his breath. "You don't know this, but after we made love, I spent the whole night awake, watching you sleep. I didn't want to miss a single moment of loving you."

Her eyes widened as she began to understand. She was hearing the confession of a man who had given his heart entirely to her grandmother. Leah had loved him, and he'd loved her.

Oh Bubbie, you loved this man, didn't you?

Playing the part of Leah, Rose wondered how she was going to figure out this man's name. She smiled tenderly at him, this stranger who'd loved her grandmother and caressed his bearded cheek. "Continue, my darling," she said softly.

Reaching for her hand, he kissed her palm. "You know it's funny the things that remain with you. We both had those fake papers showing us to be newlyweds — Lucien and Nadia Vernier — but when you saw the Nazis boarding the train, everything flew out the window. You called me Aidan instead of Lucien and begged me to run, to save myself. I loved you for your bravery, for your honesty, for your passion. In that last frantic moment, what did it matter? All that mattered was who we really were and what we meant to each other. We were Aidan and Leah, who'd fallen in love at the worst possible moment. In the middle of a bloody war."

Thank God, he mentioned his name. "Aidan, there are no bad times to fall in love. It's a precious gift." *I must be channeling you, Bubbie, because I sure as heck never felt that precious gift. I wish I had. I wish I will someday.*

"Of course it is, my darling," he agreed. "Now that we're together again, I'll keep you safe. I promise." He stubbed his cigarette out and sat up. Wrapping his arms around her, planting delicate kisses along her brow and down her cheek. "I wish I could make you Mrs. McQueen right now, but we'll have to wait until this goddamn war is over."

Aidan McQueen. She could understand why her grandmother had fallen in love with this man. Aidan was strong, brave, and unafraid to love. Trembling like a leaf in the wind and fighting back tears, Rose closed her eyes as he tightened his arms around her.

She had no idea why the blue coat had transported her back. What her purpose was. Leah and her friends believed Rose to be the next chosen one, but what was her mission? She knew quite a bit about the War from her studies and her job as a librarian, but what would happen if she revealed what she knew to Aidan? Would he think her a spy or a crazy person? She couldn't do that to him — to his memory of Leah. *Bubbie, what should I do?*

Her instinct told her it was only a matter of time before the coat would return her to the future. At least she hoped so. She could not stay with her grandmother's lover. "Aidan, this can only be a brief reunion. I can't stay."

His body tensed. "I understand. Your welfare is my first priority. You're not safe in the middle of a forest with a band of partisans. A rag-tag army at best of morally suspect desperados." His brows drew together. "How did you get here anyway?"

"Before I tell you, please finish the end of your tale."

His tone softened. "Sorry, but the thought of losing you again tears me apart."

She took his hand, her fingers twining with his. "Go on."

"I managed to get into the flat, and I spent the night there. But Henri Dupris never returned. I figure whoever denounced us, denounced him. It was only a matter of time before the Germans figured out where the safe house was. In the morning, on foot, I headed to Saint Jean de Luz, hoping I could find my way to the Basque smugglers, and they could safely get me over the Pyrenees. But it seems my luck abandoned me. The Germans arrested me just outside of Bayonne."

"How did you get away?"

"Lucky for me, my transport carried a couple of resistance fighters they'd just arrested. We were on our way to an internment camp when the convoy was ambushed. Sloppy bunch of fighters, these frogs. It was chaos. But I saw an opportunity. I wrestled a German, got his gun, and put a bullet in him. In the end, the good guys won. The partisans were impressed and took me in. And here I am, in this godforsaken no man's land. I prefer His Majesty's Royal Navy, but I haven't figured out how to get back home yet." He rolled over and pulled her into his arms. "God, I wish I had me a shower and a razor, but I'm a bit of a varmint right now. I wouldn't dare contaminate you. But dear Lord, how I want to. You know your scent, darling, is enough to drive this man wild. Now be a love and tell me how the hell you got here?"

Do I dare tell him the truth? There had to be some kind of unwritten law that when you go back in time, you don't interfere with events. *Did I really think that? Rules or laws about time travel? Isn't that what straitjackets are for?*

And then it hit her, a flash of an idea, but maybe Aidan would buy it. It was as if the words channeled through her from Leah.

"After you fled, the Germans went through all of the compartments on the train. I was terrified that one of the other passengers would denounce me. After all, they all heard me tell you to run and saw you flee. You can imagine how scared I was. I tried to be brave like you, but I was shaking and terrified. But my fellow countrymen came to my rescue. No one in my compartment said a word. They made no contact with me, nor did they denounce me. They didn't look at me or acknowledge me. Every one of them said they hadn't seen anything unusual. I don't think I took a breath until those German officers moved on to the next car."

"I'm so sorry, my love, that you had to go through that. You must have been terrified. If it wasn't for me—"

She put her fingers to his lips. "Don't even say it. I had already made my decision to do what I had to do. We both knew what we were getting into."

He kissed her finger. "One day, I'm going to make it up to you. All I want is to spend my life making you happy. Promise me you'll sing for me every day."

If she'd had any doubts that his Leah was her grandmother, they disappeared with that request. Her grandmother had always had the most beautiful singing voice. Why she didn't pursue a career in music was a tragedy. Rose wondered if it had anything to do with losing Aidan. Singing would always be a reminder of the love she'd lost. *Oh, Bubbie, my heart is breaking for you. Aidan loved you so much, and you lost each other.*

"Did you return to Paris?" Aidan broke into her thoughts.

She hated lying to him. With every word, she was digging a deeper hole for herself. "Yes. I was devastated that I'd failed to get you out of France. I spent the rest of my time until now trying to find you. I heard a rumor that there were British fighting with the *maquis,* so I volunteered to deliver a message. I'd hoped you were among the fighters. The Germans are planning major raids in this area. They're planning to come down heavy and clean out these woods. You're all in danger. You need to break up and vanish into the surrounding villages."

His thick straight brows drew together. "You shouldn't have taken such a risk, Leah. You need to get away from here before any fighting begins —" The crackle of gunfire cut short his words. Winston's low growl warned something wasn't right. Aidan shot up and grabbed his gun. "Quick, we've got to move!"

"What do you think it is?"

"I don't know, but we're not waiting to find out." He flipped open the tent flap, grabbed her hand, and pulled her out. "Let's go."

Rose froze in place at the rat-a-tat-tat sound of machine-gun fire. The shouts and screams that followed scared her senseless.

"Leah," Aidan shouted. "Move!"

Everything became a blur after that. They ran and ran. Aidan's hand gripped hers so tight she lost all feeling in her fingers. Winston, the most brilliant dog in the world, never barked once and stayed right behind them, protecting their backs. Rose stumbled, but Aidan managed to keep her upright. She couldn't breathe, she couldn't think. Every muscle in her body strained to keep up with his punishing stride.

I'm going to die here in the past.

The sharp report of a gun echoed in the night, and Aidan fell forward, collapsing on the ground. She screamed and dropped to her knees beside him. Blood gushed from his shoulder, but his chest continued to rise and fall. *He's alive.*

"Run," he panted.

Run where? "I'm not leaving you," she cried.

"You have to go. Find a place to hide. I'll delay them."

"I can't!" A torrent of tears wet her cheeks.

"Leah, bloody do as I say. Remember what you said to me on

the train. 'Live for both of us.' I'm saying that to you now. Please darling, if you love me, go and live for both of us. If I survive, I promise I'll find you."

She was hysterical, sobbing. The shouting was getting closer, and the barking of dogs grew louder. Winston stood by his master stoically, looking back toward the sounds and growling.

"For the love of God, Leah, do this for me. Kiss me and go. Please!"

Blinded by tears, she kissed him, then stood and ran as fast as her wobbly legs would carry her. She had no idea where to go. Already her guilt was wreaking havoc with her mind. How could she leave Leah's Aidan like that? Was she reliving something that had already happened? Or was this something being revealed to her that she needed to know? The snow was deep and blanketed the ground, making it harder for her to run.

A gunshot echoed through the winter landscape, and she stopped. She turned around and looked back to where she'd left Aidan and Winston. *Please, God, don't let them die.* She squinted, trying to see through the blackness of night. A shadow approached from the trees, holding a rifle pointed directly at her. *This is it. This is where I die.* She was too tired to run, too tired to fight. The loss of Aidan pressed heavily on her, crushing her spirit.

She didn't understand German, but she understood the soldier motioning with the barrel of his rifle for her. Trembling from head to toe, she raised her hands in surrender. She wanted to ask the soldier if Aidan was alive but was too terrified.

Her knees knocked together, and her mouth was so dry she was tempted to scoop up a handful of snow and stuff it in her mouth.

The soldier motioned for her to walk back to where she'd left Aidan, but she couldn't move. She was dizzy and breathless. The soldier's face contorted with rage. His mouth moved, but it sounded as if he was talking in slow motion. She stared at his lips, trying to make sense of what he was saying. All she could hear was the deafening whizz of wind screeching like a tornado around her. She lowered her hands to cover her ears, and the soldier must have shouted something at her. His mouth twisted and his eyes narrowed. His face mottled with anger, he aimed his rifle at her and pulled the trigger.

Rose saw it all in slow-motion. The bullet emerged from the barrel in a burst of sparks and flew toward her. It was inches away when her body began to disappear. She couldn't see her hands. She was fading away. The bullet passed through her chest, but nothing happened. The look on the soldier's face went from fury to confusion to fear as golden threads of light wrapped around her.

And then she was gone.

The pulsing bright light carried her forward once more for what seemed an eternity. It was like being pinned to the wall of a Gravitron amusement ride. The centrifugal force held her in place, hurtling her through what looked like a shimmering wall of water. She closed her eyes and held her breath, hoping she wouldn't drown. She landed with a thud. She sat up and screamed, expecting to be eviscerated by the shards of glass that flew through the black hole of the mirrorless frame. The shards froze midair, then turned molten, wavering, and then they sealed solid. Unbroken. Fixed.

Rose gaped at her reflection in the smooth mirror. She collapsed onto her back, gulping air as if she'd been drowning. She could feel her hands, and when she raised them, they were no longer see-through, but they were icy cold. Confusing thoughts and images swirled in her mind. Overwhelmed, she kept taking deep breaths to calm herself and her churning thoughts. Finally, her mind cleared, and she remembered everything. "Aidan

McQueen." She whispered his name if only to prove he'd existed. Had he? And if so, did he survive that night or the war? *Why didn't you find each other after the war, Bubbie?*

Rose unpinned the brooch, afraid that it might send her back in time again. Mesmerized, she watched the coat return to its tattered state.

How had a girl who had never sought adventure in her life suddenly fallen down the rabbit hole? She held the brooch in her left hand. "What do you want from me?" She felt the brooch grow warm, then hot in an instant. She dropped it on the floor. Blowing on her palm, she watched with disbelief as words began to appear on her skin: *The Lord himself will fight for you; you need only to be still.*

How? What? Her heart somersaulted in her chest. *Biblical?* She ran to her computer and booted up and typed the words that had been burned into her palm. Exodus 14:14 popped up. The Israelites stood before the Red Sea, and Moses directed that the people must place their trust in the Lord, who would see them freed from the land of Egypt. Pharaoh and his armies were on their heels, but the Lord would vanquish them. It was a leap of faith for the Jews to walk across the bottom of the sea between massive walls of water. To trust that the magical hands of God would hold the walls of liquid at bay until they safely reached the shore.

But why this message to her? What was she being asked to do? Was she supposed to place her faith in an inanimate object? Hadn't the Jews been punished for their worship of the golden calf, which was an inanimate object?

The message on her hand became an indelible tattoo. There was no pain or burning sensation, but fear churned in her gut.

Rose had to figure out what the hell was going on. She had five more days of shiva, and then she'd get in touch with her grandmother's friends. She needed answers, and they had some explaining to do. Without any directions, they'd dropped a hot potato in her hand, literally. She wasn't going to take up some cause that would put her life in danger without good reason. So far, all she'd been given were dreams, nightmares, hallucinations, and now she bore a brand on her palm. Her life had been completely upended, and she wanted to know why.

CHAPTER 14

January 20, Present day
New York, New York
David Berg Rare Book Library

The pneumatic motor lifted each delicate page of the glass-encased ancient tome with a soft whisper. Scholars and visitors read in silence, accompanied by the light tap-tap-tapping of laptop keyboards. Hundreds of books lined the glass-fronted shelves in the reading room of the David Berg Rare Book Library.

Rose glanced at her watch and noted the time was approaching noon. In between assisting patrons and switching out the books and manuscripts, she'd spent most of the morning searching through the digital archives for any mention of an Ark of the Covenant brooch. None of her keywords had turned up a thing. There was plenty of information on the ark itself but nothing on the magical brooch. Wherever the brooch had come from, there was no mention of its existence in the most extensive collection of Jewish history in the world.

Frustrated, Rose phoned the only person who could offer some guidance.

"Hi, Frida, this is Rose Levi, Leah Manheim's granddaughter."

"Rose, my dear, how are you doing?"

"Confused, upset, grieving, worried—"

"Oy vey, that's understandable," Frida interrupted.

"I have questions about—"

"The brooch," she cut in again.

"Yes, and the blue coat, and all the other things that Leah never told me."

"Of course, of course. You must have a thousand questions." The crinkling sound of rustling pages came through the phone.

"I do. I feel like I've been tossed out to sea without a life jacket."

"Oh, dear, God forbid! Let me get back to you in one hour. I need to make some arrangements. Let me try to arrange a meeting at Esther Finklestein's apartment for tonight. She lives in Williamsburg. I'll text you the address and time. I'm glad you've decided to pick up the mantle."

"I-I haven't decided anything yet."

"No need to discuss this on the phone. I don't trust these high-tech gizmos."

"Oh...right...of course. I'll wait to hear from you. Goodbye, Frida."

"*The Lord himself will fight for you; you need only to be still. Shalom*, Rose."

The line went dead. Rose's heart nearly jumped out of her chest. She pressed her fingers against the bandage on her left hand that hid the tattoo of the Biblical passage. The last thing she needed was probing questions from coworkers or raised eyebrows from patrons.

She sure as heck wanted to know what she was getting into. If her grandmother's gray-haired cronies didn't have the right answers, she'd give the damn brooch back to them. So far, she'd been hauled back to World War II, kissed by her grandmother's lover, chased by German soldiers, shot in the chest, and tattooed on the palm of her hand. Leah may have been a brave resistance fighter, but Rose could barely throw a punch — how in the world would she be able to accomplish whatever her grandmother had wanted? She was just plain, ordinary Rose Levi — librarian, reader of books, and drinker of tea. *I'm sorry, Bubbie, but I don't think I can live up to your expectations.*

ROSE DROVE OVER THE WILLIAMSBURG BRIDGE ACROSS THE EAST River and followed the navigation system's directions until she arrived at a red brick building on Berry Street, walking distance to McCarren Park. Rose knew the Williamsburg neighborhood and Brooklyn bordered one another. She parked and took a deep breath. *Frida, I hope you and your friends can help me.*

Rose took the elevator to the fourth floor and was about to knock on the door when it swung open. Frida, like Leah, was always elegantly attired. Wearing a winter-white pantsuit with navy ballerina slippers and a thick rope of pearls around her neck, she smiled warmly. "Rose, darling, come in." Frida embraced her and kissed her on both cheeks. Rose followed her into the apartment, discreetly wiping her cheeks clean of the heavy red lipstick that Frida had left behind.

Scented candles burned around the living room, and a gas-burning fireplace supplied flickering flames of warmth. The cozy room displayed numerous items that pointed to its Jewish ownership, including a Chanukah menorah on a side table. A shofar, the ram's horn that is blown on Rosh Hashanah to welcome in the New Year, rested on a Lucite stand on the mantle. The walls were decorated with what had to be Esther's own creations of needlepoint tapestries proclaiming familiar psalms and the Ten Commandments.

Beautiful Chagall prints danced across the walls with images of flying lovers and fiddlers on rooftops, and on every tabletop were photographs of family celebrations. Yes, the forward motion of time could not be arrested, even by genocide. Life continued and could not be lassoed by the vagaries of death or doubt. As certain as the sun rising and setting at day's end, or the circular cycle of birth, aging, and death, life continued for better or for worse.

Rose smiled at the array of old ladies seated in the living room. They were all dressed up as if they were the attendees of a party. Sugary sweetness perfumed the air from an array of cakes and cookies on the coffee table.

"Darling, you must have some rugelach before we begin. You remember at the shiva I told you about Sonia's pastries. I tell you they're irresistible. Just like the commercial says, I bet you can't eat just one." Frida began loading a plate before Rose could even think of lodging a protest.

"I...uh..." Rose realized that a bunch of Jewish grandmothers wasn't going to forego the social aspect of communing, especially being Holocaust survivors. They couldn't forget what it felt like to be starved to death. There was no saying no when it came to food. She smiled. "It all looks amazing."

Rose sat in the floral print wingback chair, setting her plate and cup of tea on the side table next to her. She smoothed her hands down the plain white shirt and black skirt, her usual working attire. She felt a bit self-conscious, as compared to the other women, she was underdressed. She'd met the six women at various times while sitting shiva, but it was another thing to stand before them, their gazes evaluating her. Aside from Frida, Esther, and Sonia, Rose could not recall the names of the other women and was relieved when Frida introduced the ladies once more.

"Rose, dear, I want you to meet Dr. Ruth Dreyfus. She's our historian. Ruth was a professor at Columbia University."

"I'm pleased to meet you, Dr. Dreyfus."

"The pleasure is mine, child. Call me Ruth, my dear."

"And this is Clara Gabor. Clara is a survivor from Hungary who owned Pages. You remember the bookstore on Grand Street in Williamsburg."

"Yes, of course. Leah took me there all the time. It's where I fell in love with books." She jumped up and shook Clara's frail hand. Clara's eyes were the size of saucers due to the strong magnification of the eyeglasses perched on the end of her nose.

"I remember you as a little girl, so well behaved and observant," said Clara.

Returning to her chair, Frida took a seat on the sofa and continued, "When we formed the sisterhood after the war, we numbered in the thousands around the world. Sadly, that number has greatly diminished to less than a few hundred. We've lost many good friends over the years, including our dear Leah." Frida said in a husky voice.

Handkerchiefs dabbed at teary eyes, and prayers were whispered for the women who'd passed.

Rose's heart grew heavy, and she found herself forgiving the bunch of meddling old birds in failing to warn her in advance about the brooch or the blue coat. "Thank you, ladies, for putting this together so quickly. I've been anxious to talk to all of you."

"We expected you to be confused," Esther said. "But we wanted to give you some time to get through the shiva."

"You might have warned me about the brooch and the blue coat," Rose said, leaning back in the chair.

Sonia's hands fluttered, jangling the collection of bracelets on both of her wrists. "Did you pin the brooch to the blue coat? What happened?"

Rose's eyebrows lifted. "What do you think happened?"

Six elderly heads exchanged wide-eyed glances.

Frida's hand fluttered against her pearls as she fingered them. "We didn't dare believe, but Leah was right. Dear Rose, you are indeed the chosen."

"Chosen for what?"

"Please be patient, Rose," Sonia added, jangling her bracelets once more. "We want you to understand everything, but there is much to be explained."

"I'll say."

"This is what we prayed for, Rose," Frida said. "Leah was sure of it, about you, but all of us were too afraid to believe."

We're sorry we didn't warn you," Sonia added. "We thought you wouldn't do anything until after sitting shiva."

"It seems the brooch and the coat had other plans for me," Rose said. "I never really had a choice. I tried to throw the coat away twice, but it miraculously reappeared in my closet. I thought I was losing my mind. As for the brooch," Rose peeled the bandage off her hand, "I now bear this tattoo, and I'm not very happy about it."

Gasps echoed around the room. Frida's eyes grew round, and she whispered. "The brooch will only speak to the one."

"I'm not interested in being 'the one' or the chosen or whatever you call it. I need answers."

"Rose, before you decide anything, you must understand who you truly are." Esther, the bird-like woman who'd fretted and kvetched her worries about Rose at the shiva, now gave an entirely different impression. She seemed to be self-possessed and in control perched on her high, wing-backed chair near the fireplace.

Esther cleared her throat and asked everyone to rise and link hands. Rose pictured them playing the childhood game of "Ring Around the Rosie." Esther remained seated, and Rose recalled she'd been in a wheelchair at the shiva. The nine women formed a circle and locked hands. "Please join us, Rose."

"I-I...yes, of course."

Esther intoned the words in a thick Polish accent, "Sisters of my spirit, we gather tonight as we've gathered for the last sixty-five years to keep the words and deeds of our mother Miriam alive. We are all daughters of Israel, as were our mothers and sisters. We are the defenders of the righteous and the keepers of the memories. With our dying breaths, we will bring vengeance upon any and all who seek to destroy our people. With heavy hearts, we have said farewell to our precious sister Leah, but with great joy, we welcome her granddaughter Rose into our fold. We pray she will find her place among us, renew our commitment, and join us in our mission to protect the Jewish people.

"As it has been throughout our history, our enemies are great and powerful, but we possess the power and blessings of our ancient ancestors and know that they guide our hands in all that we seek to achieve. From an old enemy, a new enemy has arisen that threatens our entire nation, and we, just as Moses, Aaron, and Miriam did, must act swiftly and decidedly to bring about their destruction. Let us close our eyes and allow the wisdom of the ancients to flow into us and manifest in deeds. Amen."

"Amen," the women chorused.

Rose didn't know what to think about the strange oration, but there was no mistaking the surge of energy that flowed through the circle of clasped hands. Electrical pulses raced around the circle like electricity conducting through wire at the speed of light.

Rose's heartbeat accelerated. Sparks shot from the tips of her fingers up her arms, like the feeling of walking across a carpet and then turning on the lights. Next, she began to feel like she was floating. She looked down at her feet — nope still on the floor. She peeked through semi-closed eyes at the elderly ladies around the room. They swayed back and forth, their eyes closed, but they wore beaming smiles. Rose sniffed at the scented candles. Were they made of CBD?

An overwhelming sense of elation and purpose filled her. She peeked again through squinted eyes to see if everyone else was feeling what she was. She was stunned by what she saw and blinked rapidly. In their elated repose, Rose saw each woman as she must have looked in her youth. They say inside every older woman is her younger version, but to see their vibrant faces as they'd been was heart-stopping. The grandmothers were somehow transformed by their connection. Even more enlightening, the colorful auras emanating from the crowns of each woman's head lit the room in a rainbow of color. Each aura was unique. The kaleidoscope of colors wavered above the circle, and Rose saw each woman's face glow with radiance and serenity. Was she sporting a colored aura too? For several seconds the women communed in a perfect state of parity, as if they were of one heart and one mind. Rose was transported with elation.

Esther broke the circle of hands, and the auras disappeared, as did their younger selves. But the sense of tranquility remained. "Please be seated, my sisters."

When everyone had taken their seats, Esther asked. "Who wishes to share the story of who and what we are to our new inductee, Rose?"

"Wait. I haven't agreed—"

"Please be silent and listen, Rose. Soon all will be known," said Frida.

Frida's rebuke reminded her so much of Leah, or maybe it was just the Jewish mother control thing. Rose bit her tongue. *There's obviously more to this than I imagined.* She held her peace and waited.

"I would speak, sisters," said Ruth, the retired professor who'd taught history at Columbia.

"Ah, yes, Ruth, you are the perfect spokeswoman. Enlighten our fledgling daughter and sister. Let her learn of her powerful lineage and the blessing that has been passed to her."

Ruth had hair dyed black as a raven's wings with a white streak on the side. From beneath her blunt-cut bangs, her piercing brown eyes shone with intelligence. Ruth's dark gaze commanded attention. Like the best of teachers, her voice held her listeners rapt and attentive, and like all good storytellers, she began at the beginning. "Over three thousand years ago during what is called the New Kingdom of Egypt, the descendants of Jacob, our patriarch who wrestled with *Malak,* the Lord's angel, lived as slaves. By that angel, Jacob was given the name Israel, and his offspring lived in Egypt for four hundred fifty years, where they grew into a great nation called the Israelites.

"The Egyptians saw the Israelites as a threat in their midst and, over time, enslaved them. From these slaves was born Miriam, who, with her brothers Aaron and Moses, would break the bonds of slavery and lead the people to freedom. Her father was Amram, grandson of Levi, who was the son of Jacob. At God's will and blessing, Aaron and his scions would assume the mantle of the holy priesthood as Kohens, and from Miriam's issue would arise the Davidian dynasty.

"Miriam was a prophetess even as a child. At six years of age, she was already called *puah,* meaning 'whisperer' for her wisdom and visions of the future." Ruth continued her retelling of the ancient biblical story, after which she leaned forward, her gaze sharpening as if emphasizing the importance of her next words. "All that I have told you is known to you, Rose. It is the same story told to every child in Bible school. What I tell you next is not known. It is a revelation of a story, handed down by mouth, from mother to daughter through the generations."

Ruth's face glowed as she continued. "From the gold used to build the sacred Ark of the Covenant, Bezalel kept a small amount and used it to fashion a golden brooch, which he gave to his grandmother, Miriam. There is nothing written about the powerful amulet, but the legend has passed in story and song through the generations of daughters and granddaughters of Miriam. It was a magical gift. The brooch contains the power of sight, vision, and the ability to move through time. The power can be used only by 'the chosen one' of every generation. Leah was the previous protectress, and you, Rose, are 'the one' chosen to follow. You share a direct lineage to Miriam and the house of David. For it is only to 'the one' that the brooch will respond. There is no other to assume the mantle, Rose. It must be you."

Rose might have stood then and told them they weren't making any sense, she might have fled, but she didn't. She couldn't. Heat coursed through her as though she were sitting in a sauna, and perspiration dampened her forehead. The candles around the room flickered and burned brighter as if upholding the truth of Ruth's story. The power of the brooch could not be denied. "But what about the blue coat?" Rose asked, her voice sounding strange to her ears.

Clara spoke with reverence in a lilting, Hungarian-accented, whispery voice. "The blue coat is one with the brooch. It is made from Miriam's blue prayer shawl, and neither has ever been far from the other. The answer to that riddle is sacred and lies with Miriam. We only know that together, their power is unlimited. They have the power to decide, and they've chosen you, Rose."

Rose looked around at the faces of the sisterhood, each reflective of their belief. "What does the brooch want of me? What am I supposed to do with it?"

"In all of our history, the Holocaust was the closest we have ever come to complete annihilation," Frida said. "Our people were nearly wiped from the face of the earth in the gas chambers. All that was left of them were the ashes that rose from the towers of the crematoriums. Millions of voices silenced forever. We are their voice, and each one of us has sworn an oath that we will never forget them, nor will we allow the world to forget them."

"We faced down evil," Sonia continued, "and the Nazi stain was eradicated from the earth, their civilization destroyed, and the *Tausendjähriges Reich*, 'Thousand-Year Reich,' is no more. But a new threat has arisen, and it is no less sinister than the genocide that preceded it. There is a plan afoot to finish what Hitler failed to do. This plot is so insidious, but so well administered, that no one suspects it exists. It dwells in the shadows and grows like a cancer."

"Rose, you are the chosen one," Esther said. "Your mission is to expose and destroy this plot and the mastermind behind it. His goal is the fall of Israel, and he intends to eliminate all memory of the Holocaust. He will stop at nothing to bring about the isolation and eventual destruction of the Jews." Esther's pale blue eyes softened with her tears. Grabbing a handkerchief from her pocket, she dabbed and sniffled.

As if on cue, Ruth picked up where Esther had left off. "We warn you, this man and his evil cabal will do whatever it takes to stop you. When our nemesis discovers you have the brooch, he will covet it and do whatever it takes to possess it. If it were to fall into the cabal's hands, it would be catastrophic. The problem has always been we've never discovered his identity. The leader of this cabal remains unknown to us. We don't know where he lives. We only know Leah faced the father of this snake in Auschwitz and believed his evil was forever silenced. But his son, like Pharaoh's son, plots the destruction of Israel."

"I thought you said the power of the brooch can only be used by 'the one?'"

"Those who covet the brooch don't understand or believe that to be true," Frida added. "Why would they? They crave power and believe they can possess that power by possessing the source. He might even try to control it through you."

Rose's thoughts were spinning out of control. "B-but I'm not some kind of superhero or spy. I'm not trained to fight, and I wouldn't even know how to shoot a gun. How in the world would I be able to find such an adversary, let alone stop him?"

"The brooch and coat will guide you," Sonia replied. "Put your trust in their power. They will lead you."

"I can't do this alone. I have no idea where to begin."

"Follow your heart, trust your inheritance," Esther said.

"Leah believed in you — she still exists on the other side, ready to aid you on your quest. You need only reach out to her," Frida assured.

"You're telling me my grandmother exists? That's insane."

"Miriam is with her — her work is not over, and yours has just begun."

CHAPTER 15

January 20, Present day
Brooklyn, New York

Rose drove home more confused than she'd been before. Why hadn't Leah confided, shared, or alluded to any of this? How could she have left so much unsaid? The woman who'd been the bedrock of Rose's existence was now a mystery to her. Rose wanted to feel elation at being a thread in the rich tapestry her ancestors had bequeathed her. She'd felt such energy and power with the sisterhood. Where did it go? All she felt now was empty and inadequate. The enormity of the task that had fallen on her shoulders made her queasy and frightened. The gray-haired sisterhood meant well, but she couldn't imagine what help they'd be in destroying the forces that threatened them. She had never felt so alone in her life.

Rose dragged herself upstairs and noticed the door to the attic was open. The door was original to the Victorian era house.

Massive, it was carved of dark oak. The hair on the nape of Rose's neck prickled and her hand shook as she pushed the door open. "There's nothing in this house that will harm you," she whispered, reassuring herself. The scent of Chanel No. 5 tickled her nostrils, and she closed her eyes and smiled. *Okay, Bubbie, I guess there's something up in the attic you want to show me. Hopefully, it will help clear this muddle I'm in.*

Rose ran her hand along the wall beside the door and found a light switch. She flipped it, and the room lit with a soft glow from an old crystal chandelier. Leave it to Leah to illuminate even the attic elegantly.

She glanced around, shivering. She'd been right; the attic was not only cold but a tad creepy. Because of the gabled roof, the line of the ceiling slanted down toward a row of dormer windows facing the street. Rose's gaze swept the room. The old and the discarded were artfully arranged in the spotless space. Her hand touched a rocking chair tucked between two of the windows, kindling an image from childhood. Rose remembered snuggling against Leah, listening to her grandmother read *Grimm's Fairy Tales*.

The past is never far away.

She was amazed at how real the recollection manifested. The human mind indeed was a storehouse, and you never knew when your mind would stumble over a long-forgotten treasure.

Against the back wall stood a massive cabinet with a beveled glass front. Rose padded closer, her fluffy slippers sliding along the shiny hardwood. On a shelf behind the glass sat an assortment of knickknacks and framed photos — frozen-in-time moments from Rose's mother's life. Everything from baby pictures to prom pictures. Aside from the photos of her mother, she found a gold-plated frame containing an eight-by-ten portrait of her grandparents standing under the chuppah at their wedding.

Rose opened the cabinet door and picked up the wedding photo. She turned it over and on the back was written the year nineteen fifty-six. Leah hadn't married until eleven years after the war. Was it because it took that long for her to believe Aidan was gone forever? Rose turned the photo back over and studied it. Her grandfather, Bernard's face, beamed with adoration, his gaze locked on his new bride. But not so the bride who gazed out from the frame as if caught like a deer in the headlights.

Rose's heart went out to the young woman in the photo. Leah's eyes were wet with tears. Rose could only guess as to what emotions were captured when the bulb flashed. Was her grandmother dreaming about what might have been with Aidan, or was she just a nervous bride overwhelmed by the pomp and circumstance of the day?

Rose had never been in love, nor had she ever nursed a broken heart or worse — lost the one person who completed her. She swallowed a lump in her throat. *I don't think I'll ever be as lucky as you were, Bubbie, to have loved so deeply.*

Rose wondered if her grandfather Bernard had known that his bride would never fully be his. *They say in love, one person loves more than the other.* Maybe that had been fine with him. Perhaps he'd loved Leah so much that he had been willing to accept only a portion of her heart. It didn't matter in the end, did it? Leah had been a devoted wife and mother, and by all accounts, Bernard had been a happy man. Rose placed the framed photo back on the shelf and closed the doors.

Three rows of drawers under the glass cabinet drew her attention. Rose opened the top drawer to find rows of letters, stacked carefully and faded with time, tied with ribbons. She carefully picked up the first stack, unsettled about prying into Leah's private correspondence, but Leah was gone, and Rose needed answers. She searched the room looking for something to carry the letters in. Spying a woven basket, Rose set it on the floor next to her and emptied the drawer, stacking the letters neatly. She was about to open the second drawer when she heard a sound, and whipped around, trembling.

In her peripheral vision, she glimpsed a movement in the shadowy corner beside her. She hated being a nervous ninny. *Bubbie, you invited me up here, but I can't help feeling like I'm intruding.*

Gathering her breath, she walked toward where she'd heard the sound. She repeated to herself that there wasn't anyone in the house but her. But attics and ghosts went together like peanut butter and jelly, and after her recent life-shaking adventure, or whatever it was, she wouldn't be surprised if the house was haunted. *On the other hand, it could just be mice.* If so, she'd need to bring in the exterminator to catch the little devils. Ghosts or mice? She wasn't sure which would be worse. She chuckled at her foolishness as she realized the mysterious figure was a dressmaker form draped with a sheet. She sighed with relief. *So much for ghosts.*

Rose returned to the armoire and opened the second drawer. It contained a photo album Rose had never seen before. She opened the brown leather folio, and a photo took her breath away. It was of the gray-haired sisterhood, but not the sisterhood she had come to know. The photo was old, taken maybe fifty or sixty years ago. The women had posed on a picnic table, some standing, some sitting, and at their center seated on the table was Leah. Scattered on the ground, piles of fallen leaves, and behind the women were leafless trees stripped bare by the winds of approaching winter.

All her life Rose had been told that she looked like her grandmother. But in this photograph, she could see just how much. It was no wonder Aidan had believed her to be Leah. The photo was black and white, but Rose knew Leah's hair had been as red as hers. It wasn't the identical arrangement of genes that stole her breath though, it was the coat. In the photograph, Leah wore the blue coat. Rose squinted, trying to see if Leah was wearing the brooch. *No brooch, at least visible.* But then again, it would have been too dangerous to pair the two in public, especially if there was something magical about their combination. Rose had found that out the hard way.

Rose tried to open the third and final drawer, but it was stuck. She jiggled it, and it opened enough for her to slip her fingers in. Clawing her way deeper inside, her fingers touched something wedged in the back of the drawer. Fingering it, she gently maneuvered it back and forth until it came free, and she slid the drawer open. Inside was a small leather-bound book. Rose opened it and turned to the first page. *My Diary by Leah Manheim.* It was written in French. Thank goodness Leah had insisted Rose study French. The first entry in the diary read the seventeenth of July, nineteen forty. Rose quickly did the math. Leah would have been sixteen years old.

So, her grandmother had kept a diary. But how had she held onto it during the war when she'd been sent to Auschwitz? Rose fanned the pages forward. The diary stopped at nineteen-forty-two and didn't resume until nineteen-forty-five. *She must have hidden it somewhere.* Rose closed the book and ran her hand over the soft leather. *Maybe some of the answers I'm looking for are in the pages of your diary, Bubbie.* Rose closed the drawer and yawned. Glancing at her watch, she noted the time was well past midnight. Between her meeting with the sisterhood and her Nancy Drew foray into the attic, Rose was wiped. She needed to grab a few hours of sleep before work.

Well, Bubbie, you've given me a lot of reading to do, but it'll have to wait until tomorrow. She needed to grab a few hours of sleep before going to work.

The diary joined the letters in the basket, and Rose carried her precious cargo downstairs to her bedroom.

CHAPTER 16

January 21, Present day
Brooklyn, New York

She walked toward a white tent shimmering in the blinding sunlight. At its peak flew a pennant, the Lion of Judah, rippling in the breeze. Sand warmed her bare feet. Her gaze scanned the horizon, taking in a vast desert rimmed by purple mountains.

The flap to the entrance of the tent floated open and closed as if waving her in. She stepped through the opening and hesitated just inside the threshold, allowing her eyes to adjust to the darkness. The coolness of the dim interior enveloped her in a welcoming embrace. She let out a breath she had no idea she'd been holding. The perspiration down her back cooled, and goosebumps prickled her skin.

Out of the shadows came a voice. "Daughter, sit with me."

Rose turned, spying a woman reclining against a pile of pillows on a colorful woven rug. Had the woman appeared out of thin air like an apparition, or had she been sitting there all along? Rose wasn't sure. The woman's beguiling voice tinkled like chimes, drawing Rose closer.

A leather thong held the woman's thick braid of snow-white hair in place. Her age was indeterminable — her skin glowed with supple beauty. A royal blue shawl that matched her striking blue-gray eyes draped her narrow shoulders, the loose fringes fluttering around her. On the ground before her lay a parchment opened for study, and beside it sat a tray with an array of dried fruit, herbs, and flatbread. Most extraordinary was the fountain that hovered free and unencumbered, floating beside her. Rose could see no source, yet water splashed into a basin as if from out of thin air in an endless stream replenishing and recycling itself.

The woman's eyes turned steel gray when she asked, "Do you know who I am?"

"I-I'm not sure..."

"Ah, well, we can't have that, can we?" Fine lines crinkled around her eyes with her smile. "I think if you open your heart, Rose, you will know me just as your grandmother did."

"My grandmother?"

"Yes." She chuckled. "Your grandmother Leah was a priestess and prophetess who served her people well."

"I know nothing about that."

"Yes, neither did she until she was called. It is the way it has been since the beginning, and it is the way it will be until the end of time. You see, it is better this way."

"Why? Why keep it a secret when you know the secret will eventually be revealed?"

"Would you wish to know your future before it happened? The length of your life? The time of your death?"

"No, I would not. But this is different. There are so many questions I could have asked her. She would have helped me prepare."

"She did. You have all the tools necessary to wage this battle. You have the heart of a warrior. The determination of a survivor. The beautiful soul of a butterfly."

"Me? You are mistaken. I'm no warrior. I'm a librarian, a preserver of the written word and history. The furthest thing from a warrior there is."

The old woman chuckled. "You are the perfect warrior, for much of what you fight are words and lies. A warrior must be cunning of mind and believe in themselves against all odds. Before he was king, David was a boy who faced the behemoth, Goliath, with a slingshot. Yet, against overwhelming odds, he triumphed. Here, refresh yourself." She filled a bowl with water from the magical fountain and handed it to Rose. "Quench your thirst." She ran her hand above the basin, and the fountain ceased its flow. "This is the fountain that quenched the thirst of the Hebrews and their beasts when they wandered in the desert."

Rose gasped. "You are Miriam."

"Yes, my child. I am the prophetess Miriam, and you are my descendant. It is your birthright to protect your people from the darkness that seeks to spread and destroy the world. You must not fail."

"That is exactly what I fear. That I will be found wanting and fail."

"The sisterhood believes in you, as do I. Trust in yourself and reach out to those who are trustworthy. There are those who will help you."

"Who are they?"

"You will find them, and you will know them when you look into their hearts." Her eyes twinkled mischievously. "Think hard. You may have met one already."

Was Miriam referring to Ethan? It seemed a bit much to imagine. "But where should I start?"

"Listen to Leah — she is your guiding light. She speaks to you in your heart. You have all you will need. I will bless you now, child. Bow your head unto me." Rose knelt before the regal being, bending her head and closing her eyes. Miriam placed her hands upon Rose's head, and her prayer echoed to the heavens. Her voice was as sweet as a comb of honey, the purest of voices lifted in a mesmerizing singsong chant. An aura of pure white light emanated from the crown of her head.

Y' varechecha Adonai v'yish'mv'yish'm v'yish'm v'yish'm 'recha.

Ya-er Adonai panav eilecha vichuneka.

Yisa Adonai panav eilecha v'yaseim l'cha shalom.

May God Bless you and keep you.

May God's light shine upon you, and may God be gracious to you.

May you feel God's Presence within you always, and may you find peace.

Rose opened her eyes, the prayer reverberating through her dream into her waking reality. The tent was gone, as was Miriam. Pure energy flowed through Rose's veins, pulsating through her with a power she'd never believed she possessed. Clarity of purpose filled her vision and a way forward opened to her.

Boy, that was some dream. Rose chuckled, got up and stretched. She hadn't felt so calm and rested since before her grandmother's illness. She recalled everything Miriam had said to her. It was almost too fantastical to believe, and yet here she was, with a mandate to fight against a growing evil in the world, just as Leah did during World War II and after. Padding to the window, Rose opened the drapes and gazed out at the beauty of the morning. *Time to get to work.* She glanced at the bedside clock. It was just after six a.m. She had a couple of hours before heading out to the library.

Rose picked up a stack of Leah's letters from the basket. She crawled back into bed and carefully opened the first letter. The top was stamped with an official seal of The British War Office, the Royal Coat of Arms flanked by the lion and the unicorn.

Dear Miss Manheim,

We regret to inform you that Captain Aidan McQueen went missing in France in 1944, and we believe him to have been killed in action. As of this time, the whereabouts of his remains are unknown. Captain McQueen served honorably, and he gave his life as a hero. He will always live in the hearts and minds of a grateful nation.

Rose's hands shook, her eyes blurred with tears. *Oh, Bubbie, you must have been heartbroken.*

The letter was written on June 1, 1945, five months after Leah's liberation from Auschwitz in January 1945. From what she knew of her grandmother's tale of survival, she was ill for the last few weeks leading up to liberation. Lying on her bunk, feverish, and left to die when the SS force-marched sixty thousand other Auschwitz prisoners to Silesia. Fifteen thousand died on that death march. For Leah, being left behind had turned out to be a blessing. The Red Army entered Auschwitz on January 27th, and Leah was liberated with seven thousand others who'd been abandoned and left to die when the Germans fled. She recovered in a field hospital and then made her way back to Paris. Leah must have tried to find Aidan. This letter must have ripped her heart in two.

Sorting through the pile of letters, Rose came across one with the return address from Grantchester, England. In her excitement, Rose nearly ripped the pages from the envelope. Maybe it was all a mistake, and Aidan had survived, but as soon as she began to read, Rose knew he hadn't.

My dear Miss Manheim,

Aidan's mother and I were very moved by your letter. It brought us great comfort to know what you did for our son during the darkest hours of the war. We knew little of his heroic deeds as the ministry of defense is spare with their communications. So very busy, I suppose. A generation laid to rest on foreign soil. So many broken hearts left to mourn those that will never come home.

With time, I'm sure we will receive a full accounting. Thank God, this war is finally at an end. So much of our youth have been lost. A high price indeed, we have paid for victory.

Anne and I were very moved by the conversations you shared with Aidan. So much of what is in your letter are things only Aidan could have told you. Everything you wrote sounded so much like our boy. It is clear to us how much faith he had in you and how close you two had become. I can tell you his mother, siblings, and I laughed through our tears. Aidan was always a bit of a rebel. We know your friendship with Aidan was deep and profound, and I know you will miss him as much as we will.

If ever you find yourself in Cambridge, we would be most pleased to welcome you to our home. Although we mourn our loss, we rejoice that you and Aidan found each other and shared something few are lucky enough ever to find.

May God Bless you,

Pastor Fraser McQueen

The letter fluttered onto the bed from Rose's hands as she remembered the gunshot she'd heard when she ran from Aidan in the snow-covered forest. Tears slipped down her cheeks. Had Aidan died that night in the forest? How desperately sad that their lives were irreparably damaged, and their future erased. She wiped her eyes.

I have so much more to learn about you, Bubbie.

She opened another letter dated June 5, 1945. The return address read Le Chambon-sur-Lignon, France.

Dear Mademoiselle Manheim,

I praise God that you have survived the war and are safely back in Paris. Your parents never stopped praying or believing you would return.

I received your letter addressed to them, and I hope you will forgive my opening and reading it. I cried, thinking of what joy your parents would have known to learn that their precious daughter was safe and well. They spoke of you daily and praised you in every way imaginable.

I know your heart is breaking, and that you have surmised that both Adam and Estelle, your blessed parents, have passed on and are with God in Heaven. When I see you, I will provide more details of the difficulties we faced without proper medicine and supplies. Your mother caught a chill during the winter, and it turned into pneumonia. When she left us, your father was despondent without her. I believe he died of a broken heart.

I can't tell you how sorry I am. Your father was such a brilliant man. I spent many enlightening hours philosophizing with him — one of the only bright spots in my existence during a most challenging time.

My dear Miss Manheim, I know it is difficult to travel at this time, but I urge you to visit our mountain village when you are able. I have several things to convey to you from your mother and father. Your mother left a letter for you in my keeping, and some other personal items that I know will be precious to you. You are welcome here in Le Chambon-sur-Lignon whenever you can arrange passage. We are a small village with modest facilities, but I am certain our alpine landscape and the fresh air will be restorative for you. My wife and I will happily accommodate you in our home.

Your humble servant,

Minister André Trouvé

Rose folded the letter and slipped it back into the envelope. She pressed her fingers to her trembling lips. She squeezed her eyes shut, holding in her tears as she contemplated the losses Leah was forced to endure. Losing Aidan and then her parents' passing must have been overwhelming. She shuddered, remembering the forest where Aidan must have been killed.

Of course, she would have gone to Le Chambon, but what did

Estelle leave her daughter? She was reminded of the strange dream of Miriam. Had Leah's mother left her the inheritance that now determined Rose's future? Had she left the brooch in the minister's keeping?

Rose plowed through the letters, skimming through those that weren't pertinent. She found a letter tied with a blue ribbon. It was yellowed and stained with drops of faded tears. Estelle's hand must have shaken when she wrote this final letter to her daughter because the words were wobbly and erratic.

Leah, mon enfant,

How does a mother say farewell? I hope you can read this letter stained with my tears. My sorrow at not being able to say goodbye to you in person devastates me. If you are in possession of this letter, then you know your father and I are no longer of this life. Please do not mourn, for Papa and I are in a better place. I'm afraid our hearts could not bear to live in a world of such unspeakable cruelty. Even with the Nazis gone, the disappointment of our own countrymen's response to our plight did irreparable damage to our belief in humankind.

You have a full life ahead of you, but our best years are behind us. You have always been the light of our lives, the child of our love. You gave us so much more joy than we ever deserved. I regret only that I won't see you married or know the pleasure of being a doting grand-mother to your precious babies. Promise me you will marry and have children. You are all that remains of our families.

I have left several things for you with Pastor Trouvé. André is a courageous man who did so much for us. He helped save thousands of Jews. So few stood up against the Nazi evil. His name will eternally be written among the righteous. You can trust him completely, Leah.

I know you think you lost your blue coat after it was taken from you, but it is safe here in Le Chambon. That coat has a mind of its own (pardon me my humor, but I think you understand). It has a way of turning up. I have also saved a piece of jewelry for you. It has been in our family for generations and will now reside with you all the days of your life. Be sure to wear it on the blue coat, the two go so well together. Keep it safe, Leah, until it passes from you to your daughter. The brooch is your precious inheritance, and you are its steward.

In our journeys through this life, we are all given a mission. I was called to be a protector. You, however, are destined to be an activist. The inheritance does not always pass in a direct line. What is required is decided by what is needed. Your role in the future of our people should be clear to you by now. You are the chosen. Chosen to guard our stories, our identity, our very existence. You must pave the way for the one who comes next. Be it your daughter or your granddaughter. It is not within your power to decide, but one or the other will undoubtedly be called.

It seems the Nazi scourge nearly put an end to us, but God would never allow his promise to his people to be broken. I don't pretend to know why this tragedy befell us, nor is it my place to question God's reasons. I think it would be wrong to assume God doesn't care. Remember, he works in mysterious ways. I know you are reading this letter because the allies are victorious. His hand is in everything.

I also left in the care of the kind pastor a key to a security box at Credit Suisse in Zürich, and a file with all the documents you will need to claim what is yours. The contents should be enough to begin your life and give you financial freedom. Your papa and I prepared for this day for you. It saddens me to think of how many others prepared too, but in many cases, there is no one left to make a family claim. The fruit of their labors will lie untouched or worse.

Papa and I bless you, Leah, and wish you a long and happy life. Know that we love you and always will. Someday I pray we will see each other again.

Love,

Maman

P.S. Your papa insists I remind you to keep up your reading and finish your education. He kisses you a thousand times.

Rose held the delicate letter to her heart as she wept. Her grandmother and great-grandparents had suffered and borne unspeakable sorrows to provide her with a bright future. *I hope I can be half as brave as they were.*

It occurred to Rose that her grandmother had made a trip every year to her beloved Paris. What if there were other purposes to her visits aside from visiting old friends and childhood haunts? Leah was an avid hiker and always made side trips to the country-side, mountains, and lakes in the summer. Could she have gone to Zürich on a side trip? Rose recalled a few ski vacations to Switzer-land she took with her parents and Leah, all beginning in Zürich. Did Leah use that opportunity to visit the bank and check on her security box? Or had she also searched for other boxes that had slipped away from their rightful owners? *If I had a secret bank account in Switzerland, I sure as heck wouldn't close it. Where did you hide the key, Bubbie?*

Rose kept reading and sifting through the letters until she came across one that made her gasp. A letter addressed to her. Rose's fingers trembled as she extracted the pretty sheet of lilac-print stationery from the light blue envelope. Her pulse pounded in her ears. Her grandmother was a prolific letter writer and had written her many letters over the years while Rose was away at college and then grad school and from Leah's many travels. Rose had kept them all. Her grandmother had prepared this final letter for her knowing she'd find it. Perhaps she had sensed the cancer had returned and knew she had only a limited time left on earth. The more Rose found out about Leah, the more she was cloaked in mystery.

Ma chérie, Rose,

My dear granddaughter and keeper of the light of truth. By now, you've received all that I bequeathed to you. Ahead lies the unknown, behind you stands a long line of women who answered the call to serve

Miriam. I know you are saddened and confused that I did not share your legacy with you in life, but remember that even though I am not with you in flesh, I am never far away.

The gifts I have left you are of potent power — bound together by a source as old as time itself. Do not fear their energy. In your hands they are safe, but beware the danger from others who might crave their power. The evil that was unleashed by the Nazi regime is alive and well. Others have picked up the mantle of hatred and destruction. They are cunning and have adapted themselves in our modern world to manifest in different ways. They seek power and domination over the world order. Their plans are already in motion. You need to be brave. Vigilant. And do not fear that you are alone in the battles to come, for potent forces align with your cause as well.

Promise me you will not take up this cause alone. There is someone I believe you can trust. His name is Ethan Blackwood. I have been in contact with him for some time. He may need some convincing, but you have the gifts of Miriam, and these will persuade him. He resides in Georgetown, Washington — you should have no trouble finding him. His heart is pure, and I trust him emphatically. Tell him my wish is for you and him to embark on this journey together.

As soon as you finish reading this letter, go to my folly, as your mother called it. You recall the music box on my desk that plays La Vie en Rose? Wind it three times and listen and then turn the key in the reverse direction. A surprise awaits you.

After the war, I lost everything or thought I had. It was a sad and lonely time for me. For some reason, when I heard this song, I found myself and learned to live again. After traveling to Le Chambon, a windfall came to me. When I returned to Paris, I purchased this music box from an antiquary on the Left Bank. I have kept it with me all these years, and now it is yours.

Our memories are so often tied to a song. Music can turn the tide of sorrow and bring comfort when all seems lost. I'm sure you've heard me mention that your mother was named after Edith Piaf, and you were named for this, my favorite song. Think of me when you hear the refrain, "Je vois la vie en rose." "I see life in pink." Know that I am with you.

Ma chéri, I know you are suffering from guilt, afraid to read my diary. There is nothing about my life I do not wish you to know. You are so much a part of me.

I'm also sure you have asked yourself why you have been chosen and not your mother. I shouldn't even have to explain it, but I will. Edith found her passion in life. She contributes to the betterment of humanity as a therapist. It is most fitting because she has always been a pragmatist and not a dreamer. These supernatural experiences you have begun to have would have been construed by her as a mental illness. I needed to protect her, and so I kept the truth from her. She and I have rarely seen eye-to-eye. However, I have loved her no less. She is more of her father's child and always has been. I am happy she is happily married and proud she has accomplished so much, but the blue coat would never have fit her, and the brooch would never have pulsed with power in the way that you have already witnessed. You may think this brutal advice, but for her own good, and yours, tell her as little as possible.

The future is in your capable hands, ma chéri. I bless you.

Grand-mère

Rose laid the letter on the bed, trying to order her chaotic thoughts. Leah had anticipated many of Rose's questions and fears in the letter, but it was just like her grandmother to leave her with more, like an ongoing puzzle to be solved. The specificity of winding the music box three times was enough to capture Rose's imagination.

Okay, Bubbie, I'm on it. Rose ran down the stairs and opened the carved wooden doors to the library. The entrance to Leah's office was hidden behind a panel of books. She'd built the secret annex as a saferoom when she'd remodeled the house. It was her private refuge, and only Rose and her parents knew of its existence. Rose removed a leather-bound volume of *The Three Musketeers* from the shelf that hid the lever. She pulled it, and the bookshelf swung open, triggering a switch that lit an antique French torchière. The light illuminated the secret chamber in an amber glow. Next to the old lamp was a French Empire daybed upholstered in sage green and gold striped satin jacquard. The wood-paneled walls were soundproof. Entering the jewel box of a room was like stepping back in time. Rose's mother, Edith, considered the secret annex to be her mother's folly, built to reproduce some fantasy of a bygone era where Leah would take refuge from the real world and her own failings. But Edith had learned early on that arguing with her mother produced no good result, and despite her protests of the unnecessary extravagance, the room was built.

On the delicate, antique writing desk was the Louis XVI style blue porcelain and gilt music box. Rose picked it up and turned the key until it came to a stop. She lifted the lid, and the familiar song filled the silence. How many times had Leah experienced emotional relief when she wound the key and listened to the plaintive melody over and over again?

Two more times, Rose wound it and listened to the pins pluck the tuned teeth, eliciting the chimed notes of *La Vie en Rose* until the strains faded and the room returned to silence. Then she reversed the key. The box clicked and the artisan's signature plate popped open, revealing a tiny velvet-lined compartment. Rose was dumbfounded. In it rested a key.

CHAPTER 17

January 21, Present day
New York, New York
David Berg Rare Book Reading Room

H i Ethan, I hope you're well. It's Rose Levi, Leah Manheim's *granddaughter. You will recall we met at Leah's shiva. You asked that I get in touch if I came across any information that might shed some light on what you and Leah had been working on. I have. Please get back to me ASAP.*

Since finding the key in the music box, Rose couldn't focus on anything else. Like the first clue on a treasure hunt, it could lead to another, and then another. Not that this entire experience had been anything other than confusing, scary, and an emotional roller coaster, it nevertheless captured Rose's imagination, as if her grandmother had awoken a yearning in her to see this to the end.

Rose dragged herself to work even though she considered staying home and skipping a day, but she didn't dare. She'd missed enough time during the shiva and didn't want to take advantage of her generous boss. The Center for Jewish History had been more than accommodating. Besides, she was already worried because she sensed that eventually, she was going to have to take time off to travel to Zürich. With or without Ethan, she had to find out what was in Leah's box.

Rose typed mindlessly on the computer, her thoughts a million miles away when a teasing voice snapped her back to reality. She looked up into Ethan's smiling blue eyes. She blinked, all thoughts flying out of her head in one big swoosh.

"I said, I don't suppose you can get away for a bit? I could use a cup of coffee."

Goosebumps prickled her skin. Ethan's smile turned into a Cheshire cat grin.

"Ethan?"

"None other."

Flustered, Rose stood and offered her hand to shake. "Why didn't you text me and tell me you were coming?"

"Consider me careful. I have encryption on all my tech but don't trust it. Been burned before, and I prefer face to face."

"Well, that's way beyond my understanding. Most of my life is on my phone and laptop."

"If we end up working together, we'll put an end to that. About that coffee?"

"Sure. How about I take an early lunch?"

"Perfect, I'm hungry too. Caught the first train out of Washington."

He spoke in a rather truncated way as though he were texting. *He's an odd one.* But her grandmother had insisted he was the man for this mission.

He was also better looking than she remembered — tousled

hair the color of autumn leaves, and his cobalt eyes were set deep beneath black brows, which at most times were furrowed in scrutiny. Funny, she'd thought his eyes gray, but she'd been wrong. They were an extraordinary shade of blue. She almost wished he was gray-haired and thirty years older with a paunchy belly and nose-hairs in need of a good trim. He shifted his backpack from one shoulder to the other — she suspected everything he needed in life was inside.

"As I recall, you said you were starving last time we met."

"Did I? Well, I'm a growing boy."

"And I remember you don't do deli but enjoy decorating your plate with a jar of pickles."

"At least I'm not going to have to submit you to a senility test. Your recall seems fine. Can we get this show on the road?"

She rolled her eyes at the cliché.

"What, you don't like idioms? Tell me it isn't so." He crossed his arms over his chest and flashed his signature taunting Cheshire cat grin.

If he kept this up, she might have to strangle him. "You clearly watch too many old TV shows."

He wagged his finger at her. "Uh-uh, remember I'm the other book lover in this dynamic duo. The telly holds little fascination for me."

"Clearly, you didn't gain my grandmother's trust by peppering her with clichés."

"For Leah, I was as erudite as Professor Higgins." He slipped seamlessly into an upper-crust British accent.

Rose couldn't help but chuckle at Ethan's reference — *My Fair Lady* had also been her grandmother's favorite musical. Leah obviously had been quite taken with Ethan, even though she'd never met him in person. Rose could only imagine how charmed she would have been gazing into his cobalt eyes. Rose understood his appeal. How many people would receive a text, then catch a train so they could respond in person? She wanted to know more about him.

"Just give me a few minutes. I'll convince Agnes to leave the computer lab and have her cover for me."

"Righto. I'll just lose myself in the ancient Aramaic of that scroll over there." He pointed to one of the cases that held an ancient parchment.

Rose shook her head as she entered the code on the touchpad opening the door that led to the lab. "Aramaic, really?"

"Just one of several languages that I've aspired to and mastered," he called after her as she disappeared into the vault.

Ten minutes later, they were sitting at a table at Boqueria, a Spanish restaurant on West 19th Street that Ethan had scoped out on Open Table. Ethan refused to speak before ordering. He read the menu with such an intense look on his face, it was as if he was reading the Dead Sea Scrolls.

"I'm impressed with your focus," she said in a dry tone.

He lowered the menu, focusing that intense gaze on her. "I love Spanish cuisine. This is a tough decision."

She burst out laughing. "I can honestly say I have never had to make a tough decision when it comes to food."

"You should feel confident in knowing I don't jump headfirst into anything, that I consider all the options." He swept his hand in a broad arc for emphasis.

Were they still talking about food or something else? She'd certainly been wrestling with her dilemma since she pinned the brooch onto the blue coat and was flung back in time. Leah had trusted Ethan, and Rose needed someone to trust. Could she take a leap of faith and confide in him?

The waiter, who couldn't have been more pleased with their

order, delivered the first course — *espinacas a la catalana* — a simmering blend of sautéed spinach, garbanzo beans, pine nuts, garlic, and golden raisins. The scent of garlic was enough to stimulate Rose's hibernating hunger, and she leaned forward, gathering in the aroma. Ethan had paired that with grilled stirato bread rubbed with tomato, garlic, and olive oil. He wasted no time in grabbing a chunk of bread and loading it with the stew. Chewing, he waved the bread at her. "Come on, dig in."

"Are you sure you'll have enough? I don't want to deprive you." She grinned.

"Cute. Don't fret, there's plenty more a-coming. Now eat! Oh, and no business conversation while we eat — disturbs my digestion. When I'm working, I work, when I'm eating, I eat."

"I guess you can't walk and chew gum at the same time."

"Now look who's throwing out clichés."

"I just can't believe you're not dying of curiosity as to why I texted you and summoned you to New York." She picked up a slice of bread, laid it on her plate, spooned some of the bean concoction on top, and picked up her knife and fork. When she looked up, she found Ethan staring at her with his mouth hanging open.

"You're kidding, Rose. Are you a direct descendant of Emily Post or something?" He didn't wait for her to reply. "Live a little. Pick the bread up and take a bite. Indulge yourself in the sensuality of losing yourself in the flavor."

It was futile to argue with Mr. Knows Best. She picked up her stew-soaked bread, and the juices slid down her hand. She leaned in to lick them away before they reached her blouse cuff. Taking a sizeable bite, she had to admit it was delicious. She let the aroma and taste invade her senses. "Wonderful," she mumbled between chews. She met Ethan's gaze and was greeted by his grin of approval.

"Now you're eating with gusto and passion, which I suspect

you rarely do." He dunked another slice of bread directly into the earthenware casserole and scooped up the stew and popped it into his mouth. "Mmm." He wiped his lips. "Tell me, Rose, have you ever taken a leap of faith? Jumped without a net? Risked everything for something you believed in?"

Now it was her turn to stare at him with her jaw hanging loose. Conscious of how foolish she must look, she closed her mouth. "Why are you asking me this when you know I probably haven't? I'm a librarian, after all. The only danger I'm apt to experience is a paper cut, which, by the way, can be extremely painful." She could feel her cheeks reddening with her annoyance. How was it that with every compliment he blessed her with, he threw in a criticism? How was she going to work with a man who was such a know-it-all? He didn't seem to have much faith in her. *Am I that much of a wallflower?* Then again, what did she have to show for her life? Yes, she had a satisfying career — a job that enabled her to help support the Jewish community and help educate the world. But other than that, she had nothing else to show for her twenty-seven years on this earth. No husband, no children, no passionate hobbies that involved trekking up a mountain or running a foundation. *Heck, I don't even have a pet.* How could she expect to take on such a monumental task of keeping the world safe from present and future Nazis? Rose felt naked under Ethan's probing gaze as if he could see the emptiness and the missing pieces of her life, her failure to find her place, and her insecurity to step out on a limb.

You're the chosen one.

Could she do this? Could she really do what Leah did? Could she be as brave as Leah? Rose set down her half-eaten bread and took a sip of water to calm her nerves.

The waiter returned and placed a steaming paella pan between them that took up most of the table. "Your *paella mariscos*, señor. It's a specialty of the house. Our chef reduces the bomba rice in a saffron-infused broth, and simmers the monkfish, sepia squid ink, squid, shrimp, clams, and mussels together and serves it with a side of salsa verde. I'll be back with more bread. Please enjoy. Oh, can I bring you a glass of wine?"

"No, thank you. I'm afraid we have work ahead of us." Rose nodded her agreement and thanked the waiter.

Ethan hadn't lied about being a gourmet. He indeed was a foodie, and she certainly couldn't fault him for his taste. The meal was perfection, even though her stomach churned at what was to come — what she had to talk to Ethan about.

"Why don't we go for a walk and have us a chat," Ethan suggested when they'd finished.

"Good idea." The walk would help clear her head. *Fingers crossed!* She hoped her grandmother was right about Ethan and his ability to help her.

They walked through the marble triumphal arch into Washington Square and found a park bench. The air was brisk, but the sun was shining through the clouds, and the patches of snow that hadn't melted from the last snowfall sparkled luminously in the golden light. Ethan sat back, his arm casually draped over the back of the bench, but she noticed his eyes never ceased searching everyone and everything around them. *Clearly, a James Bond complex.*

"Ethan, I know nothing about you," Rose blurted out. "Except that you work for an NGO that studies anti-Semitism. I'd be grateful if you'd fill in some of the blanks."

Ethan stared ahead, his face displaying nothing of what he thought about her request. He turned to scrutinize her, which only served to make her fidget. And then as if he'd come to a conclusion about her and resolved his own misgivings, he blew out a breath. "Until two years ago, I worked for the CIA. I was recruited in my senior year of college. It's customary for the agency to latch onto young people who display qualities that mesh well with intelligence gathering and show leadership skills. I fit the bill, and they came a-calling. The fact that I was a linguist was a huge bonus. Eventually, I became an operations officer overseas involved in intelligence and asset gathering. We parted ways two years ago when my goals changed — I wanted to focus my energies on anti-Semitism. My NGO is funded by a wealthy consortium of individuals. Its purpose is to rout out and expose anti-Semitic groups like the neo-Nazis, underground organizations that prowl the Dark Web, anti-Semitic and anti-Israel political players, and powermongers or groups who seek to do harm or violence to the Jews. Your grandmother reached out to one of my sponsors, and they put me in touch with her. Now tell me why I am sitting on a cold park bench in New York?"

Rose watched a flock of pigeons take flight, considering how best to begin. *He's ex-CIA?* She shivered, and not from the cold. Despite her recent supernatural experiences and everything she'd learned about her grandmother — finding out that Ethan was a spy made this all too real. *Bubbie, you were right. Ethan possesses every skill I lack.* Rose had been wrong about Ethan — he was far better suited to this challenge than she was. "My grandmother left me letters instructing me to take on her work. She believed an evil man was — is working with a secret cabal, bent on finishing what Hitler began — the destruction of the Jews.

"Eventually, there won't be any survivors left, and the living memory of the Holocaust will pass away with them. With their voices silenced and with growing anti-Semitism, my grandmother feared that an opportunity will exist to poison the minds and hearts of the next generations of humankind and open the door to another genocide. I understand her fears because she lived through it. She was witness to the horrors that befell the world when those who could have prevented the Holocaust failed to act."

"I couldn't agree more. Please continue."

"In the last weeks, I've been researching and tracking news reports — violent acts against synagogues, hate crimes against Jews, shootings, knifings, beatings around the world, and blood libel allegations. Academics who deny the gassing and the cold-blooded killing during World War II. The growing online rhetoric against Jews around the world."

"A recurring theme throughout history as I'm sure you've studied," Ethan said. "Jews have always been singled out as the scapegoats for every economic ill that has befallen man. The revisionists want to re-write Hitler's regime in a positive light as a man who sought to lift his people from poverty. Even if these people are in the minority, they're the ones you hear from incessantly, and as they say, those who scream loudest are heard the most."

Rose nodded in agreement. "As you know, Leah was a resistance fighter in World War II and was captured and imprisoned in Auschwitz, but her work did not end with the war. She continued her mission to fight anti-Semitism up until her passing."

"Yes, Leah told me about some of her experiences during the war. She was a courageous woman."

"Yes, indeed." Leah swallowed the lump in her throat and looked into Ethan's eyes. "My grandmother asked me to reach out to you and — and work with you to further her cause."

Ethan stared back at her with a gaze so intense she forgot to breathe.

"Leah trusted you," Rose whispered. "She told me I could trust you too."

The intensity was gone; his cobalt eyes softened. "Your grandmother was right. You can trust me. And I think you're going to need my help more than you realize."

"I'm sure you're right. I'm new to all this saving the world business, and I've never fired a gun, or leaped from a speeding car, defused a bomb —"

Ethan threw his head back and laughed. A laugh so rich and deep and velvety that it enveloped Rose in a warm glow. "I'm sorry," he said, touching her shoulder. "Your examples seem right out of a James Bond movie."

"Well, heck, am I far off?"

He tilted his head back and forth. "Yes and no, but I understand your point."

"Look, I'm a damn good researcher and I know every book, every document out there about Jewish history and culture. I've seen the documentaries, read most of the books about the Holocaust. This is my area of expertise. But I don't have your knowledge and — and abilities. My grandmother was clear that she wanted me to take up her mantle, and I don't want to let her down. I want to do what I can to carry her legacy forward and make her proud." Tears sprang to her eyes, and she poked in her purse for a tissue, but Ethan was quicker and handed her a packet from his pocket.

"You come prepared." She smiled.

"Did I forget to mention I was also a boy scout in my youth?"

Now it was her turn to laugh. "Would you like to come over for dinner at my place? I want to show you a letter Leah wrote to me, and there's something else I need to show you. If I tell you about it, you'll probably think I'm mad, but if you see it for yourself..." She bit back a rueful smile. "...You'll probably still think I'm mad."

Ethan reached for her hand and held it between both of his. "It's okay. I promise not to think you're mad. Besides, I've experienced some pretty unbelievable stuff in my life. I wanted to help

Leah, and I want to help you. Thank you for the invitation. I'm sure between us, we can figure out a plan of action."

Rose's eyes filled with tears again. Did she dare tell him about the blue coat and brooch? What about the gray-haired sisterhood and the legacy of Miriam? If she did tell him, would he believe her and still be willing to help? That would be the real test. If he didn't pass it, she had no idea what she would do next.

Please, Bubbie, please be right about Ethan.

CHAPTER 18

January 21, Present day
Brooklyn, New York

The battle between good and evil had never seemed so real.

Ethan gazed up at the fanlight stained glass window above the door to Rose's brownstone. It occurred to him that he and Rose shared a common goal to eradicate evil, she being the newcomer and finding herself in need of reassurance, and he being the dedicated one who had made this quest his life's work.

"I now understand why she had it made," said Rose. "It was something that never left her thoughts, and the window was a physical reminder of what was at stake. It bothers me that we never talked about any of it while she was alive." The regret in Rose's voice was palpable.

"I'm sure she wanted to avoid casting a shadow over your life for as long as possible," Ethan said.

Rose met his gaze. "That may be true, but now she's left me to fight a battle I may not possess the ability to win."

"Don't sell yourself short. Leah believed you to be equal to the challenge, and from what I knew of her, her judgment was sound."

Rose rewarded him with a smile, and it got to him. She was as lovely as her name. He followed her into the library.

She didn't have to ask him twice about losing himself in Leah's library. He'd been dying to explore the collection more fully since the shiva. His fingers lightly traced the spines of the books in each row. Like a divining rod, his fingers led him to leather-bound volumes about the kabbalah, spirituality, reincarnation, and ancient myths. He was surprised to find so many metaphysical topics, as he'd perceived Leah to be a pragmatist. But then again, acquiring knowledge should never be limited to one's personal preferences. Opening your horizons is what learning is all about — knowledge for knowledge's sake. Especially when one made their life's work the preservation of knowledge and the eradication of evil.

He set down the book he was reading as Rose entered, balancing a tray. "Can I help?"

"Could you bring the wine and glasses from the kitchen?" she asked, setting the tray down on an ottoman while she draped a tablecloth over the chess table. "I don't see any harm in us having a glass of wine with dinner, do you?"

"None whatsoever." He grinned. "Back in a flash." He chuckled at Rose's expected cringe, her annoyance at his use of clichés. He'd have to stow that one away for future use. He carried the glasses and bottle back to the library "Your choice of wine is perfect."

Rose was already sitting at the table, and she looked up, smiling. "Another thing Leah left me was a well-stocked wine cellar. She was a French snob when it came to wine. I'm partial to the lightness and crispness of a Chablis."

Ethan opened the bottle, poured, and sat, admiring the presentation on the plate. She'd sprinkled chives over the yellow omelet, and the contrast of color was appealing. "So, what kind of omelets have we here?"

"We have a goat cheese, spinach, and diced tomato omelet. I hope you like runny and soft. If not, I can pop yours in the oven and ruin it." Her humor was accompanied by a teasing smile.

"Spoken like a true French chef. I've heard about meat cleavers being thrown when customers send their meat back asking for the "well-done" treatment in France. I wouldn't doubt they feel the same about omelets. Runny is fine, and arugula salad is my favorite. Bon appetite." He took a bite and washed it down with a sip of the wine. "This is great. You've been holding out on me; you know how to cook, and your wine pairing is perfect."

"A girl's gotta keep a few secrets. Leah taught me the basics when I was a kid and added to my knowledge as I grew up. She always told me that any grandchild of hers — male or female — would know their way around a kitchen."

He raised his glass first toward heaven and then to Rose. "To you, Leah, and to us."

Her cheeks brightened to a rosy hue. She met his gaze and clinked her glass against his.

"To Leah and us."

After dinner, Ethan insisted on cleaning up while Rose ran upstairs to get the letter.

He read Leah's letter in the library while Rose made them coffee. When Rose returned to the room carrying the tray, he was chomping at the bit. "Did you find it? Did you find the key?" He looked around the library, wondering where the entrance to the "folly" might be.

She nodded, concentrating on the tray and its contents. Ethan jumped up and helped her unload the tray. "Can I see it? And what was she talking about when she said gifts and powers?"

Her hand trembled as she poured. "A lot has happened since I last saw you. It's made me question everything I've ever been certain of."

Rose took a slow sip of the rich, dark brew. Her deep sigh made him wonder if she was trying to prepare herself for what she was about to reveal.

"I've known for years about grandma's secret office, but I never thought much about it." She stood and strolled to a wall of bookshelves and removed a book. Ethan noted the title — *The Three Musketeers*. He grinned at Leah's cleverness.

"I always chalked it up to my grandmother's eccentricity." Rose pulled the lever, and the shelves swung open.

Ethan's eyes widened. "Okay, that's way too cool." He followed behind Rose, waiting as she switched on the light. His gaze swept left and right, finally resting on the desk and locking on the music box.

Rose wound the music box and the room filled with the melody of *La Vie en Rose*.

"Talk about suspense," he breathed.

"I know." When the last of the notes rang out, she rewound it.

"The three times thing is pretty clever. But a real thief would just smash it."

"Only if the thief knew about a hidden room and a hidden compartment, which he wouldn't. Besides, the key wouldn't be enough. I did some research on Swiss bank accounts. For me to access the safety deposit box, I'm going to have to show official documentation attesting to Leah's death and that I'm her sole heir."

When the final refrain ended, she reversed the key, and within the music box, the mechanism clicked, falling into place, and the secret drawer popped out. The small key gleamed under the glowing light of the crystal chandelier. Rose lifted it out of the drawer and handed it to Ethan.

He rested it in his palm and studied it. "It's definitely a bank safety deposit key." He looked up and grinned. "We have to find out what's inside that box."

She nodded. "Bring the key. I have more to show you."

"More?"

"You have no idea."

ETHAN'S BRAIN WAS FIRING ON ALL CYLINDERS AS HE FOLLOWED ROSE up the stairs. He focused on the target that had consumed the past two years of his life. Given a different frame of mind, he'd be ogling every detail of the meticulously restored classic old house, but his preoccupation with hypothesizing where this was all leading shut down his appreciation of the beauty of the old brownstone. One thing was for sure, Leah had been onto something. Rose didn't know the danger she was heading into, but she also didn't know anything about him.

Leah had intimated that she'd been collecting damning documentation on a cabal and its leader for years. She'd also mentioned to him she'd received anonymous death threats over the years if she ever released the proof she'd accumulated. It made perfect sense to Ethan that Leah was reluctant to trust any institution and had kept everything in a secure numbered account.

Swiss accounts were impenetrable. If Ethan had his way, Rose and he would be leaving for Zürich tomorrow. But arrangements had to be made before they could make that journey. He needed all the pieces in place if they were going to bring down some of the most influential people in the world — people who were hiding their evil intent in plain sight.

Their lives would be in danger. He had to get this right, and that would require planning and organization — safe houses, weapons, untraceable communications, and backup support armed and ready. Contacts had to be put on alert — funds transferred and available. Ethan didn't want to spook Rose and send her running for the hills. He needed her help, but he had to proceed with caution.

Leah's bedroom was now Rose's, but the elegant furnishings and décor had no doubt been Leah's. Ethan's senses filled with the heady sweet fragrance of French perfume. *Rose's scent.* Each time he'd met her, he could smell it lingering on her peachy cream skin. He admitted to himself he had a penchant for the romantic scent.

A Biedermeier desk polished and waxed to a glimmering sheen sported photographs of Leah with her daughter Edith. It still gnawed at him the way Rose's mother had mistrusted him, making him feel like a thief or worse. For a psychiatrist, or whatever she was purported to be, she'd read him wrong.

He was struck by a stunning picture of Rose dressed in a sexy black dress, and he itched to pick it up and study it closer, but he didn't dare. He'd sublimated his attraction to her under cover of the investigation, and he wasn't about to let his unbusinesslike interest in her open the door to anything that might cause her discomfort.

He needed to gain her trust, not her lust. *Trust and lust, not bad, doofus.* He often wondered where his strange sense of humor came from. Neither of his parents had a funny bone in their bodies. An unhappy child's coping mechanism, he supposed. One thing was for sure, Rose didn't seem to be getting his offbeat humor. *How many vacant stares does a guy have to contend with?* He turned, taking in the rest of the bedroom. And her aversion to idioms and clichés only reinforced the fact that perhaps their chemistry was off, and she wasn't in the least bit attracted to him.

Ethan picked up the heightened coloration in Rose's cheeks

when she caught him gazing at the bed. He literally had to suck in his cheeks to keep a straight face and not embarrass her with another silly joke. Distraction seemed a better ploy. He scanned the room in appreciation. "This is a beautiful room, Rose."

Rose looked around, and tears of emotion reflected in her eyes. "Leah had such flair and good taste. After the losses and difficulties of the war, she must have needed to wrap herself in a blanket of beauty. Even so, I don't think she ever rid herself of the ugly imprint of death."

Ethan's chest constricted. He hated to see her sad, and he was tempted to take her in his arms and hug her just to let her know she wasn't alone. But again, he restrained himself. Instead, he walked to the window, putting some distance between them and peered outside. "Mind if I close these drapes? Whatever you're going to show me doesn't need an audience."

"Yes, please close them. You never know anymore who has binoculars, telescopes, or even drones. I've heard all kinds of tales about peeping Toms, especially in high-rise apartments."

"And we can't be too careful when it comes to protecting Leah's work," Ethan said, wanting to steer the conversation away from creepy men, especially because he was a virtual stranger she'd allowed into her bedroom.

Rose blew out a breath. "I agree...though, I have to tell you a little about what I've discovered."

"Okay, shoot." Ethan sat on the overstuffed velvet chair next to the fireplace and turned his full attention on Rose, who began to pace. *Whatever she's hiding has her wound tighter than a cuckoo clock on amphetamines.*

As if the overflow on a dam had been opened, Rose's words tumbled out. He watched her wring her hands as she spoke, her brows raised in consternation. She proceeded to deliver a tale about a group of old women, Holocaust survivors, who were in some kind of secret sisterhood they believed originated in Biblical times. The more he listened, the more worried he became. The stress of her grandmother's passing must be getting to her. It was the only explanation.

When she paused, he did his best to hide his growing concern. "Rose, this gray-haired sisterhood as you refer to them means well, I'm sure, but why do you believe this tale of ancient talismans and mystical bloodlines? Pretty far-fetched, I'd say. Seems like border-line fantasy. Next thing, you'll be calling on the leprechauns to meet us in Zürich."

Rose's face reflected disappointment. "Ethan, I know this sounds crazy, but I've had visions, dreams, and I've..." She clamped her mouth shut, cutting off the end of the sentence. Frustration sparked from her eyes. "I can see the only way you're going to believe me is if I show you."

"Show me what? How can you show me? Rose, you're worrying me."

Rose disappeared inside her closet and returned, holding a blue coat. A coat that had definitely seen better days. It was faded, worn, and tattered. He was confused by the way she treated it with such deference as if it was made of gold. She laid it on the bed, and his curiosity got the better of him. He got up from his comfortable seat and stood beside her. "Okay, I see an old blue coat that's pretty worn out. Am I missing something?"

"I see there's nothing wrong with your eyesight," she scoffed, imitating him at his most annoying.

The sarcastic dig assured him she hadn't lost her humor. He needed to temper his habit of stating the obvious. She opened the drawer in her night table and retrieved a velvet pouch and opened it. Out came a golden piece of jewelry that he recognized immediately as a reproduction of the Ark of the Covenant. She studied his reaction. "Beautiful, isn't it?" She was luring him in, and it was working.

"May I?" He reached out to touch the glittering golden amulet. This was beginning to feel like *Raiders of the Lost Ark.*

"No! Don't!" Rose tried to pull her hand away, but it was too late.

His fingers brushed against the burnished gold, and in the next moment, something like a lightning bolt zapped him and flung him halfway across the room. He opened his eyes, and Rose was on her knees beside him, her lips were moving, but all he could hear was a buzzing sound that resembled a jackhammer pounding in his head. She jumped up and a minute later returned, holding a bottle of water. She raised his head and brought the bottle to his lips. He sipped, his hearing slowly returning to him as the room stopped spinning. "What the hell happened?" he rasped.

"I'm sorry. I tried to stop you. Are you okay?"

"Next time, try harder." He wriggled his fingers and toes. "If my hair isn't singed and you don't see smoke coming out of my ears, then I guess I'm okay." He sat up, and she helped him to his feet. "Please explain to me what just happened," he said again.

"Don't touch, just watch." She picked up the brooch from the floor and walked to the bed where the blue coat was laid out. "I found the blue coat in Leah's closet when I was cleaning out her clothes to give away. It was too tattered and old to donate, so I threw it out. But I found it back in my closet. I chalked it up to my grieving state of mind. I told myself that I must have intended to throw it out but forgot to do it. So, I threw it out again. And then it reappeared again. I couldn't think of a logical reason for how it got back in my closet. There was no logical reason for it being there. The only reason was that my grandmother wanted me to have this old blue coat.

"The brooch was given to me at the shiva by the gray-haired sisterhood. The old birds kept talking about my being chosen for something. I chalked it up to, I don't know, group senility or CBD oil. It was the same day I met you, Ethan. On my second attempt to throw the coat away, I found the brooch in the pocket of the coat. I can tell you I don't remember putting it in the pocket. In fact, I'm sure I didn't. The damn thing pricked my finger. Anyway, I finally gave up and resigned myself to the notion that the coat and the brooch were meant for me, and they weren't going anywhere. Whether I wanted them or not — they wanted me."

Ethan's head was swimming with all of this hocus pocus, but one thing was for sure, the brooch packed one hell of a wallop. There was no question, he had to find out where this was going. He'd had some wild experiences when he was in the CIA, and then after when he joined the "Let There Be Light" project. The logical side of his brain wanted to deny what was going on, but sometimes life defied logic. Leah had implied that there were things he didn't know, things one day he would find out. At the time, Ethan thought Leah was referring to the secret Nazi conspiracies hiding around the world, not this supernatural twist of events—

"I don't understand the power emanating from the brooch." Rose's tremulous voice interrupted his swirling thoughts. "But it was as if it called to me and told me what to do. Watch what happens." Rose pinned the brooch to the lapel of the blue coat and stood back.

"What the?" The coat began to change before his eyes, tatters and tears disappearing as if invisible hands were mending, darning, and re-sewing the fabric. But when the faded blue color deepened to royal blue, he rubbed his eyes, thinking he must be seeing things. *What was in that wine we drank?*

"Open your eyes, Ethan. You're not hallucinating."

He opened his eyes. "Okay, this is getting weirder by the minute."

"It's going to get much weirder when I put the coat on," she whispered.

"I don't think it can get much weirder than it already is."

"Trust me, it can."

Rose's hands shook when she picked up the coat. Ethan followed her to the full-length mirror. "I need you to step away from the mirror. It's just a precaution, but I don't want to take any chances."

"Rose, I'm having trouble understanding what's going on. Chances of what?"

"I'm pretty sure I'll be back, but I don't know how long I'll be gone."

"You're leaving? Where are you going?"

"I don't know. That's up to the coat and the brooch. Just make yourself at home. If it's anything like last time, it won't be that long. I think when I'm in the past, time is irrelevant. A minute here can be hours in the past or longer. I'm not sure. I'm new to all of this."

"What the hell are you talking about?"

"You'll see." Rose took a deep breath as though to steady herself and slipped her arms into the sleeves. She turned to face the mirror and waited.

She looks pale. Like she might faint. Ethan couldn't see anything strange, but then he hadn't anticipated the brooch launching him like a rocket across the room. And then he heard it — a sound like a teapot juddering on the stove when coming to a boil. A slight reverberation buzzed up his toes, and the hairs on his head and arms stood on end. His head whipped around as he tried to discern the source of the strange tremor. When he looked back at Rose, his eyes grew wide.

The brooch grew brighter as if lit from within, and Rose appeared ethereal. She was fading like an old photograph, and he could see through her. It was bizarre — her reflection had all but disappeared in the mirror. His jaw dropped, and he was sure he was going to have a stroke. His heart hammered in his chest as if it was going to explode, but before he could get a word out, she was gone. Rose had vanished into thin air, and he was left alone.

He was left with a buzzing in his ears, and he shook his head. Before he could figure out what was happening, the buzzing became a roar. In a deafening blast, the roar exploded through the mirror. It was what he imagined an F5 tornado would sound like. He covered his ears, expecting the worst. The mirror cracked into a thousand pieces and pointed shards of glass flew at him. He was going to be impaled. And then without warning, the jagged pieces of mirror reversed direction, and the glass and mirror melted into one again. A profound silence settled in the bedroom.

Shit! What the hell just happened?

He ran to the mirror and placed his hands on the glass. Where did Rose go? Could he get through too? But the glass had solidified once more, and the only thing staring back at him was his own reflection.

CHAPTER 19

January 21, 1944
Auschwitz, Poland

The train of time was again in motion, and Rose flew through the years at lightning speed. Her life passed by in an instant, but the scariest sight was seeing her own birth and hearing her cries when she gasped her first breath of earthly life. How it happened, Rose didn't know, but Leah was there, and she smiled at her as Rose flew by. She continued hurtling backward into a void where none of her memories could help her. Where were the brooch and coat taking her?

With great effort, Rose calmed her pulse and evened out her gasping breath. The coat and the brooch had protected her before, so logically, she had no reason to be afraid. And yet, how could she not be? This was only her second time going back, and no matter what she'd learned from the sisterhood, and from Leah's own diary and letters, she was still terrified.

The wind rushing by her ears transformed into the voice of the old prophetess, Miriam. *Trust in the power of the brooch and Leah's love for you. Call her, and she will come.*

Rose closed her eyes and breathed, "Bubbie, I need you. Help me."

As swiftly as it had begun, the chaotic wind tunnel went silent. Rose opened her eyes, and she was standing in the middle of hundreds of suitcases. Turning in a circle, she saw a line of what looked to be fifty railcars standing empty on a row of track. The silence was eerie, and a shiver crawled up her spine. She sensed that only a few minutes ago, the area had been filled with people.

Where am I?

Rose began to walk, studying the ground for what was left behind. Dolls, stuffed animals, articles of clothing, all manner of personal possessions hastily discarded or abandoned. She spied a wooden prosthesis and shuddered. *Who would leave their leg on the ground?*

Her breath hovered in the air, forming a cloud of moisture. It was freezing, much colder than Brooklyn. At first, she didn't notice it, but an acrid-sweet smell of smoke filled her lungs when she inhaled. She walked to the end of the train, and she felt a creepy sensation that she'd arrived at a crime scene.

Lifting her hand to her forehead to shield her eyes, she squinted and followed the train track as far as she could see, then she began to gag and choke as bile rose in her throat. Tears stung her eyes — she knew where she was.

In the foggy light, she could make out the guardhouse in the distance. She was standing on the *Judenrampe,* the unloading platform of — she dared not speak the name aloud. Frantic, her gaze swept the ramp again. These were the belongings of a thousand Jews, and the sickly sweet smoke was the stench of their bodies burning in the crematorium. Her knees buckled, but a voice calling her name sent adrenaline surging through her limbs, and she righted herself just before collapsing.

She turned, and a group of men and women jumped off a row of trucks. She looked from face to face trying to figure out who'd called her name and then she saw her. The woman was thin and haggard, but even in this nightmare world of living death, nothing could dim her beauty.

Rose gasped as tears blurred her vision. But there was no mistaking who she saw — it was Leah — a beautiful young Leah.

"I've been waiting for you, *ma belle petite-fille*," Leah whispered, her eyes shimmering.

Rose would have run to her grandmother, but she froze to the spot when she heard the harsh voices yelling from nearby.

"*Schnell! Schnell! Mach dich an die Arbeit!*" It was easy to understand what the German guards surrounding the area were saying, "Faster! Faster! Get to work!"

What would happen when they saw her? All she could think about was the gas chamber filled with Zyklon-B gas and the crematoriums that burned day and night.

Rose watched wide-eyed as Leah neared her and bent to fill her arms with what had moments before belonged to the living. "Don't worry, they can't see you," Leah whispered, picking up a purse jangling with coins.

"What do you mean they can't see me?" Rose glanced around and knew that Leah was right — none of the workers or guards took the slightest interest in her. She was invisible to them. She drew in a trembling breath and turned back to Leah.

"Bubbie! I'm so happy to see you. I — I...How can I help you? Can I get you out of here?"

Leah continued picking up items as if she were reaching for fallen apples. "*Cherie*, you cannot. You cannot change the past. But I am so happy to see you too."

Not wanting to lose a moment's contact with Leah, Rose followed her to the back of the truck. Leah handed what she'd collected to a man in striped pajamas.

"The coat and brooch make you invisible for your safety. You're not a reality here — just an observer."

"But Aidan saw me—"

Leah froze and turned questioning eyes to her.

"You saw Aidan? Where?"

Rose bit her tongue. Should she tell Leah what she'd experienced with Aidan? The German soldiers chasing them? The gunshots ringing out. Aidan yelling at her to run. Why would she cause her grandmother additional pain and worry? Wasn't being in Auschwitz enough tragedy for any life? And was she even allowed to tell Leah?

What are the rules for this? Are there any?

"Tell me, Rose, it's okay, I am fine."

"The first time I put the coat on with the brooch, I found myself in an encampment of resistance fighters. Aidan thought I was you." *I can't tell her Aidan died there. I can't do it.*

Leah's eyes glistened with tears, but it was her smile that broke Rose's heart. That smile reflected a love so pure, a love that Rose was sure she'd never be lucky enough to experience.

Why did he have to die?

"So, you met Aidan, my Aidan."

"Yes, he loved — loves you so much."

Leah studied her face. "What happened?"

Tears stabbed her eyes, and Rose fought to hold them in. "I'm not sure. The camp was raided by the Germans. He forced me to run, to save myself," she whispered.

"So, you left him."

"I'm so sorry, I didn't want to. He was shot while we were running away. I left him on the ground. I shouldn't have, I should have stayed with him no matter what, but he insisted I save myself. He told me to live for the two of us."

Rusty tears slid down Leah's face. She swiped them away with her sleeve. "I said the same thing to him once." She sighed, composing herself. A German shouted at her, "*Beschäftige dich!*"

"I have to keep working while we speak." Leah continued to pick up the belongings that were scattered across the ramp with Rose trailing after her. Suddenly she stopped. "What happened after that?"

"I — I heard a shot." Rose covered her face with her hands. "The German soldier must have — I'm afraid they might have killed him."

Leah pulled Rose's hands away from her face. "Look at me, Rose. Aidan didn't die, he survived the war."

"But...but, I read the letter from his father to you, the letter from the war department. Both letters confirmed his death."

"Aidan survived that night. He was wounded badly later, a head injury. He had amnesia and spent the last part of the war in a prisoner of war camp. He didn't know who he was or where he was from. The letter you saw was sent to me before Aidan returned to Cambridge. It took time, but some of his memory returned to him."

"So why didn't he find you? Why didn't you go to him?"

A bitter smile traced Leah's lips. "Some of his memory never returned to him. His memory of me, of us, was lost to him. He reached out to me after his father showed him my letter. He tried, but he couldn't remember a thing of what we shared. The Aidan who loved me might as well have been dead. I suppose I could have tried harder, but by that time, the blue coat and the brooch were mine, and I was in America. My life's calling had come for me, and Aidan was a bittersweet memory."

"But you loved each other so much. I can't imagine abandoning Aidan like that —" Rose's hands flew to her mouth — she immediately regretted saying the harsh words to her grandmother — a woman who had gone through more tragedy than anyone ought to in two lifetimes, let alone one. Her eyes filled with tears. "I'm sorry, Bubbie — I mean, Leah."

Leah sighed and gave Rose one of her quintessential wise Bubbie smiles. "I did it as much for Aidan as for me. He married as did I. We both had children. For a time, we exchanged holiday cards, but eventually, we lost touch. A part of me wished he'd one day remember, but apparently he never did." Leah handed off another load to a scrawny man who thanked her in Yiddish.

Now Rose understood why Leah and Aidan never reunited after the war. It was heartbreaking, but at least Aidan hadn't died that night in a snowy field.

"How can you be in the past, yet know what the future holds?"

"My consciousness is open to the knowledge because of the coat and the brooch. Since Miriam, the power has been passed down from mother to daughter, or in our case grandmother to granddaughter. You called me to help you, and I answered. The coat and the brooch brought you here because our people are once more threatened. You are the one who must stop the destruction from happening again."

Rose was only beginning to understand the importance of stopping the rising tide of evil. "I've confided in Ethan, and he wants to help me, although he had a hard time believing in all of this." She ran her hand down the front of the coat. "I left him back in your — my bedroom. I hope he's okay."

"He'll be fine. And you can trust him. You will need his help. He's a good man, *cherie*."

A shout rang out from the trucks, and Rose watched as the drivers began to haul the cargo away. She worried her grandmother would have to leave her soon. She hated that Leah was here — hated that the only way she could see her grandmother was in a concentration camp. Hated that Leah had been forced to witness and endure so much suffering. "Where are they taking everything?"

"Back to the Kanada warehouse where it will be sorted, packed, and eventually shipped to Germany. But you and I are going elsewhere. I have something you need to take back with you. It will give you and Ethan a good place to start."

"Where is the Kanada barrack?" Rose looked around, trying to get her bearings.

"Kanada is between crematorium three and five. As you know, Birkenau was — is a killing factory, but those of us lucky enough to be working and living at Kanada have it relatively good, except that you live every day as a witness to the systematic murder of European Jewry. The smell of burning flesh is enough to drive any decent person insane. That's why you're here to stop this from happening again. We need to move quickly. We're going to the SS barracks on the other side of the camp."

"But why? Isn't that dangerous for you?" Rose trembled at the thought of being exposed to the monsters of the SS.

"I clean the room of the father of the man we hunt. This SS doctor will never be brought to justice. He's going to escape and hide under a new identity. His son will grow up to be the man you must destroy."

Rose swallowed heavily at Leah's blunt statement. Her grandmother was a resistance fighter and far more courageous then she could ever be.

"The son is a Nazi in every sense of the word. He funds and abets the anti-Semitic movement and leads a cabal of like-minded haters. You and Ethan need to expose him and stop him because if he has his way, he'll finish what Hitler failed to do. As to the danger, this is a time for bravery, Rose. One way or another, danger will find you."

"I'm not worried about me. The coat and brooch saved my life before. It's you I'm worried about."

"Don't worry about me. How do you think I happen to be this SS doctor's cleaning woman?"

"I don't know."

"It was my intention. The coat and the brooch showed me the way to my target."

"But you never identified the son."

"It wasn't my task. My task was to compile the list and prepare everything for you."

"What list?"

"You will find out when you open the box in Zürich."

"Aren't you afraid this doctor will turn on you, harm you?"

"He's in love with me, Rose. He won't touch me, but he wants me, and it's driving him crazy." Leah waved her hand as if waving away a pesky fly. "I can certainly bear his unseemly advances in exchange for the evidence he unwittingly will give me. Now come, we'll try to get this over with before he returns to his quarters."

"You said he's a doctor?"

"Yes, he's a doctor at Auschwitz. A murderer who works with Mengele. He will escape just before our liberation by the Soviets. He's a sly one, and I'm sure he has planned everything well in advance for when the war is lost. Why do you think so many of his cohorts were not brought to trial?" Leah didn't wait for Rose's answer. "Because they knew what was coming. They stashed away the plunder from the Jews — the paintings, the jewelry, the cash, and they plotted their escapes. In the chaos after the war, the allies were more worried about the growing power of Russia over Eastern Europe — the least of their concerns were a bunch of defeated Nazis who'd scattered around the globe like cockroaches."

"It's wrong that so many of them got to live out their lives and were never brought to justice."

"Water under the bridge, I'm afraid. You and Ethan need to find the son and shut him and his co-conspirators down. The son was born during the war, and the doctor arranged for new identities for them when he left Auschwitz. I've searched his room, but I haven't found any evidence of his plans. The doctor is long dead in your time, but it is the son you seek."

"Are we supposed to kill him?" Rose whispered. She didn't know if she could kill someone in cold blood, even someone like this mysterious Nazi. Is that what Leah meant when she said she would need Ethan's help?

"You will have to decide when the time comes. You and Ethan need to build the case on the son and link him to his Nazi origins and his funding of hate groups. You must expose him to the media and the world and expose the rest of the members of the cabal and tie them to him. Their association with him will destroy their ability to affect the political landscape. I warn you, these are powerful individuals, dangerous men who won't go down without a fight — they are killers."

Leah led Rose through row after row of barracks. It was impossible to look at the suffering and impossible to look away. Reading about it, or even hearing it from a survivor was nothing compared to witnessing it. The squalor and filth, the degradation and starvation, the hopelessness and dehumanization were beyond heartbreaking. Rose shuddered and covered her face as she and Leah carefully stepped around the frail body of a woman crumpled on the ground, her dress soiled with her own excrement. Her eyes still open, even in death. *Someone's child, someone's sister. Her dreams for a future are no more. How did the survivors go on after this nightmare?*

Leah must have read her thoughts. "They went on because life is precious, and it was their duty to live, to have children, to give testament to what had happened."

Rose was humbled. *What strength it took to build a new life out of the ashes.*

Leah passed through the guard station with little scrutiny. She was obviously a familiar sight to the sentries. Even though they couldn't see her, Rose trembled as she brushed past the *SS-Totenkopfverbände*, the Death Head Units responsible for the concentration camps, recognizable by their skull's head insignia on their hats and uniforms.

Rose was struck by the disparity between the lives of the doomed prisoners and the comfort of their wardens. On a table in the entry of the SS barracks was a vase of colorful wildflowers so fresh and fragrant — the contrast between the simple display of nature's beauty and the ugliness of human suffering made Rose want to fall to her knees and weep.

Leah must have read her mind again because she whispered, "It is over Rose, and nothing can change what happened. What is important is we stop it from happening again. Do you understand?"

Rose nodded, wiping the stream of tears from her cheeks.

"Good." They climbed a wooden stairway to the second floor. Leah picked up a bucket with rags and cleaning materials and led Rose down a hallway. She removed a key from her pocket, knocked first, and when no one answered, they entered. The room was sparsely furnished but in perfect order. The bed was made with military precision. On the desk was a silver-framed photo of a baby boy. The woman holding him was thick waisted, her blonde hair in pigtails. She wasn't unattractive, but to compare her to Leah would be like comparing a rose to a weed.

Leah grabbed a rag and laid it on the desk. She began to search through the drawers. "Do you have your cell phone?"

"Can I do that, bring it with me through time?"

"It's possible. You need to think, child. Everything depends on your ability to outwit them."

Rose nodded. "I'm sorry, Bubbie. I promise I'll do better."

"I know *cherie*, I know." Leah rummaged through the top drawer. "I've got it." Just as Leah lifted something from the drawer, the door opened. Her hand flew behind her back, and she grabbed the rag and began dusting the desk with her other hand.

Rose's heart stampeded in her chest. Even though she knew the German officer couldn't see her, her fear for Leah had her trembling like a leaf. The man entered and froze for a moment.

"*Gut morgen,* Nadia." He removed his hat with the German imperial eagle emblem and SS skull's head insignia and tossed it on the bed. The SS doctor was tall and slim. His light brown hair fell in a wave on his forehead, a striking contrast to the closely shorn gray hair that sprayed his temples. The way he carefully smoothed his hair with both hands revealed his vanity. He made no effort to hide his pleasure at finding Leah in his room. He was cleanly shaven with a thin upper lip, but a generous bottom lip balanced out his face. Whatever evil he was capable of was hidden behind sky blue eyes and a handsome face.

"*Gut morgen, Herr Sturmbannführer.*" Leah inclined her head in greeting.

"What have you behind your back, *schatzi?*" He inched closer; his face transformed by his smile.

"Nothing, Horst." It was as if she'd disarmed him. His whole demeanor changed when she voiced his given name aloud. He stilled, his eyes widening.

"You know how long I've waited to hear you say my name. You've always refused. Why the change?" he asked.

Rose ran behind Leah and grabbed the brown leather object out of her hand and stuffed it in the blue coat's pocket. Leah's hand emerged from behind her back empty, and she adjusted the kerchief on her head. "I didn't think it was appropriate, but since we're friends, I see no reason to deny you that pleasure."

Looking at her, Rose couldn't tell whether her statement was sarcastic or sincere.

With his hands clasped behind his back, Horst walked behind Leah and took a quick look around. She stood like a statue staring straight ahead. Satisfied that there was nothing problematic going on, he placed his hand on the small of her back and leaned in, whispering, "I'm honored that you now consider me your friend, Nadia."

Without turning her head, Leah said. "*Bitte*, I must finish your room, Horst." Then she turned her face toward him daringly, teasingly. "You would not want your friend to be punished, would you, Horst?" Her direct gaze made Horst inch back and suck in his breath.

"You will not be punished, Nadia. I will not allow it." He composed himself and sat in his comfortable chair in the corner. Watching as she resumed cleaning, he crossed his long legs in front of him at his ankles.

Rose couldn't help but wonder how many times Leah had been forced to clean while he feasted his eyes on her? The man was clearly taken with her.

"Nadia, did you get the basket of food I sent to you?"

"Yes, my bunkmates all thank you." Leah dusted the photos on the desk, ignoring his hungry gaze.

"It was all for you. Why do you share it with the others?"

She waved her rag dismissively. "It is not good to create jealousy among the people around you. I've told you that before. I intend to survive this war and return to Paris. I'm not here to make enemies."

"Nadia, if we'd met in another place at another time — Paris perhaps — would you have been open to seeing me as more than a friend?"

"But *Herr Sturmbannführer,* we are not in Paris, we are in Birkenau-Auschwitz in Poland. There is a war going on, and you and I are on opposing sides."

"I know, but if things were different, what then?"

"You mean if you weren't married to the lovely Frau Schumacher?" Leah's sardonic smile targeted the Nazi doctor.

"You shouldn't tease, *schatzi.* We both know my wife pales in comparison to you."

Leah shook her head with amusement. "Why don't you tell me about your day while I finish cleaning?"

"Ach, my experiments continue to bring me great satisfaction. I've been injecting blood into healthy patients from typhus patients and then trying to cure them. Imagine the benefit to mankind if I succeed. I'm also exploring the body's reaction to varying doses of radiation, particularly on the reproductive organs. My work shows great promise."

Rose slapped her hand over her mouth, holding back the bile. The SS doctor didn't see her, but what if she retched on the floor? Would a puddle appear out of nowhere? She'd read that most of the women exposed to radiation experiments died agonizing deaths. From their X-ray burns, they'd be rendered unfit for work and immediately gassed. And the cruelty of performing surgery without anesthetic made the Nazi doctors Dr. Frankensteins. She imagined this particular psychopath took pleasure performing castrations and other macabre experiments on men without anesthetic. Lacking a conscience or morality, he was the incarnation of evil.

"How was your day, Nadia?"

Leah looked up and met his gaze.

Rose could see the delicate flare of Leah's nostrils as she took her time answering.

"Today I cleared the belongings of a transport of more than a thousand people. The camp must be bursting at the seams, because there was no selection, or perhaps all the good doctors of Auschwitz were too busy today conducting important scientific experiments. The unfortunate transport of men, women, and children was taken straight to the gas chamber." She swiped at her eyes. "That was my day, Horst."

He dragged his gaze away from the accusation in her eyes. "It's not you, Nadia. It's only the Jews. They brought it on themselves. They're the reason for this war."

She sighed. "Yes, I forget, sometimes. They're Jews and not like you or me."

"Exactly. One day you'll return to Paris, and you'll thank us for removing the vermin from your streets and cities."

"I'm sure there will be great parades and celebrations."

"Maybe we'll run into each other again after the war in Paris. Wouldn't that be *wunderbar*?"

"We can celebrate with champagne and toast the good old days." Leah's hands rested on her hips as she seemed to contemplate the future. "I must return to Kanada, Horst. I don't want to enrage the block master."

"If he gives you any trouble, Nadia, you let me know, and I'll handle him."

Leah picked up the bucket and walked to the door, her hand on the knob. She turned to Horst. "Horst, what's the boy's name?"

"My son?"

"Yes."

He gazed affectionately at the photo of the woman holding the baby. "Heinrich Schumacher. He's five months old."

"I wish him a long and healthy life."

"*Dankeschön*, Nadia. I will see you tomorrow, *ya?*"

"Unless some knight in shining armor appears and whisks me away, it seems likely."

Leah returned the bucket to the maintenance closet, and Rose followed her downstairs, past the guard, and out the door. She looked up at the dark gray clouds in the sky. "Snow is coming." She shivered. "Many of the prisoners will get sick and die without medicine, others will freeze to death. But in many ways," her eyes rose to the smokestacks of the crematoriums, "they'll be the lucky ones."

"Nana, it sounded like he doesn't know you're Jewish."

"He thinks I'm a resistance fighter, a non-Jew that was shipped here for punishment."

"Now I understand. You had false papers. He's a monster," said Rose.

Leah nodded. "Believe me, there are many who are worse than him." Leah placed her hand on Rose's face. It was the first time in her visit that Leah had touched her. Rose's eyes blurred with tears as she covered her grandmother's hand with her own.

"You're beginning to fade."

"What?" Rose looked down at herself, then back up at Leah. "I don't want to leave you, Bubbie." She began to sob, great heart-wrenching sobs, knowing she had to leave her beloved grand-mother in this living hell.

Leah wrapped her arms around her, hugging and kissing her on both cheeks. "*Cherie*, I am always with you. Believe me. I love you, *ma belle fille*." She stepped back, and the last thing Rose saw was her smile. The last thing she heard was, "Find him."

"Find him." The words echoed in Rose's ears as she was sucked into the vortex. She raced at lightning speed away from Auschwitz, far from the horrors of the past. Disconsolate, Rose wept and wailed as she was hurtled forward in time, unable to let go of the sheer agony of leaving her grandmother. Unable to let go of the horrors she'd witnessed.

A blinding flash of light made her cover her eyes, but a melodic voice called to her. She opened her eyes and there before her floated Miriam, bathed in white light. She began to sing, her voice mesmerizing and enchanting. She placed her hands on Rose's head and sang a blessing, infusing Rose with a sweet serenity that flowed from Miriam's hands to Rose's heart. Rose relaxed in the arms of pure love as the storm raged around her. She stopped fighting the riptide in the sea of time, giving herself up to whatever was her destiny.

Racing toward the light, she crashed through the mirror at the end of the tunnel. The mirror shattered into a thousand pieces of quicksilver. Instinctively she covered her face and braced herself for the jolt of landing on the hard floor of her bedroom. But instead, she felt strong arms enfolding her and a warm chest drawing her in.

"It's okay. I've got you," a deep voice rasped.

Her thoughts were a swirling mist as she struggled to remain conscious and then everything went dark.

CHAPTER 20

January 21, Present day
Brooklyn, New York

I *should have believed her.*

Ethan had pounded on the mirror and shouted until he was hoarse. Frustrated and guilt-ridden, he sank to his knees. His doubt and lack of trust had forced her to take a risk, putting her in unknowable danger.

Why hadn't he believed her? There was nothing normal about the rise of a new Nazi order. Why would there be normalcy in fighting it? Who was he to judge the powers of the universe? Just because something doesn't fit into what's known doesn't mean it doesn't exist. It was pompous to believe all the mysteries throughout time were explainable by the rules of science or empirical evidence.

Ethan sat on his haunches without a clue of what he should do. He was painfully aware of the minutes ticking by. If, by some miracle, she returned safely, Ethan swore never again to question what she told him. He'd already committed himself to helping her, but now that commitment shifted to protecting her.

He registered a slight tremor, almost like an aftershock beneath his knees. He stood and faced the mirror. Was his reflection wavering?

He heard it, an approaching rumble that was growing louder as if a train hurtled toward him. It occurred to him that he should take cover, but before the thought fully registered, the mirror exploded, and everything slipped into slow motion. Glistening shards of mirror floated toward him, their jagged edges on course to impale him. Through the incoming projectiles of glass came what appeared to be a blue missile.

It was too late to avoid being hit. Instead, he relaxed, hoping to absorb the impact. He'd played football in high school and college, and being tackled was part of the game. The shock of collision stole his breath and knocked him to the ground.

Ethan opened his eyes and blinked, wondering if he'd suffered eye damage. All he could see was red. He realized it was Rose's hair and she was lying on top of him.

"It's okay. I've got you."

She lifted her head, and they stared at each other, speechless. And then she fainted.

Frantic, he gently patted her face to try to wake her up. "It's okay, Rose. You're safe," he whispered. A few moments later, her eyelids fluttered, and once again they stared at each other.

He wrapped his arms around her and drew her even closer. "I was so fricking worried, Rose." He heard her intake of breath and released her. "Sorry."

She rolled over onto her back. The intimacy of having her on top of him in his arms wasn't lost on him, nor was it lost on her, judging by the rosy hue that flushed her cheeks. Rose straightened her hair, her beautiful red hair. *Don't go there, Ethan. Too much is at stake.* But he couldn't help it. He was attracted to her. Deeply.

"Are you okay, Rose?"

She nodded, swallowing. "Water, please," she croaked. "There's a bar fridge built into the armoire."

He jumped up, grateful to do something useful.

Rose gulped the water down so quickly he wondered if she'd been in the desert with Miriam again.

"I will never doubt you again, Rose. I want you to know that if you tell me that a bunch of dragons moved in around the corner, I swear I'll believe you."

She smiled. "Dragons? This isn't Game of Thrones." She chuckled. "But I can't blame you, Ethan, for believing I'd lost my head. This whole thing is pretty unbelievable." Tears rimmed her eyes. "I s-saw Bub — Leah. In Auschwitz. Ethan, I didn't want to leave her there. I — I." Rose broke into heart-wrenching sobs, and Ethan once again gathered her in his arms. All he could do was hold her and try to soothe her as she began to tell him everything she'd seen. Everything about Leah and the train and all the abandoned suitcases and belongings. They sat on the floor, leaning against her bed. At one point, he jumped up to grab the box of tissues off her nightstand and then returned to her as she continued to cry and recount what she'd witnessed.

"Whatever you've read or heard, nothing can ever capture the horror of it."

"You're right. Nothing could."

"You believe me now, don't you?" She dabbed at her nose. "I mean about the brooch and the coat?"

"You're damn right, I believe you. I believe everything you've told me." He hugged her against his side.

"I saw him. I mean — I saw his father."

"Saw who?"

"The man Leah warned me about. The man who is bent on destroying the Jews in modern times."

Rose stood, and reaching in her pocket, she pulled out a small brown booklet and handed it to him. "Here it is, I nearly forgot."

"Dear Lord, is this what I think it is?" His eyes were locked on the cover of the booklet. The black print read *Deutsches Reich* beneath a picture of the imperial eagle and the Nazi swastika. At the bottom was printed *Reisepass*, and beneath that, a set of pin-punched numbers.

"Open it. It's —" Rose's voice trailed off in a whisper.

Ethan flipped the passport open, and he stared at a black and white photo of a man. He read aloud, "Horst Schumacher, born 1, May 1906, in Halle an der Saale, Kingdom of Prussia." Lifting his eyes to Rose, he questioned, "You saw him and got a good look at him?"

"I'd know him anywhere. I saw a photo of the son too, but it was a baby picture. He did seem to look a lot like his father. That baby is who we have to find."

"You say this man was a doctor at Auschwitz?"

"Yes. He conducted horrifying experiments on Jews. He was experimenting with radiation so he could mass sterilize the Jews. The poor souls he experimented on must have died torturous deaths."

"And he was never brought to trial?"

"No. He was one of the Nazis who planned an escape route in case of Germany's defeat. They knew they'd be tried for war crimes. The father must have assumed a new identity and never looked back. Wiesenthal caught some of the murderers, but not all of them." Rose scrutinized the photo. "The baby's first name was Heinrich. If he never changed his first name, it will make it easier to identify him, don't you think?"

"We can find him. Horst Schumacher is long dead by now. It's amazing how many of these bastards got away with murder and were never brought to justice. In many ways, the allies were responsible for that. They traded amnesty for information and testimony from killers. No matter what value these murderers held, they should have been tried and, at the very least, served a sentence for their crimes." Ethan's attention shifted to Rose and he frowned. "I'd feel a lot better if you took the coat off. The last thing I want to see right now is you disappearing again."

Rose gazed down at herself. "Oh, I forgot I was wearing it." She shrugged off the coat and hung it in her closet. She returned with the brooch in her hand.

"You need to explain to me more about this time-travel stuff. What you experience and your interaction when you're there. Were you in danger? How did you manage to stay safe?" He began to pepper her with questions, wanting to understand.

She put the brooch in the velvet pouch and returned it to her nightstand drawer. "Let's go downstairs, and I'll pour us a glass of wine. I'll tell you everything I know about it, which I'm afraid isn't much. The only thing I know for sure is that the brooch and coat have the power to protect me."

They sat in the kitchen, and Rose poured the last of the bottle of wine. "Ethan, it's late, so you're welcome to stay the night."

"You're sure?"

"Yes, of course. This is a big house with plenty of rooms. We're going to be working together, and I assume traveling together. We might as well get used to close quarters."

"Suits me fine. Speaking of traveling, I think we need to leave as soon as possible for Zürich. We need to find that safety deposit box."

"I agree. Tomorrow we can book the flights and make hotel arrangements."

"Leave that to me."

He read the confusion on her face. "Why the look?"

"We'll split the cost, of course."

"This is about security and cover. I'm an expert at this. Money is not an object. Remember, I'm funded by individuals who want us to succeed. Leave this to the experts and me, please."

"Aren't you going to tell me who these experts are?"

"It's better if you don't know. Safer."

Rose frowned. "It makes me uncomfortable not knowing who these people are."

"You're going to have to trust me just like I'm trusting you."

She blew out a breath. "Okay. But eventually, you're going to have to tell me who they are."

"Be careful what you wish for, sweetheart." He smiled and winked.

Rose cringed. "What did I tell you about those clichés?"

"Can't help it." He took a sip of his wine. "Just as some people are connoisseurs of fine wine, I'm a connoisseur of kitschy clichés."

She wagged her finger at him, but her eyes gleamed with humor. "I'm trying to think of an appropriate punishment for whenever you use one."

"Just don't bring that brooch anywhere near me."

Rose laughed and sipped her wine. "That would be too severe of a punishment. Besides, the coat and brooch might decide to teach you a lesson and whisk you back to the inquisition or something."

"I'm definitely going to keep some distance between me and your time machine." Changing the subject, he said, "Do you have an up-to-date passport?"

"Yes, of course."

He arched his brow. "I'll be traveling under a fake passport. Incognito."

"Why? Are you worried about what they might find out about you? Do you think we're being watched?" She shuddered, hugging herself.

"I don't want to alert them in any way. Let them think I'm a nobody and that we're dating."

"Do you think they could find out about your ties to the CIA or the people you work with?"

"I have no idea how connected they are or whether they have people inside the government who have access to covert operations. The passport I'm using is for a Connor Hayes, I'm a stock analyst for Goldman Sachs."

"Will that throw them off our Swiss trip?"

"It'll make them wonder about it. But the important thing is that it makes our choice of Zürich seem innocent."

She studied him. "Do you have a lot of fake passports?"

"I have several alternate passports and several false identities."

"I see." Her eyes narrowed. "You are a spy, aren't you?"

"Not anymore. Basically, I'm a freelancer. But in my line of work, it's best to use a cover."

"You're not going to tell me more than that, are you?"

"Not tonight, I'm not."

She yawned, covering her mouth. "Okay." She was clearly too tired to persist in her interrogation. "Why don't I show you to the guestroom. Time travel is exhausting. I need to get some sleep."

"You lead, I'll follow."

Rose's shoulders slumped wearily as Ethan followed her up the stairs. At the other end of the hallway from Leah's bedroom, Rose opened a door. She switched on the light, and the room came into focus. The bedroom could aptly be named the blue room. Everything from the wall coverings, carpets, upholstery, bedding, and drapes were in various shades of blue. Rose entered and opened another door that led to the bathroom and switched on the light. The bathroom was modern, all white and blue tiles with chrome fixtures.

Rose's gaze swept the bath. "Everything you need is here. Leah kept this home like a boutique hotel." She smiled. "This was my room when I visited."

Seeing the wistful look in her eyes, he rubbed her shoulder. "It's lovely. I'm sure I'll be very comfortable. Thank you for letting me stay. It's been a long day, and I suspect the following days are going to be even longer."

She nodded. "Good night, Ethan.

"'Night, Rose."

When the door shut behind Rose, Ethan stared at it deep in thought, contemplating everything that had occurred. The potent force that emanated from the coat and the brooch bewildered him. If he hadn't witnessed Rose's disappearance and unexplainable return through the mirror portal with his own eyes, he would never have believed it.

Thank God, she came back.

Thank God he'd been there to catch her. He hadn't been there for her that first time. But if she ever had to go back, he'd be damned if he'd let her go alone. At the very least, he'd be there to catch her when she returned.

Everything had changed. Everything.

He closed the door and settled in for the night. Rose needed her rest, but he had work to do — emails to send and plans to make.

The hunt was on.

CHAPTER 21

January 25, Present day
Zürich, Switzerland

Sunrise over the snow-covered Alps, reminded Rose of traveling with her grandmother.

Rose had always been amused at the contradiction that was Zürich, a jewel of a city nestled in a pristine landscape whose sole existence was dependent on money and banking. The irony was as inescapable as the beauty of its mountains, lakes, and valleys.

It was heartbreaking to imagine never again sitting across from Bubbie and sharing a fondue on a sunny wooden deck in Zermatt beneath the stunning, towering summit of the Matterhorn. Rose had learned to ski in Switzerland both on family vacations with her parents and with her grandmother. As she aged, Leah eventually gave up skiing and preferred to meet Rose at the day's end for après-ski drinks of peppermint schnapps and hot chocolate. As memories washed over her, Rose dabbed at her eyes, missing her grandmother and hoping they could track down their target and his cohorts.

When the crystal blue water of Lake Zürich appeared out the jet's window, she pressed her nose up close, assimilating the breathtaking views. In the distance, the familiar Romanesque bell towers of the Grossmünster Protestant Church and the green Gothic spire above the clocktower of the Fraumünster Church rose — two religious landmarks situated on opposite sides of the Limmat River, still dominating the landscape just as they had for a thousand years.

"Have you ever seen Marc Chagall's stained-glass windows in the Fraumünster Church?" she asked Ethan without turning, her gaze fixed out the window.

"No, I guess I missed that. My trips to Zürich have always been all business."

The plane banked, preparing to land. Rose pulled her gaze away from the window and looked at Ethan. "You really should, they're incredible. Maybe we can steal a bit of time and go see them."

Ethan looked at his watch. "If you're not too tired, we could go today. It's Sunday and a day of leisure in Switzerland, so it's a good day to sightsee. We could have lunch in the old city, take a walk on the lake, whatever you'd like. Tomorrow we'll be serious."

She smiled. It would give her and Ethan some downtime to get to know one another better and relieve some of the anxiety that had become a constant companion since Leah's death and discovering her mission. She'd put her life in this man's hands, and it would give her a chance to learn more about him. "I'd like that. Have you spent much time in Zürich?"

Ethan averted his gaze. "I've been here a time or two, but as I said, it was mostly for business, and I didn't sightsee much. How about you? Have you spent much time here?"

"I learned to ski in Switzerland. Leah loved to walk the lake and hike in the Alps. The Swiss respect privacy and that appealed to her. It didn't hurt that the cuisine is great. I think I told you my grandmother was a food snob."

"I get that for sure. I'm the same. I didn't travel through Europe until I was an adult, but once I experienced the food, the art, the music, and the culture, I was sold. Take Zürich, for example. I was reading about it during the flight. Zürich was founded by the Romans two thousand years ago. Kind of boggles the mind, doesn't it? And here's one for you to mull over, the Fraumünster abbey, the church with that mega-steeple, was founded in 853 by the grandson of Charlemagne for his daughter Hildegard. He granted all of Zürich and the surrounding lands to the Benedictine convent he founded for her, and in 1045 the abbess was given the right to hold markets, mint coins, and charge tolls. Until the fourteen hundreds when the convent's power began to wane, Zürich was ruled by a woman. I don't think women, in general, know their history enough. Directly or indirectly, one way or the other, they've held power many times throughout history."

"I love that you're interested in history."

"And you thought I was nothing beyond a good-looking hunk, right?"

Rose could feel her cheeks flush. "I — that's ridiculous. I saw the way you drooled over Leah's library, and you've said several times you're a bookworm."

"You're going to have to learn not to take everything I say seriously, madam librarian. Except when I am serious," he grinned.

"Either that or I'm going to have to learn to dish it right back at you. Maybe out-cliché you."

"Hah, now that I would enjoy."

The wheels touched down on the tarmac, reminding Rose that despite the pleasant conversation with Ethan, nothing about this trip seemed even remotely about fun. She was frightened, and the minute the wheels of the jet hit the tarmac, her fears ratcheted up. The reality hit her that there was no turning back now, cliché or not.

ETHAN HAD BOOKED THEM INTO THE ROMANTIK EUROPE HOTEL. The boutique hotel, a neo-Baroque castle built at the turn of the century, overlooked Lake Zürich. It was a quirky mix-and-match of French and English décor that reminded Rose of a country manor. It was elegant but not staid, and the bellman who brought their bags up enthused about the French restaurant and bar — Quaglinos, with its 1920s ambiance. "Quaglinos is considered to be one of the best French bistros in Zürich," said the bellman as he opened the door and switched on the lights.

Rose looked around the spacious suite. "Is this my room?"

Ethan scratched his head. "Actually, it's our room."

"What?" She eyed him suspiciously and tapped her foot, waiting for an explanation.

Ethan tipped the bellman and said nothing until he closed the door. He spread his hands out as if preparing to argue his case before a judge. "Back in the day, this was Rudolph Nureyev's room. He stayed here sometimes for months when he danced with the Zürich Ballet. I thought you'd get a kick out of that."

"Great. Hopefully, I'll have dreams of sugarplum fairies pirouetting across the stage *en pointe* in ballet slippers. And I appreciate," Rose swept her gaze around the suite, "that you took the trouble to pick a room that would appeal to my sensibilities. Really, I do. I love the antique pinstriped chairs and the old writing desk, and the rich tassel tiebacks, and the crystal chandelier. But Ethan, we don't know each other very well, and I think it's a bit much for us to share a room."

"There's another reason."

"This better be good."

"For security reasons, I don't want you in a room alone. I'm not sure what we're walking into, or whether we're being watched, but I assume we are. We've already established that these people are not amateurs. They're dangerous, probably well-armed, and most likely well manned. I'd rather not wake up to your screams and not be able to get through the door to save you. Besides, the longer we can fool them into thinking we're just lovers on a romantic vacation, the less likely they are to figure out what we're really here for."

She started to protest, but he interrupted her.

"I ordered the suite because it had a couch and two bathrooms. I'll take the couch, and you get the bedroom. What's the problem with that?"

Her mouth closed as she considered what he said. She walked to the window and stared out at the lake and the people out strolling along the shoreline. Everything he said made sense. She faced him, having made up her mind. "Okay, we'll do it your way, but fair warning, I'm pretty cranky until after I've had my morning coffee."

He crossed his arms over his chest and chuckled. "I promise I'll steer clear of you in the morning, or better yet, I'll soothe the beast by making sure coffee and croissants are awaiting your leisure."

She curtsied. "You've soothed my soul already. Hopefully, I won't regret my decision. Are you still up to visiting the Chagall stained glass windows at the Fraumünster Church? We can unpack and go."

"Works for me."

CHAPTER 22

January 25, Present day
Zürich, Switzerland

Ethan held Rose's hand as they walked the short distance to the Fraumünster Church. He'd explained to her that they needed to behave like a couple, and Rose put up no argument. Ethan couldn't help but think how nice intimacy with a woman felt. Not the carnal kind, but just being together. Something he'd rarely had the chance to do in his line of work, and certainly not since he'd broken with Christie and she'd moved out of their London flat. Periodically, he'd sneak a glance at Rose, wondering if she was enjoying the simple pleasure of holding hands as much as he was.

They followed the tree-lined right bank of the Limmat River, called the Limmatquai, past beautiful buildings, cafes, and restaurants that lined the eastern side of the river and reflected in the transparent aqua water. The sun was shining, and the day was pleasant. Their route took them over the cobblestoned Münsterbrücke bridge to the western side of the river, and they stood for several minutes admiring the front façade of the church. From the exterior, they could see the vivid hues of the three Chagall stained glass windows visible from the plaza in front of the church. The tall narrow arches of blue, yellow, and green glass fractured in the bright sunlight in a kaleidoscope of color.

They sat down in a chapel facing the choir and stared at Chagall's cubist styled, colored glass depictions of biblical scenes that rose above the altar. Sunshine poured through the five soaring arches, bathing the church's interior with bold color.

"Beautiful, aren't they," Rose whispered.

"I can't believe I never came here to see them before. Thank you for suggesting this."

"Chagall said, 'Stained glass must be serious and passionate,'" she read from the brochure. "'It has to live through the perception of light.' I think he experienced his own catharsis when he created these windows. He must have been inspired by the spirit of God and his relationship to man, don't you think?"

"Perhaps," he replied. "I think at a certain point in our lives, most of us seek to examine our place in the world. What else does the brochure say?"

"It just describes the windows. It says the orange and red window on the north wall depicts the 'weeping prophet' Jeremiah, who foretold the destruction of Jerusalem, and above him is Elijah soaring into heaven on a chariot. The blue window on the south wall is obviously Moses holding the ten commandments above his head. I wonder what Miriam would think about seeing her baby brother portrayed in such splendor. The three other windows represent Jacob on his ladder wrestling with the angel, and in the center is the star of the grouping and the tallest window, the green Christ. The window flanking Christ on the right is an angel blowing a trumpet signifying the End of Days."

"It reminds me of what we know about this Nazi and his organization. They seem to be doing their best to bring about the End
of Days."

"We are not going to let that happen," Leah said, her lips trembling. "My grandmother loved Chagall — she understood his
exploration of his faith and his relationship with God."

Ethan wrapped his arm around Rose, drawing her in closer to
his side. "Chagall grew up in a religious home but was a non-prac-
ticing Jew, yet his art is filled with not only biblical themes but
Jewish themes. He never really escaped his roots, no matter how
hard he tried."

"Most of us can't really escape what is in our hearts, I
suppose."

"What is in our hearts is what matters. It has nothing to do
with where we came from. What matters is what we do with our
lives." Had he said too much? He glanced at Rose to see her reaction, and he felt his insides warm. She was smiling. He couldn't
help but think about how much they'd shared in such a short
time. The serene look on her face reminded him that there were
good people in the world. Rose was one of the good ones, and he
couldn't imagine anyone wanting to eliminate someone like her.
Soon he would have to tell her the truth about who he was and
who he worked for — a conversation he wasn't looking forward to.

AFTER THE FRAUMÜNSTER CHURCH, THEY GRABBED LUNCH IN THE
old city, then jet lag kicked in, and they returned to the hotel. As
promised, Ethan took the couch, and Rose withdrew to the
bedroom. Rose stared at the ceiling, frustrated. No matter how she
pulled at the thread, she was unable to get to its end. Her ques-

tions remained unanswered. She wished she'd asked Leah when she'd had the chance. She had so many questions — how did Leah end up in Kanada, and how did she come to the attention of Horst Schumacher? Their strange relationship and its ambiguities had overtaken Rose's ability to think. Leah and this man, Horst — a strange energy had flowed between them, and it wasn't hatred. What was it, and why? But then how could any logic exist amidst such madness?

Rose closed her eyes and tried to imagine Leah, not the grandmother who was familiar to her, but the young French woman who'd been so brave in the face of evil. What drove her to such courage?

The drone of the heating unit in the suite grew louder, followed by a ghostly whistle. Rose opened her eyes and gasped.

Where am I?

Her head rested on the shoulder of a woman she didn't know. A quick scan of her surroundings confirmed her worst nightmare. She was in a boxcar, pressed like a sardine against strangers, body against body. There had to be at least a hundred other unfortunate souls inside.

She covered her nose and mouth, willing herself not to throw up. It was unbearably hot with only one window for ventilation, and what air there was smelled putrid — sweat, urine and excrement, and worst of all — the scent of death. She choked, pressing her hand more firmly against her nose and mouth. A child cried, begging for food. "How long have we been on this train?" Rose asked to no one in particular. "I've lost track of time."

"Four days," a weary voice answered.

"I know this sounds crazy, but where did we come from?" Rose asked.

The voice sighed. "You're lucky you can't remember. We were deported from France for resettlement. Drancy — we were forced onto the trains in Drancy. After four days of hell, it's no wonder you can't remember."

"*Cite'de la Muette*," she whispered. The *City of the Silent*. Drancy, although not a concentration camp, had been one of the more hideous places on earth. Cramped, it had contained thousands of inmates, far more than it had been built to hold. Inside, misery and death abounded. There was little or no food. The cries of starving, weeping children — separated from their parents and alone — was a constant drone morning, day, and night. Most of these children would end up feeding the fires of the crematoria at Auschwitz.

The wheels of the train squeaked as the laden boxcar slowed to a stop. Outside, dogs barked, and gruff voices shouted orders in German. She looked down at herself, confused. If she wasn't wearing the blue coat or the brooch, how the hell had she time traveled? It had to be a dream. No, not a dream, it was a nightmare.

The doors of the boxcar opened, and angry shouts of "*Schnell! Schnell!*" came from the armed SS guards who waited on the platform. At the end of taut leashes, German shepherds barked, their sharp teeth bared. Rose stepped over the bodies of those who'd died in transit. A baby, wrapped in a blanket, her face white as the moon in the sky brought tears to her eyes. But there was no time to mourn in the chaos and press of humanity. She jumped down, took a deep breath, and glanced around. Women and men were being separated, and she was herded to the left side of the platform.

It was difficult to watch the hugs, kisses, farewells, and the tearful cries and promises of finding one another again. Once the women and men were separated, the women were ordered into an uneven line, and two Schutzstaffel (SS) officers with the Totenkopf skull badge on the peaks of their hats began a selection, sending women and children to different sides of the platform. When it was her turn to arrive at the front of the line, she looked up and met the gaze of the Nazi officer. He stared at her, the routine boredom in his gaze sharpening. He looked her up and down, head to toe, then as if realizing how long he'd been observing her, he waved her to the right.

Panic gripped her. She recognized him. It was Horst Schumacher. She'd arrived at Auschwitz.

Terrified, Rose's gaze spun from her new position to the other side. She knew what fate awaited those who were sent to the left. The mothers with children, the infirm, and the elderly would be funneled to the delousing chambers and showers. Stripped naked, they would be herded into one of the below-ground windowless chambers. There were eight of them. Eight gas chambers. Forty-six ovens that worked around the clock, incinerating four-thousand-four-hundred corpses per day. The numbers were too huge to comprehend. To the SS, this small group would seem no more than a shovel of ash, rid of quickly by their efficient German protocols. Twenty-four hours a day, every day.

When the doors of the supposed showers were locked and bolted, a select SS detail would insert the Zyklon-B crystal pellets down shafts in the ceiling, and a horrific death would rain down on the victims. Scratching and clawing, crawling over one another, trying to breathe, their cries and shouts must have been unbearable, but not, of course, for their executioners who carried out their merciless job day in and day out. The death-squad SS were hardened to the routine of murder, and if they weren't — they drowned themselves in alcohol when their day was done, dulling any trace of humanity left within them.

Twenty minutes and it would all be over.

Another train of Jews dead and ready for the flames.

It was a factory, a factory of death.

The industrialization of mass murder.

Rose tore her eyes from the condemned as her group was marched away. She would be tattooed, her head shaved, her naked body deloused. She would be given a bar of soap and told to take a two-minute shower before donning the striped prisoner uniform called a *pashak*.

Before Rose reached the building, a guard ran to the front of the line, stopping the processional of women. Everyone waited as he searched down the line, then stopped before her. He pulled her out of the group and led her away in another direction. She looked back toward the platform where the selections continued. Schumacher, the SS doctor in charge, pinned his gaze on her. Only when he saw her pulled from the group and led away did he return to the selection.

The guard led her in the same direction as the women and children destined for death. For a moment, she feared she was being taken to the gas chamber. But the path detoured, and she was led to another building. She glanced back at the building of death. The chimney spewed smoke. The air was heavy with an acrid, sweet smell, and at first, Rose thought it had begun to snow. But when she held out her hand, and feathery weightless particles landed in her upright palm, she realized it wasn't snow that rained over her, it was ashes.

The guard brought her to the "Kanada" crew and left. Another armed and uniformed officer strolled up to her, his eyes peering into hers. "You are fortunate to have been selected for this duty. Behave yourself and follow orders, and you might live to see the end of this war." He allowed her a few minutes to shower and then put her to work in the warehouse sorting the transport's baggage.

She gazed around the warehouse, trembling at what her job entailed. Heaps of shoes of different sizes and styles, scarves of many colors, flowered dresses, bright rubber balls, dolls with blonde curls and unblinking blue eyes — vast piles of personal belongings of men, women, and children who'd been marched into the brick building only a few yards away. Tears rolled down Rose's cheeks as she began to sort through the remnants of so many lives.

She was glad when an SS guard came and pulled her off the detail. He escorted her across the camp through endless barracks and endless misery. The lump in her throat was so large she could barely swallow. Two women dragged the body of another woman out of a barracks and left her outside. No burial, no prayers, no dignity. They expended no more emotion than if they were taking out the trash. In the camps, it was easy to become indifferent to the suffering of others. In truth, it was a necessity.

Rose averted her eyes.

The guard led her through the misery without pause. When she looked up, she recognized where they were going. The building where Horst Schumacher resided. They passed the security detail with barely a glance, and the guard escorted her upstairs and down the hallway to Horst's rooms. The guard knocked, and a voice instructed them to enter. The SS doctor dismissed the guard and told him to wait downstairs. Rose froze, waiting for instructions — her eyes locked on the floor.

"What's your name?" Horst asked.

"Nadia Vernier."

"Where are you from?"

"I was shipped from Drancy."

His French was faultless. "Where are you from before, Drancy?"

"Paris."

She stood still as he paced around her, his hands clasped behind his back.

"Look at me," he ordered.

She met his gaze. "I am SS Sturmbannführer Horst Schumacher. I'm dissatisfied with the woman who cleans my room. Tell me about yourself."

She related the story of Nadia Vernier, a French resistance fighter who'd been caught up in a Nazi sweep and deported to the Drancy internment camp.

"You're not Jewish?"

"No." How simple a word. How great its meaning.

"Excellent."

If she grabbed his gun from its holster and shot him dead — how many lives would she save?

Nothing will change. He will be replaced by someone else. And you will be dead. What purpose would that serve?

"Start now."

"I'm sorry, Commandant?" Caught up in her thoughts, she hadn't heard him the first time.

"You can start now. There is a maintenance closet with supplies down the hall. Go and fetch what you'll need."

Rose returned a few minutes later with a bucket, mop, rags, brushes, and cleaning solvents. Horst sat in a chair, smoking a pipe and reading a newspaper. She cleaned. Every time she stole a glance at him, she found his gaze on her. The paper was a ruse. He hadn't once turned the page.

Breaking the silence, he asked. "Do you hate us?"

"Hate who?" she asked innocently. *Yes, I hate you, you bastard!*

"Us, we Germans."

"Hate is a strong word. Do I wish you hadn't invaded my country? Yes, I wish that."

He nodded, puffing, a plume of smoke rising in the room that reminded her of the smoke rising from the crematorium. "Understandable. Such is war. I'm only a cog in the machine. I do what I'm ordered to do."

Ah, yes, the disclaimer of every Nazi. Everyone was just following orders. She refused to acknowledge his pathetic excuse and said nothing.

"It is better to be here than on the Eastern front where the poor bastards are dying like flies. I intend to survive this nasty war."

"As do I." That, at least, was true.

"Good. Then we're in agreement. An excellent place to start our friendship."

Friendship? She swallowed the bitter taste of bile that rose in her throat. Rose wanted to scream, to claw his eyes out. She was ashamed that her only response was to continue to clean.

When he threw the newspaper down and stood, her curses on him faded into fear. He strode to the desk where she was dusting and leaned in, his breath warm in her ear. "Do you know how beautiful you are?" He lifted a strand of her hair, running his fingers through it. "Your hair is like silk. Red silk. It's extraordinary, very rare, genetically speaking. Green eyes and red hair. I will have to do some research on the statistical probabilities of the combination."

She couldn't breathe. She couldn't move. Horst was so close to her, unbearably close to her. Then as if possessed, she raised her hand to slap him. He caught her hand before Rose made contact. He gripped her wrist so tight she could feel the bruise that would be there when he let go.

Rose met his gaze, unflinchingly.

He grinned, and a ruddy red hue colored his face and neck.

"You are beautiful and brave, Nadia. I've heard it said that redheads have a short fuse and are quick to anger. I had no idea how truthful it was." His grip remained firm; he was much stronger than she imagined he would be. But then again, his immaculately manicured hands were those of a surgeon.

"You know I hold your life in my hands. I could order your death in an instant." He snapped the fingers on his other hand.

Her first instinct was to shirk her gaze and acquiesce to his threats. Her eyes burned into his. "Go ahead. Kill me."

It was a face-off — she could feel his pulse racing through his fingertips just as she was sure he could feel her pulse racing through her wrist. A dark storm brewed in his eyes and then faded. "You're magnificent." He released her wrist, and she fought the desire to rub the pain from it. "I will save you from yourself. Finish your work, Nadia, and return to Kanada. I will expect you here tomorrow. I'll send a guard to escort you until we've established a routine." His hand cupped the back of her neck, and he pulled her in close. His blue eyes gripped her as tightly as his hand on her neck. "You are magnificent," he said again, this time in a lover's whisper. His lips hovered over hers. "I haven't felt this alive for a long time."

She had no idea what he was talking about — or did she?

Her heart thumped wildly in her chest. "No! No! No!" she shouted. She reached out and wrapped her hands around his neck, knowing what she must do.

"Rose! Rose! Wake up!"

Opening her eyes, she saw Ethan hovering over her, holding her down.

"Ethan?"

"Thank God, Rose, you scared the living daylights out of me. You were yelling in your sleep. It must have been a horrific dream because you wrapped your hands around my neck when I tried to wake you. You're a tough cookie for a petite woman."

She covered her face with her hands. "I'm so sorry. I —" She took a cleansing breath. "I thought you were him."

Ethan sat on the bed and pulled her into his arms. His kindness released a torrent of tears. Sobbing, she pressed her face into his chest.

"It's okay, Rose. It was just a bad dream. I know you weren't trying to kill me."

"But what if I hurt you by accident?"

"Hey, I've been in a few scrapes in my life. I don't think a hundred-and twenty-pound woman is going to do much damage. The important thing for you to know is you're safe. I'm not going to let anything happen to you."

When her sobs receded, he lifted her chin. "So, who was the lucky chap you tried to do in? Anyone I know?" He smiled.

She knew he was trying to make light of the moment. "Horst Schumacher."

"Ahh, couldn't happen to a nicer guy."

She nodded. There was no way she was going to tell him about the strange magnetism she'd felt between the SS doctor and Leah.

Just a bad dream — a reflection of her anxiety over everything that was going on.

Later on, when she was in the shower, she noticed the black and blue hue on her arms — Horst's fingerprints.

How is that possible? Dreams don't leave physical imprints. But there could be no denying that she carried the proof of her vision on her arm. It was a terrifying possibility. Did it mean her worst fears were real? The thought of Leah in an illicit relationship with a Nazi murderer was insufferable. It couldn't be true.

Dear God, please don't let it be true.

CHAPTER 23

January 25, Present day
Zürich, Switzerland

"She's here."

"Hold on," Heinrich spoke into his cellphone and turned to the patient who reclined on the sofa for their morning therapy session. It was the son of a hedge fund manager who had a penchant for Vegas showgirls, alcohol, and sadomasochism. His family was in an uproar and had insisted he sign himself up for behavioral therapy. He was spending a fortune at the clinic, and Heinrich was sure he wouldn't be cured in the one month he spent on the couch. Recidivism among sexual deviants was like money in the bank. Repeat offense was nearly guaranteed. "I'm sorry, Andrew, but I have an emergency call. Would you mind if we resume our discussion later this afternoon?"

"Not at all, doctor. I'm feeling better, and the sun is out. I'd like to take a stroll outside."

"An excellent idea. You've been cooped up for weeks. A healthy body leads to a healthy mind. Enjoy your walk."

Andrew rose and exited Heinrich's office. Heinrich wondered how long it would take for the deviant to make a move on the svelte blonde massage therapist he'd booked for a daily massage. He made a note to forewarn her and instruct her on how she should handle the situation.

Heinrich waited for the door to shut securely. "Give me the update," he said into the phone.

"The granddaughter arrived in Zürich this morning. She's traveling with a young man."

"She's her grandmother's heir. Do you think it's possible she combined a romantic getaway with the business of switching the Credit Suisse account into her name?" Henrich had been tracking Leah for years and was aware of her yearly visits to the bank. "It would make sense. Who's she traveling with?"

"It's possible, but I suspect there's more to this visit. The granddaughter's male companion is a stock analyst, and his name is Connor Hayes. He might be helping her with her investments, but he's also sharing a suite with her at the Romantik. I did some checking on him, and he seems legit."

Heinrich pulled on his trimmed goatee. "I'm worried about what might be in the security box. The old girl had a lot of years to compile her database. And I suspect my foolish father was more than eager to please her for her favors. When I discovered his diary, I assumed he'd never found Nadia, but now I know otherwise. What do you think are the odds that the granddaughter knows about us or what's in the box?"

"I don't imagine the old lady would have endangered her by telling her too much. We just have to make sure whatever she has doesn't see the light of day. How do you want to handle it?"

"Whatever she finds in that box, we need to steal and destroy before she has a chance to figure out what she's looking at."

"Are you talking about kidnapping her when she exits the bank?"

"I think kidnapping her would solve the problem permanently. But if we can snatch her purse and briefcase when she leaves the bank, we might not have to kill her. Our mole in the bank will notify us when she goes to open the box."

"Sounds good. I'll have a team inside and outside when the bank opens tomorrow. It'll look like a common theft, rare in Zürich but not unheard of with all of the riffraff inundating Europe."

"Perfect. If we get what we need, Rose is a free bird. But if anything goes wrong, we'll reassess our options. Remember, Ernst, everyone is flying in next week for our annual meeting. I do not want this threat to upset things. Don't let the lovebirds out of your sight."

"Yawohl, mein führer."

Heinrich snickered. "I like the sound of that."

CHAPTER 24

January 26, Present day
Zürich, Switzerland

"Hi, Mom."

"Rose, where have you been? I've been out of mind trying to reach you."

"I'm in Zürich."

"Zürich? What are you doing there?"

"Grandma left some unfinished business for me to take care of. Besides, I needed to get away from New York, needed some time to myself. I thought I might go skiing."

"Skiing? What about your job? You've already taken off quite a lot of time lately, are they okay with this?"

"Everything's fine with work. My boss understands."

"Are you alone there? I've never known you to travel alone, especially so far away."

"I-I," Rose hesitated. She was keeping enough secrets from her mother. She couldn't bear to add another. "I'm here with a friend."

"Who?"

She tried to keep her voice light. "You actually met him once, at grandma's shiva."

The silence stretched out on the other end of the line. *Silence isn't good.*

"Mother?"

"Rose, are you saying you've left the country with a stranger — a man you barely know? Have you lost your mind? I'm going to hire a private detective to investigate who this man really is."

"Mom, I'm not sleeping with a guy I barely know. Give me a little credit. Besides, Leah knew him quite well. They spoke often, and she trusted him. I sought him out, so if anyone is the aggressor here, it's me."

"Rose, I've told you this before, relationships built in cyber-space have no credibility. They're false indicators of who people really are. Believe me, I have more than enough patients who come to me with broken hearts and bank accounts that have been emptied from being duped online. You know nothing about this young man, his family, or his background. You can't trust the judgment of a ninety-six-year-old woman. For God's sake Rose, use your head."

"Mom, his name is Ethan. He's educated, well-traveled, articulate, loves books and food, has a job. What more do I need to know about him? This isn't a cyber-relationship — we met in person and went out several times. And grandma read people better than anyone. Let's not forget she survived not only the war but the Holocaust. Besides, he was kind enough to accompany me on this trip when I mentioned I was nervous about going alone."

"For God's sake, he could be after your money. In case you haven't figured it out yet, overnight you became an heiress. That makes you a desirable target for a flimflam man."

"Flimflam man? Mom, really. This isn't the 1950s. And I resent your insinuation that Ethan has some devious agenda. My money is the last thing on his mind. He has plenty of his own money, believe me." Rose suddenly realized that this conversation with her mother was more about convincing herself than Edith. She liked Ethan more than she wanted to admit, and she had the strangest sensation that maybe he felt the same. Maybe Ethan Blackwood, ex-CIA operative, spy, man of mystery — liked her too. Maybe she wasn't just a nerdy librarian who lived her life wrapped up in books. Maybe he saw more in her. Maybe she was starting to see more in herself. Maybe her grandmother had placed Ethan in her path for a reason.

"Don't be naïve, Rose." Her mother interrupted. "You're a desirable commodity, and I mean that in all the right ways. You're steadfast and devoted. There are plenty of men who are going to want to hook up with you but not necessarily for all the right reasons. That's why you need to be more careful than ever as to the intentions behind the men you involve yourself with."

"Wow! That's quite a list, Mom. I sound like a veritable St. Bernard."

"Don't be silly. You're a lovely young woman, but let's be honest, darling, you're not a social butterfly. You're a bookworm and, well, somewhat of a recluse. It will take a special type of man to be right for you. An academic or research scientist. Someone comfortable with a quieter and more insular life."

Rose couldn't help but compare Ethan with the type of man her mother was suggesting for her. He certainly liked books, but that was the only thing Ethan had in common with the dream man her mother had conjured.

"On top of everything else, Ethan Blackwood is not Jewish. You come from different worlds and sensibilities. Relationships are hard enough. The extra pressure from dissimilar backgrounds can only, down the road, eat away at what you mistakenly considered to be love."

"Mother, there are no guarantees in life or relationships. That's an antiquated supposition more in line with old wives' tales. Even grandma understood that love was greater than those kinds of prejudices."

"Rose, you can't base your life on the judgment of a ninety-six-year-old woman with the beginning stages of senility, not to mention she was an incurable romantic with ideas that had no basis in reality."

Tears welled in Rose's eyes as she thought about the difference between her mother and her grandmother. Leah would be pleased with Ethan as a prospective love interest, and she would encourage Rose to follow her heart. Leah fell in love with Aidan, a man she'd only known a very short time.

Leah and Aidan had shared a grand passion, not only for each other but a passion for everything they did. Their relationship may have existed for only a brief moment, but their love had lasted a lifetime and beyond.

Even though that horrible dream she'd had about Leah and her first meeting with Horst continued to haunt her, Rose knew that Leah had truly loved Aidan. Rose needed to remember that Leah's relationship with Horst was based on survival. "Mom, I have to go."

"Promise me, Rose, that you'll proceed slowly with this young man. Get to know him better. You don't have to rush into things."

"Why? Maybe I've been a recluse, as you say, for far too long. Maybe what I need to do is jump in and to hell with the risk."

"This doesn't sound like you at all, Rose. What's gotten into you?"

What's gotten into me? A magical blue coat and brooch, time-traveling through a mirror, stopping an evil conspiracy, prophetic dreams — the list went on and on.

Rose's life had changed since Leah's passing, and she would never again be the same. Her grandmother had lived an empowered life, why couldn't she do the same? Why couldn't she be a woman who initiated change instead of a woman who feared it?

"Don't worry, Mom. I'll be fine. I'm Leah Manheim's granddaughter. I've got tough genes. Have a good day, and I'll talk to you next week when I'm back in the States."

"Rose —"

Rose clicked off the phone. It was useless, continuing the conversation with her mother. It wasn't going anywhere. The fewer words between them, the better. She plugged her phone back into its charger. And lay back against the pillows in the hotel bed.

It didn't take but a minute for her insecurities to kick in and for her to start questioning her own bravado. Maybe her mother was right. Not about Ethan. She was sure his intentions were aboveboard. Maybe Rose was reading more into their friendship. He hadn't made one inappropriate move toward her. He'd been kind and solicitous. That thought alone was enough to sink her confidence.

Getting out of bed, she walked to the window that opened to a view of the river. Snow flurries fell at an accelerating pace, blanketing the Limmatquai. Her stomach growled a complaint. The cold outside and falling snow put her in mind of French onion soup. The very thought of a slice of French bread smothered in melted Gruyere cheese floating atop a rich broth of caramelized onions lifted her spirits. "Bubbie, I'll never be as strong as you were, but I know I'm changing. Thank you for trusting me with your legacy," she whispered.

CHAPTER 25

January 26, Present day
Zürich, Switzerland

"What did she say?"

Ethan couldn't help but wonder how Rose's mother took her announcement of being in Zürich with him. After all, this was the woman who'd made him feel as if he might walk off with the sterling silver stuffed in the pockets of his coat.

"I didn't tell her anything about why we're really here. I think she came to her own conclusions."

"What did you end up telling her to cover the truth?" he asked, taking a spoonful of the French onion soup Rose had suggested.

She gave a non-committal shrug that made him wonder who she'd inherited that move from. Maybe Leah.

"Soup's great, by the way."

"I know, totally yummy." A thread of cheese dangled from her lip, and he was tempted to wipe it away. Instead, he raised his napkin and wiped his own mouth. The subliminal message worked, and she rolled her lip, delicately dabbing her mouth, and the cheese disappeared. The thought of kissing the cheese off her lips was a dangerous place to go.

Something had changed since she'd spoken with her mother. Her body seemed less tense, and he noticed she was smiling a lot as if she was revisiting some private joke in her mind. If he didn't know better, he'd swear she was flirting. Not that he was complaining, he just wondered what precipitated this change in her behavior.

"Okay, now you've spiked my curiosity, you have to fess up. What did the good doctor Levi think of her daughter skiing in the Alps with the disreputable Ethan Blackwood? A goy no less."

"She says I can't possibly know you well enough to be in a relationship with you. She thinks you might be after my money." Her gaze fell to her bowl as she stirred the thick cheesy broth. "She suggested men like you don't go for women like me."

"What the hell does that mean? She knows nothing about me." He was pissed. "And one more thing, are we having a relationship? Because if we are, I'd like to know."

Rose's cheeks flamed red. "No, but from her perspective, why else would you and I be in Switzerland skiing?"

"Aha, so I'm a gigolo to boot. Boy, for a psychiatrist, your mom has some problems reading people. God knows what she'd do if we really were an item. Doesn't she have any faith in your judgment?"

"It's embarrassing to admit, but apparently not."

He watched her fold into herself like a flower in a cold snap. That flirtatious spirit that had made a brief appearance dimmed in her eyes.

He had a sudden yearning to hold her in his arms and reassure her that she was an amazing woman, and he'd be damn lucky if someone like Rose cared about him. Instead, he reached for her hand. "I couldn't figure out what was different about you today, but now I think I get it. It's time I told you how special you are, Rose. Don't let your mother or anyone else tell you otherwise. I think you're beautiful, smart, and gutsy. And I'm damn attracted to you. Hell, I have been since you first opened the door at the shiva." He was happy to see the glow creep back into her eyes.

"There is something between us that goes beyond this mission, and I like it. And I like you," Rose whispered. "A lot." Her cheeks bloomed with color at her admission.

At least he didn't have to pretend anymore that he wasn't attracted to her. Better yet, he now knew the attraction was mutual. "Ditto. We'll table this discussion for now. We need to stay focused on what's in the safe deposit box and what our next step is. Keeping you safe is my priority. Everything else takes a back-seat. But I really like you, and you can take that to the bank." Ethan burst out laughing at her exaggerated eye roll. But she was beaming, and he could see her confidence had returned. That million-dollar smile of hers took his breath away.

He wanted to do more than hold her hand. He wished he could do more. Guilt washed over him. Her mother was just being protective. And she had a point — Rose was not only smart and funny, but she had a vulnerable, delicate beauty that was damn appealing. Still, he was going to have to fess up soon, and he was worried that once she found out who he really was, she might never forgive him for keeping it from her. She seemed to believe he was more involved in administrative fact-gathering and not in life-threatening missions, and he'd done nothing to dissuade her from that belief. A dark cloud passed over him. It wasn't just that the less she knew, the safer she was, but he couldn't forget the hurt he'd suffered from Christie when she dumped him like yesterday's news.

Rose is nothing like Christie. He raised her palm to his lips and kissed it. "Let's finish up lunch. I want to go over our tactics for this afternoon. But I'm warning you, there's a kiss in your future."

CHAPTER 26

January 26 Present day
Zürich, Switzerland

S he was nervous.

Rose looked up at the neo-classical sandstone exterior of Credit Suisse located on the Paradeplatz. Its impressive colonnade conveyed a classical elegance. Just as Ethan instructed, Rose had taken the ten-minute taxi ride alone while he'd snuck out the back of the hotel and grabbed his own cab.

She knew Ethan was being cautious, and this way, he could keep an eye on her from a distance and observe the bigger picture. In case of trouble, he'd have the element of surprise on his side. But she'd begun to depend on his steady calmness, especially since her life had been completely upended by her grandmother's blue coat and brooch.

Rose had dressed to please the standards of her grandmother in a blue tweed suit and black knee-high boots. The outfit gave her a sophistication that seemed warranted for dealing with bankers.

She couldn't help but smile, remembering Ethan's clichéd response when she stepped out of the bedroom. "Dressed to kill." It was a compliment, and there was no way she was going to issue a complaint at that cliché.

The skies continued to dust the streets with flurries. The snow wasn't sticking yet, but it was cold — so Rose wore the blue coat. She wanted to believe she'd worn it merely for its warmth, but in truth, Rose wore it because she felt safe within its folds. Rose had pinned the Ark of the Covenant brooch to the inside lapel of the coat. If she believed the brooch and the coat held the power to protect her, then she needed to avail herself of that power.

She kept reminding herself that she was the chosen, the one who was intended to inherit the coat and its powers. The coat and brooch would do nothing to compromise her mission. After all, they were handed down to her by her grandmother, the sisterhood, and Miriam.

She walked through the entry arch of the nineteenth-century bank building and was pleasantly surprised. The historic building's interior was modern and just as impressive as the classical facade. The entry atrium towered above a geometrically patterned marble floor and a surround of gray-veined marble columns.

Getting her bearings, Rose's gaze swept the reception area and her surroundings. She found herself drawn to the center of the space where a hexagonal etched glass water fountain was installed. A small placard near the art installation read, *Fontaine du Désir.*

There was something odd but captivating about an area of commerce inviting visitors to stop and contemplate their lives, purpose, and dreams. An LED banner at the bottom of the basin streamed ever-changing good wishes in five different languages. But the ones that appeared as she observed the tape seemed custom fit for her. "To have more time," and "to be invisible." She shivered at the coincidence. Had Miriam conveyed the custom message to her? After all, it was Miriam's fountain that replenished the Israelites during the Exodus in the Bible.

"Mademoiselle Levi?" a voice called out to her, distracting her from the fascinating art exhibit. A tall, thin man with close-cropped gray hair and wearing a pin-striped suit strode to her with his hand extended and a smile on his face. He looked like the poster boy for what she imagined Swiss bankers should look like.

"Mr. Bollinger, a pleasure to meet you." She took his hand with a placid smile.

"The pleasure is mine. Call me Franz. If you will come with me." He gestured toward a set of sliding glass doors. "I see you took a moment to admire the wishing fountain."

"Yes, I think it's a wonderful work of art. Very clever the way it encourages the viewer to interact with it."

"I hope you made a wish. I've been told the success rate of the fountain is overwhelming."

He was teasing, of course. But Rose imagined his playfulness humanized him to his clients. "I did make a wish, but you understand I can't tell you what it is, or it won't come true."

"*Ja,* I've been told that is the way it works." He grinned. "Just like the wishes when you blow out the candles on a birthday cake."

They took an elevator to the second floor, and Rose followed Franz into his office. Franz Bollinger was a vice president, and she was surprised that someone so high-ranking was her grandmother's personal banker.

"I was very fond of your grandmother; she was such an elegant lady. I was very sorry to hear of her passing."

Rose sucked in a breath, fighting to hold back her tears. Would she ever be able to hear her grandmother mentioned without her eyes tearing up? "Thank you, she was very dear to me. I haven't yet come to terms with losing her."

"You were fortunate to have her. I know it sounds cliché, but time will heal."

"That's what they tell me." It seems Ethan wasn't the only person fond of clichéd phrases.

Thirty minutes later, the paperwork was done, and Franz led her to a private elevator. Rose was so stunned by the amount of money in her grandmother's account and the diversity of her investments that she paid little or no attention to whether the elevator went up or down.

"This elevator goes only to the vault and the private client rooms," Franz clarified.

They exited into an area that was so quiet you could have heard a pin drop if the floors hadn't been covered with luxurious thick carpeting. Franz accompanied her into the vault, which was enormous and filled with hundreds of metal safety deposit boxes in various sizes. He led her down a long line of boxes, stopping at one that was numbered 4216. Franz checked the key she'd given to him and said, "*Ja*, this is it."

He handed her the key. It was a large box. First Franz inserted his key and turned it open. Then she inserted and turned her key, and the box popped out from the wall. She went to lift it out.

"Here, let me help you." Franz hefted the heavy box out of its cubby, and he carried it for her. She followed him down a hallway to an intricately carved door where he stopped. "If you would, please open the door." He smiled. "My hands are full. This is a private client viewing room. I'll leave you with the box for as long as you need, and then when you're finished, press the buzzer on the wall, and I'll return to help you carry the box back to the vault."

The room was aesthetically pleasing. The walls were decorated with photographic art prints, beautiful shots of the year-round beauty of the majestic Alps. The centerpiece of the photos was a mist-covered photo of the Matterhorn. Franz placed the box on a carved wood desk with a red leather desk chair pulled up to it. "Can I get you anything else?"

"No, thank you, Franz. I'll buzz you when I'm ready."

"Excellent." Without further ado, he let himself out of the room. The door whispered shut, and she was alone.

Rose sat down and stared at the box. Her hands trembled, and she wished Ethan was there. She slowly lifted the lid, afraid that, like Pandora, she was about to release all the evils of the world on humanity. Everything inside the box was wrapped in tissue paper and plastic bags.

One at a time, she removed each item and laid it on the table. It was a large box with a lot of things inside, including manila folders stuffed with documents. When all the wrapped items were removed, she stared into the box, understanding why the box had felt so heavy. The bottom of the box was filled with gold ingots, stacked several layers high.

What the —? What was she to do with gold bullion? Where did it come from? It dawned on her that during the war, all currency would have been untrustworthy. The only thing sure to hold its value would be gold. This was her great-grandparents' box, so it made sense that they had converted all their money into gold. This was what her great-grandmother had referred to in her letter to Leah as the nest egg, and now it was hers.

Rose had no idea what this treasure was worth, and this was no time to think about it. She turned her attention to the tissue-wrapped objects. She couldn't help but recall her mother's words about being a target for flimflam men. *No one on Earth knows about this treasure. Certainly not Ethan.*

She had to smile because this was so Leah. It reminded Rose of her birthday parties as a child. There was always some game, courtesy of Leah, with a hidden prize or a treasure hunt. Rose unwrapped a velvet jewelry box and opened it. Inside was a beautiful white gold Jewish star with a bezel-set edge of diamonds. It was beautiful, and she wondered if it was Leah's or her great-grandmother Estelle's. She fastened it around her neck and slid it inside the neckline of her blouse. It made her feel closer to her grandmother.

Ethan is outside, waiting. Concentrate on finding the list.

She ran her hands over the tissue-wrapped items and closed her eyes, sensing the shape of each object through her fingertips. As a child, she'd played a game of trying to discern what an object was with her eyes closed. Hoping for an *aha* moment, she concentrated. Her eyes blinked open, and she began tearing away the tissue, anxious to see what was hidden inside. A soft covered book about the size of an old-school address book. She opened it, frowning with disappointment. It was filled with writing and a numbered list, but it might as well have been written in hieroglyphics. *Maybe it's a code she used in the French resistance.* Maybe Ethan would know someone who could decode the writing, or perhaps someone in the gray-haired sisterhood knew the code system. She'd text Frida tonight. She stuffed the book in her pocket and continued to search.

Next, she opened one of the manila envelopes and, sighing with relief that the pages weren't written in code, she began to read in French what her grandmother had written. It was the testimony of a Hannah Epstein, an indictment accusing Horst Schumacher of war crimes. Rose scanned the pages that charged Horst with working with the infamous Doctor Josef Mengele at Auschwitz and conducting savage experiments that resulted in the deaths of dozens of twins and the maiming of hundreds of other people. Rose flipped through at least fifty pages of testimony by different individuals. None of this had seen the light of day because Horst Schumacher had never been brought to trial, and now it was probably too late. Horst Schumacher was undoubtedly dead. Nonetheless, Leah made sure to document Horst Schumacher's depraved conduct during the war. Nothing in the paperwork revealed why Leah hadn't ever brought Horst to the attention of the authorities, or why he was never brought to trial.

The hairs on Rose's nape rose, and the eerie, disconcerting sensation from her dream returned. Why hadn't Leah turned Horst in? She prayed there had been nothing between Horst and Leah and prayed Leah hadn't helped him remain hidden from what should have been his just punishment.

Rose began ripping the tissue off of objects she hadn't unwrapped. Most of what she found was jewelry that had been purchased in Europe and was probably destined to be given as gifts to Leah's friends. Rose was hoping for a breakthrough, something that would be of help, and then her breath caught in her chest. *Another book.* A red softcover address type book like the black one. She turned the page. The handwriting wasn't Leah's, which was curious. *Thank God it isn't in code.* It was a list of names and addresses. Turning the pages, she read Syria, Sudan, South Africa, Argentina, Cuba, Brazil, Columbia, Ukraine, U.S., Germany, Switzerland, Egypt, Australia, Canada, and other random countries from all over the globe. Under some of the countries, only one name was written, and in others, several names appeared. She turned back to the first page and studied the names more carefully. Every name had a red line through it and a date. No, not every name. A few were not scratched out.

What does it mean?

She turned the pages, searching for one name that she knew for certain. Then the name she hoped would be there jumped off the page, beckoning her. *Horst Schumacher, 1973.* Horst's name had a red line through it. It was the only name in Leah's handwriting. The list was beginning to make sense.

It has to be.

Leah had somehow managed to compile a list of SS officers, high-ranking Nazis, concentration camp guards, and *Einsatzgruppen* squad members. The fearful names of squad members whispered on her lips and made her shudder. Beads of moisture dampened her brow as she pictured the black and white photographs she'd seen of Jews digging their own graves. Around them stood Germans with rifles pointing, the Nazi death squad called the *Einsatzgruppen*. Terrified, and ofttimes forced to undress, the Jews stood naked at the edge of large pits, row after row of the condemned. They waited their turns, watching as the murderous squad mowed them down with rifles. Driven from their villages into the forest, helpless men, women, and children falling into mass unmarked graves, body upon body, at places like Babi Yar in Ukraine. When it was over, mountains of dirt were shoveled over them as if nothing had ever happened. A million or more Eastern European Jews had met their fate from these squads.

Rose realized this was a list of murderers who'd escaped after the war and scattered to all parts of the globe with their bags filled with the stolen spoil of Jews. Rose's stomach clenched.

One by one, the monsters on the list had died or been eliminated or brought to trial. But Leah couldn't have done this by herself. She must have been working with someone. *Nazi hunters or Mossad?* Did she work with Simon Wiesenthal, or whoever carried on Wiesenthal's work after his death? How did she get the list? Did she make a deal with the devil and sell herself for Horst's cooperation? She dropped the book, sickened. She clasped her hand over her mouth and swallowed the sour taste that made her choke.

It can't be, I don't believe it. Leah would never do that.

But how else had she gotten this blacklist? Rose stared down at the book, trying to put some order to the chaos of her thoughts. Whatever was the case, it only served to reinforce her determination to bring the monster Nazi's son down. The old man might have escaped justice, but the son would not.

Rose returned everything to the box. She took only the coded black book and the red book of Nazi criminal refugees — most she was sure were dead. The coded book had to be the key to the present threat. She buzzed Franz and waited.

Franz carried the safety deposit box back to the vault. "Everything was as you expected, I hope?"

"Yes, I found just what I needed. Thank you."

"*Gut.* I have one more thing to give you before you leave."

Minutes later, she was given a debit card. She shook hands with Franz and said goodbye. Pausing at the fountain, the message caught her eye, "The darkest hour is just before the dawn."

Exiting the Credit Suisse building, she found the skies had darkened, and with the end of the day and coming of evening, the snowfall had steadily increased. She hoped a blizzard wasn't in the forecast. She scanned the plaza in front of the building.

Where is Ethan?

CHAPTER 27

January 26, Present day
Zürich, Switzerland

"We found her. She's here," said Ernst.

"Where did you find her?" Heinrich asked.

"She's inside the bank. I got the call she'll be leaving momentarily. Hans says she's been with the banker and went to the box."

"Did you set up the decoy?"

"Yes, everything's in place and ready. How should we handle this?"

"Pick her up and sedate her. We can't take any risks. Bring her to the clinic. I suspect she poses a significant threat to our upcoming meetings in Brussels. It's time to clip her wings."

Heinrich hung up with a curse. The call had interrupted an email exchange with his offshore trustee. He and his trustee were discussing the bank accounts scattered around the globe under phantom corporations. Using bank accounts intricately hidden beneath layers of legal paperwork and false identities made it easier to allocate funds to political campaigns, terrorist organizations, and hate groups. Nothing was traceable to him.

Through the legitimate arm of the organization he led, his agents were free to post on Facebook, Twitter, and the rest of social media where followers could be mined, influenced, and recruited. Facebook was his favorite because its algorithms helped Holocaust deniers. If a user clicked on any type of Holocaust denial, the algorithms would make sure they'd get a steady stream of similar material. It made him want to clap his hands together with delight. Run by a Jew too, but then again, Jews had a nasty history of being their own worst enemies.

Recently he'd begun funding research into subliminally influencing the minds of gamers and recruiting them. The young boys, teens, and men who lived on these platforms interacted in chat rooms and game rooms. Many of these kids were alienated from the outside world, where white males were often excoriated. Planting the seeds of dissatisfaction was proving to be easy in the violent world of gamers, and the gaming world was becoming a fertile ground for recruitment into groups of white supremacists, anarchists, and revolutionaries, the disrupters of the world who were intent on shifting the axis of power.

With time, the young, discontented minds ripe for exploitation would be more than ready to harness their futures to a new rising Reich. A new order that would achieve what the old order had failed to finish.

What did the girl find?

He needed to know just how much she knew and how much danger she posed to his plans. He would prepare a serum, an intravenous cocktail guaranteed to drain the truth from her. Things were too far in motion to call off what was already in progress. Members were arriving in Brussels for the European Council meetings, with outside guests from the U.S. having been invited to participate in this year's forum. Among those guests were two members from the House of Representatives and one from the Senate who'd received major campaign gifts from the cabal and its subsidiaries. They were of like mind with the cabal in their hatred of Israel.

Heinrich had found plenty of ways to funnel money to politicians through their campaigns. Also in attendance would be other politically like-minded, motivated members from around the world. Heinrich had been planning the launch of a new hate campaign against Israel for months. The meeting in Brussels was the result of months of planning. But the full scale of what he intended he'd been nurturing for years, and he'd be damned if he'd allow the granddaughter of his worst enemy to destroy it all now.

Once and for all, he was going to rid himself of this tie to the woman who'd ruined his mother's life and destroyed his father. His hatred burned like an uncontrolled wildfire, threatening his sanity. He needed to reel in his hatred and keep hold of reasonable judgment, or he'd lose the most crucial battle of his life.

Heinrich unlocked the door to the pharmacy and strode to the refrigerator where the psychotropic drugs were kept. He entered the code on the keypad, and the fridge unlocked. He grabbed a bottle off the shelf.

Scopolamine, a truth serum drug favored by intelligence organizations, was used to extract information from a detainee. Legal authorities used it when matters of life and death demanded information and lives were at risk, but Heinrich had no such restrictions. Scopolamine would loosen her tongue, and no one would be the wiser since it was tasteless and odorless. The drug had little or no side effect, with the added benefit that the girl wouldn't remember a thing about the interrogation or who administered it. Not that it was likely she'd be alive to tell. It was time to find out what she knew. What she was looking for, and how much of a threat she posed to his plans.

Getting rid of a body in the Alps posed no problem when one considered the sheer quantity of crevices and ravines. It might be years before a body was found. As for the man who was helping her, making two bodies disappear was just as easy as one. Perhaps they could contrive a lover's quarrel that resulted in a murder-suicide. That would tie things up nicely.

He filled six syringes with scopolamine, pocketed them, and locked up the pharmacy. Returning to his office, he glanced at the screen. Live video from the front gate security cameras displayed an increasingly white screen. The snow was coming down in blankets, and visibility was almost nonexistent. He made a cup of coffee and returned to his emails. It was going to be a long night.

CHAPTER 28

January 26, Present Day
Zürich, Switzerland

Ethan ran like his life depended on it.

Rose was in imminent danger. He'd been standing outside the bank in the plaza, waiting for Rose to exit when he heard a woman scream his name. His gaze swept the Paradeplatz. Only minutes before, the buildings and businesses around the plaza had begun to empty out, and now hundreds of people rushed about on their way home.

And then he saw her, red hair and blue coat across the plaza with her back to him. *How the hell did she get past me?* A group of dark clothed men surrounded her, and they were tugging on her purse, trying to steal it from her. He was running, darting around strollers and elderly people with walkers. When he got to her, the assailants scattered, and she turned toward him. Ethan skidded to a stop. It wasn't Rose. He whipped around — his gaze zeroing in on the front of the bank building. Rose stepped out the building's door, texting on her phone. His phone buzzed in his pocket with her incoming text.

Glancing back at the redhead who'd taken flight and was running away, he saw her disappear down a side street. The thugs in black had all vanished.

Shit, I've been had!

"Go back inside!" he yelled.

Rose looked up from her phone and waved to him.

"Go back inside!" He was running and yelling like a madman. She put her hand to her ear and shook her head.

A black Mercedes pulled up with a screech of tires, and a public transportation electric trolley came to a stop alongside the Mercedes, blasting its horn at the car for stopping illegally in the auto-free zone. The trolley blocked Ethan's view of Rose.

Ethan's legs and arms pumped as fast as they could go in the crowded maze of people in the plaza while his gut churned with anxiety.

Hang on, Rose.

A moment later, the Mercedes flew from the plaza, turning the corner and whizzing away. The trolley edged forward.

She's gone!

He bent over, his hands on his knees, gulping in air. He scanned left and right but Rose was nowhere in sight.

It was his fault. Subconsciously, he'd known he was putting her in danger. Rose was the key to drawing out the cabal, and he suspected the only thing to destroy them was in the box. Of course, they would try to stop her. They had this planned from the start.

His crucial error hit him like a bludgeon. The redhead had screamed the name *Connor,* not *Ethan.* In a moment of panic, Rose would have screamed *Ethan.*

Stupid! Stupid! Stupid!

Rose had become a target the minute she'd entered the building. They knew she was in Zürich and that she was Leah's heir. They were watching her. He was dealing with professionals, criminals. The only element they knew nothing about was the coat and brooch.

How did they get Rose in the car when she wore the coat and the brooch? He, like Rose, believed the sacred articles would keep her safe. Based on what happened to him when he'd touched the brooch, the assailant should have gotten a shock that would have sent him flying, or at the very least, knocked him off his feet. Ethan had come to believe that the coat and brooch were protecting her, that they'd whisk her away to another time if danger threatened. It was a stupid assumption, and now Rose was in the hands of the enemy, and chances were she carried crucial evidence that they'd kill her for. But what did any of it matter if Rose was in danger? The only important thing was rescuing her.

He checked his phone and was relieved to find the tracking device he'd loaded into her phone was working. He could see the blinking signal of the locator moving away from the plaza. For now, he could find her, but he'd need help rescuing her. It was time to bring in the outside team. He couldn't risk attempting this on his own.

He punched in the number on his cell phone and walked to the cab stand. On the second ring, a voice picked up. "We'll call you back."

"Give me ten minutes, and I'll be in my hotel room."

Just as the door swung closed in the room, Ethan's cell rang. "Blackwood here."

"*Shalom*, Ethan. The line is secured, report."

"They have her, but so far, the phone tracking is working. She's on her way out of the city."

"We have a team in Zürich on high alert and ready to assist

you. You've worked with them before. They'll pick you up in front of the hotel. Our radar shows there's a major storm hitting. The roads are going to be treacherous. It should slow them down."

"Yes, but it will slow us down, too, and we have no idea where they're taking her. If they figure out there's tracking on the phone, they'll dispose of it. We'll lose her." Guilt and anger formed a knot in the pit of his stomach.

I let her down.

He'd kept her in the dark from the beginning, and now her life hung in the balance. And it was his fault. He should have antici-pated all the potential threats. He'd inadvertently allowed her to become the bait.

"I just received a notification. The team will be there in ten minutes. Ethan, you need to stay calm. We've been waiting for this a long time, the proof and evidence linking this Hitler-wannabe and his cabal with high-ranking officials and politicians around the world. They must exposed. It's possible the evidence we need was in that box. If Rose found what we believe her grandmother possessed, we can bring the whole house of cards down around their heads. They'll be discredited and finished, and we'll have stopped a pandemic of anti-Semitic, anti-Israel attacks around the world. You did the right thing."

"I understand the mission, sir, but I care about this girl. I can't let anything happen to her."

"And you won't. Rose would have made the same choice on her own. Believe me, she's Leah Manheim's granddaughter. Leah never stopped fighting against evil, and neither will her grand-daughter."

CHAPTER 29

September 21, 1948
Paris, France

L eah walked with a decided bounce in her step. In the pocket of her blue coat was a letter from the US Embassy saying her immigration papers had come through, and she was free to travel to the United States. Nothing but heartbreaking memories remained here in Europe, and although she would miss Paris, she had to leave and make a new life for herself. In a week, she would sail to the U.S., leaving the bitter memories behind, or at least, putting thousands of miles between her and the war.

She swung a satchel of books she'd purchased at one of the *bouquiniste* that plied their trade on the left bank of the Seine. With a tearful farewell, she'd said goodbye to her lifelong friend. The bookseller remembered her father and had asked after him. They'd shared a sad remembrance of those who'd been lost. Few people in Europe hadn't lost someone. He'd wished her luck and made her promise to visit him when she returned to Paris because, of course, there was no way a born Parisian could ever entirely leave the most beautiful city in the world.

She skirted along the Quai de la Tournelle to her destination, the Café de Flore. It was a twenty-five-minute walk along the Seine past the Cathedral Notre-Dame. It was also the same path she'd journeyed hundreds of times with her father. Just as it should, it would end with her treating herself to quiche Lorraine and salad. Then she'd splurge on a dessert of *café liégeois,* a coffee sweetened with ice cream and Chantilly cream — her dessert obsession. She giggled to herself at her choice of words. Only a French person would obsess over food. People from other countries like Italy might adore food or know nothing about cuisine like the English, but *haute cuisine* was a point of pride for the French and one of the hallmarks of their culture.

Leah anticipated savoring the flavors she was sure she'd never find in New York. It would also afford her one of her favorite pastimes — observing the colorful artists and writers who frequented Café de Flore.

The fresh fall air was like a heady perfume. The three years since the end of the war had been an adjustment for Leah. Her dreams of making a life with Aidan were over, and her beloved parents were no more. She was now on her own, but there was nothing in this life that she couldn't handle. She'd seen the worst, and whatever the future might hold could only be better.

Thinking about her upcoming passage aboard an ocean liner to New York filled her with excitement. She had several girlfriends in New York, all survivors, and then there was Bernard, the young man she'd met in Paris just after the war. She'd written to him to tell him she was moving to New York, and he'd written her back immediately that he couldn't wait to see her again. She wasn't in love with him, but she liked him very much, and maybe her feelings would grow. He wasn't Aidan, no one would ever be Aidan, but as much as it pained her, Aidan was in her past.

She blinked back the tears and wiped at her eyes. Even the merest thought of Aidan brought it all back. The unexpected splendor of finding love during the most difficult of times. After the war, Leah had written to Aidan's parents, desperate to learn what had happened to him. The day she received a return letter from his father confirming his death, she'd collapsed in sorrow.

It came as a surprise a few months later when Leah received another letter from England. She'd ripped the letter open, her heart pounding in her chest. It was from Aidan. He'd survived the war but not its horrors. The shock of his words had brought her to her knees. A head injury had affected his memory, and of all the things he might have forgotten — she could not have anticipated she would be one of them. His apology was more deadly than if he'd stabbed her with a knife. He'd forgotten the love they'd shared and his promise to find and marry her. It wasn't so much that he'd forgotten his promise that broke her heart, it was that he'd forgotten the love they shared.

In his letter to her, he explained that his father had given him the letters she'd sent. He confessed to having no recollection of her or the time they'd spent together. He offered to come to Paris to try and recover his memory, but she'd refused him. The pain of seeing him and having him not recognize her would be unbearable.

Whenever she thought of him now, she reminded herself what she'd said lying in his arms. Even if this were *une brève affaire*, she would never regret it. Even now, after losing him, she didn't regret loving or being loved by Aidan. It was the sweetest memory of her life and one she'd never forget.

The bustle of Paris returned her thoughts to the present. She smiled at the levity around her as she waited for a table. Paris was alive again, and the streets were filled with magic. Everyone was out and about enjoying the beautiful fall weather and celebrating the return of peace and prosperity. After six years of war — four of which had been spent under German occupation — Paris was once more the City of Light.

"Nadia, is that you?"

The breath froze in her chest.

It can't be.

The voice dragged her back to the darkest days of her life. She blinked and shook her head, banishing the images of suffering and death. Her first impulse was to shout for the police or run. Finding a Nazi in their midst, people would most likely tear him limb from limb.

Instead, she forced a smile and turned to meet her nemesis.

"*Oui,* it's me."

She studied him, wondering how he'd managed to look so well. He wore a gray fedora and was dressed immaculately in a tailored blue suit with a red tie. The gray hair was gone from his temples, and his face seemed altered, his nose more aquiline and his jaw squarer. He barely resembled the man he'd been.

She felt it immediately, his eyes drinking her in. "It's amazing, is it not, running into each other in Paris. How are you?" he asked.

"Very well, thank you. And you? How have you been?"

Am I really having this mundane conversation on the street with my tormentor?

"Much better now. Please, join me. I have a table over there." He pointed. "I'd love to hear all about your life since last we saw each other."

I believe the last time was in Auschwitz.

He placed his hand on the small of her back. When she stiffened, he pulled his hand away.

"Please, Nadia, join me. You have no idea how I hoped I might run into you."

Without a word, she walked to the table and sat down.

"You must join me for lunch." He beamed, his eyes glowing. "I have so many questions."

He is as excited as a young man on his first date.

He raised his hand, and a waiter rushed over.

"Oui monsieur." The waiter nodded, *"Madame."*

Bile rose in her throat that the waiter called her *Madame. Does he think I am married to this monster?*

Grinning, Horst had no idea of her thoughts and asked the waiter for menus.

Leah pretended to study hers. In truth, she knew it by heart. She was keenly aware of Horst's eyes on her. She did her best to ignore his hungry gaze. When the waiter returned to take their orders, she ordered a quiche and salad.

As if awakening from a dream, Horst asked him, "Do you have duck foie gras?"

"Oui monsieur."

"Bien, I'll have that and a salad. Also, bring us a bottle of your best champagne."

The waiter left to place their order. An awkward silence settled. Leah glanced around at the other customers, anything not to meet Horst's gaze.

"Nadia, I need to tell you that I'm a changed man."

Her attention jolted back to him. "Are you? If you asked my mother, she would say, *ce qui est élevé dans l'os va sortir dans la chair,* what's bred in the bone comes out in the flesh."

"Your mother is a very wise woman, but sometimes people change."

"Both my parents died during the war." *Control your anger, Leah.*

"I'm so sorry. Life must be hard for you."

She shrugged, feigning indifference. "I manage."

"But of course, you do. You are not only beautiful but resourceful."

Yes, I am resourceful, you evil madman.

A plan was quickly forming in her mind — was there a possibility of destroying him? Even inflicting an ounce of the pain he'd tortured others with would be worth it. "*Alors,* tell me about your life Horst, but don't tell me any specific details." She leaned forward, resting her chin on her hand, and a smile flirted on her lips. "Life is better with secrets, *n'est-ce pa?*"

He grinned when she smiled. "I have remade myself and begun a new business, and it's thriving. I should be happy." His gaze traveled beyond her as if deciding whether to share one of his secrets. He leaned across the table, his voice barely above a whisper, "I've been searching for you."

"Me? Why would you search for me?"

He grabbed her hand between both of his. "I've never been able to get you out of my mind Nadia. There's a reason. We were fated to meet, I know it. I remember when you said we were enemies and on opposing sides, but that's no longer true. We can be friends now, can't we, Nadia?"

"Is that what you want, Horst — my friendship?" *Yes, Horst, I now realize we were fated to meet so that I could inflict on you some of the pain you wreaked on others. You tortured thousands of innocent men, women, and children, and here you sit with a smile on your face, flirting with me like we are long-lost lovers.*

His face flushed red. "I-I..."

She leaned in seductively. "You want me as your lover. Is that not the truth? Say it."

His face grew redder, but his gaze stayed riveted to hers. "Yes," he rasped.

"At least now we can be honest with each other." She leaned back and sipped her champagne, enjoying the power she had over him. "What would you think if I said yes? That I wanted you, too?"

She could see the possibility light his gaze, sparking like embers in a fire.

"I'd say there is nothing I would deny you," he whispered. "Not today, tomorrow, or in the future."

"Will you leave your wife?" She couldn't keep the smile from tickling her lips.

"I can't leave because of Heinrich, but the woman is nothing to me. Ask me for anything else."

She now knew what she wanted. "I require a list."

"A list? What kind of list?"

"I want to know where all of your partners in crime in the SS disappeared to. Those that weren't picked up by the allies or brought to trial. All the devils that planned their escapes well in advance and disappeared to the far corners of the earth. I know you know where they are." Goosebumps rippled along her skin as she waited for his reply.

"What will you do with such a list?"

"I will see that they pay for their crimes."

"And me, Nadia, will you also see that I'm brought to justice?"

"No, Horst, I will protect you. Why would I turn in my lover, especially if he helps me make so many others pay? Besides, you've changed. By your own admission, you're not the same man." It took all her effort to disguise the revulsion inside of her. *It's worth it. Eventually, you will destroy him too.*

He reached across the table, covering her hand with his. "When? How soon can we meet?"

The waiter interrupted to serve their lunch. It wasn't the way she'd expected to enjoy one of her last meals in Paris, but the possibility of being handed a list of Nazis and where they had escaped to was an excitement she found hard to suppress. She drank deeply and smiled at Horst as the waiter refilled her glass. She wasn't sure whether it was the champagne or her nerves that made her light-headed. "How soon can you get me the list?"

"I must go home to compile what you're asking for, but I could be back in a week."

"What hotel do you stay at?" she asked, taking a bite of the delicious quiche. She purred with delight. "*Digne d'un roi.*" It really was food fit for a king.

He smiled as if he'd handed her the world on a plate. "This is how I imagined it would be between us. Enjoying all that Paris can offer, together, hand-in-hand, heart-to-heart. Friends and lovers." He spread his *foie gras* on the toasted French bread. "I'm staying at the Ritz." He stuffed the bite in his mouth, nodding with appreciation. "It's a lovely, romantic place for us to begin the next chapter in our lives."

It was hard to stomach, but the bastard was turning rhapsodic and poetic on her. It was all she could do to hide her revulsion. "Perfect. I will meet you at the end of the month on September 30th at the Ritz Hotel at 5:00 p.m." She raised her glass, "*A notre brève affaire.*"

"No, Nadia. I have not made myself clear. I wish more than one night from you." She had to stop herself from barking out a bitter laugh, the look on his face was so earnest.

"So, you think possessing me will bring you happiness?" She continued to eat the savory egg and bacon quiche.

"I'm sure of it. I feel joy when I'm near you. The first time I saw you, I was struck, somehow changed inside. I knew I had found what was missing from my life. I don't know why — but making you happy is what I've dreamt about for three long years."

She wanted to bite her tongue before she spoke but couldn't help but dispel his fantasy. "You cannot erase or redress your past sins by giving me all that I desire. It doesn't work that way, *mon amour*. You will not assuage your guilt by loving me."

The effect of her using the endearment must have eased the sting of her words as he leaned in and planted a kiss on her palm.

"You will make me a better man, Nadia. I know that. Your honesty and candor are unlike anyone else's I have ever known."

Honesty? What would you do if you knew I was a Jew?

"As you wish, Horst. If you believe that I am the answer to your dreams, then who am I to argue?"

When you find out the truth, as I'm sure you will, you will regret this more than you can imagine. I hope it kills you!

CHAPTER 30

January 26, Present day
Rapperswil, Switzerland

O *h, Bubbie, you reeled him in, didn't you? That day in Paris.*
Rose's eyes flew open.

Her heartbeat pounded in her ears like a bass drum.

She took slow, deep breaths as she tried to get her bearings and shake off the effects of the drug. It had happened so fast she didn't know what hit her. One moment she'd stepped out of the bank and texted Ethan, the next moment, she was being dragged into the black Mercedes. She'd struggled, but when she felt the prick in her arm, she knew in an instant that they'd drugged her. So strong was the drug, it had knocked her out completely — she'd even had a vision of her grandmother and that maniac, Horst.

Rose shrank into herself so as not to touch her two abductors — sandwiched between them as she was. A third man was driving, leaning forward, his face almost flush with the windshield as he maneuvered the car through the heavy blizzard. The wipers swiped at full speed, scraping the frost away before it stuck to the glass. It sounded like fingernails grating on a chalkboard, making her skin crawl. It was only possible to see a few feet in front of the car. With little traction, the car swerved in and out of the lane as the driver struggled to maintain control of the Mercedes.

Rose was scared. She didn't know where they were taking her, but she had a good idea who was behind her abduction — Heinrich Schumacher.

How am I going to get out of this? She couldn't even text or call Ethan. If she tried, her abductors would certainly grab her phone or worse. She kept taking slow deep breaths as she tried to calm her growing panic — *Bubbie, please help me.*

A figure appeared suddenly in the glow of the headlights. The silvery strands of her hair lifted in the wind like the snakes of Medusa's hair, alive and writhing, her silvery-white gown billowing around her. The woman ignored the vehicle coming toward her, her arms and face raised in supplication, a goddess calling on the Almighty to intervene.

The driver tried to avoid hitting the wraith, and he turned the wheel at the last second and hit the brakes. The woman disappeared in a puff of smoke. Rose screamed as the car went into a spin, brakes locking, and everything began to whirl. She was thrown against one of her large male bookends and then the other. The vehicle fishtailed across the icy surface. The Mercedes could no more stop than take wing and fly, and though the driver kept the pressure on the brakes to stop the car, the heavy vehicle kept going, spinning out of control.

Rose raised her hands, covering her face to protect it from what she sensed was coming. The Mercedes hit something and flipped, sending them flying. With a loud bang, it hit the snow-covered slope, tumbling down an embankment. Over and over it flipped, the terrified screams of everyone in the car echoing until they hit a tree with an ear-splitting crash and came to rest upside down. The last thing Rose heard was the sound of the tires spinning, then there was silence.

Rose awakened to the tickle of snowflakes on her skin. She stared up into a cloud of white. *Am I dead? Am I in Heaven?* She raised her head. The Mercedes was upside down, smashed against a tree. *How did I get out of the car?* She lay on her back in a drift of snow. Tentatively, she moved her fingers and her toes. She sighed with relief after finding everything in working order. Rolling over, she heaved herself to her feet and looked down. She noticed a tear on the blue coat, and then magically, it mended itself.

Taking a small step, she gasped at a sharp pain in her right knee. She opened her coat and saw a deep cut oozing blood. Then the blood vanished, and the skin healed. She took another step, and the pain disappeared. She lifted her lapel and saw that the Ark of the Covenant brooch was just where she'd pinned it. The two mystical talismans were as one — executing their magic as she'd come to expect.

Her gaze was drawn to the wrecked Mercedes, but she hesitated to inspect it, afraid of what she might find. Swallowing her fear, she moved closer. She knelt to peer in the rear window. The three men weren't moving. They appeared dead, but she couldn't be sure. The airbags had deployed, and all three men slumped against them, hanging upside down. She shouldn't care, these were evil men who had probably received their just desserts, but it wasn't in her nature to leave them. She needed to call for help. She reached in her pocket and searched for her cell phone, but it wasn't there. Pressing her face again to the glass of the rear window, she spied her cell phone, its LED signal blinking. There was no way she could get inside the car. The doors were crushed inward, and the handles broken. She'd have to try and find a house nearby to call for help. She walked away from the car and began to climb back to the road.

She scrabbled up the embankment, slipping and falling several times before she managed to reach the pavement that was covered in snow and ice. At least the exertion had warmed up her body. Breathing heavily, she glanced around but saw nothing but falling snow. The quiet and calm allowed her to think, and she remembered what had happened just before the crash — the vision of the silver-haired woman in the flowing robes.

"Thank you, Miriam," she whispered into the wind. Rose felt a gentle warmth surround her as if from an embrace.

How far she walked, she couldn't tell. In the white-out, it was difficult to judge distances. But the warmth of Miriam's embrace along with the blue coat kept her warm, and the icy hands of the storm did not slow her down.

It was pitch black by the time she reached a cul-de-sac. A massive, wrought-iron gate appeared as though out of nowhere. Beside the gate was a sign that read: *Privatklinik für Psychiatrisches Wohlbefinden.* Rose's German was rusty at best, but she understood she'd arrived at a psychiatric clinic.

Thank God!

She could get help. She could call Ethan.

He must be worried sick.

Someone at the bank had betrayed her. She hoped it wasn't Franz Bollinger because he'd seemed so sincere not only about wanting to help her but about his admiration for her grandmother. But no one could be ruled out. The cabal had the means to buy people off, and they would stop at nothing, especially if they suspected that she possessed the power to destroy them. She reached in her pocket and was relieved to find the two small books were still where she'd stashed them and hadn't fallen out like her cell phone.

Behind the gates, she could just make out the clinic, which was built like a chalet. A steady cloud of smoke rose from a stone chimney. She could hardly wait to get inside and warm herself in front of the fire.

Beside the gate was a call box, and she opened it and picked up the phone. The phone rang several times before a voice picked up.

"Kann ich dir helfen?"

"Hello, do you speak English? I was in an accident. The car went out of control and skidded off the road and tumbled down an embankment. Three men are still inside, and I don't know how badly they're hurt. I need to call the police."

A heavily, accented male voice replied. "Yes, of course, how terrible. You are all right?"

"I'm fine. It's freezing. May I come in? We need to help these men."

"Oh, yes, forgive me. Can you walk up the drive?"

"Yes, of course. I've walked a mile already."

The gate buzzed and began to open slowly.

Rose walked through the gates and up the drive. Taking in her surroundings, she imagined that in the summer months, the grounds would be beautiful and green. The enormous double doors were made of oak. She was about to lift the knocker when they opened. A man who looked to be in his late sixties answered. He had a head of thick salt-and-pepper hair neatly groomed and brushed back from his high forehead. His gaze was direct and observant, his eyes deep blue and framed by thick gray brows. His thick lips formed a smile, and his white teeth gleamed in the light from the doorway. He was dressed precisely in a tweed sports jacket over a blue sweater from which the collar of his white button-down shirt rose. He wore gray corduroy pants, and, in his hand, he held a pipe. He pointed with the pipe, inviting her in. "I'm Dr. Brandt, *fraulein*, and you are?"

"My name is Rose Levi. I'm visiting from the United States with my boyfriend. I'd appreciate using your phone to call him and the police."

"Yes, of course, please come in."

Rose stepped inside, looking around the foyer. Warm dark wood paneling graced the walls, while an elegant oriental carpet added bright color to the dark oak floors. To the right of the foyer, she saw a large open room with windows on two walls that were draped in curtains made of heavy wine-colored fabric shot through with gold thread. Rich burgundy leather sofas and armchairs circled around a floor-to-ceiling hearth. The furnishings were elegant and inviting.

"Please follow me to my office. You can phone from there." It was with reluctance she followed him through a side door and down a thickly carpeted hallway lined with doors. She'd have to wait for the cozy warmth of the fire in the hearth.

"May I ask what kind of clinic you run?" She asked.

"It's a wellness center. Our patients come from all over the world for rest, recovery, and treatments for different medical conditions. How did the accident happen?"

"The roads are very icy from the storm, and there was something in the middle of the road. When the driver swerved to avoid it, we went into a tailspin and fell off an embankment. All I remember is the car flipping over and over until it hit a tree."

"And you were the only one not hurt. How fortunate."

He pulled a keyring with dozens of keys out of his pocket and unlocked the door. Dr. Brandt flipped the switch, and the room lit up. A walnut wood desk with an Aeron ergonomic chair faced the floor-to-ceiling windows that gave view to the grounds. Two wing-back chairs sat across from the desk.

"I'll dial the police and explain what happened," he said, crossing over to the desk. "You can tell me any details to convey to them." He picked up the receiver and put it to his ear. "Oh, dear, the phone line isn't working. Must be the storm."

"Do you have a cell phone? I think mine tumbled out of my pocket in the accident."

"Yes, I'll get it. It's upstairs. Just give me a minute, and I'll be back. Can I bring you something to drink?"

"Please, some water would be appreciated."

"Why don't you sit down and relax. I'll get my cell phone and a bottle of water for you."

"Thank you."

Alone in the office, Rose wrapped her arms around herself and studied the room. On the desk were several framed photographs. Curious, she walked over to get a closer peek.

She drew in a sharp breath.

She picked up the frame and stared at the image with horror-filled eyes. The SS doctor, Horst Schumacher, stood next to a woman who sat in a wheelchair. Her skin was pale, and her eyes held a distant, vacant look. On the other side of the wheelchair stood a young man, who could only be Heinrich Schumacher. The son touched his mother's shoulder, while the father's hands were clasped behind his back. Even his posture seemed to lean away from her.

Oh, my God! It has to be him. She shuddered at the uncanniness.

Dr. Brandt is Heinrich Schumacher! She thought she'd found a place of refuge, and she'd ended up at the very place her kidnappers must have been taking her to.

Rose sucked air into her lungs as she tried to steady her

nerves. Miriam was still watching and protecting her. Rose sensed her presence and knew she was here with her now.

I have to stay calm. I can't let him get hold of the lists. He'll destroy the evidence and kill me. I have only one advantage — he doesn't know that I recognize him.

After everything her grandmother had worked for, Rose knew it now came down to her. She would not let Leah down. She would not let Leah's sacrifice be in vain.

CHAPTER 31

January 26, Present day
Rapperswil, Switzerland

P *lease, God, keep Rose safe.*
Ethan's gaze shifted back and forth between his cell phone and the window of the white Range Rover. The tracking device had emitted a steady signal as they drove out of Zürich, but the blip had been stationary for some time, and Ethan's panic continued to rise the closer they got to the location of Rose's cell phone. It was all he could do to stop himself from imagining worst-case scenarios.

With Ethan in the Range Rover were three members of an Israeli defense force team known as the Sayeret Matkal. They were all seasoned intelligence warriors, experts in hostage-rescue missions on foreign soil. They were also deadly assassins. Ethan was not a member of the team, but he'd worked with them numerous times over the years. Ethan's secret organization was wired into every intelligence agency and pulled strings when

Ethan needed backup. He worked with Mossad, MI6, and the CIA, depending on the case. They shared a common purpose — to stop the rise of anti-Semitism and anti-Semitic violence.

The driver, Daniel, grunted as he stared out the window. "Damn, it's a bitch out there. Visibility is almost nil."

"Stop here! We're only a few meters away from her phone." Ethan peered out the window as Daniel pulled up to the side of the road. "Anybody see anything?"

The two other Israeli agents shook their heads. "That's a negative," said Noah.

Abe ejected a magazine out of his Glock and reloaded it. "We'll see better out of the car on foot."

The four men jumped out of the vehicle and went into action. Grabbing their backpacks, they suited up and checked their weapons. Each man slung an assault rifle over his shoulder. They each carried a different weapon of choice, including an Israeli Tavor Tar-21 Bullpup assault rifle, the German made Heckler and Koch's HK416, and a British made SA80 A2. It was a deadly arsenal capable of eliminating any enemy. Expertly they checked their 9 mm pistols and loaded extra magazines into their pockets. Ethan shoved his Glock 9 mm into his belt carrier. Daniel carried the M32A1 portable grenade launcher on his back. In unison, they slipped on their balaclavas, helmets, and night-vision goggles. Finally, they checked their earpiece communication devices.

Shifting their assault rifles forward, they moved in silence, searching for any sign of Rose and her kidnappers. The snowstorm had intensified to a blizzard — even with their night vision goggles, visibility was difficult. The four men resembled a team of giant white sasquatch in their camouflage tactical snowsuits. The gear — meant to protect against freezing temperatures — was lightweight and had no effect on their agility.

Noah stopped and studied the snow beneath his feet. His

English was heavily nuanced with an Israeli accent. "Swerving tire imprints. A car must have lost control."

They followed the tire tracks for several hundred feet until they disappeared off the side of the road.

"Shit! Follow me." Ethan powered through knee-high snow-drifts down the face of an embankment with the three others close behind. With their weapons aimed, they surrounded an upside-down Mercedes that lay smashed against a tree. Ethan peered through the front and back windows, his stomach tightly bound in a knot. There was no movement inside the Mercedes. "I don't see her, but this is the car I saw in the plaza in front of Credit Suisse. Help me get this door open."

Ethan's heart pounded in his chest but he couldn't afford to lose his cool. If anything happened to Rose, he'd never forgive himself.

Daniel pulled a bar from his backpack and wedged it in the doorframe. He jiggled it, and it clicked, opening a sliver of space. He stuck the bar inside, yanked, and the door flew open.

Ethan checked the pulse on the guy hanging upside down. "Dead." He unlocked the seatbelt, and the body tumbled out of the car. Abe pulled the body aside, and Ethan climbed in and checked the pulses of the other two men. "All dead and no Rose. Where the hell could she be?" He spied her phone up against the rear passenger door and grabbed it. "I've got her phone."

How could she have gotten out of this deathtrap?" Daniel asked, shaking his head.

"I don't know, maybe she was thrown somehow," Ethan replied. We better search the area and see if we can find any tracks." He prayed Rose wasn't lying unconscious in the snow — in this blizzard, her chance of survival would be slim. He pushed those negative thoughts aside. "She might have tried to find help somewhere. Let's go. These bastards don't need us, that's for sure."

"Wait." Noah pulled out his cell and took a picture of the face of the body in the snow. Then he leaned in and snapped shots of the other men in the car. "I'll e-mail these to headquarters and find out who these thugs are. Face identification through Interpol should nail them and give us an idea of who they're working for."

When Noah finished, Ethan said, "Right. Let's go."

The four men backtracked to the road and picked up where they'd left off. They walked in silence, keeping their eyes peeled for any sign of Rose.

"I wonder what made the Mercedes veer off the road like that?" Daniel wondered aloud.

"Maybe they saw an animal and swerved to avoid it. It's kind of a gut reaction," Abe contributed as he kicked snow out of his way. "We've got tracks, and they're small like a woman's boots."

They picked up the pace now that they had a clear trail to follow. The tracks stopped at an imposing gate. They all peered up at the sign. "It's a rehab clinic of some kind."

Noah retrieved his phone and read an incoming text. "Okay, the bodies belong to three thugs who have ties to the National Democratic Party of Germany, the National Socialist Underground, and several other skinhead organizations espousing white supremacy, anti-Semitism, and separatism." He snapped a shot of the sign and forwarded the pic to headquarters. "Let's see what they can find out about this place and whoever runs it."

"That's the right M.O. for what we're looking for," Ethan said, his gut clenching. Rose had unknowingly walked into the lion's den. "This guy is a monster, and she's carrying the evidence that can destroy him. Every minute that passes puts her in more danger."

Abe began walking along the fence, studying it. It was about eight feet high and made of round pipe-like stakes about six inches apart. He walked for about a hundred yards and stopped.

He tested the fence. It wasn't electrified. Daniel, Ethan, and Noah followed him. "This is as good a spot as any. Let's do this." Abe opened his backpack and pulled out a pair of gloves, slipping them on. "These should do the trick."

The other men were right with him. Each of them pulled a pair of gloves out of their backpacks and slipped them on. The gloves had a magnetic coating that adhered to the metal, and it took all four men about six seconds to scale the fence and jump down on the other side. A minute later, they were all standing inside the clinic's grounds.

They plowed through the snow as silent as Ninjas, blending in with the white frozen landscape. When they reached the building, they stopped, and Daniel took over command. "Ethan, you and Abe circle the building and determine our best point of entry." He looked at the smoke rising out of the chimney. "There's obviously someone inside. Maybe it's our prey."

"We can't just bust in. Who knows what the bastard will do?" Ethan said. "Heinrich could panic and hurt Rose." *Or worse.*

"What do you suggest?" asked Daniel. "We can't help Rose from here."

"I have an idea. It's risky, but it might work."

"I'm listening."

CHAPTER 32

January 26, Present day
Rapperswil, Switzerland

T he deadliest weapon she possessed was her knowledge. *Think!* She commanded herself.

The family photo showed the SS doctor lacked any interest in his wife or son. She knew from watching Horst with Leah that he cared nothing for human misery or life other than his own, and even less for his wife. So how did his obsession with Leah affect his son?

She needed to buy some time, and she needed to obstruct his plans. Assuming the younger Schumacher wasn't sociopathic as she suspected his father was, he wasn't immune to psychological trauma, no matter how gifted and successful. The child of such an uncaring man would undoubtedly be damaged. *Maybe I can fluster him enough to make a mistake. The worst that can happen, he shoots me sooner.*

The doctor returned and handed her a bottle of water while

studying her as if she were one of his patients. She reminded herself that she had a measure of power over him. Uncapping the water bottle, she drank slowly until it was emptied. It was best to catch him completely off guard. Rose sucked in a breath of courage. "It must have been difficult growing up with a father whose interest lay elsewhere."

"What are you talking about?"

"Your father loved my grandmother madly. She was his weakness. His love for her was greater than his love for your mother and certainly greater than his love for you. It must have been a terrible pain for you and a heavy burden to bear when it came to your mother."

"How dare you presume to know the depth of my father's feelings for me or my mother," he spat. "My mother was a gentlewoman. Your dirty Jew grandmother was a slut, merely a vessel for my father to release his baser physical instincts. He didn't love your precious Leah Manheim. Jews were nothing more to him than guinea pigs — he used them to further his important research. Nothing more than vermin."

Even though she'd hit her target, she still fought her own anger at Heinrich's blatant hatred. She wanted to lash out, wanted to run at him kicking and screaming, wanted to punish him for all of his father's sins and his own evil machinations. She calmed her breathing.

"How did your father die?"

Heinrich's face twisted as his eyes skirted away.

"Did Horst kill himself?"

His flushed face meant something. Rose had touched a nerve, a wound that hadn't fully healed — all she had to do was dig deeper. "Your father loved Nadia, knew that only Nadia could make him happy. His wife and son held no more importance than his next meal. Horst killed himself because he preferred death to a life without her. Death rather than a life with only you and your pale little mother. He didn't care about you, all he cared about was Nadia, and when Horst realized he would never have her, he killed himself."

"I know what you're doing, bitch. Don't presume you can even begin to play head shrink with me. You're nothing but a little librarian in a little Jew library." Heinrich pulled a pistol from his pocket and pointed it at her. "You'll do exactly as I say. Lie down on the lounge chair."

Rose began to tremble. *Careful. You can still do this.* Slowly, she walked to the chair and sat, her gaze fixated on the muzzle of the gun. Despite her dire circumstances, she began to feel a warming glow surround her. She took a deep breath, and a calm settled over her once more.

Heinrich moved closer to her. Rose sensed he was drawn to the brooch. It had begun to gleam from beneath her lapel.

"That's an interesting piece of jewelry. Lift your lapel so I can get a better look."

"Beautiful, isn't it? It was my grandmother's." The brooch caught the light and glowed as if made of fire.

"Take it off and give it to me."

She unpinned the brooch and held it toward him in her open palm. The brooch was now radiating colored beams of red and gold light, dazzling like the aurora borealis.

Heinrich moved to within a foot of her and pointed the gun at her chest. The muzzle of the weapon was aimed dead center at her heart. She didn't dare breathe, let alone move. His eyes burned with desire. "The Ark of the Covenant brooch," he whispered. "I've heard of its existence. Is it as powerful as they say?"

"What do you think?" *No matter what, the brooch mustn't fall into his hands.* She closed her eyes and prayed. *Help me, Bubbie. Help me, Miriam.*

With the gun pointed at her heart, he reached to touch the brooch. Rose held her breath. A blinding flash of lightning shot out from the brooch, throwing Heinrich across the room and sending the gun flying out of his hand.

Rose's fingers closed around the brooch, and she quickly pinned it back on her lapel. This was it, her chance to make a run for it. She jumped up and ran for the door, but it was locked. Her heart pounded in her chest, and she wrenched on the knob, pulling, but no matter how hard she tried, the door didn't budge. She turned and flattened her back to the door. Heinrich was laid out on the carpet spread-eagle, the fallen gun but a few feet away. His eyes were closed, but she didn't know how long it would be before he regained consciousness.

She inched forward, closing the distance between them. Heinrich's chest rose and fell with his breaths. He wasn't dead. Trembling, she knelt to pick up the pistol. Sweat beaded her brow, and a trickle of perspiration traced a path between her breasts.

Her fingers were inches away from the gun's grip.

Just as she touched it, Heinrich grabbed her wrist. A blood-curdling scream tore from her throat.

CHAPTER 33

January 26, Present day
Rapperswil, Switzerland

He heard her scream.

Ethan and the other men froze. They had just broken into the basement of the clinic through a storm window. Ethan took the stairs two at a time and reached for the door to the house itself. It was locked. He reversed his assault rifle, and using the butt as a hammer, bashed the knob. The door flew open. Behind him, he heard the pounding of feet as Abe, Daniel, and Noah caught up to him.

He broke into a run, his rifle in the ready position, his finger poised on the trigger, his senses on high alert.

He knew. He knew she was here. And he knew that bastard had her.

The men caught up with him and they broke into pairs, moving deliberately through the rooms of the house, clearing each room as they systematically searched.

Ethan focused like a laser beam. All his fears and anxiety were pushed aside. All that mattered was finding Rose. He kicked open a door within the bedroom apartments where the guest accommodations were and found a young man in bed with a blonde woman. The woman was blindfolded with her wrists tied to the bedposts.

"Well, what have we here?" Daniel said. "Put your hands up, weirdo!" Daniel sliced the ties that bound the woman to the bed.

The man's hands flew up in the air as the woman scrambled to cover her body. "Hey man, what the hell is going on?" The man was white as a ghost and trembling like a high-strung Chihuahua.

"Get dressed and get the hell out of here if you want to see another sunrise. In fact, I'd get as far as you can from this place," Ethan barked.

"But-but, What...?"

Ethan and Daniel were gone before the patient finished his sentence. Clearly, it was a slow time of the year. They found no other staff on the premises besides the kinky sex fiend and the blonde. In the living room, a fire burned and crackled in the fireplace, but they found no sign of Rose or her captor.

"I've got a text from headquarters," Noah reported into his earpiece. "The head of this clinic is a Dr. Heinrich Brandt. Rich bastard. Born during World War II in Germany. Father was Horst Brandt — most likely a false identity. They're digging deeper at HQ."

"We need to move. This is our guy." He trusted his gut. Horst Schumacher was the name of the SS doctor in Auschwitz, and Heinrich was his son. Heinrich was the head of the cabal, and Rose was his captive.

They moved silently to the other wing of the house. The laser light beams from their rifles danced on the walls like red and green fireflies. The muzzles of their guns shifted back and forth, ready to take down any opposition. They entered a hallway with doors on either side. One-by-one, the four men cleared the rooms — all offices set up for the business side of the clinic. The last door that Ethan kicked open revealed a room in disarray. Papers lay on the floor, and a lounge chair was knocked over. He dropped the muzzle of the rifle and looked around. He sniffed the air and caught a whiff of Chanel No. 5, Rose's scent. Noah, Abe, and Daniel joined him a few moments later.

"She was here, and it looks like there was a struggle," Ethan said.

"How do you know it was her?" asked Daniel.

"I know her scent, her perfume."

The three warriors chuckled. "You're as good as a sniffer dog."

Ethan's face flushed, and he shrugged. Daniel, Abe, and Noah must have figured out by now that his interest in Rose exceeded his mission statement. It didn't matter anyway. He'd failed her — lied to her. He pushed away his guilt and focused on what to do next.

He walked to the window and stared out over the frozen landscape. The blizzard had abated somewhat, and visibility had improved, but there was no sign of Rose.

Please, God, help us find her in time.

CHAPTER 34

January 26, Present day
Rapperswil, Switzerland

Rose stumbled forward, every step a struggle to stay upright. Behind her, Heinrich pressed the pistol into her back. He cursed in German under his breath, dabbing at a trickle of blood that streamed from where she'd clawed his face.

How did I end up like this? Bubbie, I'm sorry. I couldn't live up to your faith in me.

Rose had been so close to escaping, but when she'd reached for the gun on the floor, Heinrich had grabbed her wrist and pulled her down before she could pick it up. She'd nearly had a heart attack. She'd hesitated too long. She should have picked up the gun first and then run for the door.

They had rolled back and forth on the carpet, Rose fighting tooth and nail until he'd punched her, and she'd seen stars. He then wrested the gun from her, pinned her beneath him and shoved a needle into her neck. Her vision immediately went hazy, and strength drained away.

He'd stood and aimed the gun at her. She covered her eyes, certain that he would kill her. A moment later, she peeked through her fingers and giggled. She had no idea why she'd laughed, but her situation was so ridiculous that it seemed like a valid reaction. For a moment, he was dumbfounded by her response, and then he smiled. How odd.

"Would you please empty your pockets. I'm not going to shoot you."

She sat up and handed him the two small books she'd found in Leah's safety deposit box.

Holding the gun on her, he quickly fanned the pages of each book. His face flushed when he looked at the red book. He shoved it back at her. "I have no interest in this book and its ancient history."

She stuffed the book back in her pocket. "It seems your father was a traitor to his cause. This proves he would have done anything to possess Leah." *Why am I taunting him? It will only make him mad.*

Heinrich frowned, the ticking of his jaw his only response. "Do you have any idea what your grandmother wrote in code in this book?"

She shook her head, no. She wondered what drug he'd injected into her because she was having trouble keeping her thoughts straight. She felt sure the less she said, the better, but she couldn't seem to help herself.

He repeated the question in a more threatening tone. "Tell me what you think is written in the code?"

The drug he'd given her had dulled her senses — some kind of truth serum that made her feel calm and peaceful — numbing her instinct to fight and run. Even worse, she felt compelled to answer his every question truthfully. "Probably the proof we need to bring you down. I wouldn't be surprised if it contains bank account numbers, the names of your co-conspirators and minions, maybe even information about upcoming attacks."

He nodded. "Yes, I think you're right. But it will never see the light of day. Without this proof, you have nothing."

Is this it? Is this the end?

Would he kill her now that he had what he wanted from her?

"The young man you're with — Connor Hayes. Who is he, and does he know the real reason you're here?"

"Of course, he knows. He's probably searching for me now. He was with the CIA." She clapped her hand over her mouth. Heinrich didn't need to know that.

"Was he? How very interesting. Where do you think he is?"

"I — I...don't know."

Heinrich fingered his goatee. "Yes, my guess is you're right. He's most likely desperate to find you. I think it's time we left here. I have a place where we can go."

It dawned on her the only reason he didn't kill her was because of the Ark of the Covenant brooch. He couldn't take it from her without being shocked and jolted to within an inch of his life, so she figured he would come up with another way to take possession of it. Hadn't the ladies of the sisterhood said that if he controlled her, he controlled the brooch?

Heinrich held a pistol to her back as Rose stumbled down a set of narrow stairs. She had trouble keeping her balance. Her hands were zip-tied behind her back, and she couldn't grab anything to steady herself. The effects of the drug were beginning to fade now, replaced by a feeling of dread at what she'd revealed.

Confusion filled her as she replayed the fight with Heinrich in her mind. Why had the brooch, the blue coat, Miriam, and Leah all failed her? What possible advantage could there be to leave her under the control of Heinrich, a man consumed with hatred for Leah and the Jewish people?

Her chest once more tightened with growing panic. Even Ethan had failed her. In her heart, she'd held the hope that he would burst in and save her like John Wayne in the western cowboy flicks that he'd confessed to loving. But Ethan was nowhere to be seen, and she was being dragged away by a madman.

"Before we leave here, there's something I want you to see," he said. The stairs led to a subterranean level of the house. He pushed Rose against the wall. "Don't move." He keyed a combination into a heavy steel, vault-like door and waited for it to swing open. The lights in the room automatically switched on. He shoved her in front of him.

The bright fluorescent light was blinding, and she blinked rapidly. A side effect of the drug made Rose's eyes light-sensitive. When her pupils began to adjust, she gasped. A larger-than-life red flag of Nazi Germany covered one wall of the room. The flag's swastika in a white disk glowed bright and clean, like a new coin. Slowly her gaze traveled around the massive room, which she decided was some sort of museum. The opposite wall was covered with an assortment of framed Nazi-era propaganda posters. A glass-fronted cabinet and floor-to-ceiling bookshelves lined the other walls. From what she could tell, the cabinet and shelves were filled with memorabilia, weapons, and books immortalizing the Nazis. Uniformed wax figures in the likenesses of Hitler, Himmler, Hess, and Goebbels stood together in one corner, flanked by armed SS Guards holding pistols.

Rose shivered. They were so lifelike she'd thought for a split second that Heinrich had resurrected them in some bizarre human experiment. Heinrich prodded her forward with the muzzle of his pistol. "If you're wondering what this is, let's just say

272

it's one of the largest private collections of memorabilia of the Third Reich you will ever see."

Rose stumbled forward and stopped in front of one of the display cases. It contained an assortment of Nazi medals, an SS-*Ehrendolch* dagger, and a *Totenkopfring* "Death's Head Ring." The ring, designed by Himmler, was a personal gift from the head of the SS bestowed on a select few. Rose recalled seeing several of these macabre rings being auctioned over the years. There had been pushback from Jewish groups, and eventually, selling and profiting from Nazi memorabilia were banned in Europe. But there were plenty of loopholes if one claimed to be using the items for historical veracity as opposed to Nazi glorification. The ring, one of the most prized possessions of collectors, was worn on the left marriage finger.

Rose couldn't draw her eyes away from the ring. "This was your father's, wasn't it?"

Heinrich grinned proudly. "Yes, it was. Himmler presented it himself to my father, '*der Ehrenring.*' He had it specially inscribed, '*To risk our individual lives for the life of the whole.*' A most solemn pledge, don't you think?"

Rose wanted to puke. What Heinrich had assembled in this museum of horrors was dedicated to evil. "Everything in here represents a depraved regime that was destroyed forever and will never rise again."

"How wrong you are, *fraulein.* Just as the phoenix rose from the ashes, so too will a new Reich rise. There are powerful forces at work dedicated to this goal, and never before has the time been better, or the world been more ready for a true transition of power," he gloated.

Rose froze at his words and the zeal in his eyes.

"By the way," he continued, "I plan to destroy Auschwitz, Bergen-Belsen, and the rest of the concentration camps that the

Germans bungled. The German government has grown weak —
they bend over for the Jews. But we will wipe that out. In less than
a generation, no one will remember anything about the camps
other than they were used for resettlement and for prisoners of
war."

He's insane, you can't erase history. But then she thought about
the pulling down of statues, the subtle revisionist changes that
were taking place in classrooms all over the world, and she shuddered. It wouldn't happen tomorrow, or next year, but over twenty,
thirty, fifty years, who could say.

"Soon the last survivors of the so-called Holocaust will be
gone, and with their deaths, the forgetting will begin. I've worked
tirelessly to put the soldiers of the new Reich in place, preparing
for the day of reckoning —" Heinrich's voice trailed away, and his
gaze was drawn to a wall monitor in the corner of the room.

Four men in tactical gear moved stealthily through a hallway.
Heinrich snarled and pointed the gun at her. "We need to get out
of here."

Rose's hand covered her chest as she sought to calm her racing
heart.

Ethan is coming.

A second door at the bottom of the stairs led to a subterranean
heated garage. There were several cars in the garage, but Heinrich
told her to get into a red Hummer. Of course, the monster-sized
vehicle would plow through any snowstorm. Heinrich turned the
ignition, but nothing happened. *"Was zur hölle ist los?"* He tried it
again, "click, click, click." He banged his fist on the steering wheel.
Rose, who'd closed her eyes praying for a miracle, felt a prickle of
warmth surround her. *Miriam?* Was Miriam the reason the car
didn't start?

"Get out!"

Rose's eyes flew open, and fear tingled up her spine. "I — I..."

"Get out now!" The cold steel of the muzzle pressed against her forehead. She sucked in her breath and carefully slid out of the Hummer.

Pushing her up against the vehicle, he hissed, "Don't move."

Heinrich swung a bulky metal brace across the access door to the garage, making it impossible to open from inside the house. He grabbed her arm and shoved her forward out a side entrance of the garage. An icy wind whipped at her face. The snowstorm had abated enough to see beyond a few feet in front of them as they trudged through the snow. Rose stumbled, barely keeping her balance as Heinrich pushed her onward.

"Where are we going?" It was so cold her words nearly froze in her throat.

"To the boathouse where I keep the snowmobiles. There's more than one way out of here." He pressed the pistol to her back. "*Schnell! Schnell!* Move faster!"

Rose closed her eyes and prayed.

CHAPTER 35

January 26, Present day
Rapperswil, Switzerland

T*ime's running out.*

Adrenalin pumped through Ethan's veins — he wanted to run, shoot, kill. All the training from years ago came back to him as he forced himself to wait.

Daniel set the Semtex to the door's hinges, and all four men flattened themselves against the wall, sticking their fingers in their ears. The explosion blew the reinforced steel door open as if it were made of paper, and a breeze had blown through. All four men's laser pointers landed on the Nazi uniformed dummies. Their earpieces rattled from their combined sighs of relief.

Daniel chuckled, "We been had, boys." He lowered his assault rifle.

"What a sick puppy," Abe spat.

"Heinrich's House of Nazi Horrors." Noah kicked one of the wax figures, and it toppled.

Ethan's gaze landed on the monitor. "He knows we're here. We don't have time to shoot the breeze about what assholes the Nazis were. Let's go." Ethan ran from the room with the other men on his tail. The last door in the hallway didn't budge even after Ethan bashed the knob off. "Blow it!"

The explosion echoed in the cavernous garage. The men burst through, weapons raised, but the settling dust revealed no human presence.

Daniel checked his watch. "Four minutes until detonation."

Noah peered in the window of the Hummer. "Keys are in it." He opened the car door, hopped in, and pressed the ignition. "Dead."

"Okay, they can't be far." A cold blast of frigid air hit his face, and his heated breath condensed into a cloud of moisture. Ethan jogged around the building to the front of the clinic. "Wait. Down near the lake, do you see something?" He raised the riflescope to his eye and peered through the reticle. The color blue filled the scope — Rose's blue coat. He adjusted the riflescope and spotted Rose walking in front of a man who pointed a pistol at her. "It's her."

Daniel looked at his watch. "Noah, what do you think?"

The sharpshooter knelt to the ground and positioned himself. He rested his eye against the riflescope. "Like shooting candy from a baby," Noah steadied his breath and stilled his body. "Shit, he sees us."

Ethan squinted through the foggy haze. Heinrich grabbed Rose from the back and wrenched her against his chest, shielding himself. Rose screamed, "Ethan!"

"I don't have a clean shot, dammit!" Noah growled, his eye glued to the riflescope.

Ethan's heart pounded in his chest — everything was falling apart.

The explosion was deafening. The clinic ignited into a scorching inferno, and burning debris rained down on the Sayeret Matkal team. Ethan covered his head, keeping his eyes locked on Rose and Brandt. Simultaneous with the demolition of the clinic, a bolt of lightning flashed. It appeared out of the sky and struck Rose. Blinded, Ethan shielded his eyes. When he opened them, Rose was gone.

"What the hell is going on?" Noah yelled above the deafening roar of secondary explosions and fire coming from within the clinic. "Rose vanished. I don't see her."

Ethan ordered, "Don't worry about Rose. Just take out that damn Nazi!"

Heinrich's head snapped back and forth, searching for Rose, his eyes wide. With a snarl of rage, he swung back toward Ethan and the team. Hatred sparked from his eyes. "You will never stop us. There are thousands more out there just like me! I'll see you in hell!"

Ethan smiled. "You first, asshole!" The words scarcely left his lips when a single shot rang out. Heinrich's body twisted and spun, and he stumbled from the impact of the bullet ripping through his chest. He clutched his chest as if he could staunch the flow of blood with his hands. Tottering forward a couple of steps, disbelief written in his eyes, he slumped into the snow.

Ethan and the others ran to the dead man. Using his boot, Abe flipped Heinrich's body and knelt beside him in the snow, checking his pockets. He held up the black address-sized book and thumbed the pages. "Got it." When he checked Heinrich's other pocket, he held up five hypodermics. "The bastard must have drugged her."

Ethan turned in a slow circle, his gaze scanning the surrounding landscape. He didn't care about dead Nazis from the past or in the present. He had only one concern. *Where is Rose?*

CHAPTER 36

September 30, 1948
Paris, France

L eah gazed out the window of the taxi in awe.

The Ritz Hotel was stunning by any measure, and she could not help but be impressed with its opulence. When the taxi had made the turn around the Vendôme Column on the Place Vendôme, her pulse kicked up into high gear.

Two years had passed since the Nazi occupation of Paris. Hermann Göring — who'd commandeered the Imperial Suite at the Ritz during the German occupation of Paris — had committed suicide with a cyanide capsule in a Nuremberg prison cell the night before he was to hang. All of the Nazis were gone from the Ritz, except, of course, the man she was meeting.

She stepped onto the red runner that led up the steps between a row of arches crowned with a white awning. Embroidered in blue on the awning were two words that evoked the sophistication and legendry of the hotel: *Ritz Paris*. On either side was a green topiary shrub, meticulously pruned into a tapering spiral. The formally attired doorman greeted her as if she were a princess, his white-gloved fingers offering a gentle nudge on her elbow as he led her up the steps. The glass-paned wood doors opened to an intimate foyer. No guests loitered. If one wished company, several restaurants and a cocktail bar were ready to accommodate. Their willingness to uphold their guests' privacy was one of the many reasons that the ordinary and the celebrated made the Ritz their home. Leah felt as if she'd just arrived at a grand country manor, and she was the highly anticipated guest of honor.

Discreetly, on one side of the foyer, was a carved wood reception desk, and next to the reception desk, a scrolled wrought-iron staircase curved its way to the floors above. Her gaze soared up the stairwell, wondering on what floor Horst's room was.

"Mademoiselle Sauvage?"

She turned and smiled at the *Maître d'Hôtel*. *"Oui,* Monsieur." She did her best to present herself as a poised, confident woman, and not the counterfeit she felt herself to be. Only an academy award-winning performance would get her what she'd come for.

"Monsieur Brandt alerted us to your pending arrival. He is in the César suite on the third floor. The elevator is this way." The elegantly attired man indicated with his hand. *Of course, Horst alerted them as to my arrival.*

"I think I'd like to take the stairs if you don't mind. The hotel is so beautiful, and after so many years of war, I'd like to savor it."

"Please, Mademoiselle, the pleasure is ours to have such beauty grace our halls. Turn right when you reach the third floor, and you'll find Monsieur Brandt's suite."

"Merci, Monsieur." Her fingers rested lightly on the black and gold wrought-iron banister as she walked tentatively up the red oriental carpet runner centered over the white marble stairs. She needed these extra minutes to focus herself and gather her

courage. In no hurry, she stopped to admire the period antiques and tapestries hanging on the walls. When she reached the third floor, she followed the Maître d'Hôtel's directions. Arriving at the door to the suite, she wasn't surprised that it swung open before her hand touched the door knocker.

Horst's cologne assailed her nostrils, drowning out her sparingly applied Chanel No. 5. His gaze drank her in as if she were an oasis in the desert, and he a traveler who'd crawled through blistering sun and heat to quench his thirst at her well. "You came. I wasn't sure you would."

"Of course, I came. I wanted to — I had to." *Will I ever learn to lie without feeling revulsion?* "Are you going to invite me in, Horst," she purred. "Or am I to stand out here in the hallway all night?"

He helped her off with her blue coat, revealing a black satin dress with a fitted waist and a daringly low bodice. Her veiled black hat was provocative as well, shadowing her eyes with mystery. She'd chosen red lipstick and red shoes, her own way of branding herself as a woman of ill repute, which was how she felt. If things went wrong, by tomorrow, she'd truly be one. "You're dazzling, Nadia. I'm at a loss for words."

"I'm sure before the evening is over, you'll find your words," she giggled. She turned in a slow circle, taking in the lavish suite. A fire burned in the hearth in front of a sumptuous overstuffed moss green velvet sofa. The sensuously curved lines of Louis XV chairs with their ornate gilded gold and brass fittings sat upon an intricately patterned oriental rug. Her gaze traveled up to soaring ceilings crowned with gold-leafed moldings. In front of the windows that overlooked the square, a small, intimate table for two was set with white linens, sparkling china, crystal, and sterling silver flatware that glowed in the candlelight. None of it was lost on her. *This pig is reveling in these beautiful surroundings. If only it were Aidan standing across from me.*

Leah couldn't stop it, the lone tear that streaked its way down her cheek. She wiped it away, but Horst, who hadn't taken his eyes from her, strode to her and gathered her in his arms.

"Darling, why are you crying?"

Leah placed her hands on his blue velvet smoking jacket, putting some distance between them. She looked down at his chest. "I'm just so taken with how beautiful everything is, the table, the suite...you." The lie slipped from her lips with such ease, it surprised her.

He raised her chin, forcing her to look into his eyes. "All of this is nothing compared to what I have planned for you, Nadia." His gaze dropped to her mouth, and his lips slowly followed suit. He trembled when he kissed her, and she responded, kissing him back, pressing into his embrace. It was a small price to pay, and when the kiss ended, his quivering body and gasping breath told her she had him just where she wanted him.

"I'm starving, *mon amour*," she whispered.

"How selfish of me, my sweet." He released her, and she sighed with relief. "First, a toast." He pulled a bottle from an ice bucket. Removing the foil and popping the cork with a flourish, he filled two champagne flutes, handing her one. "To us, my darling, and tonight's pleasures." They touched glasses and sipped. "Ach, perfect, and now I'll have our meal sent up." He placed his glass on the table and picked up the phone. Leah waved to him while he spoke to catering, pointing to the bathroom, and he nodded. She removed her hat, setting it on a chair, and taking her handbag, retired to the bathroom.

Leah stared in the mirror at herself. *You can do this. You need to do this. For all those souls he destroyed. For all those innocents he tortured. You are the hand of the Archangel Raguel, the Angel of Justice who will deliver God's vengeance on those who transgress his laws.*

She reapplied lipstick, dabbing it with a tissue, and then

combed her hair. Her charmeuse satin dress was gathered at the waist, and she'd created a small pocket into which she stuffed two capsules. One of her friends from the resistance had helped her procure the drug, guaranteed to knock out a horse. If it didn't, she would find herself in a whole heap of trouble.

When Leah returned to Horst, he was seated on the sofa. Magically, a gloved waiter had arrived and was arranging the first course on their plates.

"Monsieur, should I return to serve the second course?" asked the waiter.

"*Non, merci.*" said Leah, "I will take care of it. We'll call and leave the table in the hallway when we're through."

Horst nodded, his eyes gleaming. Leah knew the intimate act of her serving him only intensified his desire and the romantic illusion it represented.

When the waiter left, they dined on *soupe de poisson* with garlic toasts followed by *sole meunière,* sautéed spinach, and last but not least, *crème caramel.* It was clear to Leah he'd planned a light meal so as not to interfere with the pleasures to come. Naturally, he wouldn't want anything to get in the way of the grand finale. For entirely different reasons, neither of them took but a few bites of any of the dishes, but as to the champagne and wine, that was another story. Horst imbibed deeply.

When he excused himself to go to the bathroom, Leah finally had her chance. She refilled their champagne glasses. Removing the two pills from her waistband, she split them apart and dumped them into his glass. By the time he'd returned to the salon, she'd rolled the cart outside the room to the hallway and waited on the sofa with the two glasses of effervescing champagne on the coffee table in front of her.

"*Chéri.*" She stood and placed her hands on his chest, gazing at him from beneath her lashes, her face impossibly close to his.

"Before I make a toast to us, I'd like to conclude the business part of our arrangement." She held still as a statue waiting for his response.

"Ach, yes, of course. How can you trust a man who doesn't deliver on his word?" He bent and gave her a peck on the lips. "Forgive me, my darling — allow me to retrieve it."

She'd been holding her breath, and when he left the room, she let out a sigh of relief. He returned and handed her a small red leather-bound book. She smiled up at him and quickly flipped through the pages. It was all there as promised — many of the names she recognized. It would take years to find them — and she would need help in doing so — but she had no doubt there were many survivors who would happily spend the rest of their lives bringing these monsters to justice.

"Thank you." She stored the book in her purse. Returning to the sofa, she raised her glass, waiting for him to join her. "We need to make a toast," she encouraged.

Horst sat and lifted his glass. "And what are we toasting, Nadia?"

"We're toasting the future, Horst. We're toasting you and me. Strange bedfellows that destiny has brought together."

His brows rose with amusement. "This is exactly why I am so taken with you. Your wittiness, the way your words arouse me as much as your face and magnificent body." His gaze dropped to her breasts hungrily, and then returned to her face. "To us, *liebling,* the first of a *tausend nächten!*"

A thousand nights, over my dead body. "To us!" She sipped and watched him down the champagne. Taking her glass, he placed both hers and his on the table. Then he moved in, kissing her neck, inhaling her, his shaking hands tentatively brushing her breasts. Her heart pounded, threatening to burst through the cavity of her chest. *How long before the drug begins to work?*

"Oh, I'm so nervous, Horst. Please go slowly." She closed her eyes, her head tilted back, praying for the knock-out drug to take effect before she threw up her meal.

He growled, "I'll try, but my need grows ever stronger. I have never known a more desirable woman." He grabbed her hand and pressed it to his groin. She wanted to scream. "This is what you do to me, Nadia." He stood, and she could see him protruding firmly against his trousers. He pulled her up, jerking her to her feet, and then before she could protest, he picked her up and strode to the bedroom. "I cannot wait a moment longer!"

She shook like the last leaf on a tree branch on a windy fall day. She hoped Horst would just take her physical reaction as a case of nerves, like a bride on her wedding night. Her fate was out of her hands, and the thought was paralyzing. It awoke the horrifying imagery of Auschwitz. Auschwitz, where helplessness was a debilitating disease that scarred and mutilated its victims. Auschwitz where living was a form of torture.

Horst gently laid her on the canopied bed. Surrounded by silk pillows and soft candlelight, the boudoir was designed for romantic trysts. He removed his jacket and knelt at the edge of the bed and slipped off her shoes. He kissed her feet, and she tried to hide her revulsion. Then he was beside her, his hands all over her, kissing her exposed cleavage. "Beautiful," he whispered. He raised his head and held her gaze. His eyes were dilated and heavy, and he shook his head as if to clear it.

Thank God, it's beginning to work.

"Nadia." His tongue was thick, and his words began to slur. He pulled her dress up, his fingers clumsily rubbing against her silk stockings. Fumbling, he unhooked them from her garter belt. "I need to feel you beneath me." His words had lolled out of him, barely understandable. His head bobbed backward and forward like a newborn infant without support. He groaned and lay on top of her, his hands gripping her face. He began to kiss her more deeply, his tongue seeking hers, sliding around her mouth as he rocked his pelvis against hers. Leah gasped, terrified that the drug wouldn't take effect in time. Then as if by magic, he collapsed on top of her with a grunt. His dead weight pressed her into the mattress.

Afraid to move lest he awaken, she waited. Staring at the ceiling, she could hear the seconds ticking off from the mantel clock. The weight of him was unbearable, but she knew she'd scream and die of fright if he woke, so she lay as still as a mouse waiting for her chance to escape. Snores greeted her ears, and Leah finally let out the breath she was holding. *I'm safe.*

She gently rocked him off of her and rolled him onto his side. She carefully slipped his clothing from him until he was naked. He mumbled something that sounded like her name and reached out to grab her, but then he fell back, his arms going slack. Holding her breath, Leah froze. When his snores began anew, she went quickly to work. She mussed the sheets and threw pillows here and there, finally pouring some champagne onto the sheets to dampen them.

Straightening her dress and hooking her stockings back to her garter belt, she went into the salon and opened the drawers of the Louis IV desk. She found a fountain pen and thick, creamy stationery with The Ritz emblazoned at the top. She retrieved her purse and removed a sheet of paper, sat down, and began to copy what she'd previously written back at her apartment. She'd carefully plotted her actions — no retribution and nothing to alienate Horst or arouse his animosity. The best thing would be for him to forget her.

Horst, my darling,

Forgive me, but I never thought I'd feel this way about any man ever again. Last night was enthralling. My body aches all over just thinking about what we shared. You are indeed a lover beyond compare. I thought my heart would burst with joy at the height of our union — like a glorious fireworks finale. I will treasure what we shared forever.

And now, I must ask for your forgiveness — for I cannot continue our affair. The thought of spending my life counting down the hours until your return, clinging to precious moments that will be far too few, is unbearable for me. The long days of waiting for you to return to Paris, and then creating a few dazzling memories would never be enough to sustain me. More important, the overwhelming sin of adultery and keeping you from your beloved son who deserves your attention is something I cannot live with. You have a family, a thriving enterprise, a future that you must guard and keep safe. I could not live with myself for putting your life and livelihood in jeopardy.

We were never anything other than shadows passing in the night. You saved me at Auschwitz, and for this, I'm eternally grateful, but the war is over now, and we must reclaim our lives. Despite the passion we share for each other, it is impossible for us to continue on this path.

I want a man to come home to me every day and not just a few days a month. To be a kept woman is not for a woman like me. I need to know that I am, first and foremost, the only woman in the life of the man I love. I want to marry and have children of my own, and despite your tenderness for me, that is something you cannot give me.

Please, if you care for me, let me go. I will never harm you. I care too much for you. What we have shared was une brève affaire, a beautiful memory for both of us to cherish. Find happiness in what you have.

Forever grateful,

Nadia

She licked the creamy white envelope, and tiptoeing into the bedroom, laid it on the pillow next to Horst. He slept so soundly, his soft snores ruffling the lock of hair that had fallen over his brow. *How can a monster look so innocent? Why Horst? Why could you not feel for others the way you felt for me? Why did you terrorize, torture, and kill thousands of Jews at Auschwitz and yet protect me so well? Where was your humanity for those that you destroyed? Was I simply a reflection of your own vanity? Or did you truly care? And if so, why only me? Why did you reserve what little humanity you had just for me?*

These were questions Leah didn't know the answer to, and perhaps never would.

She took a deep breath and decided she needed to let go of the hatred she'd harbored for him. She needed to relieve herself of that burden, or she could not, in truth, live her own life. Yes, it was true that she did yearn for a husband and children. But carrying such hatred inside would only infect any chance of happiness she had. And that was the difference. She would continue to seek justice, but she would do so without the hatred that had become a living, breathing thing in her soul. She had to, or she would be lost.

Nadia Sauvage has died tonight, but Leah Manheim is reborn.

Each name, each monster, would be found and brought to justice. "A fair exchange," she whispered to herself as she slipped her arms into her blue coat and quietly closed the door to the room.

I am free of you, Horst — forever.

CHAPTER 37

January 26, Present day
Rapperswil, Switzerland

Forever... *Forever... Forever...* The word reverberated in Rose's head as she was once more pulled into the light, hurtling back to the present. Seeing the fateful confrontation through Leah's eyes quashed her doubts and restored her belief. Leah had never sacrificed herself on the altar of Horst's desire. She'd beat him with cunning and courage. *Bubbie, forgive me for ever doubting the purity of your heart or the sincerity of your actions. Thank you for showing me the truth.*

Rose's heart filled with relief as a cocoon of calm surrounded her, and lilting music filled her ears.

"Rose?" A voice called to her through the mists of time in the tunnel of light. Miriam appeared an angel, beckoning Rose to join her. Beside her stood Leah, wearing what could only be described as a wedding gown, her smile like a bride uttering the words of consecration, "I do," eternal and continuous in its optimism. Rose reached out to these kindred souls as she burst through the radiant illumination into the warm embrace of her grandmother and Miriam's arms.

Who am I? Rose asked.

You are a daughter and sister of those who stand against evil. The eternal mother's hands gently landed on her head, anointing her with blessings.

But the burden is so overwhelming, how will I find my way? Rose wondered.

Your way is cleared of the detritus of cruel indifference, or the black tar of blind hatred. All who seek to maim, cripple, and strip the good from this world have no power over your life. Open your heart and love will empower your journey.

He's waiting.

A blinding flash of lightning turned the night from black to white. The past disappeared like a mole burrowing into its subterranean lair into darkness. Rose gasped, her lungs filling with precious air, her ephemeral form transitioned to the present like a winged phoenix reborn from a pyre of ashes.

Ethan was carrying her away from the burning clinic toward an SUV. A man she didn't know stood ready to help.

"Let's go!" said the stranger, hopping into the front seat.

Gently, Ethan placed her in the backseat, slid in beside her, and belted them both. He slammed the door, echoing the other man's command. "Let's roll." The tires of the Range Rover spun on the icy surface for a moment before gaining purchase. As the vehicle sped away, the driver gazed in the rearview mirror, studying her. The giant of a man who sat next to him turned his brows furrowed in puzzlement. On the other side of her, a third man regarded her with curiosity as well.

Ethan took her hand and held it in his. "You're okay, Rose. It's over. You're safe." He opened a bottle of water and handed it to her. "Drink. It'll help."

She hadn't realized how parched she was. She drank deeply, letting the water seep into the soil of her body. "What happened to Heinrich?"

"Dead. Burned in the clinic. The authorities will rule it an unfortunate gas explosion."

"But how?"

The men in the car shared a knowing look.

"Is anyone going to tell me what's going on?" She frowned at Ethan. "Who are these men?"

"They work with me."

Ethan's cryptic answers were filling her head with steam, and the vein in her temple throbbed. "Are they CIA or MI6? You lied to me. You let that monster kidnap me. You knew he was coming for me."

"Someone in the bank compromised you. This is all my fault. I'm so sorry you were kidnapped. I'm sorry I wasn't close enough to prevent it. I promise to tell you everything, but right now, we need to get you safely back to Zürich."

Rose reached in her pocket. "Where's the list, the book? Oh, God, Ethan, it didn't get lost, did it?"

The big man in the front passenger seat held up the small black book. "We got it, Rose. I hope you don't mind if I keep it. We have decoders who will figure out what Leah wrote, and our people will see that every name on this list is exposed and toppled from power. By the way, my name is Abe, and this is Daniel," he pointed to the driver. "Next to you is Noah, and we are delighted to meet you. You are one brave lady."

Rose felt the heat flush her face. It could have gone so wrong. Once again, the coat and brooch had saved her.

"We've got trouble ahead — incoming vehicles," Noah said,

checking his tablet. "Pull over on that side road ahead and kill the lights."

Daniel swerved off the road and shut off the engine. The other three men turned to watch the road behind them. A minute later, a line of police cars, fire engines, and ambulances with blaring sirens raced by, heading toward the clinic. They sat another minute, just in case there were any straggling emergency vehicles.

"All clear," said Noah. Daniel fired up the Rover and backed out, and they were on the road again.

Abe cleared his throat and glanced at her from the front seat. "I hope you don't mind my asking but are you a magician or something? How did you disappear into thin air when Heinrich was using you as a shield?"

"I-I don't know — the flash of lightning came at the right time, and I-I rolled away from him into a crevice in the snow."

The men glanced at each other, clearly not believing her story.

"God stepped in at the right place and time," Ethan said, his tone blunt.

The three other men nodded, accepting the explanation.

Rose squeezed Ethan's hand tight. "Yes, it was certainly a miracle."

The three men nodded solemnly.

Rose looked at each man and asked. "You all have accents except Ethan. You're all Israeli, aren't you?"

Daniel spoke up first. "Yes, Rose, we work for an Israeli organization, off-grid, if you will. Your grandmother, Leah, reached out to us a few months ago. She had compiled a list of possible members to a secret organization bent on the destruction of Israel and the Jewish people."

"When Leah first contacted Mossad, she had a difficult time getting anyone to listen to her," Ethan explained. "Unfortunately, the officer she spoke to thought she was just a silly old woman with crackpot ideas about conspiracies and cabals — "

"But Leah finally connected with someone who believed her — and that was Ethan and his organization," Noah cut in. "Ethan discovered that Leah had been instrumental in bringing many Nazis to trial, but her name was a secret — just another hero or heroine, forgotten to the dustbin of history."

Ethan cleared his throat. "Leah never identified or located Heinrich Brandt. She'd put together bank accounts and the funneling of money to politicians and hate groups, but she never figured out Horst Schumacher's actual whereabouts. Possibly she didn't want to for reasons we'll never understand. Without you, Rose, we would never have been able to access the safety deposit box. You were our only possible way of catching Brandt red-handed. I'm so sorry I couldn't tell you everything, but I truly believe that Leah would have wanted you to fulfill her life's work. You and I both know that. Forgive me for not confiding in you."

Rose pulled the matching red book out of her pocket. "Heinrich wanted nothing to do with the book his father gave to my grandmother. He called it ancient history — he was clearly ashamed of it. But this is the list Leah used to bring murderers to justice. My grandmother was a hero."

"She certainly was," Ethan said softly. "And so are you, Rose."

Rose pulled her hand from Ethan's grasp and shook her head. "I don't think I could ever do what my grandmother did, but I'm glad I could retrieve this evidence."

"Don't be too hard on Ethan," Abe said with a grin. "He was under strict orders from the top."

Rose looked at Ethan. Anxiety laced his eyes. She knew the kidnapping wasn't his fault, but it hurt like hell that he hadn't told her the truth. Yes, he told her he was ex-CIA, but despite her teasing comments to him about being a spy, she had no idea he actually was one. She would need to have a talk with Ethan but now was not the time. She glanced at her watch, it was after midnight. She swallowed the lump in her throat. *January 27. Holocaust Remembrance Day.* She bit her lip to keep it from trembling. *Please don't let me start crying. I need to be strong—like her.*

"Are you okay?" Ethan whispered in her ear.

Rose leaned her head back and closed her eyes.

Ethan lived in a world she knew nothing about. He was working with a secret organization, and God knows who else. His work, no doubt, kept him away for months at a time. How could they build a relationship when she didn't know when or if she'd ever see him again? Could she trust him to be honest with her?

Everything had changed, but everything was still the same. It all felt inevitable. She would go back to her job in Manhattan, back to her life in Brooklyn, back to the house her grandmother left her. Back to being alone.

CHAPTER 38

April 6, Present day
Brooklyn, New York

Rose opened the door of her old brownstone and bent to retrieve the New York Times from her doorstep. Wearing her robe and slippers, she shuffled into the kitchen and poured herself a cup of coffee. Spring had finally sprung, and the long dreary winter months were behind her. Sunshine filtered through the lace curtains in the kitchen.

She opened the paper and stared at the bold, black headline that blazed across the top of the front page: U.S. Congress Hit by Resignations in Wake of Anti-Semitic Conspiracy

For the past few weeks, the news media had been following stories of the demise of Heinrich Brandt's secret cabal. Ethan had been right. Heads were rolling around the world — top government leaders and officials, business scions, academics, even a few media giants — were being exposed and forced out of power.

Rose had returned to Brooklyn and her job at the David Berg

Rare Book Room. Her adventure had ended as quickly as it had begun. The Blue Coat hung in her closet, and the Ark of the Covenant brooch was stored in its velvet pouch in her nightstand. Rose was relieved that Heinrich was dead, and his cabal had been toppled, but her heart was broken.

As she predicted, Ethan disappeared after they returned to the U.S. That talk she hoped to have with him never happened. Just one text — stating he would get in touch once he'd wrapped up the details of his mission. But weeks had turned into months, and Rose had stopped deluding herself. Ethan was out of her life. Whatever they'd shared was no doubt a result of the intensity of their mutual goal and being in close quarters. The proverb "absence makes the heart grow fonder," in Ethan's case, had not proven to be true. For Rose, the story had played out differently. Her pain had only sharpened. She'd been slow to realize that with their enemies brought down, their story was over. If they'd been lovers, it would have been so much worse. At least that was what Rose kept telling herself.

Rose meandered to the coffee machine and placed her cup under the spout, re-tying her hair into a loose topknot while she waited for the cup to fill. Her thoughts returned to the letter she'd found. After Rose had crashed in exhaustion for a few days, she'd begun to sift through her grandmother's correspondence once again, coming across a letter in her grandmother's elegant script in an unaddressed envelope.

When she finally got around to reading the rest of her grandmother's letters, her tears had spilled in a relentless torrent, soaking the pages. She'd come across a letter to Aidan that Leah had never mailed, and reading it was heart-wrenching. It reminded Rose that she, too, may have lost her only chance for love. She wiped the tears from her eyes.

I really need to stop blubbering like a baby every time I think about him.

It was Saturday, and she was home as usual. Her days off from work were the hardest to endure. Even her mother had taken to feeling sorry for her. At last Sunday's dinner, her mother had asked about Ethan, and Rose had given her some excuse about his work. At least Edith had shown enough decency not to rub salt into her wounds by not uttering the four words no one ever wants to hear: "I told you so."

The doorbell rang, surprising Rose out of her reverie. She glanced at the kitchen clock and noted it was just a few minutes after eight. She got up and padded to the door, unable to recall making any online orders recently. Perhaps her parents had decided to pop by?

"Shit!"

"And good morning to you, too."

Rose's jaw dropped. She couldn't believe that Ethan was standing on her doorstep, let alone looking like a GQ model dressed in pressed khakis and a button-down navy shirt. Her hand went up to her topknot, and she pulled her robe's sash tighter, wishing she hadn't worn her "Mr. Darcy Is My Boyfriend," t-shirt. *Get ahold of yourself!* "Um, c-come on in." She pulled the door open wider, stepping behind it. "There's coffee in the kitchen. I'll be right back." She turned and skedaddled up the stairs.

Shit! She said again, this time in her head as she threw off her clothes and dashed into the shower. Twenty minutes later, she'd slipped on a pair of black leggings topped off with a white silk tunic. She'd brushed out her hair, put on her favorite silver hoop earrings and slipped her feet into a pair of soft leather mules. Scrambling for the stairs, she stopped herself, ran back into her bedroom, and spritzed Chanel No. 5 behind her ears. *Okay, now I'm ready.* She took a deep breath and let it out slowly, allowing herself one final glimpse in the mirror. *Bubbie, I don't know why he's here, but I'll try to keep an open mind.*

She found Ethan in the library reading, a cup of coffee on the side table next to him. He looked up as she stepped into the room, set the book down, and smiled. "You clean up good, Rose."

She swallowed hard, her hand going to her head, remembering she'd tamed her hair into some semblance of control. Seeing Ethan again brought all of her feelings back in a big swoop. It felt as though they'd seen each other just yesterday, all the weeks seeming to slip away. His casual ability to slip in and out of her life unbalanced her. "Leah always said, proper attire is a powerful weapon," she quipped, proud that her voice wasn't wobbly. "'If you don't know how to do something, dress like you do, and you'll do better out there.' It's time I incorporated all of her wisdom into my life." She took a seat opposite his and crossed her legs, lifting her chin in an imperial manner, determined not to let her nerves overwhelm her. "What are you doing here, Ethan?"

"I was in town, and I thought — scratch that." He shook his head. "Truth is, I've missed you, Rose."

"That's a shame." She cast her eyes on the wall of books before her, anything not to look into those steely blue eyes that seemed to see right through her. "I've been so busy since I got back, I hadn't realized how much time passed since we last saw each other." *Liar.*

"Wow! I know I deserve that, but it still cuts deep." He scrubbed his hands over his face. "Look, I'm not good at the sorry thing, but I am...uh...sorry, that is."

She looked at him, keeping her hand on the throttle of her emotions. "How is it you're even managing to screw up an apology? What is wrong with you?"

His face flushed red. "I am sorry. Truly sorry. I've brought you a peace offering. I was away and investigating something for you, and I found it."

"Me? Now you're using 'something for me' as an excuse for the phone calls you never made, the texts you never sent, or the emails you never wrote? You really have some nerve, Ethan Blackwood." It was all so overwhelming, having him just show up out of the blue. He looked so...so damn good, while she'd spent the last months an emotional wreck. She couldn't contain it, and the dam burst, tears pouring down her cheeks. She jumped out of the chair, ran from the room up the stairs to her bedroom, slammed the door, and threw herself onto her bed weeping. *Damn him, damn him, damn him.*

ETHAN SCRATCHED HIS HEAD. HE WAS IN A POSITION HE WASN'T USED to being in. He didn't know what to do. He foolishly thought that when he showed up, Rose would greet him with open arms like a returning hero and forgive him.

Smooth move, Sherlock.

Damn! She was right. He'd been a complete asshole. Using his "mission" as an excuse, telling himself he wanted to surprise her. But the truth was, he'd been scared shitless. Would she understand and forgive him if he admitted that visions of being dumped by Christie still haunted him? Relationships were difficult for him and the more he procrastinated, the easier it got to make excuses. Maybe she was better off without him.

His feelings for her were confusing. Trusting someone with his heart again was hard.

She's not Christie, you idiot. Stupid! Stupid! Stupid!

Still, if she thought for one minute that he would walk away, she was wrong. Ethan Blackwood never walked away, despite how things appeared. He marched up the stairs, determined to make things right with Rose. He'd mistreated her and, dammit, he missed her, needed her, and had spent too many sleepless nights thinking about her.

He pushed open the door to her bedroom, his heart clenching when he saw Rose curled up on the bed. His ex-girlfriend Christie had never shed any tears for him, but seeing Rose's slender frame shake with sobs gutted him. Rose was different, and a tiny glimmer of hope sparked in him — maybe her reaction was because her feelings for him were as deep as his for her.

He sat on the edge of the bed and gently ran his hand over her back. When she didn't slap his hand away, he kicked off his shoes and lay beside her, curling up against her back, molding himself to her body. Her shaking seemed a bit less now, and her sniffles were few and far between. He continued to hold her, even though what he wanted more than anything was to kiss her.

Sweeping aside her thick red waves of hair, he whispered into her nape. "I'm sorry, Rose. Please forgive me. I've been a selfish fool. I know I've made a mess of things, but..." *Say it, say what you're feeling.* "I'm in love with you. There I've said it, and you can't imagine how good it feels to admit it." She didn't answer, but her body stilled. Ethan counted the seconds, hoping she'd say she loved him too, scared that she wouldn't.

"Will you hold me for a bit? Just like this," she whispered.

"The way I feel about you, I could hold you for an eternity."

She sighed and relaxed, and except for an occasional quiver, neither of them moved.

He snuggled closer.

I think I finally did something right. "Rose?"

"Hmm?"

"You haven't told me what you're feeling."

"Ethan Blackwood," she whispered, "am I detecting a touch of insecurity?"

"Maybe...uh...yes."

She turned over and cupped his face. "Tell me again that you love me."

Desire and warmth engulfed him with confidence. He slipped his arms around her, pulling her flush against him. "I could go on for hours about why I love you, Rose Levi, but you know I'm a man of few words, and a lot of them are clichés." He brushed his lips against hers. "I love you, Rose, and if you'll have me, forever seems like the perfect length of time for me to prove it to you."

The dimple in Rose's left cheek deepened with her smile. "Ethan Blackwood, I think you finally got it right. I love you too."

EPILOGUE

April 16, Present day
Grantchester, England

R ose wore the blue coat with the Ark of the Covenant brooch pinned to her lapel. On her lap, she clutched her purse, which held Leah's letter, the letter Leah had never sent.

For the umpteenth time during their drive up to Grantchester from London, Ethan reached for Rose's hand and gave it an encouraging squeeze. "You okay?"

Rose glanced at Ethan and nodded with a smile. Not only had Ethan found Aidan, but he'd arranged for them to meet. Besides his admission of loving her, which had changed her life forever, Ethan had told her everything about his past and his work. She told him about her past too — which was about as exciting as the pneumatic page-turner at the library. Good thing Ethan was into books.

The anticipation of their meeting with Aidan had her emotions strung taut as a tightrope on which she balanced precariously. Ethan had phoned Aidan's daughter Tess with a request to visit her father, and as unbelievable as it seemed, she and Ethan were on their way to meet the man Leah had loved all the days of her life. Tess had warned Ethan that her father's memory wasn't good. But what did that matter? He'd lost his memory of Leah long ago. Before Aidan passed from this life, she wanted to deliver Leah's letter to him. She had to do this for Leah, and for Aidan, and for the memory of the love they'd shared.

"Don't worry, I'm just nervous," Rose said. "I want so much for him to remember Leah."

"You can only do so much. Leah's gone, and Aidan is a very old man. Whatever they shared is alive in you, my love."

God, will I ever grow tired of him saying "my love?" Never, never, never.

Ethan tuned in a radio station, and by coincidence, Pink Floyd's song-poem "Grantchester Meadows" came on the air. The sound of birds chirping led her mind to drift over everything that had happened in the last month. Ethan had shown up at her door, and she'd let him in, not only into her house but into her heart. In those first few days, they shut out the world, not answering phones, texts, messages, or the door. Nothing was allowed to interrupt their magical period of discovering love. And discover they did, making love in every room of the old Brooklyn brownstone. She suppressed a giggle. The library, naturally — being Ethan's favorite room — had figured prominently in their love trysts.

Every minute of every day was spent gloriously in each other's arms. Rose had never been so happy in all her life. Leah had been right. When Rose finally opened her heart, she'd found the one man to complete her. Rose had the sneaky suspicion that Leah had chosen Ethan for her and that neither she nor Ethan had much to say about the matter. It was all a fait accompli on the day they met, which was just fine with Rose. She'd never tell this to

Ethan, of course, he wouldn't enjoy the thought of being manipulated. Some secrets were best kept to oneself.

They took the scenic drive up from London, passing through Essex and some of the greenest countryside on Earth. They stumbled on a field of saffron crocus growing near Saffron Walden, a village in the Uttlesford district of Essex. Ethan was driven to near frenzy by the possibility of purchasing English saffron, which in Tudor times had been considered the finest in the world. Ethan took the turnoff and detoured into Saffron Walden to buy some ridiculously expensive vials of the spice from a specialty food shop. His passion for cooking was a running joke between them. But Rose had no complaints about that quirk since Ethan had done most of the cooking during their impromptu week together.

"You're going to thank me for stopping here when we get home."

Home. Such a beautiful word, especially coming from Ethan. The Brooklyn brownstone had always been Bubbie's house, a special place where Rose had collected lovely memories over the years. Even after Rose moved in and discovered her grandmother's secrets, it still hadn't sunk in that the house was hers. But now, it was starting to feel like their home together. "And why would I be thanking you?" She chuckled at the cheeky grin on his face.

"Because I am going to make us a paella you will never forget, and you're going to bless your man with kisses all over his body in thanks."

"I don't think you had to spend a small fortune to get me to do that."

His eyes widened. "Don't get me all flustered and aroused, Rose. I'm driving."

"You're the one who mentioned bodily kisses everywhere."

"That I did, m'darlin'." Ethan slipped effortlessly into an

English accent and threw an exaggerated wink her way. "And, a jolly good thought, indeed."

Before Rose knew it, they were driving down a long, gravel, box-hedged driveway to a farmhouse surrounded by venerable old trees and sweeping emerald-green pastures where Red Poll cattle grazed in contentment. Tess cared for her father in the English Tudor farmhouse where he'd been raised.

Aidan's daughter was silver-haired and seventyish, dressed in a mid-length gray skirt and twin-sweater set — very English and very proper. She was warm, yet reserved in her greeting, the way the English tended to be. Leading them into the house, she bubbled on about the chilly and rainy spring they were experiencing.

"I do hope the weather isn't too dreary for you during your visit," said Tess, sticking her hands in the pockets of her sweater.

Rose took in the house, imagining how different things could have been. Aidan and Leah might have lived out their lives here. "Your home is lovely."

The house of stone, wood, and plaster, though weathered outside, was modernized within. Smooth plank flooring and sleek modern lighting contrasted with the well-worn, well-loved, and well-cared-for furnishings. In the corner stood an elegant antique grandfather clock whose pendulums swayed and whose tick-tock echoed around the great room. Tess looked around, smiling. "This house has been in the family for generations. I hope it will be for many more." She took Leah's hand and squeezed it. "My father is in the garden. He's always a bit more responsive when he's outside. I was just going to put the kettle on. Would you like some tea?"

"That would be lovely," said Rose.

"Why don't you go join Dad and introduce yourselves. I can't promise you he'll remember your grandmother, but one never knows, he drifts about in time so much."

"We'll be very gentle with him, Tess," said Ethan.

She smiled. "Honestly, I think the stimulation will be good for him. He doesn't receive many visitors — just family gatherings when the grandchildren and great-grandchildren try to make it down from the city. Most days, we have a full-time nurse here with him, but she's off on Sundays, and I spend the day here. My father's probably forgotten more than I'll ever know, but he does surprise us now and again."

"It doesn't matter, we're just happy to meet him," said Rose.

"Go on now, I'll join you in a few minutes." Tess opened the heavy slider, and Rose and Ethan stepped out into the garden. Pink roses lined the path, and the bees buzzing and birds chirping joined with the distant ripple of a river flowing over rocks. Beyond the garden, a lawn sloped down to a stand of trees. In a wheelchair sat a white-haired man wearing a blue sweater with a red and black plaid blanket over his lap. He stared ahead, but there was no way of knowing what he saw.

Rose knelt before him and took his hand. "Aidan, my name is Rose Levi, and I'm Leah Manheim's granddaughter."

Aidan didn't look at her, and he didn't answer — she might as well have been invisible. But nothing was going to dissuade Rose. She'd come a long way to see him, and regardless of his response, she was determined to try and reach him through his fog of lost memory. Tess joined them with a tray in hand and set it on a picnic table that sat beneath an umbrella.

"May I roll him over to the table for you?" asked Ethan.

"I'd be pleased if you did," answered Tess. Rose stood, and Ethan pushed the wheelchair so that Aidan's legs slipped beneath the table. "Did he say anything yet?" Tess asked as she poured the tea and sliced a cake that smelled of vanilla and lemon.

"No, not a word."

"Well, don't lose heart. You stay a bit and visit and keep up both ends of the conversation. I believe he hears more than he lets on. A bit of the devil he has in him. I'll be in the kitchen if you need me. It's probably better if I'm not here. It might give Dad a bit of a start and wake him up. Be patient, there's still some of the old fire burning in him somewhere."

With Tess gone, Rose opened her bag and pulled out Leah's letter. Aidan lifted his cup of tea to his lips, and his hands shook, but he concentrated on not spilling a drop and smiled as if pleased with himself when he didn't. However, he seemed utterly unaware of Rose and Ethan.

Rose unfolded the letter. "Aidan, I found this letter addressed to you among my grandmother's correspondence. She never mailed it, but I know she meant you to have it. You and *grand-mère* met a long time ago during the war. I believe it will mean a lot to you." Rose took a deep breath and began.

"My darling, Aidan,

How do I begin to tell you the story of us?

If the young man I fell in love with was sitting before me now, he'd say, "Get on with it, Leah, for Christ's sake. Time waits for no one." And that I must do because I know that deep inside of you, though you may not be aware of it, lives a memory of a young couple who once upon a time not only found comfort in each other's arms, but found the courage to fight on when war tore them apart. The love they shared for each other could never be tarnished by war. They were soulmates and nothing would ever change that simple truth. That was you, Aidan, and me.

My God, we were so young and brave and grasped what little time we had together in both hands. We loved unconditionally, with complete abandon and passion in that cold and dreary one-room flat — our only witness the darkened silhouette of the Eiffel Tower. We were two hearts that stumbled onto love amidst the chaos and uncertainty of war. We had no guarantees of tomorrow, just a few precious moments to be trea-

sured for whatever time allowed. Vows, promises, and pledges were made, but neither you nor I could have envisioned what would come to pass.

You forgot me, and I never tried to make you remember. We married other people, had children, and made separate lives for ourselves. But even with all of the good in my life, I never forgot you, nor will I ever. Your memory filled the empty space in my heart and refused to budge. The years have come and gone, but that love still burns like an eternal flame, forever young. You may not remember, but I keep the flame alive for both of us. Because I know how much you loved me, there is no regret. I shan't forget the hours we read to one another, the hours you held me in your arms, our scents mingling, and the taste of you on my lips. No one can ever take that away from me.

I write this letter only to remind you of how dearly you've been loved in this life, whether you know it or not. You might recall someday my saying to you that I would never regret our brève affaire and I wouldn't change it for the world. I told you after we'd made love that first time that I felt as if I'd lived a lifetime in those few weeks and that I would treasure this time we shared forever. I will never forget your answer, your kisses, and your proposal of marriage. Yes, Aidan, though, you may never remember — you loved me with every ounce of strength in your body and entrusted your heart to me forever.

Mon amour, I wish you every joy. I wish — no, I hope one day we'll be reunited, if not in this life, then in whatever comes next. Remember, darling, my last words to you and yours to me, "Live, my darling. Live for both of us."

Until we meet again,

Je t'aime,

Leah

Rose carefully smoothed the delicate pages on the table. She turned to Aidan and found his watery blue eyes fixed on her. Tears slipped down his cheeks. She clasped his hand in hers. "You remember, Aidan, don't you?"

"Yes. Thank you." He smiled and closed his eyes, whispering, "Leah. Leah, I'm coming." Then his head nodded forward, and he seemed to fall asleep. Rose didn't know what to say. She waited, hoping he'd open his eyes, but instead, she felt his grip lessen with every second until his hand went limp in hers. "Aidan?"

Ethan, who was standing a few feet away to give Rose and Aidan privacy, turned, reacting to the panic in her voice.

"Ethan, something's wrong. Call Tess." Rose pressed her hand to Aidan's cheek. "Aidan?" she repeated. Ethan ran toward the house, calling for Tess. Rose's eyes filled with tears. She knew he was gone, but she also knew he'd passed peacefully with a smile on his lips. But, most important, Aidan had remembered.

The scene turned chaotic with Tess crying and calling to her father, who, with a smile on his face, was no more. Ethan took charge, but nothing about the present felt real to Rose. The din of their voices faded away, and she stepped back as the paramedics arrived and went to work. She was barely aware of Ethan, who held a weeping Tess in his arms.

A movement from the corner of her eye caught Rose's attention and she turned. A mist had come up from the river, and out of that mist emerged a young woman wearing a blue coat. Her hair, a vibrant red, flowed down past her shoulders. She stood still as if she were waiting for someone.

"Leah," Rose gasped, her hand covering her mouth as a ghostly Aidan stood up from his wheelchair. He looked at Rose, and she was struck by his youthful beauty. He was exactly as she'd remembered him in the forest of France — tall and dashing — a courageous man who saw the future and embraced it. A man who loved with every fiber of his being. With a wink and a salute to Rose, he turned toward the young woman in the blue coat.

Tears streamed down Rose's cheeks as she watched the young couple that neither time nor death could keep apart. Both running now, they fell into each other's arms, their lips meeting in a deep kiss. Their kiss ended but not their embrace. They gazed at one another, and Leah raised her hand to Aidan's cheek. Rose knew what she said to him. She felt it right down to her soul. Aidan wrapped his arm around Leah's shoulder, and they turned toward Rose. Leah pressed her hand to her lips and blew Rose a kiss. Then with her head on his shoulder, Leah and Aidan strolled into the mists of eternity.

Rose stood there, her eyes looking beyond the mists.

"Are you okay, love?" Ethan asked, slipping an arm around her waist.

She leaned her head on his shoulder. "Better than okay. Everything is as it should be."

The End

Dear Reader:
I hope you enjoyed *The Blue Coat Saga*.
If you would like to leave a review,
please visit your favorite book site.
Or you can *scan the following QR Code.*

Keep reading for a FREE PREVIEW of *Mona Lisa's Daughter* — a compelling, riveting dual-timeline historical novel intertwining the mystery of Leonardo da Vinci and the Mona Lisa in Renaissance Florence with the story of a courageous nun risking everything in World War II Florence.

A Heart-wrenching World War II Novel

Mona Lisa's
DAUGHTER

From the bestselling author of
THE GIRL WHO KNEW DA VINCI
& THE LAST DAUGHTER

BELLE AMI

FREE PREVIEW

MONA LISA'S DAUGHTER

*NOVEMBER 15, 1925 ~ SANTA MARIA DEL CARMINE ~
FLORENCE, ITALY*

Valentina Amato saw only blackness. She shivered, huddling
deeper into the folds of the damp blanket. She couldn't tell
whether the frigid temperature or her fear of the unknown caused
her to tremble. Rain battered the tarp she sheltered under, and she
worried the heavy winds would carry it away. She prayed for the
old farmer who drove the cart and the old donkey who pulled it.
She tried not to think of their destination or why she was forced to
leave her home in Fiesole. In her short life of only fifteen years,
Valentina could not imagine why she deserved this fate.

"Hai portato vergogna alla famiglia! Dio mio, che maledizione!" Her
mother's screams had shaken the walls of their house. "You have
brought shame on our family! Dear God, what a curse!"

Her mother, Giulia, had repeated the words over and over as
she tore at her hair and rocked back and forth in her chair. Giulia
never held anything back when it came to her temper. Her

outbursts were legendary. Valentina often wondered if her mother believed she stood on a grand stage with an audience watching her perform.

For Valentina's crime, Giulia had declared banishment was the only recourse—both for her and her bastard unborn child.

"Mamma, please," Valentina had begged. "Let me stay. I promise to hide in my bedroom until the baby is born. No one will know. I promise not to tell a soul."

But Giulia would not be dissuaded. Valentina was to blame for the tragedy that had fallen upon their heads and must pay the consequences.

The pelting rain and icy wind certainly felt as if God agreed with her mother's punishment. Valentina wiped her tears with the back of her hand as she contemplated why her mother hated her. Giulia's anger seemed to have simmered for years, just beneath the surface, like a dormant volcano. Valentina's pregnancy had caused the volcano to erupt, giving her mother license to proclaim what an ungrateful, wretched girl she had for a daughter.

The more Valentina had pleaded and wept, the angrier Giulia had become until the words between them became a flood of rebukes and vituperations that neither mother nor daughter would ever forget.

Hateful words, once spoken, can never be forgotten. It was a lesson Valentina would always remember.

The cart came to a stop, and Valentina's heart wrenched. Tommaso pulled back the tarp to help her descend. In an instant, the rain soaked her. At least the nuns would think her face was wet from the downpour and not from tears.

"*Madre di Dio,* what a storm," Tommaso said, the rain spilling over the brim of his hat. "Come, girl, make haste. I must find shelter for the donkey and myself on this wretched night."

He held her by the arm, escorting her to the massive double

doors of the convent. He pressed a button, and a bell echoed on the other side of the thick, heavy wood. Valentina's legs shook, and she pulled the wet blanket tightly around her with one hand and clutched her small suitcase with the other. Finally, the door groaned open, and a nun appeared, holding an umbrella.

"Don't just stand there, girl, come in. Come in. We've been expecting you." A flash of lightning lit the sky, illuminating the nun's face. Valentina's gaze skittered away at the condemnation she read in the sister's eyes. Her gut twisted in despair. *Am I to be judged guilty without the benefit of a trial, even here under God's own roof?*

Tommaso lifted his hat respectfully. "Where might my donkey and I find shelter?" he shouted above the thrashing rain.

"The caretaker's cottage is behind the church. Giuseppe will put you and your donkey up for the night."

"Grazie, grazie."

The nun shut the heavy door, sliding the bolt in place. She hurried through the cloister, her black habit billowing in her wake. Valentina scampered behind, trying to keep up. She caught a shadowy glimpse of frescoes on the walls while the sweet scent of grass and freshly tilled earth hinted at the presence of a nearby garden.

The nun broke the silence by introducing herself as Suor Emilia. "Get a good night's sleep. Tomorrow, you will learn your duties."

"Duties?"

"Yes. Everyone here works, and so will you." Suor Emilia glanced back at her. "Of course, we will take into consideration your condition." She shook her head, her gaze dropping to the barely visible bump of pregnancy. "Why you girls don't realize that your silly fancies will lead to ruin is beyond me."

Valentina said nothing. She would not give this black crow the satisfaction of a reply. She may have been ruined, but not by her own silly fancies.

APRIL 1, 1503 ~ FLORENCE, ITALY

Gentile Signora Giocondo,

> *The first time I saw you, time stood still. Do you remember that day? If only I had wings, I would have followed you home. Your beauty had arrested my senses, nearly stealing my voice...*

The Mercato Vecchio teemed with Florentines who walked about smelling and sampling the vast array of fruits, vegetables, olives, cured meats, and cheeses on display. Every few feet, a vendor called out, hawking his wares.

"*Fichi* with pulp as sweet as sugar!"

"*Pesce fresco!*"

"*Polli* for sale!"

"*Formaggi* fit for a king!"

Their voices raised in a cacophony, each trying to outdo the other, competing to grab the attention of prospective buyers. Many of the vendors called out to Leonardo by name, having known him since he was a boy. His father, Ser Piero, had brought him to Florence at the age of twelve and apprenticed him to Master Verrocchio's workshop when he was fourteen. Leonardo's genius drew recognition early on, surpassing his master, and he reveled in his status as Florence's favorite son.

But not all boys are created equal in temperament. Leonardo, as a youth, was nothing like his companion Salai. The beautiful boy with curly hair and hazel eyes who'd arrived at Leonardo's household when he was ten had grown into a fetching albeit vexing young man. Leonardo couldn't help shaking his head as he recalled Salai's impish behavior from that morning.

The young man had strolled into Leonardo's private rooms with a sly grin. "Shall I go to the mercato, Maestro? We are running low on food." In addition to serving as his assistant, Salai took on duties that would otherwise cost Leonardo precious time away from his work.

For fourteen years, they had been inseparable. A devoted attendant and student in his household, Leonardo had used Salai, now twenty-four years old, as the model for his Vitruvian drawing of a man encircled by a square—well, not quite. In his quest to draw a masculine figure that would symbolize a blend of art, science, and perfect proportion, Leonardo combined Salai's splendid physique with his own in one unique sketch. The drawing was based on first-century Roman architect Vitruvius' treatise *De Architectura* and his principle that architecture must reflect man and nature in its harmonious proportions.

"Maestro, I am here only to serve," Salai had said as he leaned down to give Leonardo a playful tug on his beard while his other hand had slipped into Leonardo's pocket as stealthily as a seasoned pick-purse.

"Yet you often serve yourself first," Leonardo had countered, slapping Salai's hand and gently cuffing him on the head. "I will go myself and find the most perfect eggplant for our meal."

"*Ahi!* You wound me, Maestro," Salai had huffed, his hand going to his chest in a show of pretended innocence. "Besides, I was hoping for a juicy roast."

"No one I know has a taste for meat as you do," Leonardo had said in irritation.

Salai had erupted into a ripple of giggles, and Leonardo couldn't help smiling at his unintended double *entendre*. But the truth was, the young man was as defiant as a toddler when it came to eating any vegetable or legume. And yet, Leonardo found it impossible to deny Salai much of anything. His friend's real name was Gian Giacomo Caprotti, but Leonardo had nicknamed him Salai—*little devil*. The moniker had fit like a pair of new silk tights, as the hellion loved to stir up trouble and reveled in the nasty habit of stealing.

"You will turn my hair white before its time," Leonardo had warned with a shake of his head.

"And yet, what a splendid mane it would be, Maestro," Salai had quipped. Kissing Leonardo's forehead, he spun and danced out the door.

Leonardo expelled a deep breath as he strolled by the meat seller stalls, knowing his precocious friend would pout for a fortnight if he did not buy him the *spiedini di carne*. He would give in, as always, but only after purchasing his own dinner. He stopped at a vegetable stand and picked up a dark purple *melanzana*. The skin of the voluminous gourd-shaped fruit was as smooth and shiny as a newly minted florin. He held it to his nose, inhaling its ripe scent. Giving it a gentle squeeze, he tested it for firmness. "*Squisito, amico mio*—such vivid color. As beautiful a specimen as I have ever seen," he proclaimed.

The vendor took a bow. "Perhaps you will paint this perfect eggplant, Maestro."

Leonardo chuckled. "It will be painted in *olio d'oliva* and fried to perfection for my dinner." He patted his stomach. "A glorious end for a glorious creation." Paying the merchant, Leonardo tipped his hat and slipped the melanzana into the cloth sack with his other purchases.

His mood had much improved, a welcome relief, as his

thoughts often shifted like the moving parts of the machines he designed. Leonardo's endless curiosity supplied the replenishing fount from which his innovations took shape. But such boundless inquisitiveness exacted a price—principally the continual strife between creativity and completion. The excitement of a nascent idea called to him like a siren's song, luring him away from one project to embark on another, stealing from him what he desired most—time.

He continued his stroll, his senses attuned to the sights, smells, and sounds floating around him. A distant chorale of angels tickled his ears. The Santa Maria del Fiore Cathedral bells rang for the Angelus at noon. Despite the tension between his religious convictions and his feelings about the Church, hearing the familiar bells further buoyed his disposition. He hoped his decision to return to Florence after seventeen years under the patronage of Duke Ludovico Sforza would prove a wise one for both his financial and artistic standing.

Rounding a corner, Leonardo came face-to-face with a winged orchestra of caged birds. The percussive honking of geese and quacking ducks underscored the symphonic squawking of quail, partridge, pigeons, and doves. Lending a dramatic crescendo to the performance was the robust flapping of wings of hawks and falcons, as though the large predators lamented their frustration at being so close to plump prey and yet hindered from hunting it.

At that precise moment, he saw her through the cloud of floating feathers. A young woman stood as still as a statue, watching a pair of turtledoves cuddling like lovers. The young woman watched the birds, her gaze enthralled. The feathery lovers cooed and fluttered, fluttered and cooed. Their wings, the color of roasted cinnamon bark, touched and glided in a delicate dance. A few feet away stood her maid, holding a basket. The servant shifted her feet and leaned the basket against her hip. She heaved a sigh, clearly chafing at her mistress's delay.

Leonardo bit back a smile and resumed his study of the lady. She wore the latest fashion from Spain, a forest green gown of silk. He observed the swelling of her bosom pressed against her bodice and the fecund fullness of her face and surmised she had recently given birth. With his painter's eye, he subconsciously calculated the miracle of muscle, skin, and bone that resulted in such an unusual face. A delicate auburn wave of hair fell across her high forehead. Leonardo followed the course of the curl that meandered like a river through pristine countryside. Her bold, high cheekbones lifted her eyes into an intriguing slant, forming a shadowed surround that, had he not known better, would suggest she'd applied ancient kohl to enhance them. His gaze traveled to her mouth, and he lost his breath. While not overly full, her lips curved up in a gentle arc. Gentle and yet sensual at the same time. *A smile that is not quite a smile.*

"I feel such profound sorrow when I see winged creatures so confined," she said in a mellifluous voice. "To be deprived of flight, once having tasted it, seems cruel beyond reason."

He hadn't expected her to speak, and even less did he expect her words to match his sentiments.

Her eyes met his, their burnished beauty pensive.

Struggling to put thoughts into sentences, he answered, "Animals, like us, reflect the perfection of nature. And yet, they survive only at the whim of men. It is an affront to imprison any creature. But I will further suggest that killing and eating them is an even greater tragedy. It is for that reason I consume neither meat nor fowl nor fish of any kind—" He stopped himself and mused that for a man who had trouble conjuring clever words to say to this young woman, he'd managed to provide a loquacious revelation and a heart-held truth about himself.

Her fine, dark brows rose. "How curious you should say this, for I, too, have lost my ability to consume animal flesh." Her lips turned up in that shadow of a smile. "Unfortunately, my husband —indeed my entire household—is not convinced that a diet composed of pasta, beans, vegetables, and fruit could be sufficient to placate one's hunger."

Leonardo laughed. "Alas, my own household would concur. I have come to learn that one cannot force a belief or a way of life on another."

"I could not agree more. Better to keep one's counsel if one wishes to preserve a happy home." Her eyes dropped to his hands, covered in red dust. "You are an artist."

Looking down at his hands, he grinned. "It seems I have betrayed myself." He hadn't realized he'd plucked a piece of chalk from his pocket and had been fidgeting with it. "Among other things, I paint." He patted the sketchbook that hung at his waist, generating a cloud of chalky dust. "Forgive me." He rubbed his hands together, brushing it away.

"You do not use a stylus and ink?"

"I find the chalk more conducive to capturing a moment, especially when away from my desk. I can model the features more accurately with chalk, something impossible with ink. It allows me to create greater dimensionality to the face in the fullness of the moment. I call the process *sfumato*—to evaporate like smoke." His hands circled expressively, causing more puffs of red dust to float around him.

She watched the floating swirls and then met his gaze. They both burst into laughter.

The birdseller interrupted their shared mirth, his broad girth suggesting that a good amount of meat formed the foundation of his diet. "Maestro, may I ask your patience while I see to the lady's request?" At Leonardo's nod, the vendor turned to the young woman with a deferential smile. "Signora, how may I be of service?"

Leonardo took the opportunity to study the olive-skinned beauty more closely. She carried herself as regally as a queen, yet she possessed an intriguing spirit that captured his inquisitive nature. He found himself drawn to her pleasing manner and the way her midnight eyes focused intently on the vendor as she coaxed him into giving her the best price. Her high forehead spoke of intelligence, while the gentle slope of her aquiline nose gave her profile an elegant silhouette. But it was the pertness of her rounded chin and the teasing curve of her rosebud mouth that captured his artist's eye. He was mesmerized by how her lips almost, but not quite, committed to a smile. What thoughts lay behind her curious expression?

Leonardo had an overwhelming desire to sketch her—quite surprising since portraiture was his least favorite medium. He pondered if he should ask her to pose for him. Would she think him impertinent? He quickly dismissed the notion as inappropriate, given her obvious standing as a lady of quality.

Even so, he'd rarely met a woman who reflected his own thoughts so well. He would have leaped into a lively discussion if she had been a man. He was used to men's blunt and often coarse camaraderie; women, on the other hand, required a more delicate dance. While the lady's candor bemused him and her beauty enchanted him, other qualities fascinated him as well—the cadence of her speech and, more subtly, the pauses between her words. And, of course, her attentive regard as he spoke attracted him most of all.

"Will you purchase any birds today?" she asked Leonardo as the vendor disappeared to the back of his stall. "What will you do with them since I know you do not eat them?"

"Why do you ask?"

She shrugged, and yet her eyes held a challenging sparkle. Leonardo recalled something his friend Machiavelli once said:

Men generally judge more by the eye than by the hand, for everyone can see, but few can feel. Everyone sees what you appear to be. Few really know what you are.

Leonardo sensed this woman was unlike most people.

The birdkeeper returned and opened the cage that held the turtledoves, scooping them into a small, slatted box. The signora pulled an intricately embroidered *borsetta* from a pocket in her skirt and removed a florin, handing it to the vendor. He counted out her change, and she thanked him, dropping the coins into the small, draw-stringed pouch and tucking it back into the folds of her gown.

She turned to Leonardo once more and inclined her head in a slight nod. "I bid you a good day." She turned to her maid and said, "Come, Estella, we must be on our way."

"Sì, Signora." The young woman bobbed her head, seeming to snap out of a dazed reverie.

The lady hesitated as though she might say something more to Leonardo but then seemed to change her mind, offering up one more almost-smile instead as she picked up the box with the turtledoves and walked down the lane of stalls, her maid, now rushing to keep up.

The impression she made might have ended at that moment, yet Leonardo's gaze followed her as she stopped at a quiet spot where no vendors hawked, no buyers gathered, and no awning cast a shadow. The servant girl, once again, stood a few feet away from her mistress, holding the basket on her hip.

The warmth of the sun's rays bathed the regal lady in a golden glow. She slid open the wooden slat and coaxed the turtledoves out with a few whispered words of encouragement. They hovered before her, cooing as their wings flapped in tandem. It was as if they thanked her, and he half expected them to embrace her with their wings. She waved them off, wiping her tears with a handkerchief. Leonardo watched, mesmerized not only by the duo that took wing and disappeared into the blue sky but also by the woman who freed them.

Dear Reader:
I hope you enjoyed this FREE PREVIEW of
Mona Lisa's Daughter.
If you would like to keep reading please scan
the following QR Code.

ABOUT THE AUTHOR

BELLE AMI

Belle Ami is an award-winning and Amazon bestselling author who captivates readers with her breathtaking historical fiction, compelling historical romance, and gripping romantic thrillers. Known for creating unforgettable characters and weaving complex, emotionally resonant stories, Belle masterfully combines passion, suspense, and history into tales that reflect the redemptive power of love, the resilience of the human spirit, and the triumph of hope against all odds.

Her works include *Mona Lisa's Daughter*, a mesmerizing historical thriller set in WWII Florence, Italy, where a young nun must protect a 500-year-old secret—a cache of letters between Leonardo da Vinci and Lisa del Giocondo—while confronting haunting truths from her past. *The Last Daughter*, inspired by the true story of Belle Ami's mother, Dina Frydman, is a heart-wrenching WWII novel chronicling the horrors of the Holocaust, following the Nazi invasion of Poland and the unimaginable struggles of Jewish families during the reign of terror.

Belle's bestselling *Out of Time Series* is a time-travel art-thriller collection that includes *The Girl Who Knew da Vinci*, *The Girl Who Loved Caravaggio*, and *The Girl Who Adored Rembrandt*. Her *Blue Coat Saga* is a gripping time-travel suspense series set in WWII and modern-day, featuring *The Rendezvous in Paris*, *The Lost Legacy of Time*, and *The Secret Book of Names*.

In her *Tip of the Spear Series*, Belle delivers contemporary international espionage thrillers with romantic elements in *Escape*, *Vengeance*, *Ransom*, and *Exposed*. She also delights readers with her *Lost in Time Series*, a historical romance time-travel series published by Dragonblade Publishing, where three friends journey from modern-day America to 19th-century London, Paris, and Tuscany to unravel ancient mysteries, battle dark forces, and discover love.

Rediscover Belle's debut series, now revised and re-released under the new title *Toxic Love*. This gripping romantic thriller trilogy includes *Toxic Attraction*, *Toxic Deception*, and *Toxic Redemption*. The series delivers an edge-of-your-seat experience, following a passionate love triangle between a captivating young woman, an enigmatic billionaire, and a fearless FBI agent.

Belle has contributed to Dragonblade Publishing's *Lion's Den Connected World* with *Luck of the Lyon*, a romantic Regency-era tale filled with intrigue, a dashing hero, and a beautiful widow. Her novella in *Night of Lyons: A Lyon's Den World Anthology* is another highlight of this beloved series, offering an evening of unforgettable romance and adventure.

A former Kathryn McBride scholar at Bryn Mawr College, Belle Ami is the proud recipient of the RONE, RAVEN, Readers' Favorite, and Book Excellence Awards.

When she's not writing, Belle enjoys hiking, boxing, skiing, cooking, and travel. A passionate home cook, she loves creating delicious meals for her family, especially Italian cuisine—a fitting pastime given her deep connection to Italy, which features prominently in many of her books. Belle lives in Southern California with her family, where she crafts her next story while exploring scenic trails that fuel her imagination and her love for storytelling.

Belle loves to hear from readers. You can reach out to her via her website: **belleamiauthor.com**.

Sign up for Belle's newsletter: **The Belle Ami Journal** for exclusive giveaways, contests, sneak peeks, and no spammy stuff. Scan the following QR Code to sign up:

You can also connect with Belle on social media:

BELLE AMI BOOK LIST

BELLE AMI COMPLETE BOOKLIST

HISTORICAL FICTION

The Last Daughter

Based on the remarkable true story of Belle Ami's mother, Dina Frydman, one of the youngest survivors of the Holocaust, *The Last Daughter* is an unforgettable tale of resilience, courage, and the unbreakable will to survive. A heart-wrenching and inspiring story that reaffirms the power of the human spirit.

Mona Lisa's Daughter

Spanning the golden days of the Renaissance and the harrowing shadows of World War II, *Mona Lisa's Daughter* weaves together the lives of two extraordinary women who find their strength and courage in the face of unimaginable challenges.

TIME TRAVEL HISTORICAL FICTION

OUT OF TIME THRILLER SERIES

She can see into the past. She can see the truth. But the truth can be deadly.

When art historian Angela Renatus partners with Alex Caine, a former Navy SEAL turned private detective, to recover stolen art, her dreams begin pulling her into the past—where danger awaits at every turn.

Multi-award-winning and bestselling author Belle Ami presents a mesmerizing blend of time travel, historical romance, and edge-of-your-seat mystery in this gripping series.

The Girl Who Knew da Vinci—Book 1

The Girl Who Loved Caravaggio—Book 2

The Girl Who Adored Rembrandt—Book 3

THE BLUE COAT SAGA

Two extraordinary women. One shared destiny. A captivating time-travel mystery thriller that spans generations.

The Rendezvous in Paris—Book 1

The Lost Legacy of Time—Book 2

The Secret Book of Names— Book 3

Boxed Set: The Blue Coat Saga (Books 1, 2, 3)

LOST IN TIME SERIES

Published by Dragonblade Publishing

Three paintings. Three best friends. Three incredible time-travel adventures across three iconic cities.

London Time—Book 1

Paris Time—Book 2

Tuscan Time—Book 3

HISTORICAL ROMANCE FICTION

Part of the Bestselling Lyon's Den Series World published by Dragonblade Publishing:

Luck of the Lyon

Night of Lyons

Published by Dragonblade Publishing and featured in the anthology:

Lords of Midwinter's Festival: A Historical Romance Anthology

The Earl's Dilemma

CONTEMPORARY THRILLER FICTION

TIP OF THE SPEAR THRILLER SERIES

Mossad agent Cyrus Hassani and his elite team of courageous men and women embark on dangerous missions to thwart the ever-looming threat of deadly terrorists and nuclear attacks. Award-winning and bestselling author Belle Ami delivers a fast-paced and thrilling international espionage series interwoven with complex and compelling love stories about the heroes and heroines who work deep undercover to keep the world safe. Guaranteed page-turners you will want to read all the books in this series.

Escape—Book 1

Vengeance—Book 2

Ransom—Book 3

Exposed—Book 4

TOXIC LOVE SERIES

Obsession. Seduction. Danger.

Love has never been more intoxicating—or deadly.

Toxic Attraction — **Book 1**

Adelia Lindstrom, a rising star in the equestrian world, is swept into a whirlwind of passion and obsession when she meets the dangerously seductive billionaire, Miles Bremen. But as their fiery connection deepens, Adelia discovers that surrendering to him may cost her everything.

Toxic Deception — Book 2

Adelia thought she could move on, but when her children are kidnapped, she's thrust back into the orbit of her enigmatic ex-husband, Miles, and an FBI agent who's fallen for her. In a race against time, Adelia must navigate a web of danger and betrayal to save her children—and her heart.

Toxic Redemption — Book 3

Haunted by heartbreak and consumed by danger, Adelia's life is thrown into chaos when she becomes the target of a killer. Caught in a love triangle between the dark, passionate Miles and the steady, protective David, Adelia must choose between redemption and ruin as the clock runs out.

The *Toxic Love Series* delivers an electrifying mix of passion, suspense, and obsession in a dark romance saga that will leave you breathless.